PENGUIN
BOUGAINVI...

Kalpana Swaminathan is a surgeon... include the novel *Ambrosia for Afters*... *Cryptic Death*. She has also written si... pseudonym Kalpish Ratna with Ishrat... the arts and literature appear in seve... publications.

PRAISE FOR *BOUGAINVILLEA HOUSE*

'A brilliant study of obsession and betrayal, an utterly absorbing tale'—rediff.com

'Imagine a mixture of both Bette Davis and Joan Crawford's characters in the 1962 classic film noir, *Whatever Happened to Baby Jane?*, add a dash of post-Rhett Scarlett O'Hara, and set in a house that would spook even the guests of Norman Bates' hotel, and you have something of the flavour of this disturbing and brilliant novel. If this makes *Bougainvillea House* sound like a melodramatic Grand Guignol, I have done Swaminathan a disfavour. The plot, characterization and style make [her] characters seem all too real, and if the themes she tackles—adultery, divine justice, homicide, sex and death—have the air of Greek tragedy, the style she employs is thoroughly contemporary'—*Outlook*

'Clarice Aranxa will likely go down as fictional India's darkest heroine...But it is Swaminathan's language which is the most seductive element of the book...Swaminathan teases the story along till you are fully absorbed in the tangled webs of evil and destruction'—*Business Standard*

'A psychological thriller and [a] subtle probing of the dark recesses of the human mind...The style, complex, sometimes lyrical, sometimes earthy...holds the attention of the reader'—*The Statesman*

'Kalpana Swaminathan takes the reader into the twilight zone of [the] human psyche. With the precision of a surgeon with a scalpel, she lays open a world where sanity and dementia meet, where the physical disease becomes a symptom of the diseased psyche...And yet the book is more than just a psychological drama. It is a creative rendition of the final journey towards a "menaced, angry and solid" death'—*Tribune*

'"Original" and "graphic" are the two words that instantly come to mind...Swaminathan's descriptions of all things intangible are comparable to those of [the] classics'—*Dawn*

'Kalpana Swaminathan builds the story with haunting use of language and imagination. With mastery over the plot she takes the reader on a complex roller-coaster ride...Swaminathan has used her medical experience and knowledge to construct a superb psychological drama with chilling effect'—*Free Press Journal*

'Kalpana Swaminathan is back with her trademark rich, hypnotic prose...The storyline is gripping, the writing style immaculate'—*Financial Express*

Bougainvillea House

KALPANA SWAMINATHAN

PENGUIN BOOKS

PENGUIN BOOKS
Published by the Penguin Group
Penguin Books India Pvt. Ltd, 7th Floor, Infinity Tower C, DLF Cyber City, Gurgaon 122 002, Haryana, India
Penguin Group (USA) Inc., 375 Hudson Street, New York, New York 10014, USA
Penguin Group (Canada), 90 Eglinton Avenue East, Suite 700, Toronto, Ontario, M4P 2Y3, Canada
Penguin Books Ltd, 80 Strand, London WC2R 0RL, England
Penguin Ireland, 25 St Stephen's Green, Dublin 2, Ireland (a division of Penguin Books Ltd)
Penguin Group (Australia), 707 Collins Street, Melbourne, Victoria 3008, Australia
Penguin Group (NZ), 67 Apollo Drive, Rosedale, Auckland 0632, New Zealand
Penguin Books (South Africa) (Pty) Ltd, Block D, Rosebank Office Park, 181 Jan Smuts Avenue, Parktown North, Johannesburg 2193, South Africa

Penguin Books Ltd, Registered Offices: 80 Strand, London WC2R 0RL, England

First published in Viking by Penguin Books India 2005
Published in Penguin Books 2006

Copyright © Kalpana Swaminathan 2005

All rights reserved

10 9 8 7 6 5 4 3 2

ISBN 9780143062264

This is a work of fiction. Names, characters, places and incidents are either the product of the author's imagination or are used fictitiously and any resemblance to actual person, living or dead, events or locales is entirely coincidental.

Typeset in Sabon by SÜRYA, New Delhi
Printed at Repro India Ltd, Navi Mumbai

This book is sold subject to the condition that it shall not, by way of trade or otherwise, be lent, resold, hired out, or otherwise circulated without the publisher's prior written consent in any form of binding or cover other than that in which it is published and without a similar condition including this condition being imposed on the subsequent purchaser and without limiting the rights under copyright reserved above, no part of this publication may be reproduced, stored in or introduced into a retrieval system, or transmitted in any form or by any means (electronic, mechanical, photocopying, recording or otherwise), without the prior written permission of both the copyright owner and the above-mentioned publisher of this book.

A PENGUIN RANDOM HOUSE COMPANY

*For my parents,
Savithri and Swaminathan,
in celebration of their fifty years together*

Clarice, Tape 1

It rained the night they brought me to Bougainvillea House.

Rain dripped. Limp, gray strands combed out straight from the algid scalp of the house. It flashed silver, barred bright as water by the jeep's headlights.

The jeep roared as it swung out of the drive. For a little while, the roar filled my head. Then I lost that too, as it emptied into the hollow night. Only the rain stayed, hanging at the window, whispering scandal, a neighbour who would not go away. Beyond the mesh of water, darkness tucked the world out of sight.

It was like how it will be. Soon now, very soon. It comforts me to think how near it is.

It did not comfort me that night. I sat on the edge of the bed—I could still sit up then—and strained my eyes against the night.

I must have fallen asleep, for I woke up in the cobwebbed light of dawn, a chill spray of rain pricking my toes. I had left the window open and my clothes on the chair were soaked. The numbing exhaustion I felt every morning kept me in bed till Pauline came in, scolding.

These days, Pauline does not scold. I miss that. These days she glides through the room like a fat black moth, her eyes escaping mine.

That first morning, Pauline scolded me for leaving the window open. She brought in tea, blistering hot, fragrant and weak, the way I like it . . .

But nine months in Bougainvillea House has changed all that. These days I crave the mild astringency of tea, but I don't ask for it. If I do, they will push it into my stomach through a tube.

Don't they know I might want to taste it?

They know, all right.

'You'll drown in it,' Marion said last week. She saw my eyes plead for a taste of tea. 'You'll drown in tea. Imagine drowning in tea!'

She's right. If I sip tea, I will drown in it. I don't like the word *drown*. It has the sound of falling down, down, endlessly down the shaft of a dark well. Marion's right. Drowning in tea will be like drowning in a well. My lungs will fill with thin sludge, it will bubble out of my nostrils as I struggle to breathe. No. I do not want to drown in tea. I want to die here, in my bed. I will not make a fuss about it. And I will not make a confession. I will go unprepared into whatever lies beyond death: a coffin from Cajal Mendonca, a wooden cross on my grave.

That first morning in Bougainvillea House—how I keep going back to it! How far back it seems. Nine months. Very nearly nine months, the time it takes to grow a baby. It could just as well be nine years. A lifetime ago. A dying ago. It has taken me all this time to make my peace with truth.

I have always told the truth, haven't I? The last time I saw Baga promontory, I had a glimpse of what truth is all about. This is what I'm trying to tell you. Not about my life or my dying, but about truth. I have to tell somebody. And you, faceless, nameless, formless as the air, you can hook and reel in the twisting words caught cross-wise in my wasted throat, fling them gasping and twitching on the page and look at them and read them for what they are.

The last time I saw Baga promontory was over a month ago. I haven't left the house since. We went for a drive in Xavier's taxi: Marion, Pauline and I. It was late afternoon. The world was washed and ironed, happy as a party dress. The clouds were crisp ruffles on a stiff taffeta sky, the palms a fringe of deep green lace. I made Xavier stop near the promontory. I wanted to see the sun lower itself into the wide lap of water, while the sheer cliff stared, unafraid. That's courage. That's endurance. That's what I've endured all my life because I've never had it—the ability to stare without dread. Dread that what you see might start up a landslide in the heart.

That's what happened to me in the peaceful country where nothing had happened before.

Rocks toppled, uprooting great chunks of earth, gouging out wounds. Bleeding runnels of water swelled into a flood and then sulked in a stagnant pool in which trees floated, their roots blaming the sky. Everywhere was tangled in wire; telegraph wires, telephone wires, television aerials, lamp posts, a high voltage snarl that none could approach. None could help that devastated country I called home. I carried it within me. I carry it still, with all its dislodged rocks, uprooted trees, its wires still careening with current, live. It rumbles within me like a storm although it is long past, and I will never see such storms again.

To quiet it, Clive died. That did not help.

With the Baga cliff, it is no such thing. It endures. It has seen more than the petty lifetime of Clarice Aranxa . . . It's a long time since anybody has called me by my name. Clarice. Somehow, it seems a difficult word to say. My friends, if they can be called that, call me Mrs Aranxa. I tried—once—to get Justin to call me Clarice, but that died too, like his touch, like the song in my blood at the sight of him.

As I watched the cliff that evening, it changed. Or did the light change? Blue disappeared. A low orange took its place. The air grew thick. Leaf and grass and twig disappeared. Trees lost themselves in rock and hollow. Then the air turned green, brooding olive, the colour of memory. The green air of the coconut grove. Now the cliff was more real. It was black, all black, and yet the eye could trace contour. It menaced, angry and solid. I knew then that there was no going beyond it. It was the truth. It was death.

Truth is a cliff at sunset. It depends on when you look at it. It's different every time, and each time, as true. It depends on the audience. The audience is the air, the light, the time of day. That decides what the cliff looks like. That decides the truth.

The truth, then! The truth that I have always spoken; so many truths, to so many people—which one shall I choose for you?

My first day at Bougainvillea House, and I was tired before it had begun. No matter. I told myself what everyone seemed intent on telling me: I was here to rest, to recover. Wasn't that what Marion wanted me to believe?

But what did *Marion* believe? Looking back, I think she believed it would be an easier life for me here. Correct that. She believed it would be an easier death. Not that any of us spoke of dying then. It was all *getting better*. And I wasn't even ill, was I? Just tired. I broke things. I was clumsy. I hadn't been that way before. Dainty Dolly, my Daddy used to call me—funny, me remembering that now. I don't remember him at all. I can't remember his voice. When did he disappear from my life? Who can tell? Not that I care! That lot went out long ago, mother, father and all the rest. They haven't left any memories behind.

So my move to Baga was all about getting better. But she didn't seem to think about how long that would take. And when I *got better*, what then? Would I be back in my own home? I did not ask. Marion did not say. It would be no use even if I did return. It would no longer be my home. It would be Marion's. But at Bougainvillea House, for better or worse, I could stay on as undisputed queen.

I think that's the offer Marion made that day.

It was stupid of me not to have seen it then. Would I have fought off her suggestion if I had? My mistake all along has been to think of Marion as a child. Marion is thirty-eight. *Old.* An old maid. Old maids are children till their parents die, aren't they? Then they can't wait to grow up, run wild within the week. That's how it's always been. Money has nothing to do with it.

In the old days, they lived on sufferance, cooking, cleaning up, looking after other people's babies, washing the smelly old, offering themselves to passing uncles, cousins, brothers in the mad dark scramble of family sin, till they were too old even for that and took to religion. Wasn't very different when they went to work, was it? Everybody's sweetheart from the boss to the chaprasi, and don't tell me otherwise. Half of them went mad, took to drink and hanged themselves.

My Marion, now—she's clever. Real brains, real beauty. And look at her. An old maid. Brings home a packet every month, lives lush too, nothing of the miser about Marion. I keep her sweet. I keep her young. In my home, she's the child, I'm the mistress, Pauline is our servant. I like things to be clear. I've kept things clear so far. But they will blur, now that I'm ill. Marion knew that long ago. She knew that Pauline would grow from servant to— what? Keeper? Marion gives the orders now. Even if I recover my strength and return to Bandra, that house will no longer be mine. It will be Marion's.

We were alone in the living room that morning. Let me see, I have the date: the fifteenth of September. 'You'll be so happy in Bougainvillea House, Mummy,' Marion said in the ardent voice she reserves for lies. Pauline was out, buying fish. Melissa was in Surat, with Tom and their snivelling kids. I was entirely at Marion's mercy. 'You'll have a lovely rest in Bougainvillea House.'

My cheek went cold. My hands were steel claws digging into the sofa. My toes were ice chips. My tongue a thick paperweight of glass, words snowing within it with each noiseless shake. Marion often has that effect on me. The affection of an unloved child is a chilling thing. Marion has no restraint, none. When she was little, she would rush to hug me every time she entered the room. I would put her away from me gently, and tell her that was quite enough, there was no need to make such an exhibition, but she never got the message. Poor Marion!

With pity, my chill thawed. I felt, without fear, my first intimation of death. That first glimpse was like peering through a hole in a crumbling wall, and seeing a grassy plot with sleepy crosses planted askew. I yawned a little. It was . . . cozy.

It had rained all morning. Marion had taken the day off from work. That should have warned me. Silence stretched expectant hands across the room, hunger awaiting charity. The window slid in a cold slice of sunlight, and silence was dismissed.

I was sitting on the sofa. When Marion began to speak again, I felt the need to get up and walk a little, but I found my legs would not obey. I had to think, to deliberate quite a bit on the natural act of standing up, to coax my legs into obedience. But I had to sit right down again as Marion chose this moment to spread her arms dramatically across. She was kneeling, as if in prayer, her beautiful eyes wide with pleading. She scared me, Marion did.

Think, then, of that morning, of the gelid rain-light pooling on the floor, and my daughter kneeling before me, telling me I must die.

Marion said, 'You will be safer there, no traffic, no dangerous roads to cross. And you've always loved it there, haven't you?'

So I was meant to end my days at Bougainvillea House.

I hadn't been there in years. That one month was the last time—1962. Melissa was six, Marion two. There isn't much Marion could know about Bougainvillea House, could she? It brings in a good rent, or did as long as Mr Gomes stayed. Mr Gomes was in Australia, but he would return, he would want his home back. Perhaps Marion only meant it as a holiday! I couldn't stay for ever in Bougainvillea House.

Then I remembered how late Marion had been the previous evening. A date, she said. It was a lie, of course, Marion never stayed out late with Keith.

It was no date that kept her. Marion had been to see the neurologist.

Let me say this right away. I have no quarrel at all with Dr Khan. I don't blame my illness on him now, and I didn't then. He is a good man. Is it his fault that his Allah forgot to give him a heart?

Dr Khan's office is a hushed room full of shadows. There is a steep couch, more like a ledge than something to lie on. I was never asked to. Behind his desk is a tall window with a deep sill. On this stands a vase like a saint in his niche. The vase is of milky green porcelain. There are no flowers in it. Dr Khan likes beautiful things. He likes Marion.

It is easy to imagine their conversation:

'How much longer before she's bedridden, Doctor? She can still walk, but she tires easily.'

'Difficult to say. A month, perhaps two.'

'Will she be able to care for herself? Eat on her own? Dress?'

'Not for very much longer.'

'And then?'

'I'm sorry.'

At this point, Marion would have shed a few tactical tears. Dr Khan would have hesitated over patting her shoulder. These days, men—even old men—have become wary of beautiful girls like Marion. Who wants to pay for a minute's tingle with public shame? Sexual harassment it's called, like a disease. We used to call it getting fresh, or making a pass. We used to giggle over it. We made them pay, too, but covertly. Now it's all open. Naturally, Dr Khan did not touch my daughter and must have rung for tea instead.

Marion pleaded with me. She never can speak a sentence without that whine for approval. 'You'll have all the rest you need to get well again, Mummy.' Liar. She was waiting to get rid of me.

Dr Khan must have told her how long it will take for my breathing to stop. That's how the end will come, I have been told that already. Those unseen muscles that push my ribs in and out will flop from fatigue. I will strain to fill my lungs with air, but my ribs will stay rigid like hoops of cane in third-rate furniture. Only my caged heart will plod on regardless.

Then that, too, will cease.

'Marion, please.' It's true, it's God's truth that I pleaded with my daughter, I who had never yielded to her pleas. 'Marion, please let me stay, let me stay where I can go to hospital. Respirator—Dr Khan said they have that machine here to help me breathe. I'll die without that machine, Marion.'

Were there tears in my voice? What do you think, you nameless, shameless scandalmonger to whom I address my memories? Do you know me at all?

'You'll never need a respirator.' Lies, lies again! 'And if you do, we'll have one right there in Bougainvillea House.'

Lots of money, my daughter makes, and she's never grudged me a thing.

How long can I breathe on a machine? How will I breathe? Will I have to wear it like a bra that pumps me in and out? I won't have an iron lung, I've told them that. I've seen those in the hospital, when I had Marion. I'll die if they put me in one. But Dr Khan said the iron lung is a museum piece now. Get me something up-to-date, I said, something modern, something—what is that term again?—yes, something state of the art; I'm no antique, I said.

Marion will never buy that respirator. There won't be time.

Marion is a good daughter. She does not like to see me die by inches. It was good of her to send Pauline with me.

But it was Pauline, wasn't it, who started the idea in Marion's head? Pauline was here with me that other time too, that long-ago time I was first at Bougainvillea House. It was Pauline. She started it. She changed my Marion.

I thought Marion might take the week off to see me settled here. But no, she was all haste to be rid of me. We can go together at the end of the month, I said, but that would not do for Marion. She shopped feverishly for me, with mindless extravagance, everything imported, not even the towels Indian: lacy lingerie, sheer, silky stuff, soft flowery chiffons, comfortable shifts, fluffy mules. Perfume. Rainbows of lipstick and eye shadow. Such luxury! She made up pretty packages with tinsel and satin as if they were birthday gifts.

They're all still unopened, in that drawer there. They can fill my coffin, like fistfuls of bonbons. I take up very little room, and lesser every day.

I did not expect visitors on my first morning at Bougainvillea House, I didn't want any. But I did have one.

Pauline bathed me and I dressed in the powder-blue chambray with ivory buttons, the one I had made for Marion's going away—for that disastrous wedding that never took place.

I told Marion it was bad luck to shop for clothes six months ahead of time, but did she listen? She was so eager to do things right. She couldn't possibly have been in love with him—oh there's no such nonsense about Marion. But she likes to keep up appearances. She's my daughter in that, if in nothing else.

I couldn't bear perfume that morning. I dabbed eau de cologne on my neck and my wrists and the back of my knees, the way I was taught a lady should. My shoes gave me trouble. I would soon be wearing flat shoes, or else—horrid thought—chappals! I had made up my mind to take to bed once I could no longer wear shoes—better that than shuffle around in chappals like an Indian.

I wore my amethyst—for luck. Why did I need luck that morning? I didn't stop to ask. The flat stone sulking behind its tracery of gold wire comforted me.

I had to rest a few minutes after getting dressed. I made myself up carefully. A little of that apricot blush Tom gave me last Christmas. And just a trace of blue-grey round the eyes.

I've always liked eye make-up. Clive thought it strange that I should use eye shadow at home. Clive hated make up. He was cold, unimaginative, correct, selfish.

That month in Bougainvillea House was his stolen moment of passion. But that was thirty-six years ago. Is it so long ago? I feel Clive's presence here, with me, now. *My* Clive. The cold, unimaginative, correct, selfish man I married. That *other* Clive was a stranger, and I was best rid of him.

I returned that other Clive to his family, boxed neatly, home delivery. He must have been a surprise. You see, I didn't call his family, I didn't tell them what Clive had done. I'd been brought up never to speak ill of the dead, and I wasn't going to break that rule for my husband, was I? And the fates, too, conspired, as they say. There were no phones working.

I didn't accompany him in the jeep. I couldn't bear the thought of bumping up and down with him one more time. And if you think that's a ghastly joke, let me tell you it was I, not you, whom Clive bumped for seven years. I took the train with Pauline and the kids. You had to change trains, then take a ferry those days. There was a six-hour delay, too. So Clive reached Bandra ahead of me. Just after Sunday lunch he must have arrived, and all the old folk too dazed with xacuti and sorpatel to know what was happening when Mendonca's men pushed him into the living room. They must have thought their darling daughter had sent them something from Australia.

Funny, I couldn't see then how comic it was. All of them clucking over the crate, urging Mendonca's man to open it, open it. Not letting him speak his lines the way they were always yacking. And when the crate was peeled away—a coffin, and no mistake!

I bet they hoped it was me.

Looking back, I can see it was a thoughtless thing to do, sending him on with no explanation. It was the only detail I slipped on. Otherwise, I did everything right. I like order. I like ceremony. I like a lace doily on the tea tray, a rose in season, the newspaper crisp as toast, though I never read it. I like these things because they are familiar to me, familiar from doing them for Clive. To this day I insist on my tray of morning tea with the lace doily, the rose, the newspaper. Although I do not drink tea any more, although the newspaper is a week old. There never is any news in Bougainvillea House; every day repeats itself. Pauline cooks and cleans, the gardener waters the plants, Marion comes and goes like the tide, I wait. No, there's never any news in Bougainvillea House. We do have roses, though ...

But to return to my first morning in Bougainvillea House.

I had a visitor. There was a young man in the living room when I got there.

I've thought a great deal about how words might twist that moment, but that sounds about right. It's the closest to truth. That was all I knew then, at that moment, you see.

There was a young man in the living room when I got there.

He was at the bookshelf, with his back to me. So there was nothing to warn me. All I saw as I entered was a stocky man, swarthy as most people seem to be these days. So few have that delicate bloom of true Portuguese skin. Clive had it, as do our two girls. I, like all the Aranxas (oh yes, my born name was Aranxa too), I'm tinted like a magnolia.

He turned.

Clive!

I was ambushed by pain. Savage fists pummelled my heart, threshing my blood till everything was a crimson haze. I knew I was staring at him. I could not stop. I watched his face blur and melt into another set of features, similar, yet distinct.

That face brought with it an odour of green things, sharp and wet, the wild scurrying of tiny feet in rough places. It brought the wetness of mud and rain, the sharp slap of a wet skirt on my calves. It brought terror. It brought time. I had thought that time was over, for these were things I had known and forgotten. There was no chance of forgetting any more. Memory rattled a loose pebble in my skull, jolted and skidded by cold white bolts of shock, as though I were strapped, tied and nailed down to the electric chair. There was no stopping it now. From that moment on it has kept up its convulsion in my brain.

I swear he noticed nothing. Did I hide my distress so well? He smiled and held out his hand and the voice that came out of those familiar lips was not Clive's. This man is a stranger, I remember telling myself, as I acknowledged his greeting. He said, 'Welcome to Bougainvillea House.' He was to say many things to me after that, but whenever I think of him now, which is often, that's what he says: 'Welcome to Bougainvillea House.'

Who was this stranger to welcome a woman to her own home? 'I did not catch your name,' I said. I think I must have narrowed my eyes. Don't do that, Clive used to say, it makes you look like a cat.

'I didn't catch your name,' I repeated, a little slower and louder this time to make the words come clear.

'No. I never confess to it till I've had my first drink.'

'You won't get that here,' I said.

A warm brush of laughter, a capful of breeze, the kind of laugh that would make him friends for life. Not with me. It struck a chill in me. He had the grace to look ashamed. 'I only said that for effect. Isn't it the sort of thing a gentleman says? I've been quite nervous about meeting you. I don't touch the stuff, actually. My father died of drink.'

'How dare you—' the words escaped me, but he seemed to accept the rebuke.

'I didn't mean any disrespect. That's one thing good about being dead, isn't it? People are forced to respect you. I'm Justin

Borges. Dr Justin Borges, actually. Marion told me about you.'

Marion! Just like that—Marion!

'I was Dr Khan's student, you know. So you're in safe hands.'

'Nobody thought it necessary to ask my opinion.'

'I'm the only doctor for miles.'

'I won't need one.'

'Great! We can be friends, then.'

Presumptuous brat! I liked him, though. And then, suddenly, I remembered that old drunk Borges, and I understood. Justin Borges, Doctor Justin Borges, the son of that old drunk Borges! Oh it was too much! I laughed out aloud, and that was not odd because he thought he had rescued me, a dying old woman, out of the sourness of dying. That was not wrong either. I laughed for him, then, and for Clive, for the joke old man Borges had played on Clive. I laughed for all the years I had never dreamt what was growing here in Baga, in the very place where Clive died.

Dr Justin Borges! Oh he was gorgeous, a great big clumsy boy with eyes that turned my bones to water, the way Clive's should have but never did.

'Are you from these parts?' I asked.

'Where else? There are few imports to Baga, believe me.'

'Except the old, the sick, the dying.'

'I prefer to think the brave, the kind, the gracious.'

'You are quick with compliments.'

'I have heard much about you, from Marion!'

Another of Marion's conquests. It did not surprise me. I was pleased for my daughter. She has good taste. 'Is this a consultation?' I asked. 'I'm not ill today.'

'Wonderful! We shall walk, then.'

'We?'

'Sure. Best way for me to check your muscles.'

'Muscles! I haven't any!' But of course I did then, though I knew I wouldn't soon enough. But I wasn't thinking of my illness when I said that. My protest was purely feminine outrage. Do you understand, then, how this young man, this dashing young man, this son of Borges, this Clive-returned, made me feel? He made me feel sixteen, he made me feel fluttery right through. I only had to hold his eyes and the world would be made safe for me. Above his collar, his skin was chocolate.

'Too muddy,' I managed to say.

'That's how it's going to be for the next three months.'

Three months from now I won't be walking anywhere, I thought, but did not say.

As we went down the steps, I slipped and caught his arm to break my fall. It felt strange, that warm chunk of life beneath the sleeve. I could not let go. My fingers caressed him. I held that solidity with the greed of a lifetime of waiting.

Are you shocked? I could, of course, explain it away. That's not why I'm talking to you, is it, for explanations? No. I'm talking because I want to tell the truth. There are so many truths I have to tell. I'll come to those presently. To go back to that moment, that is what I did. That is what I should have done to Clive but never did because I could not. Clive did not deserve it. And so I waited all my life to bestow this caress on—no, not my son, my own blood, as I was about to say, but on another woman's son, and there can be no sin in that.

There—I've begun to explain already, and what's the use of my talking to you, then? From now on I'm just going to stick to what happened. There will be blanks. You can fill them or you can leave them. They aren't important. I'll tell you all that is.

Before I could take my hand away, his own flew down like a bird and covered mine.

Joy broke free like a shout in me. That rush of life so long left unkindled, that ache to bruise with pain and dread and happiness, it was worth many deaths to feel that again. Then he looked at me, and my heart stilled.

His brown eyes were tight with light, their centres opening like black doors. The whites had turned pink. It was Clive's face hanging above me in the awful dark, and I turned my face away as I used to—but there was no pillow now, no soft nest in which to cup my cheek. Now I could shut my eyes and wait and wait and it would never be quickly over.

I freed my hand. 'Thank you, Doctor.' And that, as Marion says about her boyfriends, was that.

We walked along the creek. They have tarred a narrow strip of road since Baga became a money spinner. In the old days there was no road here. It was just a stretch of mud.

That was how I found out. From the mud on Clive's gum boots.

It was curious, that expedition to buy gum boots. We went to

Calangute, to the shops near the temple and the vegetable market, such a dirty place! Clive suggested I should spend the hour with Sister Arabelle at St Anne's near by while he went to Ribeiro's. 'I want to come too!' I cried. I was being petulant, a spoilt child. He liked that sometimes, as though two weren't enough. Clive put me off that time, saying it would be all man talk at Ribeiro's, no place for a lady.

He came back with a sari for me from Ribeiro's shop. A sari! What possessed him! A piece of cloth like a shroud, I always think. Who's going to wrap up in a blessed relic, not me! Anyway, he bought me a sari. I didn't look at the bloody thing, did I? Put it away to give as a Christmas present. Lots of sari-wearers came up for Christian charity round Christmas time.

And then I noticed those gum boots. Why do you need those, I asked, don't you have a perfectly good pair back home in Bombay? I asked against my better judgment, I must add. Clive disliked questions. I was careful never to question him—usually. That's what made ours such a happy marriage.

Quite early on in our marriage I taught Clive manners. I knew what he wanted: a house that made him feel a real fidalgo. Furniture gleaming with that solemn glow of old wood. Waxed floors. Gladioli in tall vases. Lace doilies. Porcelain, white and empty as dismembered bones, skeletons on display. Music on the piano, always 'Isle of Capri', the only tune Clive could recognize. I kept the house as he liked it, but I let him know nothing came for free.

I broke a rule when I asked about those gumboots. After that, Clive was cold and remote all day and I was cold and remote all night.

Clive wore those gumboots on his afternoon jaunts. Rain or shine, he always took a walk after lunch. He said it was good for his digestion, but he had a paunch like a Christmas balloon. Stupid, balding, ugly Clive.

I thought of those gum boots as I walked down the tarred road with Justin. His steps had slowed to match mine, and we walked close, the air a warm sheet between us.

'I've walked this way before,' I said.

'Before the road was made?'

'Hmm.'

'Must have been slushy.'

'I wore gum boots.'

That was a lie. I had followed Clive barefoot, afraid my shoes might give me away as his had. I can hear the sound now, the suck of the mud, smacking its lips at the taste of my feet. Mud spattered my calves, the hem of my skirt, lemon Tricel, already stained beyond repair. Lovely yellow it was, pale, but with a shine to it like lemon curd in a tart. I wore it with a flowered shirt, and a matching band in my hair. It made me feel like Ava Gardner.

'There's a coconut grove ahead.' Why did I tell Justin that?

'This is hardly the hour to visit the grove!'

'Why?'

'It's haunted. You should go there at dusk. That's when the ghost walks.'

'Your ghost keeps early hours,' I said lightly, with the kind of laugh the magazines call girlish, the kind of laugh men like to hear from a woman. And all the while the bomb was ticking in my brain: *We're talking now, we're talking about Clive.*

'It's not a proper ghost, you know. The body isn't here. He died here, but they took him away.'

'Who was he?' You would expect an old lady like me to be a little frightened of such morbid talk, wouldn't you? You won't hold it against me that my voice trembled.

'I don't know,' he replied, 'somehow, the older people don't like to talk about it. Some tourist, perhaps, drunk or hopped out of his mind.'

'Suicide?'

'Accident, more likely.'

I've always considered there's nothing in the world you can't joke about. Kidding Justin made it easier for me to take those last steps to the grove. 'You're scared, Doctor! Sit here, then. I'm off to explore!'

I set off at a brisk pace, trying not to notice the wriggly feeling in my calves that warned me my knees would buckle any moment now.

The rain had stopped over an hour ago, and a yellow light seeped through the wadding of wet cloud. The grass steamed. Coconut palms towered, graceful pickets. Just outside the grove, delicate grey shadows trellised the wet grass. The ground was hard beneath my feet. This was a rocky place once, before the palms were planted.

How deep do their roots plunge beneath the turf, I wondered. Of late I had begun to worry about such things.

How light will the turf lie on me?

Lighter than Clive, for sure. He was a heavy man. Fat.

I am not going to join Clive at St Andrews'. I never did like his family. I have no intention of letting Uncle Bosco's skeletal hand creep up my skirt like it used to beneath the lace tablecloth crocheted by his wife. No. Not up my best black skirt of raw silk.

I've laid out my wardrobe for my positively last appearance above ground: Black raw silk suit, the one Lydia tailored for Christmas (*charcoal* she calls it). Ivory crepe blouse, with lace cuffs. Mother's cameo brooch—neither Melissa nor Marion likes that, so there's no sense in leaving it behind, and I can't meet my Maker with no jewellery on, can I? Black court shoes, not suede, I hate those. It's always been patent leather for me, with a black satin bow. Marion says patent leather's not quite as classy as real leather. Gucci, then, I said, no Indian cow's going to cover my feet, sacred or otherwise. Indian leather stinks.

Do you know I actually got Marion to plan my wardrobe? Not that she knows what it's for. And that's another joke, isn't it, calling it wardrobe—my shoulders will be like coat hangers soon enough.

I ought to say I got Marion to plan my coffin, but that sounds a bit mean on my daughter.

Heaven knows how they'll get the shoes on, though. I don't like to think of that. They say Mendonca is very clever. He'd better be. I can't meet St Peter barefoot.

You've heard what Mendonca did to Annie Athaide's face? It was like a jigsaw when they brought her in from the hospital, blown to pieces, they say, but Mendonca did a good job. Peaceful she looked, if a trifle pink—and that's another thing I've made sure of. No Indian brands. You know what people like Mendonca are like, they'll use any cheap thing, it's a business after all.

I've kept a box of stuff for Mendonca. It's packed and ready, though I hope I won't need it just yet. And I hope they find it. No point posting me off to Panjim in the jeep and then finding the box got left behind. Estee Lauder it's always been for me, same as Elizabeth Taylor, and I'm not changing brands now. Hypoallergenic, odourless: cleanser, astringent, foundation, matte powder, highlighter, blush, both creme and powder. And all my eye make-up, including the brushes, with special instructions to use the electric-blue eye shadow—it sets off the gleam of black silk. The lipstick I've chosen is a soft brown—it won't do to be too brash. With all those sickening lilies they're bound to pile me with, I don't want him to skimp on perfume. A whole bottle of Chanel 5 I've put in, for a good dousing with it before I meet my Maker. Let's hope Mendonca doesn't steal it.

Lingerie, too, I've put aside with the suit. Fresh and sweet in its white satin case, with the pomander stitched into the lining. Apricot lace camisole, pure silk, of course, from Paris. My underwear must be white, of cotton. No slinky whorish stuff in the presence of Our Lord. I don't mind a little borderie anglaise let into the cups, it's not disrespectful, but nothing beyond that. Not like Angie D'Monte, remember? They buried her in her nightie and you could see right through—the dark bits of her tits and everything.

I walked to the coconut grove forcing myself to think of these things because I wanted to refuse memory.

Memory is striped grey and black. It stalks, patient as a cat, lean and randy. It thrusts into me, fur, claw and needly white teeth, licking the back of my eyes with its rose-petal tongue. Memory is a cat, a thieving homeless beast that leaves behind fleas as it leaps from brain to brain. A wild, harsh, solitary thing.

My feet took me to the edge of the grove where trees stand hunched together, the space between them a secret. There used to be a coarse tangle of bush here, but now it has been cleared away. The space gleams, bald, brown, wedged between smooth tree thighs, a blue shadow creeping beneath the shaved mound.

That's where they were.

In that space, within that bramble bush, that's where they were. At first I saw only her. Just her back in a red print dress of the sort servants wear. Her back was arched over him, and I remember thinking: She's only a servant, she's doing what servants are meant to do.

'Would you like to rest a little?' Justin's hand hovered on my arm, flattening the film of air between us. My arm grew rigid. I willed his fingers to touch me, and they did. I needed that touch.

I needed more than that touch at that moment.

I let Justin lead me to a little seat there, an old bench cracked in the sun and now sucking damp into those crevices, sucking in rain. Sit I had to. By now my legs were sponge. I was beginning to have trouble holding my hanky, so I let it drop. Justin picked it up, shook it out, put it in his pocket. I pretended not to notice.

'This is where lovers sit,' I said. Had they been sitting here that day? I could not tell, I could not remember.

I did not care.

My heart drummed in my throat, a sparrow thrashing against a glass pane. I was with him now, this new Clive, *my* Clive, the one I could have lavished a lifetime of love on, if only he'd been there before. But he was here now. He was with me in the coconut grove, in that very same place. He was here with me, not her. And all the wasted days of our marriage came rushing at me, all the vengeful nights. I could say penance for them now, kiss for kiss.

If only he had understood that moment! But Justin was no Hollywood hero. He didn't know what to do. He picked up a small stone and shied it at a coconut frond, the kind of stupid aimless thing small boys do all day.

Dr Justin Borges, the small boy. Nothing was the same. I was a fool to think it could be. He was just a boy, younger than my Marion. A servant's bastard, jumped-up gentleman-doctor of charity, kept on a leash by my daughter till he could declare me dead.

That was why he was here, this aimless boy sitting with the rich dying widow from whom he had no expectations. He was here to make out my death certificate. To stick a little piece of paper beneath Mendonca's nose and cause him to hurry me underground. This little bastard would make out the certificate, and his mother would hear: *That old woman died today, the rich widow I told you about.* And the poor widow would smile and sleep in peace.

That was the moment when I decided that Justin would never sign that certificate. He would never have to drop my pulseless wrist and say 'I'm sorry' to Marion, people in a film both of them, for neither would be sorry I was dead.

I picked up a pebble too. The effort tired me. The pebble slipped out of my grip. Tears bubbled in my eyes, they boiled beneath the whites, blistering them. They spilled, scalding my cheeks, they splashed on my wrists like hot rain.

Justin did not move. But I knew that he would, eventually, and I knew exactly what he would do. Suddenly all his movements became familiar, every one of them took on a well-remembered rhythm. Now he would offer me his handkerchief. Now he would get up abruptly, swing his arms, shake his head like a pup in from the rain. All the gestures a man makes when he wants to ventilate his thoughts, he made them all.

My resolution hardened like toffee. It always does, once an idea is past the messy stage of hesitation. Its caramel stickiness balls up, toughens, tightens into a thick, slick slab of sweetness I can taste for a long, long while.

I dried my eyes with his kerchief. 'Enough of this nonsense!' I said briskly. 'Come, Doctor, help an old woman walk back to her house.'

His eyes were surprised—and relieved. He took my hand gently, with the timid touch of a callow child.

I prepared to play mother. 'So you know Marion.'

'We've met.'

Oh the primness of the young! They think the clipped phrase and brusque answer can conceal their hearts. Not their hearts, exactly. We know what they think with, these young people nowadays. Not *my* girls, don't make that mistake, my Marion's pure. I brought up both of them pure and good. Melissa, now, that's different, she's married to a sailor and you know what sailors are. I knew exactly what Justin was thinking when he said that about Marion—'We've met.'

I said: 'I wish you'd write and tell her I'm doing fine. She worries so. You could phone her one of these evenings.'

'If you want me to.'

My! Edgy, wasn't he! 'Oh she'll believe you. She never believes me when I tell her I'm well. It's fuss fuss fuss all the time. She's become broody as a hen since her disappointment.'

He kept quiet. So he knew about it.

'She's an unlucky girl, my poor Marion. All the boys run after her, but somehow they don't click. I wasn't too fond of that boy, mind you. Very good family, but there's always some imbalance in these people, converts, you know. It's the blood, it doesn't mix well with ours. They say his grandmother went mad.'

'Suicide is often more from despair than madness.'

How dare he! Again I tasted the sweetness of my resolve. 'A textbook sentence, Justin! They must have taught you that in medical college. You have a lot to learn in life. Despair? He had everything—money, career—and now Marion for a wife. What reason could he have had for despair?'

'Who can explain despair?'

'It was inconsiderate of him. Cowardly. Selfish. A mortal sin.'

And messy. He had to be picked up piecemeal from the tracks, and guess what the Ferraos did. They stacked the pieces in a child's coffin, so I heard. To save space. Space costs, if it's a suicide. I didn't go to the funeral. How could I with Marion in hospital with those sleeping pills and all? But I did hear it was a shabby affair.

'Think of what he did to my daughter.' Anger made my voice harsh. 'He spoilt her life. She'll never know what it is to be happy.'

'Oh you mustn't think that! She'll find her happiness one day!'

Not with a fool like you, I thought.

'How old are you, Justin?'

'Thirty-five. Why?'

'Marion's older. When she turned thirty, I told her to hurry up or she might miss the bus.'

'Maybe she didn't want to take it.'

'It begins to look that way, doesn't it?'

I took his arm as we walked home. There was nothing to fear now, nothing to thrill to. It was a crutch. I could move it at will to match my gait. A bar of flesh no longer linked to mine.

'Do you have a girlfriend, Justin?'

'I do now!'

We both laughed, for different reasons.

After Justin left, I sat a long while on the patio.

I still do, if this can be called sitting—floating on cushions, every limb at the mercy of Pauline's whim. My nerves, that brown and yellow tangle of strings in Dr Khan's picture book, all of them have been taken over by Pauline. She holds them in her pudgy grasp, and I flail and jerk about in sympathy with each tweak and twitch.

The sun comes in through the trellis, pushes past the pink bunches on the Rangoon vine and leaps in my lap like a kitten. It curls up against my stomach and purrs, spreading its warmth like a blanket on my thighs. Comfort? It's the kitten that's cozy, not I. My arms droop, heavy pillars suspended between air and earth, holding up nothing, rooted nowhere. My head sinks into the yielding cushions, and I am no longer here.

I am in the coconut grove. I am always in the coconut grove these days, behind the bush that has been cleared away, peering through the brambles that aren't there anymore.

Her dress is a red slash, shiny, wet. She is holding up her wound to mock me. Her fingers brown ribs in a black fan of hair.

His hair was always oily. Coconut oil, just like an Indian—can you imagine how shocked I was! And then I made him change to Brylcreem. I never had to touch his hair, thank God.

Her fingers travel the wide, boring map of his back.

It makes me shudder now, more than thirty years away from that day. Clive's back was always clammy with sweat. A queue of suitors a mile long and I had to marry a man who sweats like a pig, I used to tell him bitterly. It made him nervous, baths three or four times a day, talc, cologne—no deodorants those days, none of your fancy aerosols. He still sweated. Change your shirt, I'd tell him, six times a day, we have Pauline, thank God ... Funny how often I have to thank God when I think of Clive. Yet I never thanked Him for Clive.

In the grove, shadows knife her face.

My knife is memory, my shard of broken glass, cutting grey-brown cross-hatched scars of shadow. No blood. Blood will never stain these hands of mine.

On her face, knife cuts, shadows. Her eyes are drowsy. Now his face—rapt, anguished, pushing against her as she rubs her cheek on the black dome of his head.

Clive's head, full of dullness. Stupid Clive. Had a head fit for a servant, lacked gumption for his wife.

I never saw more than that, JesuMarieJoseph, I came away. They couldn't have done more in broad daylight. Clive always liked the lights off.

Every day now, I peer through the brambles. There were brambles then, a bush you could hide behind. There was shame.

There are no brambles now. Things are different now. There is no longer shame.

That morning, my first in Bougainvillea House, I lounged in the chair a long time after Justin left, till Pauline brought lunch.

It was a delicate meal Pauline brought. Just right. None of that spicy Goan food I can't digest. There was soup, cream of mushroom, out of a tin. Pomfret, lightly grilled. Thin slivers of toast, lavish with butter. And from Fortino's, a lemon tart, a twirl of sunshine. Rich, glistening. I sank my mouth in it, flattening the ridges with my tongue, all tickle and slap and honey it was, I can hold its smoothness now, sweet prickles in my mouth, I am spilling on my bib, Pauline will scold, Pauline will rub my mouth with a dry towel till my lips crack bloodily, she will, she will. Oh why did I think of that tart! Yes, I remember—because of what happened soon afterwards, Pauline never brought me pastry from Fortino's again, she always made some excuse or another when I asked her. These days, she goes oftener to Fortino's. When I ask her where she's off to, she pretends as though she can't understand what I'm saying. Sometimes the question amuses her. She pats her stomach and says, 'Fortino!' Sometimes she brings the flat white box to me. She holds it under my nose so that I can smell it. But it is always empty.

I don't like Pauline, you think? Let's get that straight, then. Pauline is my servant. *I* pay her, Marion doesn't. She takes her orders from *me*. One does not like or dislike servants. One manages them.

That afternoon, when Pauline had cleared away, she helped me upstairs without a word.

It was one of her 'down' days. Her mouth hung like a shark's, downturned and lipless. She took off my dress and hung it up. I needed help with the shift, a soft pink cotton with a drawstring. She eased off my shoes, and dusted my feet with talc and massaged my soles as I had taught her to do. And all the time I saw only the top of her grey head or her sagging chin, or her thick bolster arms. Never her face. She plumped my pillows and was about to leave the room, but I wanted to crack that glass pane of silence. I wanted to touch her.

I said, 'What a nice boy he is, that Dr Borges.'

She stopped at the door and gave me a sharp look. For all her doughy appearance, Pauline is far from stupid. She waited, knowing I had more to say. 'Handsome, too, don't you think?'

'Like his father.'

I laughed. 'Why that old drunk Borges, I remember his ugly face! Some fool married him and this boy is the result. You call old Borges handsome? You've got bad taste, Pauline.'

Her pouchy face set with resentment. 'Borges was a good man. The face of a good man is good to look upon.'

The face of a good man—

Clive was a good man. He was not good to look at. Big jowly face. Pop eyes. Within a year of our marriage, he was bald. Make money, Clive, I told him. You look prosperous; now *get* prosperous. And did he! You can see how we live. And it's all my own money, what Clive left me when he died.

I made myself a short white tennis dress and twirled my racquet at the Gymkhana every evening. If he hadn't started making money right away, I would have taken swimming lessons. There wasn't a man in the Gym who didn't marvel at my being married to Clive. (That didn't stop them from trying, but I showed them quick enough that I wasn't that sort.)

I kept Clive on his toes. I made it quite clear to him where his happiness lay. Was I wrong in that?

I've always believed in honesty. I've raised my daughters that way too. Nothing like clarity, I tell them. Melissa learned that lesson well. Not Marion.

Marion! My proud, beautiful, good girl. All the boys were crazy about her, but she was picky. Too picky, perhaps. 'I don't know, Mamma,' she told me, 'I simply don't care enough.' But with Keith it was different. She knew he was right for her. The Ferraos were *nortera*, East Indians, good folk who knew their place and were respectful. It was a great honour for them to get a bride like Marion, and I made it clear that they should know it. I was happy about the marriage. Marion was getting on, wasn't she?

And then I dropped the crystal vase.

It wasn't the first thing I'd smashed. Of late, cups and plates slipped from my grasp and I was always dropping spoons. Marion called it 'nerves'.

She couldn't say that when I dropped the vase. Real Belgian crystal it was, not the sort of stuff you find in Indian shops.

And that's how I landed in Dr Khan's clinic. 'He's a nerve specialist,' Marion said, irritating me no end. There was nothing wrong with my nerves. I told him that too, the minute I entered. 'There's one thing I want to make clear, Doctor.' I said. 'I'm not the nervous sort at all.' I was surprised when he seemed to believe me. He said he agreed, the illness didn't have anything to do with being nervous. 'I'm not a clumsy woman, either,' I said. My voice had begun to tremble by then. Dr Khan made no attempt to soothe me. He probably left that sort of thing to the family doctor. 'It's not clumsiness, I'm afraid,' he said quietly. Oh well, pills and needles, I thought. But it wasn't that either. My mother used to rap me on the knuckles with a spoon when I smashed a glass or a plate, but Dr Khan's brand of justice was much worse. I was awarded a life sentence for smashing that vase.

Yes, it was Belgian crystal, I told you that. I would have paid the price five times over, gladly. But this I did not deserve. I did not deserve to die. Punishment or curse? I remember thinking if the first, it was too large for so small a crime. If the second, and surely it was that, then I was powerless against it. I had a disease that would kill me, Dr Khan said. It would kill me slowly, tiring me out muscle by muscle. He explained very carefully, as though to a child or a dimwit, that my body moved because of muscles. I had—how many did he say?—oh hundreds of muscles, big and small, and all of them were going to quit on me. Not all at once, but one by one.

'Paralysis? Stroke?'

'Not exactly,' he said.

'Then what? Like polio? But I am over sixty, Doctor.'

Who would think that? his eyes said, lingering on the lace insertion in the V of my new beige silk. But what he said was: 'No, not polio.'

Even saints hadn't reported this complicated form of martyrdom. 'Does it have a name?' I asked wearily. 'Or should I just call it torture?'

'It's totally painless,' he said. His eyes glittered with conviction like a priest's. Totally painless, like the kingdom of Heaven they promise you if you don't sin.

'Totally painless,' Dr Khan repeated. Then he said, very slowly and carefully, like a spell or an incantation: 'Motor neuron disease.' At first I didn't have a clue what it meant. It sounded like a bus. He picked up a pencil and began to draw a series of gruesome pictures, but I stopped him.

'I'd rather not see them. I've lived sixty years without knowing what's inside my spine, and I'm going to die that way. My muscles are just as good as yours, Doctor, though I suppose you're ten years younger.'

He left it at that. But there were tests. 'What's the point in doing tests just to find out I have something incurable?' I told Marion. So you see, I had begun to accept my illness already.

Motor neuron disease. It sounds like a bus, but it isn't taking me anywhere. I have learnt what will happen soon. My lips will fall silent. My mouth has already begun to fall open, and I slobber. My eyelids will refuse to open. My eyes will loll like a doll's. My tongue began its sloth a while ago. You can say that you don't understand what I say, and I won't think you rude. I can't swallow too well. Sometimes I even choke on water.

What's that you're thinking? Cheeky, aren't you? No, I have no problems of that sort, how dare you!

Everything tires me. I cannot hold a book. Soon I will have to give up breathing too. Yes, that's going to happen to me, but not just yet.

I'm talking to you now of what it was like just before they brought me to Bougainvillea House. They said I had a terminal illness. All I'd done so far to prove that was to smash crockery. I walked, talked, ate, and took very good care of my appearance. Shoes were beginning to be a problem, though. But that was all.

Marion wanted to call off the wedding. I wouldn't hear of it. I made her promise not to tell Keith about my illness. My 'nerves' we called it when we spoke about it at all. In those early days, we did not tell Pauline. If she knew about it, she did not comment. You see, it's only in Bougainvillea House that Pauline is part of my life. Earlier, she only kept house.

What if Keith thought Marion might inherit my illness? What if their children got the disease? Keith is your last chance, I told Marion—I never am one to mince words. Marry Keith. You're thirty-seven this year, that's late for a woman.

Marion wept. Marion agreed.

I was disappointed in Marion.

I liked Keith. In some ways he was good for Marion. I liked his spirit—daring and adventurous, just the opposite of quiet, safe

Clive. He had a pilot's license and nagged me to go up with him in a plane that looked like a plastic toy. Not on our life, I told him. I'd cautioned Marion against it as well. Oh, it was safe enough. He'd never let her take risks, he was that deeply in love with her. But there's the other thing, isn't there—you never know what he'll get you to do once you're up in the clouds with him, I told Marion. I had to tell her because she has no experience of men. Very few working girls have, I notice. That's because in all these high-up jobs men and women are so busy being polite to each other, there's no room for that sort of thing. But get them at an office party and you'll see their true colours quick enough. High in the sky there's no one to hear you scream, I told Marion. Something told me, though, that Marion might not scream.

Anyway, I know for a fact that she never did go up with him, or anywhere for that matter, my girl is still pure as the day she was born.

Keith and I had long talks about Marion. You must be patient with her, I told him straight. Her father was very patient with me. He agreed, embarrassed. He was lucky to be marrying Marion. She could have had any boy she wanted, but she had kept herself pure for him, I said.

Keith often helped with my shopping. There were last-minute purchases, the wedding was just a month away. That's why he was with me that afternoon, though nobody knows that, only you do, now. I can tell you, I regret Keith. He had the makings of a man.

The twenty-second of September. Marion was to be married on the eighteenth of October. I wanted Keith to help me choose curtains. I called him at work, at half past twelve, and asked him to meet me at Santa Cruz during the lunch break. You see, I wanted to save myself disappointment. I would never have got over the disappointment of not finding those perfect curtains—they were for their new flat in Worli.

The flat was a gift from his parents, and why not? But make it in Marion's name, I said. Keith didn't hesitate. We didn't tell Marion. Everyone knew it was all Keith's money, but it was gracious to maintain the fiction that his parents had paid for it. They were simple folk, really. Naive. My heart bleeds for them. But as these Hindus say, who can quarrel with fate?

I'd called Keith close on lunchtime because I knew then he wouldn't have time to wriggle out of it. There was no question of him telling Marion. I made it quite clear those curtains were to be a surprise. I met him just outside the Club. I was a little late, hurrying from my previous appointment, with the Sisters of Charity.

I tell you this only to clarify that it was pure coincidence that nobody knew I spent that afternoon with Keith. I never meant to conceal it.

Later, it upset me too much to talk about it.

I wouldn't let Keith drive that afternoon—parking can be such a problem in Santa Cruz! So he left his car at the Club and we took a rickshaw.

We walked along the market for a while, and I remember asking Keith if he wasn't hungry, it was his lunch break, after all. I'd had mine before I left home, just an omelette and some soup, nothing heavy. Keith wanted to eat pani puri. I can never abide street food. Have you seen the way the bhaiyya dips his hand into the pot when he fills the puri with that hot stuff? I didn't want to sit on that narrow wooden bench next to the cart, but I did need to rest my legs, didn't I? There was a walk ahead of us. So I sat, and watched Keith wolf down twelve puris. Twelve times the bhaiyya dipped his grimy nails into the pot.

I wondered if Marion knew she was marrying a pig. I said, 'Your wedding suit's going to be a tight fit unless you walk off those puris. Come along, I'll show you a jacaranda tree.' He tagged along good humouredly. He was a sweet boy.

There was a jacaranda in bloom near the railway track. It was the only jacaranda in Santa Cruz. I hadn't seen any other that bloomed so late. We were in September, past the rains, and the tree still carried a soft dusting of violet blossom. I have never known that to happen before. Surely, then, it was all ordained.

It was awful near the railway tracks. It always is. Where do you expect people shit every day—in their pockets? There's one toilet to forty families and you can imagine the mess. Naturally, the tracks are more convenient. Keith grumbled, but I was resolute. He couldn't even tell frangipani from gulmohur, and as for jacaranda, he'd never heard of it before! Besides, if anybody had to grumble, it should have been me. I was wearing the most unsuitable shoes for such an adventure. Dark blue court shoes with satin rosettes.

I had on a narrow skirt of the same blue with a soft blue

blouse and a Dior scarf knotted loosely round my neck, a bold swirl of black and gold. It was genuine Dior. Tom bought it in Paris, a gift for my fifty-eighth birthday.

Strange about that jacaranda! A sign, wouldn't you say? Growing the way it did just beside the fast track. I'd never have known about it if I hadn't glimpsed it from the train the week before, going to Bombay Hospital for those tests. I'd met Marion at her office at lunchtime, and she was all for taking a cab, but I said the train was good enough, besides the appointment was for three and we'd never make it by road. That too was a sign. I took that train. I noticed that tree. And everything that happened later was meant to be.

Keith crinkled his eyes against the sun but still couldn't spot the sparse blossoms at the top of the tree. 'Turn to your left and step back a little,' I suggested, so that he could have a better view. The sun was fierce, drilling into my temples. I retreated to the cool shade of a wall. Keith, his back to the fast track and one hand clutching his neck that was clearly protesting, cried out, 'Ah, I found them! There they are!'

A lie, of course. It wasn't that easy to spot small violet flowers against the dazzling ultramarine sky.

How hot it was out there beside the railway tracks! How close and sticky the scarf felt against my neck. I tugged it loose, and at that instant, a sudden breeze swept it right off my shoulder . . .

Off it fluttered, a strange black-and-gold bird flapping across the fast track, a black haze in the staring eye of the thudding train. I cried out in distress: 'My Dior, my only Dior scarf!' thinking all the time what a waste it was. I wouldn't dare buy one in Heera-Panna, not unless Marion paid for it.

And you know what Keith was like. Full of daring. Impulsive. Like an old time hero: Cary Grant, Errol Flynn, Stewart Granger, though nowhere near as handsome. I was still wailing over my scarf when he darted across the tracks for it.

The brakes screamed. They caterwauled. They shrieked like a cat outdone in battle. The train overshot, thudded, stopped. Silence for an eternity before the babble of voices erupted.

I kept in the shadow of the wall. I didn't turn back once, but crept quickly away along the quiet lanes till I emerged near St Teresa's and took a rickshaw home.

I really can't stand complications.

From that moment on, I did everything to smooth matters, but they stayed wrinkled, they stayed awry, the creases never really went away. People die every day on the tracks. People in a hurry. Desperate people. Mad people. Keith might have been in a hurry. He might have been desperate. He might have been mad. Who could tell? People must think as they please.

Who could tell? That's what I said when people asked. Who could tell Keith had it in him to do that? Handsome isn't everything, I said, rich isn't everything. It's a taint in the blood that led him to commit a mortal sin. My Marion's had a lucky escape.

I did my best to smoothen things. I really cannot stand complications.

There will be complications at Bougainvillea House. I knew that the moment I recognized Justin. One thing is certain. I am not going to have a quiet death.

The week after I arrived at Bougainvillea House, Marion turned up.

She burst in one afternoon when I was strolling back from the coconut grove with Justin. She was standing at the top of the road waiting for us—I found her there like a warning as I turned the corner. I disengaged my hand from Justin's arm and waved.

That wave bothered me. It meant that I was losing control. I had responded without thinking to a familiar face. It wasn't as though I was glad to see Marion. Her sudden appearance cracked the eggshell tenderness that was growing between Justin and me. And yet I waved to her.

Marion, my beautiful daughter. She has inherited my looks. There's very little of Clive in her. That's Melissa. Her father all over, pop eyes, and, of late, even his paunch. Earnest. Plodding. Biddable. But she doesn't have Marion's despair. Marion has always desperately wanted to be loved.

Justin was pleased to see Marion. He didn't say much, but I could see it. Marion ran down the path to meet me. She linked her arm firmly in mine and we tottered the rest of the way to the house. Funny how I always seem to totter with Marion. I walked well enough on Justin's arm.

'Don't fuss, Marion,' I said crossly. 'You can see how I've improved. I walk almost a mile every day. Don't we, Doctor?'

'You shouldn't tire her out like that,' she reproached. Justin shrugged. He was tongue-tied in her presence.

'You're here to rest, not train for the Olympics,' Marion scolded when Justin had left. She was thinner than she had been a fortnight ago. Her hair was dull and limp. There were lines on her face I hadn't noticed before. My daughter was an old woman. Silently, I cursed Keith Ferrao.

'Why don't you visit Melissa for a while,' I suggested later. 'You're all worn out. You need a holiday.'

She was at the dressing table when I said this. She was brushing her hair, standing in her slip. Her shoulder blades stuck out like fins. She stopped brushing. We were used to each other. She knew what I was really trying to say.

In the mirror her jaw tightened. It was the old look I had learned to dread. It meant she was going to stay. 'I'll be here at least a fortnight,' she said, and I knew that was final. It is futile to cross Marion's will. Though I have learned to bend it over the years.

I knew the peaceful pattern of life at Bougainvillea House would change with Marion there, and it did.

Perhaps I haven't quite told it the way it was. Let me try again.

That afternoon, I ate no lunch. I asked Pauline to undress me quite early and was lying in bed when Marion came in. She had taken off the striped dress she was wearing, and stood in her slip brushing her hair. 'I'll be here at least a fortnight,' she said.

I shut my eyes. There were red and green lights flashing behind my eyelids. I was tired. I wanted to swoon into the softness of cushions, of quilts, of mattresses ethereal as clouds. I wanted to be rocked in their womb every time I breathed. Air hung heavy between my fingers. Light washed my palms. My hair was a snarl of electric wire, heavy copper filaments that cut without insulation.

Marion kept talking. Through my weariness her words surfaced in fragments, running into each other, and getting lost: ... not good ... recov ... stre ... Mor ... todwell ... past.

That's what I remember. And then I noticed she was crying.

She sat hunched in front of the mirror, tears splashing down the pale blue slip till it had grey maps all over her breasts and I could see the lace half-cups she wore. She flung her brush against the cupboard. It missed and flopped awkwardly on the carpet. She turned fiercely towards me, rage mottling her old-woman neck till she looked like a guinea-hen. 'You're all I have left, Mamma—listen, do you hear me? Don't pretend to sleep, I know you're listening. You're all I have!'

Wearily, I shut my eyes and slept.

It was inevitable, I suppose. Marion stayed the fortnight. She spent a lot of time with Justin. He no longer walked with me to the coconut grove. I hardly went there all that week. But I had dreams.

I let Pauline take me to the beach. The sea frightens me, yet I went with Pauline. I hadn't been there since '62.

There weren't any hippies on Baga then. They came the following year, and all the women topless. Clive was out of it by then, safe at St Andrews, safe from the brazen glare of rose-brown eyes and bouncing flesh.

All the men in my life have been zeros. Clive, Keith, and Tom who talks like an Indian. And now Justin—Justin who has inherited the stupidity and coarseness and the natural servility and heat of a mother who was little better than a slave.

I like thinking of her. It comforts me to see her like this: She is old. Her skin is thick and opaque and soft, with little pores and marks like a cold omelette. Her hair is grey—no, without colour, like the fuzz of maize. Some days I make her bald. She has a small solid nose, like a red-brown cube of steak. Within the red dress (she wears nothing else in my memory) her breasts hang limp like last week's party balloons. The party lasted longer than Clive, of that I'm certain. There were other masters she obeyed. And yet, here is Justin. That old drunk Borges married her when her belly was full—out of pity? Out of shame?

The first morning we went to the beach, Pauline and I, it was cool, but sunny. Pauline staggered under the load I made her carry: rug, beach umbrella, thermos of lemonade, bottles of sunscreen and moisturizer. I liked walking on sand. I took off my sandals and gave them to Pauline, and gloried in the trickle and sift of sand between my toes, till fatigue overcame me. We found a suitable place to pitch camp. I stretched out on the rug, and missed my cushion. No point in being uncomfortable! So I sent Pauline back to the house for it, and asked her to fetch some sandwiches too.

Pauline's retreating figure looked like a black gas cylinder, rolling on casters. I've always wondered about Pauline. What does she see? What does she think? Always, at all the important moments of my life, I have found Pauline. Perhaps she will be waiting for me at the pearly gates, robe and harp in hand.

She was here with me that day in Bougainvillea House.

I'll tell you the date right away: 18 June, 1962.

The clock struck four as I entered. She saw me come into the house.

That clock doesn't strike any more. I had the gong removed before we left Bougainvillea House. When they were fussing over the arrangements, I had someone come down from Calangute to fix it. He worked right here, within the sightless stare of Clive's eyes. I sat in the rocking chair, watching him. That clock never struck again.

It struck four as I entered that day. Bong. Bong. Bong. Bong. Each interval an eternity of menace. I stood there staring at its white blistered face, my feet muddying the floor. My hair was stuck to my face like a web, like a membrane. I was trapped in my own hair, in my thoughts. I could not move. Having walked so far, I could not move now. I was trapped within the tight compass of those four bass notes: bong-bong-bong-bong.

Pauline came in.

What would have happened if Pauline hadn't come in?

But Pauline did come in. She came from the kitchen, she rushed when she saw me, ran all the way from the door. She carried me, dragged me, coaxed me up the stairs. And then there was the glare of white tiles quickly lost in the fog of blessed, blessed steam. She tore the foul clothes off me, and bundled me in a fleecy cocoon, deep pile Turkish—I can never bear any other sort of towelling. How its velvet nap bristled against my cringing skin—I remember that. Yes, I remember that. My feet splayed, comforted, in a hot swirl of water. Soap on my calves. Tears of mud rolling off my thighs. My skin weeping, cleansed in the hot mist. Face sponged. Hair dried. Soft soles curling into her rough palms. Tea with rum in it, stinging the stomach like a slap.

I sipped, and the world moved again.

She pulled a flannel nightie over me. Now I was in bed, tucked like a child. *This is how life will be from now on: all Pauline, and no Clive.*

I heard my voice lie weakly, 'Where's Mr Clive?'

'He went out after lunch.'

I shut my eyes. My brain raced, clear, frightened. I had come home with my clothes caked with mud, my legs wearing a second, darker skin. I couldn't say I'd been to the beach—and in the rain? No, I had to find something else. God has always come to my aid at moments like this. 'I wanted to see the grotto at St Anne's,' I said wearily. 'Old Maria said—'

'They all say that here, Baby. They'll say anything, believe anything, these villagers! Two candles and your man forgets the taste of feni, they say. Who'll believe them? What did you want candles for, Baby? You'll go back to Bandra and Clivebab will be all right, he'll forget all about Baga, candles or no candles.'

I rose angrily on my elbow. 'What are you talking about, Pauline?'

She smiled slyly and moved away. 'Nothing, nothing. It'll get better, Baby, everything gets better if you wait. Now you sleep. The rain has stopped and the children will want to go out.'

Pauline, even in those days, was old. She has always looked like this, as long as I can remember. Stout, plump stomach and a bosom like a pillow that my daughters have cuddled up to all their growing years. Pauline must have been young thirty-five years ago. I think she's about a hundred now, strong as an ox. It's the breed. They don't tire easily. She won't admit it, but she's Indian through and through. I've taught her to speak a civilized tongue, at least to me—but her Portuguese isn't even skin deep! The moment I turn my back it's yackyackyack in her barbaric Konkani. Mind you, no Konkani with the children, I warned her when they were babies, only English, even if it must be your Indian brand of it.

By late evening, I was anxious. Clive was not back. I asked Pauline to put the children to bed early.

It had started to rain again, a thick black drool, like blood congealing, like the green slither of slime at the bottom of a well.

I wanted to shut the windows tight, bolt and barricade the door, switch off the lights and cower in the darkness for what may come. But nothing did. The lights stayed on. The rain kept up its oily ooze against the panes.

At eight, Pauline said maybe she should go and look. Where? For what? I did not ask. She did not say. We played it that way. After Pauline left, I went into the children's bedroom and sat with my hands comforted by the hot, soft rolls of their small bodies. I have never found such comfort in them since. But then, I have never again sought it . . .

Pauline returned at ten o'clock. She wouldn't meet my eye when she entered. Over her shoulder she said, 'He isn't there,' and went into the bathroom to take off her wet dress.

'Perhaps he's left. Perhaps you just missed him.'

'Perhaps.'

'Didn't you ask them?'

'No. I could see he wasn't there. There was only one person in the hut.'

How did she know that? She must have got them to open the door and let her in. There would have been some conversation. And it wasn't a hut. It was a small cottage, crude, poor, but still, not a hut. I am a just woman, and I give credit where credit is due. It was a small tidy cottage. I had been there earlier that afternoon, knowing it was Thursday and she wouldn't be at home. And what if she were? It was *she* who must tremble, not I!

How did I know her house? I had followed her once before. Now why did I say that? I don't have to explain, I don't have to tell you why. Ask no questions and I'll tell no lies, that's the deal. Your back twitches now and then. Is that a question? Leave off, or I'll fall silent and make gargling noises in my throat.

There was a chair on the porch. A thin cotton strip for curtain stirred in the doorway. Pretensions! All these Indians have pretensions. The door was open. I thought there might be someone inside. If there was, I would not need to explain my presence to a person of that class. They would ask no questions, feeling their home honoured by my presence. I might invent a story, or I need not. That's what blood is, isn't it? The ability to feel at ease anywhere. Be gracious, I've taught my girls. Every Christmas I used to send them out to poor homes, carrying gifts. Don't eat anything, I used to tell them, don't touch the cake.

The door was open. I went in. There was nobody in there. The floor felt cool beneath the wet slap of my bare feet. It was good and muddy before I left. The kitchen was in one corner, a dark angle, no more. There was a narrow bed, the mattress no thicker than a couple of sheets. Another roll of bedding against the wall. On the cot's railing, that red dress, neatly folded. Ants crawled beneath my skin as I touched its rough folds. Next to the bed was a sewing machine. That meant scissors near by. I found them. I cut the belt off that dress with one neat snip. It coiled in my palm like a hangman's rope. I did not keep it with me for long.

Pauline said: 'She's at Mapusa. They go there every Thursday to sell piece work, mother and daughter. The old woman came back today but she stayed back there. She stays with her aunt sometimes.'

'Who does?' I asked, making the rules clear to Pauline. I was back in bed by then, sipping my nightcap, luxurious, secure. Pauline should have kept to rules. She realized it too, for her face took on a sulky look, all pouch and jowl. She turned away.

I was smitten by terror. It was my first fear since afternoon, and it did not pussyfoot as dread or worry. It barged in and smashed its fist in my face, knocking me out. Terror, yes, that was its name.

'Pauline!' I screamed out. 'Pauline, don't go! I'm scared!' There are times when nothing works quite as well as the truth. This was one of them. It brought Pauline back. It replaced the sullen look on her face with tenderness, it converted me from scheming wife—or widow—into frightened woman. Pauline gathered me up, crushed me against her pillows. She had a safe smell, like a kitchen one knows.

'He'll be back, Baby,' she kept saying.

'Maybe he's gone to Mapusa too.'

'With the old woman?' We giggled, girls together. Clive was the enemy, the oddity. I was no longer the injured wife. I was, like Pauline, the gossip with a delicious secret.

Pauline brought her crochet to my room and sat by me till I fell asleep. I slept easy that night, more easily than I had in all the nights of our marriage. I woke refreshed at eight, as usual, when Pauline drew the curtains. Then I saw her face, and knew. Clive hadn't returned.

Marion was fractious, asking for Daddy. Melissa ate too much breakfast and was sick. I sat with them at the table thinking how stupid my children were. They hadn't a clue that I was dizzy with terror. Mummy, Mummy, they whined that morning. That was strange too. They never came to me until they were dressed and ready to go out. It was Pauline they usually whined for. Why was it my turn that morning?

Any moment now, there would be news about Clive. I begged Pauline to take the children away to the beach. I wanted to be alone, to think. It was nine o'clock.

The rain had stopped. It was a clear blue day with masses of fluffy cloud, clean and white. Everything looked washed and laundered crisp. I wanted to run into the garden, to laugh, to sing, to be happy. I was happy. I'll never forget that hour of solitude. My terror melted away into a cool bath of happiness in which I splashed and frolicked, knowing it wouldn't last.

At ten, Pauline came running in, dragging Melissa, and Marion on her hip. The children squirmed away from her and clung to me, whimpering. I was peeling them away when Pauline too collapsed against me, wailing. Really! They were all behaving as though the end of the world was here. I pushed Pauline from me and screamed at her to stop it and speak up. Immediately, she became the proper servant. She backed away a pace and hung her head. I could hardly make out the words.

There was news. Clive had been found. He had drowned himself in the old well.

After that, a great deal happened. People I had never seen before walked in and out of the house. Everybody was kind to me. Sisters from St Anne's took the children away, Marion still screaming for Daddy. Pauline brought me tea.

I spent the morning trying to phone the clock shop at Panjim. Nobody else seemed bothered. I kept dialling and dialling and nobody seemed to care. Finally somebody picked up the phone. I got someone who spoke English. I must have the clock seen to at once, I said. There has been a tragedy in the house and the clock must be silenced. At once.

Sometime during all this, they brought in Clive. Pauline had a sheet ready to cover him. They laid him on the floor—I made Pauline roll up the carpet just in time. 'Cover him, Pauline,' I said, looking out of the window. People crowded the road outside. All of Baga waited at the gates. I met their avid gaze unafraid, my back to Clive's glazed eyes. I couldn't bear to see his pop eyes one more time, the bulging whites glaring at me in the dark. Not one more time. I couldn't bear it. I left the room. I was sick before I reached the bathroom, sick, sick, sick.

All that time, I could only think of the mad black eye of that old well.

The creek ends at an old temple. Nobody worships there anymore. The Portuguese ravaged it, of course, but they didn't make a church of it, it could never have been grand. The local people don't think much of it. The walls are hidden under dark green slime and moss. But here and there a crack opens and a hard edge of stone catches the light. For all its decrepitude, the ruin still holds its own. You can think what it's used for, then. Wherever there are young people, that's what places like these are used for. But Clive was not young.

I can see the temple now, I can feel its air. It's a room of shadows. It's lit by a hole in the roof, a central skylight through which a sunbeam slants, flat as a slab of stone. The broken idol stood beneath the skylight. How can I tell what idol? I was brought up not to notice these things. I don't know these Hindu gods with four arms and as many heads and the strange animals and birds they keep with. I don't know their outlandish names. I can only see the gouged rock where the idol was broken. Perhaps the stones beneath my feet were fragments of that god.

I liked walking into that temple, though I couldn't tell why. In there, I was myself. Unquestioned, neither good nor evil, ugly nor beautiful, useful nor wasted. I was I. The torn ceiling, the broken wall, the riven pedestal of the idol, these fragments were complete in themselves. They spelt order in a way that Clive's spotless house never could.

And it was disorder that had survived.

The coconut palms around the temple were short and crowded, an army of midgets left behind to guard the temple with no god in it. The well was a few paces away. It was a deep well. Its throat was a black disc of glass from which the sun glittered up at me. Surely it was as old as the temple, but people still used it occasionally.

Its brick wall was crumbling.

On one of my afternoon trips to the grove—oh there had been

many over those last two weeks—I had nearly died because of a pebble in my shoe ... I gripped the well's brick ledge to steady myself as I bent to slip off the shoe. Imagine my shock when the ledge simply caved. I saved myself in time, falling on my right side to break the plunge. In my fall, I tore down more bricks. I screamed, but nobody heard me.

There was a green light around the well, cool and dark, but not menacing. A crow rattled the palm leaves, and for some reason, I laughed.

I knew what that well would accomplish for me.

I piled the bricks back carefully. Now only a gap on the edge showed where the first few bricks had toppled into the well.

I walked home thoughtfully. I avoided the coconut grove. I did not want to watch them. They would be there for certain. By now I knew the pattern of their meetings. I knew the pattern of her life. That was Wednesday afternoon. Thursdays, she went to Mapusa with her mother, to sell the rags they had sewn, crouched over the sewing machine all week. Probably sat up all night doing it, as all her afternoons were taken up with Clive.

I knew a lot about her. I knew everything about her except her name.

Clive came home at tea time. I'd never known him to miss a meal. He looked exhausted. 'You need a good long rest, Clive,' I said, handing him the plate of sandwiches. He smiled uneasily as he wolfed down the sandwiches, and patties from Fortino's—chicken, with a rich larded crust, flaky as a cloud. He ate six.

I sighed. My mouth had the sad droop of the oppressed wife. 'I wish you'd come with me tomorrow, Clive,' I said softly, 'just the two of us, please? There's something I want to show you, something I want for us.'

'Of course. Any time you say. Any time.' He stood when I left the table, like a little boy who's just remembered his manners.

That's how he agreed to go with me to the old well.

⁓

I thought about that time, I thought about Clive as I waited on the beach for Pauline to return. All that happened a long time ago. All that happened yesterday. In Baga, everything happens yesterday.

The sand was growing warmer. The sea had grown a cheap glitter, like a sari border, at its edge. It was beginning to give me a headache.

Pauline was some time bringing me the sandwiches and that cushion. She settled it comfortably, then flopped down on the sand next to me.

'You stop going to that coconut grove, Baby,' she said severely. 'Very bad for your health, it is,' she said. 'See how much worse you've grown all this week.'

Had I? That morning the lipstick was too heavy for my grip. But my legs weren't giving me any trouble. Not yet. I could still walk to the coconut grove. If I could rest there for an hour, my knees felt strong again.

Pauline hadn't spoken to me in that tone for a long while. Her words transported me back to that first time in Bougainvillea House. The sun brushed my eyelids lazily. I floated on the sand, listening to Pauline.

'You should see another doctor. Not Justin.'

'Why?'

'Don't play games with me, Baby. You play games with everybody, and you think they can't see through you. But not with Pauline. Either speak the truth or stay silent.'

That was grand!

We played a game all right—she was servant, I mistress. But that was pretence. We were conspirators. Pauline knew about the girl in the red dress (as if she never wore any other). Pauline knew why Clive had drowned in that well. Pauline knew why the coconut grove compelled my flagging feet, all these years later, towards that bald mound. But that's all Pauline knew.

I said, 'You think Justin isn't old Borges's son.'

Pauline shrugged. She dug into her pocket and brought out an old wallet. In its plastic cover was an old photograph. I was touched. I didn't know she cared so much. It was our wedding photograph. How young I looked—and how lovely! I remember how difficult the veil was, real Valenciennes lace, my grandmother's. How lovely I was.

And beside me stood Justin.

I had forgotten how like Justin Clive used to look those days. Justin had the advantage of intelligence. It lit his eyes with mischief, it made patterns of his words and gave his voice texture.

Nonetheless, that first morning, I had mistaken Justin for his father. Justin was Clive's son. I could not escape that truth.

I handed the photograph back. 'There's a resemblance, certainly. But so what? One dark stocky young man is very like another.'

'Clivebab was not dark.'

'True. What then?'

'I know what happened to her after Clivebab died.'

'Oh? And how do you know what happened to whoever?'

'You never knew her name. You never wanted to know. It was easy to forget. I found out because I did not want any trouble, Baby. I didn't want her landing up at your doorstep with a baby. I did not want the girls to know. She married that old drunk Borges. He'd been after her a long while. He didn't care that the baby came too soon to be his.'

I sighed. There was no point in pretending to Pauline any longer. 'I don't care about who she was and what she did or whose baby she bore. She has nothing to do with me, or I with her. As for Mr Clive—I've forgiven him a long time ago.'

Pauline studied her hands. Her palms are rough with calluses, cracked and harsh. They are the hands of a servant. Hands that must be put to work, or else die. They cannot exist as mine do, soft, elegant, tenderly cared for, manicured and massaged. I have idle hands. Without Pauline's hands I will soon be unable to live. Pauline's hands are my will.

Now I watched those hands shake. Suddenly I wanted to see them wrung.

'You had a warmth in your heart for your Clivebab, didn't you, Pauline? You were in love with him.' I couldn't hold back my laughter. It was such a ridiculous thought! 'You're a fool, Pauline. What made you think he would even look your way? When was the last time you looked in the mirror, Pauline? Have you ever seen your face?' I laughed so hard, I began to wet myself. This was a new worry. It sobered me up immediately. I forgot Pauline, I forgot Clive, I forgot everything but the ferocious intent of my scissoring legs.

I stopped. I unwound my legs and let the slow warmth of the sun soothe my tired muscles. Presently, my fingers felt strong enough to undo the waxed paper of the sandwiches. Cucumber, wafer-thin, with the faintest dusting of pepper. Lush with butter, of course. I like butter frozen so that it can be sliced like cheese.

Pauline makes butter at home by skimming cream. I can't stand the stuff. Nothing but Polson in the old days for me. These days you can get nothing but Amul. They say in Australia they butter the floor. I keep telling Tom to emigrate, but does he listen?

Sun, laughter, food. I felt good. I said lazily, 'Give me a glass of that lemonade, Pauline.'

She planted the thermos between my palms and went back to staring at her hands. Unscrewing the cap of the thermos was beyond my strength. That lemonade weighed like lead.

'What are you waiting for, Pauline?'

Pauline didn't move. My hands trembled. Just as I knew it would, the flask slipped from my grip and slid down on the sand. My pulse roared till my bones rattled with its thunder.

Pauline sat next to me as if nothing had happened. After a while, she rose and walked away.

Do you know what it feels like to be left lying on the sand, unable to rise? In some time the sun will bite through the umbrella. The white glare will grind its thumbs into your eyeballs till you want to vomit. You will feel yourself sinking millimetre by millimetre into that soft lap which will pull you right into the centre of the earth's hot breathless dark from which there is no repeal.

You can never know what it is to be left lying in the sand, unable to rise. You can get up and walk unaided, run, stride after Pauline and grip her fat neck and force her head down among the dunes and sandpaper her eyes. You can do that when you have a will.

You can do that if you don't have motor neuron disease.

I do.

When Pauline walked off like that, I had to look at what my world had become. It had become a yo-yo and Pauline held the string. I could have opened that flask. I could, with freakish courage, have hooped my wrist with steel. But Pauline robbed me of will, and I let the flask roll heavily, muffled by the sand, like a funeral drum.

Lying there in the sand, my eyes flattened by the looking-glass glare of the cloudless sky, death began to enter me. I saw it at that moment for what it is, stripped of ornament and glamour. A slow bloat with the ooze of corruption.

Death began in me.

When you feel death enter you, you suddenly see how trivial everything else is. You see the pettiness of the goals you strived to reach. The people you loved seem strange to you. You watch them through the sheet of glass that is your body, the glass that is beginning to crack in stars, in spidery circles. Everything outside the glass is unreal. Real is inside the glass. Real is you, and fast dwindling. Nothing is important but to keep real. There are no loyalties except real. There are no relationships. There are no principles except one: stay real. Stay.

Pauline would return. Even through my panic, I knew that. She had to. Pauline lacked nerve. More, she lacked experience. I possessed both in equal measure. I would have planned it differently, had I been Pauline. Now she would have to return—or lose her place. Disgraced, who would have her then? She had no family, no home, no income but what I promised to give her. The truth was that she needed me as much as I needed her. But now the game would be played differently. Pauline would continue to keep up a pretence, and so would I, though this time, pretence of a different sort.

So when Pauline returned, as I knew she would, I was humble with her. Nothing was said. When she picked up the thermos, I grasped her rough hands and shed a few judicious tears. She began to cry too, and for some time we kept at it, two old women sobbing in the sun.

Then she unscrewed the cap of the thermos and poured me some lemonade. I made her have some too, and with that, my act of contrition was complete.

I said nothing of this to Marion.

~

Marion was spending a lot of time with Justin. I couldn't see what for. Justin came to lunch and stayed for tea. Justin took Marion out to dinner. They went for long walks on the beach. They spent hours on the telephone.

'Am I your only patient, Doctor?' I asked Justin one afternoon.

'No, but my most important one.'

Glib, that boy was.

I remember that afternoon. He was waiting for Marion to fetch her umbrella. They were on their way to the canoe rest. Marion wanted to do the canoe trip. So did I. I wanted to the first time too, but Clive never took me. Neither did Marion—both Justin and she said it would upset me. 'I won't spoil your fun,' I said. 'Pauline can take me some day.'

Naturally, after that, Marion didn't do the canoe trip, either. When they reached the canoe rest, she felt giddy and they had to turn back.

While they were away, I had Pauline bring me lunch in the patio. I asked her to sit with me while I ate. I wanted her to feel my friendliness. Lunch was a dull affair: steamed mullet, tomato soup, sanas, caramel custard. A lunch that didn't tire my jaws. Very soon, the sanas would become difficult to tackle. I had taken to using a napkin all the time.

Looking back, I see where I made a mistake. It would have been cleverer to ask Pauline to bring her own lunch to the patio, too, but I can never stand the way Indians eat, dabbling their thick fingers in rice and gravy. It makes me sick to watch them.

'Pauline, I'm worried,' I began when she had adjusted my cushions. 'I'm worried about Justin.' I saw the sulky look come upon her face so I went on hastily: 'Yes, I know you got angry with me the other day on the beach. But you know what we old women are . . .' I paused for the loyal protest—'You're not old, Baby'. It did not come. I was still on shaky ground. 'Marion's not going to see what you and I can see. Marion doesn't even remember what Clive looked like. Photographs? She'd just dismiss it as a passing resemblance, no more. You see, Pauline, it's Justin who is real to her.'

Pauline nodded. It was Clive who was real to both of us. 'I heard she has a house in Anjuna,' she said hesitantly.

'Still stitching, I suppose!'

Pauline refused to meet my gaze for some moments. Then she said in a strangled voice, 'She came here that night.'

'Here? To this house? How she dared!'

'She came the back way. I saw her just as I was setting out towards her hut. You remember, Baby, I said I was going to look for him? She also had come here, looking for him. She clutched at me, jabbering wildly. Her words made no sense. "He cut my dress," she kept saying. I understood that Clivebab had been in their house when they were gone to Mapusa. "He cut my dress! He cut my dress!" She was shaking with fear. How could I pretend, Baby? I calmed her down. I said I understood . . . I told her Clivebab was not home yet. That made her wring her hands and whimper. I did my best to soothe her. I went back with her to her hut. He had never come there, her mother said. He was too grand for a humble place like theirs, she said. "My daughter is like a mango," she said. "When he has sucked her dry of juice he will spit her out like a stone." But something was up, all right, she said. Why had he come into their house when it was empty, why had he cut her daughter's dress?

'"How do you know it was him?" I asked the girl. She said nothing. She only looked at me, Baby, and a knife went through my heart.

'Early next morning, long before you and the children woke up, I went to her house again. I went because I was afraid, and you were sleeping like a baby in your innocence. With whom could I share my fear? I found them, mother and daughter, sitting on the porch, staring into the black dawn. It wasn't yet five. They hadn't slept all night.'

'What did she say?'

'She showed me a red dress. He had cut the belt off it, she said. It frightened her, and it frightened me. Why should he do a thing like that, Baby? Then in the morning, by ten o'clock, everybody knew. And she was right about that belt.'

'What do you mean?'

'They found it with Clivebab's body, a limp piece of red cloth. They thought it was just rubbish. People use that well as a dump. But I remember, it was stuck to his shirt when they laid him on the grass.'

You're lying, I wanted to scream, you weren't there!

'Surely you imagined that, Pauline!' I said scornfully. 'Why, you weren't even there. You were with the children.'

'No. I left them with the cook and ran back there after I told you. I knew you wouldn't ask questions. You were like a statue that day.'

'Did you know then?' There was no need to elaborate on that. Pauline understood.

'Too early to tell, wasn't it? Then the old one must have made Borges marry her before it began to show. Now we know, but who else will? It was so many years ago.'

'A very long time ago.'

Time unwound itself in silence. I saw the endless procession of days that marched like mutes after Clive's cortege. They were black days, muffled, slow-paced, leading up to me, to this moment, and past it, and past the well again, towards the churchyard at St Anne's.

It would be St Anne's, I was sure of that. I would never see Bandra again. My heart griped with sudden anguish. Bandra was home. I should be dying there, not here in Bougainvillea House.

Tears fell unbidden into the caramel custard. The spoon slipped from my fingers. The endless moment when the cup toppled was crowded with the grief of a lifetime. It was coming to a finish, this life of mine, and what had I to show for it?

The question echoed in my hollow skull all the time that Pauline was cleaning up the mess, walking me up the stairs, undressing me, getting me cozy among the cushions. Dr Khan had given me pills to save for really bad moments. I asked for them now, two discs of dreamy blue. Tickets to oblivion.

The flat is silent.

There are no sounds from the kitchen.

I've got the bathroom tap fixed, so the drip doesn't set my nerves on edge.

It's peaceful now.

Yesterday I got rid of the bai. I don't need any help with the housework. There's just me. The house is neat as a pin, not a grain of dust anywhere.

I've stopped thinking about food. I forget to eat some days. There are sandwiches curling in the fridge.

The flat's too quiet.

I'll get a bird. Two birds. Lovebirds, lime green and sky blue. I can have them now if I'm careful. He wanted to buy me a pair, but I said no. I didn't tell him it was because she would never stand for it. I didn't tell him. It would have led on to something, something nasty he would have said about her. Something like a dagger in my heart.

I miss him. I didn't think I'd miss him so much. I miss him.

I'm getting rid of all the stuff. I gave that silly girl the box of Body Shop bath salts and gel and that expensive creme de mer. She was so thrilled, it was pathetic. What's the point my hoarding all that stuff?

There's still the little satin bag at the bottom of the cupboard. What a time I had hiding that from her.

Now I can keep things anywhere I please. What's the use, though, it only makes me sad.

What shall I do with this little bag? I've emptied it on the bed. All these pretty things look so silly now, all their bright cheeky colours so cheap. I wish I hadn't bought these things. Really, some of them—but it felt different then.

Harlot, she'll say if she sees them. Silently, shaping her lips. *Harlot*. That's the word she'll pick, it's in the Bible. *Harlot* she'll say. She'll laugh. She'll dangle the stuff before him next time.

What am I saying. There is no next time.

I mustn't let her know. There is nothing to know, actually, just my fear. I am afraid all the time.

I can't bear it. I can't bear to think of what's next. I can't bear it.

Clarice, Tape 2

Where did those pills carry me that afternoon? I've often wondered. It was a long way I travelled: it was two when I went to bed and a little after four when I awoke. I hurtled through miles, an astronaut in the void between worlds. Perhaps I died. Perhaps this is death and that—the transient flash—was life.

I felt time, or time felt me, for I felt myself held and kneaded and moulded into ... what? It was Time with a capital T, Einstein's Time. They gave him the Nobel Prize for that, imagine. I remember taking up a lesson on him when Marion was in school. She could never spell Theory right. The Theory of Relatives, she wrote in her test. How all of us laughed! I don't know why they made such a fuss about Einstein, he only gave a fancy name to a common truth. Five minutes in Clive's company was like a lifetime or two. If that isn't Relativity, what is? I got no prizes for that, though.

Time, I was telling you—my faceless, nameless confessor—I was telling you about Time. Time stretched or bent or opened out for me in that pill sleep. I dreamed. Long cushiony colours. Deep green with a sheen to it. Satin blue. Black—thick velvet black. A deep and dangerous red that flashed every time my eyeballs roved. I saw all that. I was led down thoughts that twisted through the snarls and ravines and crevices of my brain. I slipped and slid with my thoughts, careened with them.

Thoughts are different from feelings. Feelings are inside my blouse. Not within the ribs, not that deep where the heart has its trampoline. Feelings are on your chest, where your breasts are. Bad feelings are like wearing a tight bra, and good feelings like no bra at all. Most of the time our feelings are disciplined in a well-fitting bra with good support. Styles change. Feelings, too, go out of fashion. But they come back, yes, they do, look at that Madonna in those kulfi cones we used to stuff ourselves into in the sixties. Feelings shouldn't be allowed to bounce about. I've never allowed that. I take a 36 C underwire, cotton always, Triumph mostly, though I'm not against a good Marks & Spencer when I can get it. Indian brands are for Indians. They're shaped differently, have you noticed? Maidenform's good enough for *them*. The shops on Hill Road have Korean, all frothy lace and heartbreaking pastels, but the sizes are all bonsai. Or is that Japanese?

I'm telling you this about thoughts and feelings because these ideas meandered through my sleep. I saw no pictures. The ideas shrank one beyond the other as colours, not as words. How far I travelled that afternoon! And when I awoke I found that I hadn't moved at all.

It all wheeled slowly back into place. The gears engaged noiselessly and locked. If I were to rise, life would begin its smooth glide into death. So I lingered, wishing to delay by a minute more the moment of departure. My mind fluttered, full of falling things like plastic bags, toffee wrappers, old torn shreds of lace. Shiny, brittle, useless things. Waste. These things were trash. My trashy thoughts. While I slept, the top of my head exploded like the scab on a pimple and this was all that shot out, this handful of scrap. I waited for these stray thoughts to settle. They fell to the floor eventually, almost as if they were real. Pauline could pick up the litter afterwards.

When I had tossed out this trash, I felt cool and clear, a clear green through and through. I tasted toothpaste. My arms and legs were crisp sticks of some faint green vegetable—asparagus perhaps, exquisitely tender. I was a shrub, a seedling, the first new leaf. I was nascent. I was born.

I got up and dressed myself without Pauline's help. I hadn't done that in a long, long while. When would I do that again?

I chose my best cotton frock, the apple-green seersucker with green braiding. I used a dash of emerald green on my eyelids, and a burgundy blush. For my lips I picked a soft plum, just a hint beyond natural. No perfume. Nothing that would interfere with the dark stains of my life.

I found Marion and Pauline in the kitchen. Marion put her arm around my shoulders and drew me to a chair. 'Stop treating me like an old woman,' I grumbled, but it was all pretence. I enjoyed being loved.

I sipped tea, grateful for its clean flavour, its mild sweetness and sharp warmth. I ate nothing. There was work to do. As yet I had no plan, but it would emerge. The best plans, I can tell you, come from inspiration, not deliberation.

'I've made up my mind,' I announced as I set down my cup. 'I'm going to live!'

They stared uncertainly at me.

'Oh yes, I am. Dr Khan is not going to cure me, neither is Justin. God is going to cure me. Sweet Jesus is going to cure me. I have faith.'

Pauline crossed herself fearfully. Marion said, 'Of course, Mamma'—loyally, but without conviction.

'And you're going to help me, Marion. You must be my arms and legs, carry my heart and soul with you to Panjim.'

'We'll go early tomorrow morning, Mamma. We'll take the car. We'll make a regular picnic of it.'

'Oh I'm not coming, Marion. I will offer a novena at St Anne's. And tomorrow will be too late. Don't argue with faith, Marion. Go today to Our Lady of the Rosary. Go now and offer my prayers to the Virgin. Go.'

I urged Pauline to make the trip with her. They could be back by dinner time. It was barely four now. I hurried them with my newfound hopes. They cowered before the effulgence of my faith. Pauline gave up conversing, and prayed audibly.

They left at last, and I was all alone at Bougainvillea House.

I telephoned Justin. I said I needed to speak with him urgently. He hesitated. Couldn't it wait till morning?

That decided me. Till then I hadn't been certain of exactly what I should do. I knew now. That second of hesitation cost Justin his life, I suppose—but it made mine.

It can't wait, I told him. Now.

Then I sat down to wait for him. A curious immobility possessed me. But it did not frighten me. It was lightness. That compelling force which makes a duty of the crazy dance of life had drained out of me. Nothing mattered if I did. Nothing mattered if I didn't.

Justin arrived at last.

When he had exhausted his meagre stock of pleasantries, I said, 'Justin, I have been keeping something from you. It may be vital to my treatment. I want you to know it now.'

His banter dried up. He said gently, 'You've been overdoing it of late—'

'Far from it. First, let me say this to you, Doctor, as I may not have another opportunity—thank you. Thank you, Justin. You've been more than a doctor. You've been a son to me. You've been a blessing.' I leaned across and kissed him on the cheek. He was embarrassed. I continued: 'Is it true that disease is as much a state of the mind as of the body?'

'Er . . . yes. That's true.'

'You sound uncertain. Perhaps you have no faith?'

'Faith is distinct from science, Aunty. They can coexist, but not quarrel. If they do, one or the other must quit.'

'Explain.'

'If you believe—for instance—that faith can cure motor neuron disease, then faith is quarrelling with science. One or the other will quit on you, and chances are that faith will. But if you believe that faith can help you cope with motor neuron disease—you're probably right in that. It can help you cope, but not conquer.'

'Such ideas don't cross my mind, Justin. I'm a simple woman, I can't reason the way you do. But I do believe that disease is a state of the mind as much as it is a state of the body. By this I mean that if I have some fear or guilt weighing on my mind, if I don't face it, don't resolve it, it speaks through my body. I fall ill.'

'There could be some truth in that, yes.'

'There are people who even get paralysed—when they don't speak out what's in their mind. I read that in *Reader's Digest*. Women who want children desperately begin to look pregnant, even when they aren't. I've read about these things.'

'Sure. But these are hysterical illnesses—'

'Hysterical! That's all you men ever call us!'

'I'm not calling you hysterical. There's nothing hysterical about your illness at all. And if you're a recent convert to one of these prayer groups who mumbles over you—let me warn you very seriously against them. You have motor neuron disease. You can certainly pray and strengthen your spirit to fight its ravages.

That will lessen your suffering. But it will not cure you. The illnesses you mentioned are cured once you get to their cause—the troubled mind. But you don't have an illness of that sort.'

'How do you know?'

'Because—'

'No. Let me finish. As my doctor, you should know what's been building up in my mind all these years.'

'I can arrange for you to speak to a priest—'

'Pah! I have no use for priests!'

'But you have faith!'

'Faith in the Redeemer. But I will speak to no priest.'

'A psychiatrist, then.'

'So now I'm mad.'

'Most people who consult psychiatrists are flat-footedly sane. They go to the psychiatrist because they cannot afford the luxury of madness. The smart ones seek help. The stupid kill themselves.'

'I'm smart, but not that smart. No. I don't need a psychiatrist. I want to speak to you.'

'I'm here.'

'So you are, Justin, so you are. You have your car? Good. Take me to St Anne's. Our pilgrimage begins there.'

That sounded grand. I did not want to spoil the effect by talking anymore, so when he made several attempts to start a conversation, I stopped him with a gesture of weariness. I was anything but weary. That wonderful light immobility still possessed me. I wanted it unthreatened, inviolate. I had no energy to spare for verbal combat.

Service was over by the time we reached the church. I knelt, Justin beside me, and bowed my head into my supplicant palms. I felt a fierce joy shake me as a wind shakes a tree. I was kneeling! I, who found walking difficult—I was kneeling in the full confidence that I would be able to rise and walk without hindrance! I prayed for strength. I prayed for determination. Suddenly, it was easy to believe in miracles.

I touched Justin's sleeve and felt a wave of pure love for him. His eyes travelled my face in wonder. I knew he would feel the force in me. Soon, he too would believe in miracles. I whispered, 'Lourdes is here.'

I rose, purified in the white heat of faith. I was calm and strong. My legs walked firmly, the prayer book was secure in my clasp.

The interior of the church was murky, lit only by the tall candles at the nave. When we entered, there had been a shadowy figure a few pews ahead of us. We were the only worshipers there. Not surprising, for people worship by schedule, not need. Now, as I rose to go, the stranger rose too, and knelt at the nave. She was an omen, a black bird, a raven, a sign. She was a nun in the black habit of the Sisters of St Anne's. She left shortly, through one of the doors that opened into the vestry.

I was alone with Justin. I prayed at the Stations of the Cross, with every prayer, growing stronger in resolve. Justin was patient, still in the thrall of wonder.

We had been nearly an hour in the church. I walked out through the side door into the darkened yard.

'I am going to tell you now, Justin. Walk with me. Don't question, listen. Be patient before you judge me.'

I led him out of St Anne's, across the dirt road, to the bridge. We walked across, and entered the coconut grove. He took my arm to help me, but I shook him off. I stopped and leaned across the trunk of a palm.

'This is not a story, Justin. This happened to me. It happened a long time ago, before you were born. It happened the time we were here in Bougainvillea House—all of us together, for the first and the last time. I, my daughters, and Pauline. And Clive. Clive was my husband. My story is about Clive.

'You are young, Justin, and full of hope. It is difficult for you to imagine a marriage turned sour, a lifetime of pain and infidelity. Clive was a good man, but he had his weaknesses. I was his wife, I endured them.'

Justin's hand touched mine briefly. It was warm and soft. Clive had hard hands, and he was always cold. This was Justin, I tried to remind myself, not Clive. It was still light enough to see by. I fought my calm a little. I must hurry. The dark would alarm Justin.

'But I was young too, Justin, remember that! Younger than you are now. Youth knows no patience. It doesn't know that there's a boundary even to pain. I was bitter and reproachful. No matter. That is not what I'm here to say.

'We had hardly been here for a week when Clive took up with a local girl. He was besotted with her. They met here, in the coconut grove. They sheltered in that broken temple there, so I'd heard. I heard about them every day. From the cook, from Pauline, even the shopkeepers talked about it. Can you imagine what it was like for me?'

Again his hand, warm, comforting.

'Several times I thought of speaking to the parish priest at St Anne's though I didn't know him at all. But you know these things are best kept quiet. I was ashamed and angry. But I did nothing about it.

'And then one afternoon, I could bear it no longer. When Clive went out after lunch, I followed him.

'I saw them together, the girl and Clive. I hope you never learn the pain of betrayal, Justin. There is no pain like it, none. It is a pain of the body, yet the body is numb. It is a pain in the heart, yet the heart is as stone. It is pain without forgiveness. When you are as young as I was then, the pain of betrayal is pain without boundary. You can never cross that pain. All your life you travel it. Beyond it—is death.

'That pain entered me that afternoon. It is still here in me. It keeps me young. I have not lived beyond that day. That afternoon has stretched throughout my life. Everytime I breathe, I remember it. I came back to Bougainvillea House to exorcise that pain. Now I know nothing but death will rid me of it.

'That girl wore a red dress. They were not even decent folk, the girl's family. She wore a cheap red cotton dress. She looked like a servant girl. And if you had seen Clive! Wait—let me show you Clive.'

I rummaged in my handbag for the photograph, but didn't find it.

'They were not making love or flirting as you might have thought. They were arguing. She was screaming at him to marry her. Marry her! And Clive, a respectable man, with two lovely daughters! He was trying to get a word in edgewise, but she kept railing at him. Women of that class, the language they use! It makes my ears burn to this day.'

I walked on, led by the memory I was placing before Justin. My hand curled round the photograph in my handbag. A few paces more, and I would be at the well. If I failed, there was still the photograph.

Everything may have changed in all these years. The temple may have gone, and the old well. But for me, time had frozen that afternoon: three o'clock on the 18th of June, 1962. I expected to find everything preserved as it was the moment I turned away from the well.

I had turned away from the well at three o'clock. The clock was striking four when I entered Bougainvillea House. What had I done in the interim?

I was here, here where I stood now. I had squatted here in the slush like an Indian having a shit. I sat curled up in the mire and then I lay down in it. I did that mad, inexplicable thing, I who could never stand filth of any sort, I rolled in the mud like a pig. I don't know why I did that. It simply seemed the right thing to do.

Now I was close to the last tree in the line that led to the well. Strange how clearly I remembered every blade of grass, every leaf, every dripping twig—but I could not have, in all truth. Thirty-five years—no, more! Things might have changed within a week of Clive's death. They would have covered the well. Hacked away the bushes. Lopped the trees. Fenced off the temple. Put a blue-and-white board threatening trespassers with prosecution. They would have done these things.

Or not.

They would have done these things in Bandra. But this was Baga. People still spoke as though the Portuguese landed yesterday.

I was right.

Time had stood by me. The temple still crumbled amidst trees. The same deep green light prevailed, more sombre now, as the day weakened.

There, too, was the old well. Uncovered. Its wall long healed by creepers and grass, yet breached where the bricks had given way under Clive's weight.

I walked slowly up to the well and stood with my back to it. I placed my hand on the rim and caressed it. It was faithful to me, an old dog that would follow me to the death. My hand slipped abruptly into a tangle of weeds, into the breach in the wall, so lightly camouflaged by time. You could say, too, that I found the breach because I knew it was there.

Justin said in a low voice, 'You're tired. Let's walk back.'

'Tired! I never was so energetic in all my life!'

But he was uneasy. 'I don't like this place.'

'Don't you, Justin? Haven't you come here before?'

'No.'

'Not even while playing—didn't you lose a ball and come exploring after it?'

'No! Never. I don't like this place.'

How could he? He was made here, wasn't he? Or maybe he came about much later. Maybe she walked home, scissoring her thighs, clamping her cunt to keep in Clive. Maybe with Clive's sluggish slime she also took home the dark green slick of this oily light that never changes, never changes, no matter what the weather or time of day. No wonder it scared him.

'But I must finish my story, Justin. You owe me that much.'

He didn't answer, but I knew he felt the bars of silence give. Memory was stepping out of its prison house, shabby, inadequate, nervous—but free.

'She was shouting so loudly that her words abraded the air. Everything bled. The trees. The birds. The green sky. The grass. Their blood spattered Clive. He put his hands over his ears and staggered like a drunk. She drove him, still shouting, towards the well, and as if words were not enough, she tore off the belt of her dress and whipped him, whipped him, as if he were her slave—'

I was shouting too, yelling out the memory I was building for him. I drove him with my words and he staggered as his father had done.

'Then she flung the whip over his head and it went flying like a red bird into the well—'

I had carried it in my bag, a red, shiny plastic belt. I had held it hidden in the folds of my dress, looped and ready for him. I pitched it just so, over his head, and he ducked blindly, toppling into the breach his father had made, crashed through its tangles and went screaming and echoing into the black green depths of the well.

Those liquid sounds! Suck, gurgle, a feeble splash and then, simply, the sound of stillness. I waited. I waited a long time, till silence made my ears throb. Then I looked down into the deep mirror of the well.

Truth lives in a well, they say. Perhaps I expected to see Clive's face, back where it belongs. But a young moon flapped in an errant breeze, rippling with pleasure as the wind riffled the glass.

A young moon, and it would be over the tops of the palm trees before they missed him. Tomorrow he would float like his father, webs of corruption blebbing his skin.

⌒

I turned away, satisfied. It was quickly and efficiently done. My immobility, my lightness, were even stronger than before. I felt not calmness, but exaltation. I opened my bag and used the compact, freshened my lipstick and fluffed my hair, though there was hardly enough light to see by.

Then, with resolute step and blind instinct, I picked my way through the maze of the darkened grove. It was the longest and the most difficult walk of my life. I met nobody as I crossed the bridge. I walked into the darkened courtyard of the church. It was empty. As I entered the church, I looked at my watch. It was seven.

There was nobody inside the church, either. I settled myself comfortably, there was no longer any need to kneel, and I don't believe I could have done it, anyway. Lightness buoyed me. I floated above the hard wood of my seat, my feet were off the ground. I was far away, and floating—on the moon, drowsy, pliant, lulled by the luxury of pleasure and peace. I have never, before or after, known such pleasure, such peace.

It lasted longer than I expected.

It was still there when a priest came in at eight o'clock. I cleared my throat as he was leaving, and then, of course, he turned around. I rose—with great difficulty—and spoke to him. I explained I had come in at half past five, or six perhaps, as the service was over, and I had stayed on to pray. I was waiting now for my doctor. It was getting late, and there was no sign of him. Perhaps Father would be able to help—Dr Justin Borges, did Father know him?

Father did. 'I thought that was Justin's car outside,' he said, 'he never leaves without meeting us. I was surprised he hadn't come to the House this evening.'

'I thought he might have, Father. He told me he wanted to speak to someone and would be back within half an hour. He's been gone almost two hours—' Here was the opening I was looking for: it's no mean idea to seek in church for divine aid!

Then, of course, the tremor in my voice was evident, my legs gave way suddenly, and I had to be helped to a seat. The story of my illness came out, hesitantly, but of necessity—without Justin, I told the Father, I was stranded, and practically helpless to move on my own.

From there to the kind care of the Sisters was an easy transition. The nun I had noticed earlier in the evening brought a wheelchair. I rode in state to the parlour of the House. A novice brought tea and cake. Another, a hot water bottle. Meanwhile, the nun—Sister Domenica—with the delicate deftness of a dentist, was extracting pieces of my past. My recent past, to begin with, held everybody's interest for a while. The dying are always a curiosity. And then I told them about my newfound faith. It had come upon me suddenly. I had woken up in a state of grace. Now I knew that Jesus would cure me. Nothing Dr Justin Borges could say would shake my belief. I kept at it till I had firmly tacked on a little plastic halo.

Then my voice shook again. It faltered. I fell silent. My fingers picked at the rosary. I shut my eyes, and from beneath each emerald eyelid squeezed out one hot bitter tear.

My audience fell silent too. The air tightened with words straining to be spilt. The faces around me were grave, inward-looking. They knew they stood on the brink of darkness, and my next words would push them into it. They would hurtle down the chasm knowing there would be no rescue, no rope to grasp, no foothold. Nothing till the first crack of bone against hard bare rock.

I spoke.

I said: 'My husband drowned in the old well thirty years ago.'

I said it heavily, weighting each word with grief, as though thick tears had secretly crept into each syllable. My voice was waterlogged. I opened my bag for some tissue and blew my nose.

'They tried telling me it was suicide,' I continued. 'They lied. Clive was a good man. He would never commit a mortal sin.'

There was a murmur of approval: perhaps of assent. Clearly, I did not seem the sort of woman who would cling to the memory of a husband who had died in mortal sin. I would have divorced him before he was cold in his coffin—clammy is a better word, considering he was drowned. Sister Domenica touched me. She meant it to be a gesture of comfort, I'm sure, but her fingers felt like a gecko scrabbling up my sleeve. I can never stand being touched. Even Pauline's hands, which daily grow more necessary, disgust me.

Disgust brought tears. They slipped easily, warm as oil, coating the waterproof blush. It's always worth spending a little extra on make-up, though I can never make Marion understand. She even uses Indian brands sometimes. I found two tubes in her bag once and chucked them out before she could use them again.

I cried, enjoying the soft rush of tears. I was still light, still happy, but not exalted. I felt cozy among the cushions, the taste of tea lingering in my mouth. No, that's not true. It's just that I crave tea now. The Sisters' tea was smoky, over-boiled and it rasped my palate. The cake was worse. I felt sorry for those priests.

They were all talking, slipping me words of comfort, one by one, like coins. It is unpleasant, accepting alms. I said abruptly, 'Will you send for a taxi? I must get home. I can't wait any longer.'

They wouldn't hear of me going alone. Dr Justin was probably with some sick or dying villager, and he would never forgive them if they left me to my own shaky devices. Sister Domenica would go with me. I wasn't too pleased, but I had no choice in the matter, had I?

I had hoped she would have the grace to sit by the driver, but no, it was in the back seat, with me. The driver was insultingly solicitous of the nun, coming round to make sure her door was locked. I've always known you can never tell with nuns. Priests are different. One can't do without priests, what with confirmations and weddings and funerals. They have to be endured. But nuns, I've always felt, are a needless complication.

I pretended to be asleep, and that worked because Sister hushed the driver when he blathered. No doubt they would make up for it on the return journey, and I made up my mind right away to send away the taxi—for who knows what wickedness they might be up to in the dark?

The taxi driver turned out to be a rascal. I refused to pay the fare back, but he said not to worry, he would take Sister back for free. I tried telling Sister that she would be safer if she took the bus back, but she was all rare for it, wasn't she? It angered me, and I had walked up the steps before I realized I should have waited for her. I collapsed just in time on the top step, falling gracefully into Pauline's arms as she opened the door. To make up, I invited Sister in, and, though it galled me, the taxi driver.

By now my tiredness was no pretence. I could barely sit up. Even talking tired me. The calm had drained out of me, leaving a cringing emptiness. 'You see my weakness, Sister?' I sighed, sadly, with a bitter, trembling smile. The taxi driver looked as though he would burst into tears any minute, but Sister Domenica only looked polite.

Pauline, who loves the Church next only to pastry, brought in glasses of squash and a plate of bolinjas.

I thought it right to pass out before Marion arrived. I tell you again, it was no pretence. My head drooped, and I knew no more.

'I knew no more.' What a lovely phrase. I use it now because it makes me feel like a heroine from one of those serials in *Woman* or *Woman and Home*, back in those years when I was a girl. Lovely, romantic stuff. Later, these very magazines became unreadable. The stories were nothing but filth. Women wanting it all the time, if you know what I mean. Even our Indian magazines are catching up. The other day, I saw a copy of *Femina* with Marion, and some of those letters they print—I didn't know where to look! There's so much of evil in this world, isn't there? And in good respectable homes, so many of them Catholic!

I never look at a magazine these days, unless it's about Princess Diana, but dirty filthy gossip they print sometimes. I'm sure none of it is true. Of course she isn't a royal, not really, just a commoner, but I do like her clothes.

As I said, my head drooped and I knew no more. Pauline must have carried me upstairs somehow, and put me to bed.

A clamour of voices woke me up. Marion's voice, high, querulous. A man's, gruff, angry, insistent. Pauline, urging patience.

Marion's voice came closer. She was angry now. 'My mother is an invalid. Her doctor won't allow us to disturb her.'

'I don't want to disturb her, madam,' the man's voice turned reasonable. 'I just want to ask her a few questions. This is a serious matter. Dr Borges is missing. His car is still parked outside the church. Your mother was the last to see him, perhaps she might be able to help us.'

'So here in Baga if a man is not home by midnight they send for the police? It is not six-thirty yet, Inspector. My mother will not wake till eight. You can wait if you wish, but I would prefer it if you came back at half past eight. Besides, you must understand that my mother is Dr Borges's patient. It would throw her into a bad state to hear he's disappeared. She has a life-threatening illness. The shock may even kill her. At least let her get rest enough to face a difficult time. Please.'

Nobody can resist Marion when she's persuasive. I turned on my side and slept till eight.

Sleep is a measure of virtue. It is the sinful, the erring who are insomniac. Their evils crowd out sleep. To lie down, for them, is to count the tiny coloured bits of cloth that make up the patchwork of guilt. Shapes: square, hexagon, octagon, circle. Texture: the rough cotton of everyday guilt; the silky, slippery texture of the more sly intent. Betrayal. Lust. Spite. Ugliness. They're all in the guilt quilt. There's no sleep within the guilt quilt. Pull it up to your chin and pucker your lids till your eyelashes disappear, but there's no sleep in it.

I slept well that night. I knew that what had happened to Justin was inevitable. It had its place in the order of things. Justin was the acknowledgement of Clive's guilt. With Justin away, Clive could be at peace at last. Which widow would not wish that for her husband?

But it's difficult to make people see things your way. Very soon after Clive's death, I gave up trying to convince people. They have their thoughts; I have mine.

So when Marion finally came to me with the news of Justin's disappearance, I feigned alarm. I was fearful and cross by turn. 'Why didn't you wake me when the police came here?' I demanded, 'I could have helped. Take me there now, or call them over.' Marion bleated nervously, it was not necessary, they would phone if there was any news, I was not to alarm myself. I fell back weakly among the cushions. You must understand—the news, delivered by Marion, exhausted me. 'Call Pauline,' I quavered.

My voice sounded like the first whisper of death. Death first entered me through Pauline. In summoning her, I was summoning Death.

Pauline was not there. She had gone out early to the convent. Why did she need to do that? Perhaps to see Justin's mother, Marion said. The police said she had kept vigil by his car all night.

Justin's mother, Marion said. Just like that, uncaring of what those words might do to me.

It was Marion who bathed me and readied me for this important day. She was clumsy. She almost gave me a chill, leaving me to sit in that damp towel till she had found the dress I wanted. I had asked for a white dress with red braiding. White for virtue, red for courage. I felt clean again.

There was trouble getting my shoes on. When she began to brush my hair, I said, 'Leave me alone. I can do the rest myself.'

She stood open-mouthed, watching me. 'Close your mouth, Marion,' I said, 'or you'll catch flies.'

I did do the rest myself, with steady fingers. I made up my face, I blotted my lipstick, I did my eyes. 'You have little faith, Marion,' I said lightly, 'you don't believe in miracles, do you?' Marion crossed herself and moved to the other end of the room. She did not seem to rejoice in my new powers. She almost shrank from me. 'I shall go to St Anne's again today. Who knows, we might be back in Bombay by the end of the week. The Lord will work his miracles on me, Marion, now that he has rid me of the doctor who used to interfere.'

That was too much for Marion. She gasped and ran out of the room. We certainly are a strange family! First Clive with his low tastes, and now Marion.

Yet, could there really have been a *tendresse*—as the old magazines used to put it—between Marion and Justin? Had they too walked the coconut grove and crouched in the old temple there? Did they too swim in the rippled light, dissolving, as Clive and the girl had, into the very air, crashing through the trees, grinding into the earth, swelling past the sky? Had they? Had they had they had they?

She wouldn't dare, my Marion wouldn't go there. Even on her wedding night Melissa had said, 'What will Mamma think, what will she say!'—so that oaf Tom had told me, guffawing. You should thank me, I had said, you should kiss the hem of my robe for putting the fear of God in my girls and keeping your wife pure for you.

No, Marion was a good girl. Justin might have taken after his father—and his mother! The two of them, rutting like animals, had made him. How could he be any different? A cold water dousing, that's what you need, I'd told Clive often enough. Go take a shower. I had given him a cold water dousing, hadn't I? And now, his son.

I came downstairs slowly. My shoes were troublesome. I wished I had the sloppiness to wear chappals like an Indian. But we Aranxas have always been too proud. I shall step into my coffin in court shoes.

Marion was not in the hall, nor in the kitchen. The house was empty. I sat down in the sofa and prepared to wait. Noon passed. The clock, silenced these thirty-six years, mocked me as the light changed. We had both been silenced that long-ago afternoon. The world had raced ahead of us. The clock didn't care. But I did. I kept trying to pull back the world into my little socket, and it kept slipping out. Time was no argument. Time had nothing to do with it. Time was not the axis on which my world spun. My axis was Clive. The tide of his life was mine.

Noon passed. My stomach cringed with hunger. Hunger at a time like this! Pauline would be appalled. These Indians have a superstition that food eaten in the presence of death is tainted. Where *was* Pauline? I needed her. I needed tea. I needed an omelette, two pieces of toast and a slice of papaya. I needed the reassuring clink of cup against saucer, the tinkle of fork and spoon.

You are as old as me, Sister, you will understand this. You know too that the rhythms of the body overtake all griefs, all triumphs. Subtly, they override relationships. Relationships break. People die or leave you. But these are rites of living: dressing, eating, reading or not reading the newspaper, the meaningless phone call, the casual guest. These make up life. When they stop, when they leave you, when they cease to happen, you are brain-dead.

Brain-dead. When I first heard this, it sounded silly to me. When you're dead, you're dead, I said; how can only one part of you stay dead? They did not explain at once. They were—they still are—too kind. But gradually I learnt the meaning of the term and how it applied to me. I would stop breathing, and still not die. My heart would stop. I still wouldn't be dead. I would be threaded through with tubes and wires that flashed waves and dots on little boxes. These wires would pull my ribs in and out, filling and emptying my lungs. Into my blood they would drip magic to oil my heart springs and wind them tight enough to tick again. But when I am brain-dead, none of these things will work. My brain will write its flat autograph on the friendly machine, and it'll be time to give Cajal Mendonca my box of make-up.

When I stop breathing, I want to be brain-dead. I don't want these tubes and machines. So you see, it is actually my decision, and not Marion's, that I should stay on in Bougainvillea House, where we have no respirator, no wires to trap me, and where the only doctor for miles is bloating at the bottom of a well.

It was my decision. Marion is not really being cruel, keeping me here. But that afternoon, as I waited for Pauline and Marion to return, the keen edge of hunger slicing through my middle was the keen edge of Marion's cruelty. Pauline's cruelty began later. It began when they returned.

It was past two. They came in quietly. When they saw me on the sofa, their eyes slid away. They would have walked past if I hadn't called out to Marion.

Both women stopped. In that instant, I saw them—for the first time—as women. Not daughter. Not servant. Not family. They no longer contained innocence—one, the innocence of childhood, the other, the innocence of senescence. All these years, I had gifted them that innocence, for, to my vision, always, Marion was a child. And Pauline, she was old. That kept them always guarded from the crudities of life. But now I saw I had been wrong. They were no age at all. They were just—women. They were complicated, like me. Their thoughts were complications of love and hate and desire, like mine. Their breasts had been squeezed with the violence of dread and longing and hurt as mine had been, and the soft folds of their skirts lapped the treacherous rocks of sex.

They were women. Men died between their thighs, and there too they were born. These women had stomachs that hungered, like mine. These women had hands that cared and cherished and throttled and wrung dry.

Their blank women faces regarded me. Wordless as stone, and as unwrinkled, unlined, wiped clean of grief or laughter. Grave as judges, they stared at me. These were the faces of strangers stopped by a passerby who asks the time. They did not know me.

'It's two o'clock. Where have you been, Marion? What's happened?'

They were silent, but all the speech Marion had in her was gathered in her eyes. Her eyes drilled holes through mine. I shut my eyes to shield them against that blowtorch stare. When I opened them, Marion was gone. Pauline had stayed back, impassive as Baga promontory, bloated, unchanged, while the tides around roared their confusion. She had something to give me, though.

From the folds of her dress her fist emerged. It stood splayed like a hood for a second, then out darted a shiny snake of red and silver that stung me on the cheek. I knew it before I saw it. It was the plastic belt that sent Justin down the well. It hit me and it hit me hard, with a silver flash of buckle on my jaw.

The room exploded, and the sun went out.

How dark it was, how dark! How cool on the eyes after that blinding flash. My scream trailed, electric-blue, jagged as lightning. Then soft wads of darkness jammed tight around its fiery crack. Its fire was sealed off. The blackness bulged with silence. I could feel with my skin, but I could neither see nor hear. My tongue curled, heavy and spent, within the moist cavern of my mouth. There was no rousing it. It was past the frenzy of speech. I let darkness lap my skin. It caressed me through intruding layers of clothes. But it was not close enough. I needed to be encased in darkness, to be engulfed and invaded by dark. My fingers fumbled with buttons, hooks. My dress slid to the floor and my calves tingled with the swift brush of it. I peeled off my slip. Everything was easy in this new black world. For months I'd needed help with my bra. Now it snapped off by magic. I felt darkness take my breasts. They were feathers of darkness, taking flight with hard inquisitive beaks that pecked their way past the eggshell calm. I dug into the waistband of my panties and tore them off. Darkness whistled clean through me. It slid in like oil, it poured into me, it laved me. I was suspended in darkness, rocked as I had never been rocked, cuddled as I had never been cuddled, held and caressed and possessed, taken. I was darkness. I lost my name. I lost my memory. I lost everything but the single sensation of darkness. I lost time.

It was still dark when time returned. Voices returned. Places returned.

'Mamma? Mamma!'

'Let her sleep. The injection will take some more time to wear off. That nurse won't come here a second time if she starts acting up again.'

What nurse? Who had given me an injection? And for what? For my blindness? For I was blind now, and I had never been warned that motor neuron disease would put out my eyes. Justin should answer for that. But he couldn't anymore. Or he'd answered already. I could be generous and look at it like that. And what about Dr Khan? Or had he warned Marion, and had *she* kept it from me? Where did they find that nurse?

Questions, questions, binding my brain tight with barbed wire. And that Pauline—talking about me *acting up*? And Marion, taking it! I was bursting with words, but they would not emerge. I was dumb. Tongue-tied. I could not see their faces, so I couldn't hurt them with my eyes. I was imprisoned in night, condemned to listen and not reply, judged without defence, sentenced without trial.

'What could have happened, Pauline? Why doesn't she talk?'

'She can talk if she wants. She can hear us. She can see. This is just one more lie.'

'Pauline!'

'You know I speak the truth, child. What did Dr Khan tell you?'

'He couldn't have known anything. He didn't watch her, *we* did!'

'But you told him how she went all crazy like that, took off her clothes and all, you told him, he knows then what's wrong with her. He's a doctor, isn't he? How did he tell you what injection to give, if he didn't know what's wrong with her?'

'Pauline, you're cruel! You're mean about her. She's never told a lie in her life.'

'No? Ask me, child. Ask Pauline. She told lies about everything. She told lies about your father. She told lies about Justin. You know who Justin was, child?'

'No!' The word, catapulted by my stretched-to-snapping brain, whizzed past the walls of darkness, and in its wake, the dammed river of speech welled out in torrents. I was talking very fast, too fast for either me or the others to comprehend. Or perhaps I only imagined it and I was not talking at all. There was only the nasal bellow of No, a buffalo bray: No—o o—

It was enough. Pauline was distracted. Marion ran to me, and held me tight. Then darkness slid away and I was looking at them again.

Fast. Fast. I had to be faster still, or I would lose everything—Marion, sanity, life. This was no time for a truce. I had to attack. I turned on Pauline. 'You hit me.' The words came clearly now, coldly, calmly. 'You hit me with a belt.'

Marion gasped.

'Pauline?'

Pauline hung her head. As I expected, the fight had leaked out of her like sawdust. Marion could sack her. Where would Pauline go next? That talk of a room in her brother's house in Benolim was a fairytale. Her sister-in-law would throw her out in a week. And her savings? They were with me, weren't they? All in my locker whose key is my little secret. No, Pauline would stay. Pauline would apologize. Pauline would beg. Pauline would grovel. How long before I turned gracious and forgave her?

She said, 'It was an accident. I was trying to show you something when it slipped—'

'What slipped, Pauline?' Marion's voice had turned imperious. 'Let me see what that was.'

'You mind your business, Marion,' I said sharply, 'this is between us old women.'

Pauline's eyes welled with angry tears. She wept noisily, messily. I pretended not to notice. I turned to Marion. 'What's all this about? Please call Justin at once. Do you realize I had turned blind? None of these doctors warned me that would happen. I'm scared it will happen again, Marion! Call Justin, please!'

Marion stared at me.

'Oh yes, now I remember, Justin was missing. Has he been found?'

Justin had been found. Like his father before him, Justin had been found at the bottom of the well.

Marion could not tell me this. It was Pauline who announced it, after Marion had walked out of the room. Pauline said, 'You know where Justin is. He's where his father went before him. He's drowned himself in that old well. And that red belt was there with him. You knew that, didn't you?'

'What are you talking about, Pauline? Are you trying to tell me Justin's dead? That's impossible. We were together till six last evening. He was happy, cheerful. Not the sort of man who's going to jump into a well in the next hour. They're making a mistake. It couldn't be Justin.'

'No mistake. Justin is drowned dead. She was there. She saw the body. She saw the belt, though it made no sense to her. But you knew about the belt, didn't you?'

'I don't know what you're talking about,' I said, infusing a heavy note of patience into my voice. 'Is that the belt you scared me with?'

For answer, Pauline went to my wardrobe and brought down the empty suitcase that's kept on top of it. I did not notice what she said, what she did. I was too busy concentrating on keeping my face secret and remote.

She flung the suitcase to the floor and threw it open. What did she expect to find? It was empty. 'You are mad, Pauline,' I said, 'we'll have to shut you up very soon.'

'What was in this suitcase a week ago?' Pauline asked coldly. 'You know and I know.'

How did Pauline know? I had sneaked it into the suitcase in one of those uncanny supernatural bursts of energy that I had felt off and on this last month. A red plastic belt. I had bought it on one of my excursions with Justin, making him wait in the car while I tripped away on 'a feminine errand'. Hiding it away from Pauline was more difficult. But I was lucky that afternoon. I had sent her to Calangute for fine rice. But I was not surprised. There seemed to be nothing that Pauline did not know. Perhaps that was her real function in life. That was why she was created. To be my shadow, my watchdog, my baleful guardian angel.

'I don't know, Pauline,' I said weakly. 'I don't know what was in the suitcase. Ask Marion. She unpacked it, didn't she?'

Pauline looked as if she would throw that suitcase at me. But her face changed and grew secret. She shrugged her fat shoulders and heaved the suitcase onto the cupboard again.

I could see that things were not going to be any easier when Marion returned. The dark was a safer place to be. Almost without warning, I turned blind again.

This time I did not tell Pauline. I shut my eyes and stayed unmoving in bed till she left the room. The dark was cool and comforting, but interrupted by red jagged trails of fear. How strange! There was surely no need to fear anymore. Everything was over now. Clive was at peace.

And then I remembered Marion, and fear flashed its red slash again. Marion—was she—had she? No. It was unthinkable. And yet it was the thought that coloured my darkness an oily green like the light in the ruined temple, like the crinkled mirror of water in the well.

Two weeks already. I can't bear it.
She was upset.
She's upset.
I can never tell with her.
She is upset with me.
Lord have Mercy on my soul
Lord have Mercy on my soul
Lord have Mercy on my soul
Lord have Mercy on my soul
Lord have Mercy on my soul
Lord have Mercy on my soul
Lord have Mercy on my soul
Lord have Mercy on my soul
Lord have Mercy on my soul
Lord have Mercy on my soul
Lord have Mercy on my soul
Lord have Mercy on my soul
Lord have Mercy on my soul
Lord have Mercy on my soul
Lord have Mercy on my soul
Lord have Mercy on my soul
Lord have Mercy on my soul
Lord have Mercy on my soul.
She gets upset with me even when I do what she wants.
Why does she hate me so?
What am I saying? Lord forgive me, that's not true.
She loves me
She loves me
She loves me

She loves me
She loves me
She loves me
She loves me
She loves me
She loves me
She loves me—
If I keep writing it, maybe it will come true.

Clarice, Tape 3

I stayed blind. Marion must have returned, perhaps the nurse did, perhaps Pauline never went away. I stayed blind, I stayed deaf. I did not speak. I went away.

I travelled to a place where things were right, they were light. I did not lose time. All the while, a proximity—was it Clive, was it Justin—comforted me. But all the other names and faces I lost. There was only I, Clarice.

I thought a great deal during this time. My brain wore itself out thinking. I thought of things I had been too rushed to think of all my life. I thought of the way the breeze moved through the trees, lifting leaves. I thought of the fluted edge of the piano, dark and knowing, in the single shaft of light that struck the living-room floor. I thought of the curve of a wine glass, of the fat, ballooned cheek of a jar. These things gathered a tense life and a grace all their own. They floated in the darkness, not bothering me, not resenting that I should wear them out with my thinking. They had no meanings but what they were, or what they had been before darkness claimed me.

And threaded through all these thoughts was the excitement of death.

It was better than a movie, being dead. It felt as though a newer sense had opened up when I was deprived of all the others. And through it, I saw.

I saw. What with? Not with my eyes, for I was blind. Nor did I see form and line and colour, as I see you, my silent inquisitor ... Do you know—I worry about you. I worry about what all this is doing to you. I worry about whether you think of me when you leave my bedside. About what compels you to listen to my story. Is it curiosity? Pity? Dread? What do you feel when you walk away from me, when you walk away from a story you haven't heard? Disgust? Contempt? Anger? I worry about your appetite, your sleep, the dreams I may appear in. I worry about your silence that makes me tell and tell and tell . . .

I saw, I tell you. That sight was a knowing, a flash of understanding. With that came a sense of approval from those who breathed there in that darkness with me, Justin or Clive, both perhaps, swimming with me in the cool dark green night.

It couldn't last. Being dead gets over sometime. Armageddon, I suppose. Hindus get born all over again, recycled like plastic bags, non-what's-that-something-gradable. I woke up too, perhaps, into another life.

I woke up to the sound of Dr Khan's voice. It was very soft, very springy, like a lawn. I was hearing my name after a very long while, you understand. I enjoyed the sound of it.

The sound of my name ended death, returned me to life.

'Clarice,' Dr Khan said. 'Clarice.'

My name was warmth. My name was oxygen. My name was energy. My name was light, sound, touch. I was my name, and my name was life.

'Clarice. Clarice. I know you can hear me, Clarice, I know you can hear me. Are you angry with me, Clarice?'

'No.'

How did I find the word that meant no? In the dark green darkness it glimmered like a zero-watt bulb, a low, baleful light.

'No.'

'Do you know who I am, Clarice?'

'Yes.'

Another word. Yes. Like No, the truth. I tried it again. 'Yes.'

'Good. In a little while you will be able to see me, Clarice.'

I saw him now. He had grown fatter. Big chin he'd always had, growing like a vegetable beneath his leafy lips, ugly thing. Now he'd grown a beard to hide it. Pepper and salt. It looked artificial.

'Can you see me, Clarice?'

'Yes.'

'Well?'

'Well what? You have a beard.'

'So I have, Clarice, so I have.'

I was tired. I wanted to sleep. I shut my eyes.

'Wake up, Clarice. I want you to sit up in bed.'

I was nothing if not polite. I sat up in bed.

'Good. Now I want you to get out of bed and walk towards the door.'

That was more difficult. But to my surprise, my legs moved with more alacrity than they ever had before.

'Go downstairs, Clarice. I'll join you in the living room.'

'Not in my nightie.'

'Very well. Dress yourself, while I wait outside. Shall I send in Marion?'

'No. Pauline.'

What made me ask for Pauline? Was it the need to be comforted by her hands? I don't think so. I asked for her because I knew this was the psychological moment to reclaim Pauline. I was not mistaken. Pauline came in hesitantly, but when she saw me standing there smiling at her, she threw herself on her knees and cried out it was a miracle. Stupid Pauline plumped down on her knees right there and started an Ave Maria. She could have been praying to me, Clarice glowing in her grotto of darkness, so I made my mouth tender. My eyes were watering anyway in that wash of light after the long dark.

We wept, two old women, our secrets briefly on display.

As Pauline rose, I remembered the red belt. It lashed out of the cool nest of darkness, a gleaming scarlet obscenity. It stung my peace. I had to be rid of it now, or it would poison me for ever.

Then I noticed the suitcase was gone. The top of the wardrobe was flat and empty.

'I took it away, Baby,' Pauline followed my eyes. 'All that is finished now.'

The name shuddered in my throat as though I had swallowed a bird. 'Justin?'

'You get dressed now,' Pauline scolded, 'all your clothes have become old. Tomorrow we'll go buy a new dress in Panjim.'

I couldn't but smile at that. I was to be a child now, was I? Imagine Clarice Aranxa in a dress bought in *Panjim*! 'You get that new dress for yourself, Pauline,' I said with affection, 'maybe not a black one this time.'

Pauline looked sad. 'Black,' she insisted, 'always black.'

It was peace, then! This talk of clothes was a truce. Now we could go back to pretending. But I didn't want that. I wanted that belt out of the way. I wanted Justin out of the way. I caught Pauline's hands. They rasped my palms, but I held on.

'Pauline, tell me. Tell me Justin did not die. Tell me I had a nightmare.'

Pauline's hands slid out of my grasp. For an instant I watched her face flood with anguish—was it fury, was it grief?—and then she hurried out of the room. I sank back into bed. My moment of trust had misfired. It would have been easy for Pauline to take up my offer. I had offered her peace, sanity, safety. All she had to do was to comfort me. To tell me the world would be whole again. To tell me Justin was gone, vanished, dismissed without a trace from our lives.

But Pauline chose to make Justin stay. I want you to be clear about this. It was *Pauline's* choice, not mine. Everything that I've had to do since that moment was caused by Pauline. She was totally and unconditionally responsible for it.

For the second time since they brought me to Bougainvillea House to die, I felt my resolve harden into something solid and sweet.

Pauline returned. We worked quickly in silence, getting me dressed for my interview with Dr Khan. I could have made my legs marble, my hands slats of wood, my fingers thick woollen stumps, but I chose to be generous. I stayed nimble. Pauline dressed me without much trouble.

For that important day I chose silk, I could go downstairs in no less. A soft grey dotted silk with a gathered skirt. Agates, grey and silver. No make-up for my eyes, let them burn and sting in their nakedness after that surfeit of dark. A dull mauve for my lips. All my cheeks could take that day was a touch of Natural Rose. A dab of Zephyr, subtle, breezy. Shoes—will power was needed here—grey suede, ugly really, with round toes and stubby heels.

To complete the picture, I asked Pauline for my rosary.

My elbow nestled in Pauline's palm as we went down the stairs. I felt the familiar jump in my pulse as I entered the living room.

Sometimes I think I have only been two places in all my life: the coconut grove and the living room at Bougainvillea House. Certainly, all the important moments of my life have been divided between these two locations.

As I entered, I had a brief blackout. My knees buckled. I lost the moment. For just a thin splinter of time I had imagined Justin standing there, in front of the book shelf, just as I had found him that first day in Bougainvilliea House.

When I regained time, I was seated on the sofa. Pauline was settling a cushion behind me. Dr Khan smiled at me across the coffee.

Neither of them had noticed my moment of panic.

I smiled gaily at Dr Khan. As always, emerging from the dark, I was far from tired. Pauline's eyes were those of an enemy. Now it remained for me to learn the truth about Dr Khan.

My third, and, perhaps, last phase at Bougainvillea House had begun.

Pauline left us. The hot sugary smell of coffee disturbed me. I did not want to be distracted from my lofty mood by hunger. I could not be certain, but I felt I had eaten and drunk nothing during those long days in the dark.

'I don't remember when I ate last.' I hadn't meant to say that. I hadn't meant my words to be edged with panic.

'You had some dinner last night. Tea this morning, but nothing to eat. I know because I asked. Are you hungry, Mrs Aranxa? Perhaps some coffee and a sandwich?'

Mrs Aranxa. The brief throb of pleasure he had brought me earlier with the sound of my name left a small circle of intense hurt, like a cigarette burn. Really, these doctors were all the same!

As if by telepathy, Pauline appeared in the doorway with raised eyebrows. I shook my head and she went away.

I smiled at Dr Khan. I felt quite kindly towards him, despite everything. I wanted to hear his version before I gave him mine.

'What happened to me, Doctor?'

Dr Khan placed his cup carefully on the table. The act stretched to an eternity. My smile was beginning to ache. My legs were cotton wool already. Somewhere at the back of my head, I ached for the comfort of darkness again.

'Things became too much for you, Mrs Aranxa. You couldn't cope with the shock of Justin's death. So you retreated. Into silence, into darkness, till your mind gathered enough strength to confront life.'

'You speak like a priest, Doctor,' I complained. 'You're supposed to tell me about my illness. You never warned me I might go blind. You told me nothing of the sort when you made those drawings of my nerves and things. You told me I'd stop walking, I wouldn't be able to swallow, I'd choke. You told me I'd stop breathing. But none of that seems to be happening to me. Instead, I went blind, mute, deaf. I think I died for some time.'

He nodded gravely. Now he looked like Mendonca on churchyard duty. 'You're quite right, Mrs Aranxa. You can best think of your little interlude as a temporary death. We are all happy to see you revived. As for the rest, we must be grateful for each day won. Great things may be accomplished by faith and belief. But I cannot lie to you. You still have motor neuron disease. And the disease will run its course. But who knows?'

If I hadn't jostled the table with my knee and upset his coffee cup, he would have said Allah is merciful. I want no mercy from his Allah. Get me a good Catholic specialist, I kept telling Marion, but would she listen? This is not a Catholic specialty, she said, there are no Catholic neurologists or Hindu neurologists or Muslim neurologists; there are just nerve diseases and neurologists. Marion has the stupid notions of her generation—all mixed up with Indians they are most of the time, don't have the sense to see where it's all going to lead—mud-coloured children running about barefoot with their tummies sticking out and the tips of their weenies pink and uncovered all the time.

Naturally, as I was thinking all this, I had slid down in my chair. I felt it come on, weakness oozing out of every pore, my thighs like wet towels, just floppy and buckling, and the cushioned chair-back peeling off my spine. I slumped, conscious of how limp and helpless I must appear. I didn't want to prove Dr Khan right so fast, but there was no avoiding it.

Pauline helped me up as usual. No, not quite as usual. Something had changed. She slid a cushion to steady my back, smoothed my skirt down, massaged my calves, went upstairs for my shawl and tucked it about my knees.

But she did all this *after* she had cleaned up the coffee.

I knew then that things were going to be different from now on. The miracle had worn thin. It was no longer a matter of faith. I would have to tell Dr Khan the truth.

'Will I turn blind again?' I asked. Pauline, who had finished what she had to do, lingered to hear Dr Khan's answer.

'Not if you come to terms with what's on your mind,' Dr Khan said. 'You cannot run away from something that has shocked and troubled you, Mrs Aranxa. It must be faced.'

'Justin's death.'

'Yes.'

'Justin's suicide.'

'Yes.'

'I was the last person to see him, you know.'

'Yes.'

I stared at Pauline till she left.

I took a deep breath. I leaned forward and touched his hand. It felt smooth and hard and cool as stone.

'Do you know why Justin killed himself, Doctor?'

'No.'

'I do.'

There! That was out. I had no option but to tell the truth. I had been brought up never to lie to doctor, lawyer, or priest. But what truth could I offer him? Not the truth I had given Justin, not Pauline's truth or Marion's. Dr Khan had been kind to me. He deserved a truth of his own.

'Perhaps that's Justin's secret.' Dr Khan was going to be squeamish. 'Perhaps it should stay sacred to the dead.'

'Perhaps you have heard something already? Pauline has talked to you, perhaps?'

'No.'

'But before I tell you that, Doctor, I would like to know something. How long have I been blind and deaf and silent? Did you give me medicines or injections to recover my sight? Will all this happen to me again?'

'Marion called me three weeks ago—the day after your visit to St Anne's with Justin. This was shortly after you heard the news of his death. Marion called me saying you were talking in a confused manner and appeared very disturbed.'

Disturbed! I had taken off all my clothes, hadn't I? I remembered that.

'I told her to get in touch with a nurse in Panjim, gave her instructions to medicate you. It was clear to me from Marion's account that you were having what is usually called a breakdown, a nervous reaction to shock—'

'But the medication didn't cure me, Doctor. I did begin to see and hear, but my blindness returned. Maybe I need some tests? Different medicines?'

'No. You need to look at what's weighing on your mind. If you can come to terms with it, you won't turn blind. This is not part of motor neuron disease.'

'How many diseases is one supposed to suffer from?' I asked testily. 'I suppose you'll invent a new name for the next thing that hits me.'

'I have a cold, Mrs Aranxa, as you can see, a very noisy one.' He blew his nose to make the point. 'Now, supposing I slip on the stairs and break a leg, the cold isn't going to leave me just because I have a fracture.'

We laughed. There's nothing quite like laughter for buying time.

'But this is no laughing matter.' I dabbed my eyes and sobered up. 'Dr Khan, you are either a magician or a psychologist. Justin's death has left the burden of his secret with me. I must share it, I must confess it—but to whom? You? The police?'

'Perhaps you ought to tell Justin's mother. She has been shocked and bewildered by his suicide. As indeed have we all. He seemed such a happy young man with a wonderful life to look forward to. Yes, I think you should tell his mother—'

Tell me now, can you still blame me?

This is what Dr Khan said: *Yes, I think you should tell his mother.*

First Pauline, then Marion and now Dr Khan.

What happened was inevitable. There's an old-fashioned phrase for that kind of thing: *The fates conspired* . . .

'You should tell his mother,' Dr Khan repeated.

I followed right on cue: 'You don't understand. Justin's secret *was* his mother.'

Dr Khan arranged his face carefully, hiding his disbelief.

'I didn't put that very clearly,' I continued. 'That evening, Justin came here looking very troubled. Marion must have told you what had happened to me that day. I had woken up from a nap, curiously inspired by divine grace. I felt the strength of the Lord in all my limbs. I told Marion and Pauline to offer a prayer for me at Panjim. They left at four o'clock. Justin came soon after that. He was very upset. He said he had discovered something that threatened his very existence, and he meant to confront his mother with it. "It has infected my life," he said. "I want an end to that shame now."

'I begged him to compose himself. I told him to talk with his mother after he was calmer. Why not take me to St Anne's, I said. I wanted to pray there, to thank the Lord for my strength. Even doctors must recognize miracles, after all. Perhaps he could talk to his mother after that.

'"I'll do better than that," he said, "I'll ask her to meet me there. I must take her to that place."

'"What place?" I asked.

'"The place where my father killed himself," he said grimly. "She cannot lie to me there. She cannot lie to me anymore."

'He made a phone call from here, told his mother to meet him at St Anne's at six. Then we went to St Anne's. He kept telling me that his mother had ruined him, but would not say how. Then, just as we alighted, he said, "Would you think less of me if you knew I was a bastard?"

'"You know I don't permit bad language, Justin," I said. "I mean it literally," he said. "I'm illegitimate." It sounded strange hearing a grown man declare himself illegitimate. "That's only for babies, Justin," I said. "You're a big boy now and a doctor. You're quite legitimate!"

'I think he didn't realize how painful the topic might be for me. I hope he had no reason to find out. He left me in church. I'm sure he met his mother. If he told her what he'd just told me, then I can guess where he took her. And also what she told him. You can live all your life out trying to forget old sins, Dr Khan, but there's One Above who won't let the world forget them.'

My voice had sunk to a whisper. I was deathly tired. I had gripped the arms of the chair for support, but my fingers were butter, slipping off the rounded wood.

'You've tired yourself, Mrs Aranxa,' Dr Khan said. His voice was troubled. 'You must sleep now. You can tell me the rest when you're stronger.'

I roused myself with an effort. There were just a few more words rattling within my skull. Once they were out, I could enjoy the delicious surrender of sleep. 'That's all there is. Except to tell you that I've known all along that Justin was illegitimate. He was the illegitimate son of my husband Clive.'

Dr Khan's sharp exclamation of distress endeared him to me. He looked as if he was going to cry. 'Really, I had no idea—'

'How could you? I knew the moment I first saw Justin. The resemblance was too striking. Please call Pauline.'

Pauline had never been very far away, as I suspected. Her face looked like thunder trapped in stone. 'Bring me my bag, Pauline.'

I found the picture, gave it to Dr Khan and accepted the tribute of a gasp of astonishment. And I still would not meet Pauline's eye.

'As you can see, Pauline, I've told Doctor the truth. Now take me upstairs and help me into bed.'

She had to almost drag me up the stairs. They had warned me against taking an upstairs bedroom when I came to Bougainvillea House. 'You might find the stairs difficult, Mamma,' Marion had protested when she visited.

'Not yet. I promise you I'll switch rooms when I do,' I'd said. But I wasn't ready for the switch just yet. Not tomorrow, nor the day after, nor for several weeks yet. Not till Clive was completely free, at peace at last.

Pauline undressed me swiftly. She left me in my powder-blue slip, the one with rose lace panels, perched on the edge of the bed while she vanished on some chore. My knees were goose-pimpled with cold by the time she returned. Of late I could not bear the mildest chill. She came in with a look of triumph, ready to counter my sharp words with scorn. I did not give her that satisfaction. I had learnt I would have to endure neglect—of at least some degree, till she relented. If the fear of losing her job did not make Pauline relent, her own heart would. Pauline is easily stricken with guilt.

She peeled off my slip, unhooked my bra, pushed the soft pink cotton shift over my head. I emerged slightly dishevelled. That must have been a good moment for Pauline. For a second, we regarded each other without masks. Friends, enemies, conspirators. 'I've told Dr Khan everything,' I said. 'Told him about Clive. That Justin was his son. That Justin found out he was not the son of old man Borges.'

Pauline said, in a voice hardly above a whisper: 'Did you tell Justin? About his father?'

'No. You know I wouldn't do that.'

'That's true.' She knew I would never sully Clive's good name. 'Maybe *she* told him.'

'No. He was going to confront her with it that evening. He asked her to meet him outside the church.'

'Oh? How would you have got back, then?'

Pauline the practical. Pauline my servant. 'He said he would drop me home after that. He asked me to wait in the church for him.'

'You didn't tell the Sisters that.'

'No. How could I?'

'Did you see her then?'

'I? No. You remember what had happened to me that afternoon, Pauline. I was praying. I kept praying that I would be able to get well enough to go home again.'

At the word home, something snapped in me and I broke into bitter sobs. One by one the cherished objects in my house, the gleaming furniture, the polished stair knob, the fine linen and the tasselled curtains, the delciate china, the very pots and pans that I seldom handled—all of them rose and claimed me. The house was a physical presence, stretching its hands across the abyss, reaching for me, and I had betrayed it. A wave of sickness passed over me. I began retching. Pauline, alarmed, ran for iced water, but came back with Dr Khan instead.

I bet he got an eyeful of my powder-blue slip, with rose lace, still slung on the chair-back. What with the lace being all over the bust and up the thighs as well, all he'd need was a bit of imagination, but I didn't grudge him that. I got the iced water finally. 'I want to go home,' I said.

'This *is* your home,' Dr Khan said with intentional stupidity.

But Pauline did not add her assurance. The look in her eyes reflected mine. Bougainvillea House would never be home to either of us. We had lost too much here. But I would end my days here, and, for as long as I lived, Pauline was a prisoner too.

I wiped my tears, composed myself. Dr Khan looked away discreetly as I got into bed and Pauline settled the coverlet over me. Suddenly, I didn't want Dr Khan to leave. I asked him if he would mind sitting at my bedside for a few minutes, there were still a few things I wanted to say to him.

Pauline left us.

Dr Khan sat in the chair, his sweaty back against my slip. It was the sweat stain on his shirt, so like Clive's, that reminded me I was not done yet, there was still much to do before Clive could be at peace.

'You must have been surprised to hear that Justin was my husband's son,' I began. 'I was, too. A death sentence brought me here to Bougainvillea House. But that wasn't as shocking or as painful as meeting Justin. My first glimpse of him—I thought Clive had come back. It was a very difficult moment, Doctor. I knew the truth at once. You know my husband drowned in the same well which claimed Justin. They called it suicide. But I have never believed that. Clive was a good man. He would never commit a mortal sin. Yes, he was unfaithful to me. I had heard rumours, but I knew nothing for certain. Pauline had heard some stories, but I didn't dignify them.

'All these years I never dreamt that Clive's son was growing up here.'

Dr Khan would understand the poetic justice of Justin's appearance in my life: the son I never had, appointed to perform the last rite of writing out my death certificate. He was a man of some imagination. Some part of him saw beyond the prescription pad, the part that had spotted the reason for my blindness. When he said *I think you should tell Justin's mother*, hadn't his words meant: *Act! Act now!* I was acting on Doctor's advice, wasn't I?

Everything, I tell you, everything conspired to make things happen the way they did.

I was content to leave things as they were. Justin was with his father, their relationship acknowledged at last. I had won myself a parole from the life sentence of being Clive's wife. I would have been content to end my days in the consciousness of having done my duty. But I saw now, from the things Pauline had said, from the way events had begun to shape themselves, from Dr Khan's words about my burdened mind—I saw that my responsibilities were far from over.

'You must rest now, Clarice,' Dr Khan said absently. He was worrying over the burden I had just placed on him. He would go running now to Justin's mother and make his report. Did he know her? Listlessly, I asked him.

'Yes. I've known Justin a long time. Yes, I've met his mother before.'

'And how is she taking it, Doctor? How is she taking the death of her only son?'

Dr Khan shook his head. A non-committal gesture. She could not have felt much grief. She could have felt nothing like what *I* felt, now as I lay there recreating the truth for Dr Khan. She could have felt nothing like what I felt when the moon crumpled like a scrap of paper on the water. She could have felt nothing like what I felt that distant afternoon when the clock struck four as I dragged myself muddy and exhausted into the house. She could have felt nothing like what I felt when I watched them, watched her broad red servant's back arched over him.

'Who can explain a mother's grief?'

Did he say that, or did I? I cannot recall.

'Didn't she tell the police she met Justin at St Anne's that evening?' I asked, surprised. 'I seem to remember the police troubled Marion here because they thought I was the last person to see Justin alive. That isn't true. Justin had asked his mother to meet him at St Anne's. Didn't she tell the police what happened?'

I had said all I had to say. Words dried on my tongue now. I was tired and thirsty. I shut my eyes. Before I knew it, I was asleep.

To each of us is given, at some time or the other in our lives, a chance to ensure justice. Nobody has ever taught me that, I read it in no Bible. Events have shown me that truth. All along I have been an instrument of justice, and shall continue to be till I die.

Death is still some distance away. I can still breathe, though I cannot swallow or speak with much success. At that time—was it a month ago, two months ago?—at the time when Dr Khan restored me, I could still walk, I could still eat. Tick-tick tick-tick I heard that unseen clock within me metering the minutes I had left. Sometimes it was faster than my heartbeat, sometimes slower, but I heard it all the time. Occasionally, when I had tired myself, the clock missed a tick or two, and my heart stilled with the menace of its silence. But it always started up again, in a rapid two-step, tick-tick, tick-tick. Where was that little clock? In what part of my body or brain? Funny how I've never thought of the brain as part of my body. I think with my brain, and what I *think* with can't be the greasy grey clump they chop up to make bheja fry!

I thought a lot about Marion. Marion, my sweet beautiful Marion, the child I could not love. I gave her everything else, though. I taught all the right things, made life as smooth and pleasant as I could for her, because I knew there would be thorns, thorns and weeds always for Marion! I did all that for her, and yet I do not call it love. I gave her security. I protected her, as I protected her sister, from their father. What if she had known Clive? What if Marion had known the truth about her father?

Waking after that drugged nap, the question stared at me. What if Marion had known the truth about her father? The answer was cruel: *Had she known, she wouldn't have fallen for Justin.*

How cruel was that? Marion would get over Justin. Not that anything of that sort had happened. Marion is a good girl. Besides, she's thirty-eight. I raised both my daughters to understand that that sort of thing is for the lower classes. Women like us have to put up with it, it's one of the duties of marriage, but like other unpleasant things in life, it's quickly over. Besides, it's a question of managing, isn't it? Marion has a degree in management. She must have learnt *something* from it!

The lower classes are hot-blooded, Indians are hot-blooded. I've tried to keep my girls away from contact with that sort all those important years when they were growing up. It's those formative years that decide your life. I told them things that my mother never told me. I told them what the lower classes do, I told them what all Indians do, I told them everything, clearly. I even told them about family planning. It's a mortal sin, I told them. I had to tell them these things, because they had Clive's blood in them. They would take after me, not him, but one could never be too careful. My girls have never let me down. Marion is still pure as the day she was born, Keith or no Keith, Justin or no Justin, she's kept her knickers on.

Still, I was glad that afternoon that Marion didn't know the truth about her father. It would all come out now, wouldn't it? Marion would hear stories. Worse, she might go with Dr Khan to see *her*. Perhaps they had met already, perhaps she had touched my daughter's skin, the delicate skin that was Clive's. Would my pain never end?

'Pauline!' I screamed. 'Pauline! Pauline!'

Pauline rushed in. With her came Dr Khan. They lifted me off the floor, for I had slid down with my screaming and thrashing. They tried to calm me. Dr Khan talked to me in a low voice, soothing words that meant nothing at all. It was Pauline I wanted. Only Pauline could tell me the truth. Only Pauline could shield me from it.

I clutched at Pauline till Dr Khan left the room. I ground my tear-stained face against her soft mound of stomach, but there was no answering kindness in her. I was beyond anger now. I needed Pauline on my side.

I stopped sobbing and let go of Pauline. I blew my nose in a silky nest of tissue and pulled her down on the chair next to my bed. 'What is to be done about Marion?' I asked.

Pauline's arm beneath my hand was impassive as stone. Yet I knew it would be only a matter of time before she relented. She could never stay indifferent to Marion. There was too much of Clivebab in his daughter for that. 'Marion doesn't know anything,' Pauline said slowly. 'Don't tell her anything. She is grieving for Justin.'

'Too much,' I said, 'too much for her own good.'

'If Justin hadn't died—' Pauline's eyes trapped me with their naked question. She was daring me to say it. I took up the dare. I finished her sentence.

'If Justin hadn't died, we might have had to tell her before anything happened.'

'She was coming back to life with Justin,' Pauline sighed. 'Her cheeks had blood in them again, her hands were warm. We need not have told her!'

'Pauline!'

'She could have been happy,' Pauline insisted stubbornly. 'Why go raking up old tales? She could have been happy. Happier with Justin than with that jungli Keith.'

I was shocked, but I reminded myself that it was quite natural for Pauline, such things were known among them. In those vast sprawling families in the village, who keeps count of bedfellows? Wife or daughter, sister or aunt, it's all one: nobody asks questions. This was no time to argue with Pauline. I temporized, instead. 'True, Pauline, I wouldn't have said anything—you know that. You wouldn't have told her—I know that. But what about Justin's mother? What would she have done? She couldn't have kept quiet, could she? She may not have told Marion, but she would have told Justin.'

Pauline shrugged. Suddenly, I understood Marion would never have known, Justin would never have been told by his mother. Like Pauline, she would not have been shocked. It was common among them. Convenient, too, I suppose, all in the family till they went mad and the story got out.

'But somebody *did* tell Justin, Pauline. Perhaps somebody who had watched Justin and Marion together. Somebody who wanted to make mischief.'

Pauline nodded. I was satisfied. She no longer questioned my story of Justin's state of mind on the last evening of his life. 'But you see, Pauline,' I continued gently, 'Justin only told me he had learnt he was illegitimate, that old man Borges was not his father. He was planning to confront his mother. To tell her he had a right to know who his father was.'

'Maybe she told him.' The words stuck in her throat. Pauline was slowly facing the possibility that I might be speaking the truth. 'Maybe she met him.'

'They had arranged to meet. Certainly she met him.'

'But she didn't say so,' Pauline said heavily. 'She never mentioned she met him that evening. She never told me or the sisters or the police, I would have known if she had.'

'Why didn't she?' I let the question hover, drawing blood as its venom soaked deep into Pauline's mind. I did not need to add 'Unless she had something to hide.'

'It will all come out now,' Pauline said. 'Clivebab and everything. Marion will know. We can't keep it from her any longer.'

'We must.'

Pauline shrugged.

She was wary, very wary. I would have to make all the moves. I took a deep breath. 'Pauline, about that belt. When you said it was found with Justin, I nearly died of shock. I recognized that belt. Justin made me buy it for him, one of those days he took me to Calangute. "I need a red belt," he said, "could you please buy one for me? Just an ordinary one you'd wear with a skirt, a red one. I can't buy women's things in this place without comment. It'll be all over Baga tomorrow, Justin buying clothes for his girlfriend. But I need that red belt." Of course I bought it. I didn't ask whom it was meant for. He didn't explain. When we returned he asked me to keep it till he should need it. "Please keep it a secret," he said. Where could I keep it without you finding it, Pauline? I told him to put it in that suitcase—'

'I knew it!' Pauline broke in triumphantly. 'I knew you couldn't have put it there, or taken it down from there!'

I permitted myself a laugh. 'If only I had the strength for such things! Soon I won't have the strength even to talk to you, Pauline, nor even to swallow a morsel of food.'

She was sobbing now, falling on her knees, clutching my feet, begging my forgiveness. I let her enjoy herself. I cried a little too, from relief. I was almost through with what I had to say.

'And that evening, after he had made that call to his mother, he said, "Give me that belt now. I'll need it this evening." And he took it out of that suitcase and carried it with him. That's all I know, Pauline, about that belt! And you hit me—you hit me with it! Why, what did you think, stupid girl, what did you think of me?' Now I was sobbing in right earnest and that set Pauline off again. We cried in chorus till we were tired of it, and began laughing together instead.

You have to be as old as I am to know that laughter and grief are identical twins, just like hate and love. Even at my age you can't guess which one has grabbed you.

We laughed. Was it the laughter of relief, or of joy at our moment of understanding? Or was it simply *funny*? And Pauline? What did she see? An old woman shedding tears of penitence. Hers, then, the laughter of generosity, the light heart of compassion, the ennobling thrill of forgiveness. Of what crimes did Pauline suspect me?

Later that day, Marion came to see me. She came unwillingly, yet propelled by the same compulsion I felt: that something would have to be resolved that day. I welcomed her. I opened my arms to her. She held me lightly. My lips felt the flesh of her cheek flinch and turn firm.

Marion was afraid of me.

I decided then to tell Marion everything. It would devastate her, but it was necessary that she should learn the truth. Besides, Dr Khan may have told her already, or would soon. That was a risk I could not take. I had already resolved things with Pauline and with Dr Khan. My daughter was more important than either of them. I owed her the truth.

'You're wondering why Justin's death affected me so badly, aren't you, Marion?' I said. 'You wondered. You worried. You asked yourself, why should my mother turn blind with grief over Justin.'

Marion shrugged. She had grown a hard manner of late. She had brought home the manner she wore at work, to flaunt before her dying mother. Boss woman. Well, she couldn't be boss woman with *me*. She said, 'He was your doctor. You were afraid you wouldn't have a doctor, now he's dead.'

'Nonsense. I have Dr Khan,' I reminded her. 'Doctors are a dime a dozen. No, that's not why I suffered, Marion, that's not why I'm still suffering. I'm suffering because of you.'

'Me!'

'You. My child, my daughter, my Marion. You'll never know what I went through when we lost Keith. And now—Justin.'

'Perhaps I carry a curse,' she said.

'Don't talk like an Indian! Only Pauline says things like that. Marion, tell me the truth. What was between you and Justin?'

She stirred angrily. Her eyes were hot and flat. The eyes of a snake. 'We were friends. What of that?'

'I was worried it may have been something more than friendship. I was worried because then I would have had to tell you the truth.'

Silence stretched. Even a breath would have snapped it. Pauline appeared at the door. Her eyes slid between us, and she was about to turn away when I stopped her. 'Pauline knows,' I said. 'Pauline knows the truth, and now you must hear it too, Marion. Stay with me, Pauline. Give me strength that I may speak the truth.'

Warily, Pauline approached my bed. I reached for her hand. After a while, I felt her rough fingers grudgingly close around mine.

I prayed aloud. A Hail Mary. A contrition. As I prayed I looked at the two women who waited for what I had to say—

Marion with her head bowed, her shoulders trembling, Pauline with a quiet light in her impassive eyes. Marion would never forgive her father. She would never be able to forgive herself for unknowingly injuring me through Justin. She would blame herself for not finding out the truth about Justin before calling him to attend on me. The truth would bind me to my daughter.

I was growing tired of telling my story over and over again, and a new version every time. These stories are not of my making. It's the audience that shapes the telling. Demand and supply, it's called. Or is it supply and demand?

I finished my prayers and crossed myself, and began to tell Marion the truth.

⁂

'Marion,' I began, 'many years ago, when you were a little baby, we spent a month here in Bougainvillea House.

'You were not yet three years old, Marion, and Melissa was six. Pauline was with us too. Remember how cute Marion was then, Pauline? Pauline would take the two of you down to the beach after breakfast every day and you would play in the sand till lunchtime. You turned black as an Indian that year, baby! But no matter, it all peeled off and you had your rose-petal skin back in no time at all.

'Now don't get impatient, Marion. I'm coming to what happened. Do you remember your father, Marion? How can you! You were such a baby when he died. He died here, in Bougainvillea House.

'I've brought you up to believe he died of typhoid, but that isn't true.

'Your father, Marion, was—how do I tell you, child? Your father was not faithful to me. By the time you were born, I was resigned to it. He didn't mean anything bad by it, he was a good man. But he had this weakness. He couldn't help himself. Stop! I know what you're going to say. You'll call me a doormat, you'll tell me I should have left him. You'll tell me I never should have stood for it, and you'd be right!

'Pauline will tell you he was a good man. A loving father. A responsible, caring man, kind, generous, worthy of respect. And she will be right too!

'I thought sometimes as you do, Marion, and sometimes as Pauline does. But most of the time I didn't think at all. I simply loved him. I loved Clive more than life itself, more, God forgive me, than I loved my children. You have not known what it is to love like that, Marion. Not yet. Perhaps you will. Pauline understands my feelings. Don't cry, Pauline, we have grown old, you and I. We needn't hide our feelings from each other. Pauline understands. Dear Pauline. You are more than a sister to me, Pauline. I haven't always been good to you, Pauline, I don't deserve you. Don't leave me, Pauline. Let your face be the last one I see before I close my eyes, Pauline. Because you understand about me and Clive. Because you know, Pauline.

'Marion, your father had an affair with a local girl. There! I've said it. I've said what I've been afraid to say even to myself all these silent years. Yes, there was a girl. A girl from the village here. I learnt of it—how does one learn of these things? They say the wife is always the last to know, but that's not true. I knew the very first time he was unfaithful to me. I can tell you these things now, Marion, you're no chicken, though life has left you still untouched. I knew the first time. It was scarcely a month after our wedding. Can you imagine what I felt? Pauline wasn't with us then. She came to us when Melissa was born. She was our good angel. Clive gave up wandering then, took up the piano. He used to play "Isle of Capri"—remember, Pauline? The same tune over and over again. Isle of Capri.

'He kept straight, except for that Lobo girl in '61. You never knew about that, did you, Pauline? The thin girl with TB? He dropped her when he knew she had TB. But he paid for her medicines. She came to see me after Clive died, to demand money for injections: you were angry when I gave her the money, Pauline. But you didn't know I did it for Clive's sake. You didn't know how it hurt me. You only scolded me. I earned myself a dozen mothers-in-law the day you came here, Pauline.

'Where was I, Marion? Yes. The local girl. I even saw her with your father once. They met every afternoon in the coconut grove. Then one day Clive realized I knew about his affair. I was not reproachful, but I was sad. I'm sad now, when I think about it. He was very contrite. He promised to mend his ways.

'But he went out after lunch as usual.

'My heart was breaking. I thought of what the villagers said about the miraculous powers of Our Lady of the Grotto. That afternoon, my pain was past bearing. So I trudged to the grotto and prayed there. I was on my knees a long time, praying that Our Lady should grant Clive the courage to do the right thing.

'But that girl—

'Marion, she killed him. Oh no, she didn't stick a knife into him and murder him, but it was almost as if she had. Nobody will know what happened that afternoon. She told Pauline later that she had gone to Mapusa. She went every Thursday to sell the stuff she'd stitched through the week—cheap dresses, petticoats, that sort of stuff. It might be true, for all I know, but then whom did Clive meet that afternoon? He went out soon after lunch. I tried to stop him, but he just walked out. I never saw him again.

'Pauline had taken you girls to the beach. It wasn't raining then. The rain came pelting down as I reached the grotto. I prayed on my knees in the pouring rain almost for an hour. Ask Pauline in what state I returned to the house that evening. Tell her, Pauline! Tell her how I fainted in the hall from sheer exhaustion, how you dragged or carried me to bed.

'We waited all night for Clive. Late next afternoon they found his body. He had drowned in the old well. Just like Justin. Most people thought Clive had committed suicide, but I didn't. Clive thought suicide was a mortal sin. Clive was a very religious man. He would never commit a mortal sin.

'I think they met at the grove at the usual time, and the girl told him what I didn't know then. She told Clive she was pregnant. She must have done it on purpose—these girls know all the tricks! The shock of it killed Clive.

'Now you understand, Marion? Do you understand my fear, my dread about you? Justin was your brother, the son of your own father, Marion. He had the same blood as you.

'Can you imagine my shock that first morning at Bougainvillea House? My first glimpse of Justin! I thought Clive had come back to me. Almost at once I realized Justin was Clive's son. The world went black for me, Marion, at that moment. My heart turned inside-out with pain. He looked exactly like Clive when we were first married. He spoke like Clive. His hands were Clive's hands, his voice was Clive's voice. Even his mannerisms were Clive's. He had Clive's eyes. Only his skin was swarthy, like that girl's.

'I can't think of her with anger, Marion. I've never thought of her with anger from the moment I met Justin and realized who his mother must be. I felt pride in Justin. He was my son too. And his mother was—what? A sister, perhaps, a friend whose face I never knew. You are too young to understand such feelings, Marion. At your age, love is full of passion. It is anger and jealousy, and yes, it is hate too. There's a lot of hate in love. It's part of the package, like sex. You can't be picky. You have to take the lot or dump it. You have to suffer it. But when death is just a doorstep away, love has a different meaning. It means BIG. It means so big you can't see its borders. You can't see where it begins, you can't see where it ends. The further you look the further its borders recede, like the horizon. There is nothing you cannot do when you love like that.

'That is how I loved Justin. I warmed my soul at his smile, Marion. He was a baby, a toddler, a schoolboy, a teenager and a man all at once. I loved him for all the growing years I hadn't known him. I loved him the way I've loved both my daughters. *He was my son*, Marion.

'If Justin had lived, I would have had to tell you this truth anyway. You were growing close, but you didn't know it was blood calling to blood, Marion!

'When Pauline told me of Justin's death, I thought it was a nightmare. You don't know what had happened that evening, Marion. Listen. Listen now and remember—I've told Dr Khan, too. I've told him what I'm about to tell you. You heard me tell him, didn't you, Pauline?

'After you had left for Panjim with Pauline, Justin came here. He was very upset. He would not tell me what the matter was, but he kept saying he would have to resolve the matter one way or the other before the day was out. He said his mother owed him the truth. I asked him to take me to St Anne's. I cannot help you in any other way, I told Justin, but I can pray for you.

'That seemed to calm him. He agreed immediately. He had a better idea, he said. He'd call his mother and ask her to meet him at St Anne's while I prayed there, and have it out with her. He wanted to take her to a place close by, he said. It would be better done with me praying for him, he said. You can imagine my hesitation. I did not want to meet his mother. But I could not dampen the sudden hope in his voice. He made the phone call. He took me to St Anne's. Just before he helped me out of the car, he said, "Would you think less of me if you knew I was a bastard?"

'At first I made light of it, asking him not to use bad language. But when he persisted, I saw how it was—he must heave learnt the truth somehow. He meant now to ask his mother about it. How could I have stopped him? It was his right to know. I said nothing. But I prayed, how fervently I prayed for him. For her too, poor thing. After all these years to be reproached by one's own son! I prayed, still in that inspired mood that had set in that afternoon. When Justin didn't return, I had to ask for help getting home, as you know, but I was not unduly alarmed for him, not afraid. I thought they would have gone home upset. Very upset, since his car was left parked there. But I didn't sense any danger.

'That was why I thought I was in a nightmare when Pauline told me Justin was dead. It could not be real. I felt as though some evil magic was stifling me in its coils. I twisted and writhed against it, but there was no escaping.

'Marion, how I wished to die then! How I wish to die now. Help me, Marion, help me die.'

That is what I told Marion. It was the truth she needed to know. I'd told Dr Khan.

I lay back exhausted on the pillow, slow tears of relief cooling my cheeks. Darkness descended. I was within the wings of an enormous raven, silky black, with talons of sharp black iron. A black beak loomed hard and smooth beneath its solitary unsleeping red eye. It drove the beak into me, deep, hard, till I was threaded on it, impaled on it, filled in and out with darkness, upheld on darkness, pressed down and swaddled with feathers while its soft black down crammed itself into my eyes, my nostrils, my mouth, and my head burst with darkness into a million sparks of light.

When I opened my eyes, Marion was crying into her hanky the way she used to when she was little. The hanky was a cup her tears spilled into, plink, plink, plink. Beneath her lashes, her eyes had a look of surprise. It touched my heart, that look.

It touched my heart, but there was nothing more I could do.

Dr Liaqat Ali Khan's Casebook

July 28/'98

Mrs Clarice Aranxa, aged 61 yrs
Refd by Dr Carlton Dias, MBBS

C/O:

Weakness both ULs, duration 3 months.
Difficulty in walking down the stairs—1 month.
Tiredness and inability to keep up daily routine—1 month.
Failing grip (noticed by daughter)—1 month.
'Clumsiness' reported by patient as 'out of character'—1 month.

Early morning cramps+, LUL ++
L arm often feels very stiff.
No paraesthesias, fasciculations, tremors or other abnormal movements.
No difficulty in articulation, chewing, swallowing, no shortness of breath.
No bowel or bladder complaints.
No h/o antecedent trauma/febrile illness.
No major illness in the past.
15 years post menopause.
No relevant FH.
Widowed in 1962. Two daughters.

O/E:

Extraordinary composure.
Gait and attitude N.
Orientation, higher functions N.
BP 110/80. HR 80/min. Mild pallor+
Cranial nerves N.

Ocular movts N.
No facial weakness.
Cervical spine clinically N.
Wasting of intrinsic muscles of hand, LUL.
Thinning of thenar eminence, RUL.
Fasciculations RUL flexor compartment.
Power RUL Grade 3+ all groups distally. Proximal: Grade 4, all groups.
LUL distal: Grade 3. Proximal Grade 4.
Deep reflexes: + RUL, dampened LUL.
Mild hypotonia in RUL.

Both lower limbs show increased tone.
Power is 4+ in knee flexors, but 3+ in extensors.
Plantars extensor bilaterally. Mild hyperreflexia, deep reflexes ++ both LL.
No clonus.
Clinical Impression: Combination of LMN & UMN signs.
Fasciculation in UL, spasticity in LL.
No bulbar signs (yet).
No cervical spine pathology.
Clinically: Probable ALS.

She's so composed, one almost wishes for pseudobulbar gaiety! Corrected my spelling: 'Use an X, Doctor!'

'Oh, like the tennis star,' I said. No response. 'Can't expect Indians to know Portuguese,' she told her daughter.

Clarice AranXa: Problems ahead! Unlikely to accept diagnosis (definite ALS). Resentful of visit. Feels rebuked for 'clumsiness'. Scornful of 'nerves'.

'Never had a nerve in my life!' Somehow, I believe her. Despite all that exaggerated femininity (massaged skin, perfume, heavy make-up, slinky clothes, lace-edged slip showing), she's tough stuff. Daughters probably conceived under GA! Can't think how AranXa did it otherwise.

Accompanied by daughter Marion, big, bosomy, mid thirties, overgrown child with pre-pubertal lisp. Dressed by mummy: pants stop halfway, blouse from cake shop, six-inch heels. Diamond on engagement finger, marrying in October.

Diagnosis must be quickly established to help family plan for poor Clarice. Marion will bear the brunt. Denial likely.

her. Expected the fiancé. What a dog to let the girl face this alone! M insisted on knowing, and so M was told. A different woman today. Professional, I suppose, is the word. Lisp replaced by low intimate voice, eyes like glass, words like knives. She puzzles me.

'I've never heard of anything like this.' Rage. Denial. Expected. Normal.

But next: 'Should I buy a wheelchair right away?'

M has begun to think.

I had to choose for C then. Life? Or death? Which would help Marion more? M loves her mother. M is to be married. M is mother's sole caregiver and will not stint on creature comforts. For M's happiness, C must live.

I chose life for C.

'Since the disease started in the limbs, it may progress very slowly,' I said. 'She may not find herself very seriously limited for two to three years more, not with her sedentary lifestyle. Bulbar changes may be delayed. One can never tell.'

But Marion asked, 'How long does she have, Doctor?' And then, as if her meaning was not quite clear: 'I mean, how long before she dies, Doctor?' I said, 'Five years, maybe even—'

'Five years!' Marion's dismay told me I had decided wrong for Clarice. I had chosen to help the child I met with Clarice, not the woman who confronted me now.

I should have said: 'It's going to be downhill all the way from now on.'

Too late now.

I told M I must speak to C myself and explain the diagnosis. But I would like to wait a month before doing that, so that I can reassess her and note the progress of the illness.

Meanwhile I am to see M again next week. Poor girl. What kind of rascal is she marrying?

August 25

Consultation with Pt's Daughter.
Progress of illness explained. Discussed possibilities of Rikulid. Daughter more eager to work out plans for caring, so discussed likely disabilities. Pointed out life choices would have to be made as illness progressed.

Letter to Dr Dias. Both mother and daughter refused further visits to Dr D.

August 8

Reviewed Clarice Aranxa.
C/O Increasing fatigue. Takes midmorning nap of late.
O/E No change.
X-ray cervical spine: nothing remarkable. Osteophytes+ usual at her age. But in view of LL hyperreflexia, adv. MRI.
Refd, Dr K.T. Shah for EMG

No slip-up in C's iron control! There was a maid waiting in the foyer for her—Marion did not come. The maid fussed over C, speaking to her in Portuguese!

With C's idle, lethargic lifestyle, perhaps she won't feel the limitations of ALS so badly till the worst hits her. What does C do all day? She doesn't cook or housekeep or read or sew, and I don't think C even gossips . . .

August 16

Reports on C. Aranxa:
MRI: NAD. Cervical cord looks fine, no compression.
EMG: Suggestive of LMN degeneration in RUL flexor compartment, and intrinsic muscles of the L hand. Reduced recruitment, large motor unit action potentials and fibrillation potentials reported in both UL.

Diagnosis: Amyotrophic Lateral Sclerosis.

Diagnosis communicated to pt's daughter Marion. Suggested she return with another family member to discuss implications. However, as she insisted there's nobody else who could come, prognosis was discussed with reserve.
Appointment made for consultation a fortnight from now.

Marion without her mother is a very different woman. I hesitated at discussing the illness with her alone. Cruel to put the brunt on

Marion has grit. She made notes as we talked. Her Qs: What should I do if she stops breathing? When will she lose control over urine and stool? Will she be in pain when she dies?

But not: But she appears so strong and healthy—maybe she will overcome it!

Marion has not stayed long in denial.

September 6

Visit from Marion's fiancé with wedding invitation.

More to this visit than the invite. Marion's destiny doesn't seem so bad. Keith Ferrao seems to have C down to a T. M is fiercely protective about C, did not want Keith around at visits here. Keith's request: If C asks whether ALS is hereditary, can I tell her no? 'The Aranxas are Goan aristocrats. We're East Indians. We Ferraos are bad blood,' he said with a laugh, 'that's what Clarice thinks. If there's even a faint chance of Marion or her children getting it, Clarice will stop the wedding.'

I didn't quite get the logic of this, but told him I would deal with C.

Seems a nice guy, less pretentious than the Aranxas. Doing well for himself. Large family property—which explains C's blessing.

September 15

Reviewed C, 2 weeks ahead of schedule, by request.
Limb signs more pronounced. Easy fatigueability. No bulbar signs yet. Discussed diagnosis with patient (asked daughter to wait outside).

'We never had polio drops when we were children,' C said, poor thing. Tried to be as gentle as I could, but she unfortunately asked all the right questions, so clearly the daughter has been at her already. 'Jesus suffered for us. I can suffer for him,' she said. Assured her it was totally painless.

The look she gave me then—outrage, contempt and amusement—told me that no matter how humiliating her final indignities, they would never breach the bastion of her superiority! She refused to look at the CNS pictures to understand what was going wrong. That's better kept for a future visit, I think. I mentioned the wedding invitation. 'I hope he treats Marion right,' she said. 'Marion's always too eager to please.'

September 22

Last night just as I was leaving here, C called. Marion had swallowed sleeping pills. She was cold and could not be roused. C sounded as calm as on her visits here.

Rushed over. M comatose, cold, cyanosed, pulse thready. Choked on vomit. Colour improved on clearing airway. Likely intake: two strips of alprazolam (at bedside) 0.5 mg tablets. Shifted to hospital. Supportive measures were enough. Respiratory depression not central (vomit may have helped, though it probably took place 2-3 hrs after ingestion). Flumazenil was not necessary. Adv. counselling later.

Cause? Was told only when I asked C as I was leaving the hospital: Keith Ferrao was killed this afternoon, while crossing the railway tracks at Santa Cruz.

Accident?

C crossed herself with the suspicion of a sneer.

Perhaps suicide, then. Couldn't ask, obviously.

Hospital called today at 6 a.m. to report M was awake and threatening to go home. Spoke to her. She sounded collected. Suggested she stay in till 8 a.m. when I could see her, but she was insistent. One can never tell, she might take another shot at those pills. These darned benzodiazepines—people eat them like peanuts. She agreed to stay till C could come to collect her. Later I discovered this had already been arranged between mother and daughter. Not a little irritated to find Marion gone by 7a.m. when I made the early trip to hospital. They'd cleared the bill, thank God.

September 24

Phone call from C.
Marion weak, awake, naturally very broken by Keith's death. The police found her card in his wallet and called her at work. She gave them his home address.
C said his parents had to identify 'pieces of Keith'. Terrible.
It was all too much for M. She came home early, locked herself in her room and swallowed those pills. C said it would be impossible for them to go for Keith's funeral with M in this state. 'The last thing she needs is trouble.' Which seems odd, but not really, if I go by what that poor boy told me. May he rest in peace.

October 10

Surprised to get a call from M, asking for an appointment to discuss her mother's situation. Is C worse? Perhaps the trauma of the last two weeks has been too much.

October 11

M has planned to take C to live in Goa. They have a house in Baga. The maid, Pauline, will go with C, and M will visit on weekends. Will that be all right? C can be brought to me every three months or even oftener. Can I suggest a doctor in Goa? Yes. My student Justin Borges. Excellent doctor. As it happens he will be in Bombay next week. M arranged to meet him here.

Poor Marion is trying to put her shattered life together. Goa is a good idea, I think, as long as C feels comfortable about it. I did not ask M, but I have a feeling C will not be told till the plans are all made. M deserves some life of her own, and C may even enjoy being the queen of Baga society!

October 20

Joint consultation with Dr Justin Borges, MD, and pt's daughter.
Clinical status discussed with Dr Borges.
Anticipatory plans for caregiving.
On the last visit, C had asked me about a respirator: What will I do if I stop breathing?
I said: Although we do not anticipate such rapid deterioration, the patient's anxieties will have to be dealt with in the chosen set up.
On the whole the consultation ended with all of us feeling the shift to Goa might be best for C.

But what does C herself think?

—

December 21

Spoke with Justin about C's condition.
After 2 months in Goa, Justin says C is worsening, but slowly.
She tires more easily, but as yet there are no bulbar signs.

'I'm one of the family now,' he said, I thought, with some pride.
  I asked if M was around. He laughed.
  It might solve a lot of things for C, having a doctor in the family. But Justin deserves better.

Liaqat's Diary

I'm writing this to restore some order to the confusion of the past few days. I have to set it down, this burden of secrecy. I don't want to tell Sharifa, not yet, and unless I write it all down, I probably will.

So I'm spelling it out. For whom? For me, Liaqat.

I'm trying to work out an answer to the question Sharifa is bound to ask very soon: Exactly how do you manage to get in such deep shit every time?

Well, it isn't *every* time. It's just this one time. But it's deep, and I don't now how I got here.

Clarice Aranxa. The moment she stepped into my clinic, I fell headlong into her life. I thought I was rid of her when she went away to Goa. How could I have been so myopic?

I thought Justin would take care of her.

Justin.

<u>April 3:</u> Telephone call from Goa, from Clarice Aranxa's daughter Marion, incoherent with distress. The first fact I gather: Clarice is tearing off her clothes and screaming. I can hear her on the phone, above Marion's screams that her mother has gone mad. Apparently, she doesn't seem to be able to hear or see anything, and isn't saying anything either, only screaming.

Everything happened at once, Marion says. 'She can't see, she can't hear, she can't talk, and she's taking off her clothes.'

A dissociative reaction, then. Acute confusional psychosis.

What caused it?

Only then does Marion tell me: Clarice was upset by the news.

What news? I have to ask twice before she tells me.

I must write it now, though the words wring me. Justin is dead.

'Dr Justin Borges committed suicide,' Marion said.

He killed himself by jumping into a well.

Clarice was upset because Justin was dead.

I called Sister Salgaoncar at Panjim, requested her to visit Clarice and report back to me.

April 30: With Serenace SOS, the acute episode of 3rd April was controlled, but over these three weeks since the episode, Clarice has continued to be withdrawn. Reportedly, completely blind, mute, deaf. She swallows when fed, accepts the bed pan, and allows herself to be bathed and changed.

Last week Marion called again. I urged a psychiatric consult, but she refused. She insisted I should see Clarice.

In the three weeks between these two phone calls from Baga, I have lived out a peculiar sort of hell. I could have seen Clarice earlier. I told Marion I couldn't come to Baga because I had a critical patient. That's not entirely true. Sadiq Bhai has been out of the woods this last fortnight. I could have gone had I wanted to.

The reason was Justin. I could not bring myself to visit a place that would make his death real to me. In Bombay, his death was still rumour. The sound of his laugh was not yet memory. I expected to hear it every time the phone rang.

In Baga he would be a body. There would be a grave to visit, a shattered woman whose hand I must hold. (This was the most difficult. We knew her slightly. Sharifa and I had made a whistle-stop at Baga in '93. We didn't have lunch, but Mrs Borges said she had something better. A boy-sized jackfruit sat on the kitchen floor. She plunged a knife into its jammy heart. Such a pig I made of myself!)

And yet, was it only Justin? Was it no more than the embarrassment of grief, and that guilt at being alive when somebody younger and more vital is cruelly dead? No, there was more to my unwillingness in going to Baga, an unease to which I could not put a name.

After Marion's last call I forced myself out of lethargy. I could no longer dodge my responsibility towards Clarice.

I expected the worst. Three weeks of total withdrawal from her surroundings did not bode well: this could be more than a dissociative reaction to grief. It might be evidence of psychosis. Three weeks is a long time. And yet, surely, her distress over Justin's death is more than formal regret. Perhaps even more than the pain of losing a friend. Very likely she feels adrift, her lifeline cut, abandoned to endless days of suffering till death should relieve her. That's enough to panic about. Or is it?

I had a hard time persuading Sharifa not to come with me. She wanted to see Mrs Borges. If she'd known that Marion had offered air fare, she would have insisted on coming along—'Only one fare to pay, come on, we can afford that.' I took the wind out of her sails by opting for the bus. A foolish decision. I'm not going to admit it outside these pages, but forty-five really is too late to have your bones rattled. I've come back from the trip in a myotonic clench, my gait an anthropoid slouch, every muscle in a whimper of protest. Next time, I shall accept Marion's offer.

Mrs Borges was so pitiful. I couldn't keep from breaking down. What does one say on such occasions? Why do we mouth those futile words? Mrs Borges searched my face for clues. Her hands kept rising and falling in incomprehension. There were two nuns with her when I visited. They said Justin's death was the will of God. What makes them so bloody sure? How do they know God does not feel as angry and thwarted by death as His children do? What kind of creature is God to punish a parent with the death of a child?

Mrs Borges opened a safe and brought out her treasures for me to see—his school certificates, a silver medal for science, the school shield for football, his degrees, the parchment rolled and packaged carefully in a silk shawl. All the while her tears rained on them. The nuns tried to make her put away the things, but I restrained them. Be brave, the sisters whispered, be brave, Arula. What *for*? Presently she collected herself and her face assumed a stony gravity. We sat in silence for a while, then I came away. The nuns opened their prayer books several times during my visit, to prompt my departure. Maybe I stayed too long. At first I could not bear to enter that house and then I could not bear to come away.

I had gone straight to Justin's home from the bus station. After I left there, I didn't have it in me to face Clarice. I needed a hot bath and breakfast after that bumpy night ride. The rickshaw driver suggested Palm Door, and Palm Door it was. The

Palm d'Or gives itself three stars, but nobody else will. I got a room with clean sheets and cockroaches and no water in the bath. By the time I had bath and breakfast organized, I had reached that state of nervous expectation when every possible complication becomes a certainty.

If Clarice needed special attention, I would advise Marion to shift her back to Bombay. With Justin gone, I knew nobody in Goa I could trust.

My rickshaw driver had turned extortionist in the tedious hour I spent at Palm d'Or. He frowned at the notes I gave him. Other tourists, he said, were paying much more. One hundred and fifty he took off me—and they say Bombay's expensive.

We didn't have to ask the way to Bougainvillea House. The thick vine that crept up the whitewashed walls was a brilliant splash of magenta and lilac. It must have been Clarice who named the house. The woman has no imagination, no imagination at all.

The maid received me. Marion, she said, was in the bath—please wait in the parlour. I was intrigued as I had never been in a parlour before—but it was only a living room, a bit gloomy for my taste. The maid was about to leave when I stopped her with a request. Could she tell me about Clarice's present state?

At first the woman was noncommittal. Her shrug and nod of helplessness came with formal words of woe—O that it should come to this, etc. With a little prodding, she said Clarice had been all right, a little weak may be, but all right, till she heard the news of Justin's death. She grew sullen after this statement, simply stood there glowering. Clearly a storm was gathering, for she burst out belligerently, abandoning her execrable Hindi and lapsing into the richer English of everyday exchange—'I tell you what she got! Rich people disease she got! Too much laad becoming. She see everything, she hear everything, she know everything! She become blind and deaf and dumb—for what? All natak.' Then her hand flew to her mouth and she hurried out of the room.

I looked around me. Justin must have sat here often in these last few months. In this very chair perhaps—no, Justin liked his comfort—he would have preferred that squashy sofa, where there was room enough for Marion, too. I could hear his hearty laugh wake up the still air. I'd grown to enjoy our conversations on the phone. Ten minutes with Justin could put a man in good humour for the rest of the day—made him very popular with his patients, too. Even the worst curmudgeon in the ward made an effort to smile after a therapeutic dose of Dr Justin.

Why would a man as genial as Justin kill himself? What hid behind that mask of good cheer? Justin was a little too old to die of a broken heart—thirty-four or thirty-five, I think. And in any case, one cannot connect the torment of unrequited love with happy Justin. Justin tormented would lash out, not hurt himself further. The baffled look in his mother's eyes told me she too could not understand what had crushed the real Justin, for surely, she knew the child behind the laughing man.

The utter misery of loss overcame me. Is it not true that in mourning one death we mourn all the deaths we have lived through? When we weep, do we not dissolve those bitter crystals of pain that distort our adult vision? Perhaps we do not. Those crystals remain, prisms of menace, cracking the flat white light of ordinary day into a hallucinogenic fringe of dread. And yet, we see because we permit grief. To block grief is to block vision. As Clarice has. Clarice has survived the moment by turning blind.

Marion came in. She was thinner. That, and the absence of make-up, made her less overwhelming. I had been dreading this moment. I had no idea if Justin's enthusiasm for Marion was reciprocated. Anything can happen on the rebound. Justin had charm. It could be hard on Marion: the girl had attempted suicide once.

That morning, though, nothing seemed further from Marion's mind than the death of Dr Justin Borges. She did mention him once, a little peevishly: 'If only Dr Justin had noticed some warning sign, it wouldn't have got so bad.'

Marion, I realized, was suffering from that most mundane of human responses—embarrassment. Why had I thought her above it? She was ashamed as hell about her mother's 'madness', as she had called it on the phone.

'Your mother has suffered a severe shock,' I told Marion. 'She's trying to come to terms with a tragedy.'

'I don't see why Justin's death should be a tragedy to her,' Marion snapped. 'Of course we're all very sorry and all that, but it isn't a personal loss; it isn't as if he were one of us.'

Patients often expect their doctors to be patterns of good health. Most are reproachful if you so much as sneeze. Drowning in a well is extremely unprofessional. Survivors can expect to be sued.

'She's had tragedies before,' Marion said. 'She was twenty-five when my father died of typhoid. She didn't react then by going crazy. And now she's blind and deaf and dumb as well. What kind of disease is this anyway, Doctor? Why didn't you warn me that this might happen?'

I smelt litigation and resolved to hold my peace till I had seen Clarice.

'I'm really glad you're here, Dr Khan,' Marion said as a sop. 'Justin was very sweet to Mamma, but he really didn't know much about the illness, did he?'

Upstairs, Clarice was lying in bed with her eyes closed. This was the first time I had seen her without make-up and was surprised at how young she looked. She lay in the classic pose of martyrdom, with her legs crossed at the ankle, her hands steepled in supplication, the face upturned with a look of beatific calm.

'Mamma, look who's here to see you.'

No response. A slight but definite increase in rigidity. I signalled Marion to leave. She shrugged, but obeyed, banging the door behind her.

I pulled up a chair and began talking to Clarice.

After a few words, I registered a change. Soon she began responding in monosyllables. Then she could see me, and very soon she was able to get out of bed. I had performed a medieval exorcism.

I left her in Pauline's care and returned to the living room to await her.

I didn't have to wait long. She had dressed for the occasion, but had worn very little make-up. She walked without aid, if a little cautiously. Her perfume was delicious. Her manner hostessy. I did not miss her moment of panic when she entered the room: she too felt Justin in that room.

Presently she asked, 'What happened to me, Doctor?'

I explained. She protested that this couldn't happen on top of ALS, but of course it can. We talked. She was making a superhuman effort to control exhaustion. Soon the coffee was spilt, and Pauline summoned. After she had been soothed and made comfortable, Clarice startled me by announcing she knew the reason for Justin's suicide.

My first reaction, I'm ashamed to say, was to silence her. It was Justin's secret, I told her. But I knew she would tell me. She did, and this is it: Justin is—was—the illegitimate son of her late husband Clive Aranxa.

I was inclined to discredit this. There was a definite paranoid feel to her story. The exalted language of spiritual experience, the blindness, the dissociation—all pointed to an acute psychosis. But the damned witch pulled out her wedding photograph—and it could have been Justin there next to a very young and ravishing Clarice.

A little heavier, a little fairer, but Justin still.

Now I blame myself severely for having visited this trauma on my patient. I was the unknowing instrument of a most unkind destiny. I cannot even begin to imagine her tumult when she first saw him. Apparently, she had known of Clive's liaison, but not of its outcome. Justin's uncanny resemblance to her husband must have triggered upheaval on a seismic scale.

Clarice was impressive. She did not reject Justin as a physician. She overcame her difficult feelings and was gentle with him, never letting her distress show. He had been happy with his patient. That iron control of hers again! Or her innate kindness, I must admit. Her generosity of spirit. Whichever it was that helped her rise to the challenge, it had failed her after his death.

Worse follows. Clarice is certain that Mrs Borges was the last person to see Justin alive. I was shocked to hear what Clarice had to tell me about that evening. She was in the grip of some sort of exalted feeling that made her certain of total recovery; all she had to do was pray. She sent Marion and Pauline to Panjim for the evening service. She was alone at home when Justin arrived in a high state of agitation. He had just learned that he was illegitimate. He was in an ugly mood. He wanted to confront his mother and demand the truth. Clarice calmed him down, suggested they take a drive to St Anne's, as she wanted to pray. Perhaps Justin could meet his mother there. Naturally, she would not intrude. But she felt the atmosphere of the church might calm Justin's rage. Justin agreed, and made a phone call to his mother.

When they reached St Anne's, he left her in church and went outside to meet his mother.

Clarice never saw Justine again.

At 8 o'clock, worn out and frightened, she had been rescued by the priests there and sent home in a taxi. Justin's car was still parked outside the church. The news broke the following afternoon. And then—Clarice reacted.

What should I do now?

My first responsibility is towards my patient. But I have a loyalty towards Justin too. Perhaps I should have gone back and warned Mrs Borges about mad Clarice and what she had said. But Clarice is not mad. What does that make Mrs Borges? I'm not talking about Justin's birth—who cares about that—she gave Justin a marvelous life. But—if she met her son that evening, why is she silent about it? Embarrassment? Shame? After all these years? Despair? Or guilt?

How could I face Justin's mother with my mind full of these questions? I know I should have gone back. I should have spoken with her. But I ran away. This is why I am writing all this down. This is what I do not want Sharifa to know. I'm ashamed of showing myself as the coward I truly am.

As yet, Marion knows nothing. But Clarice is planning to tell her. About Justin, about Mrs Borges. She has no choice now. Marion must hear the truth from her, she says, and not from strangers.

What does Clarice expect me to do? I get the feeling she wants me to convey all this to Justin's mother. Her last questions drill into my skull: 'Didn't she tell the police she met Justin at St Anne's that evening? Justin had asked his mother to meet him at St Anne's. Didn't she tell the police what happened?'

Why didn't she?

She had told me how she had spent that evening—watching the sunset as she always did, from the top of the Baga cliff. Walking home slowly in the twilight with no clue that at that very moment, perhaps, her son was walking to his death.

Yet, Clarice is certain she met her son at St Anne's.

I can't think. I can't reason anymore.

My duty towards Clarice Aranxa is over. Physical deterioration has been slow, but bulbar signs are evident now. Soon there will be problems of speech and swallowing. In a few months, probably, hastened by these traumatic events, Clarice Aranxa will die.

Physicians are supposed to like all their patients impartially. Or rather, we're not supposed to like or dislike them. We're not supposed to react to them. At all times and at all costs we must maintain the abyss between *them* and *us*. Early in life I learnt that the abyss must be bridged if I was to help at all.

How many of his patients *can* a neurologist help? Anything even remotely curable is surgical these days, and not even a fine, frank hinge-open-the-skull-and-view-the-contents operation, but some sidey hole-in-the-corner tinkering with tubes and TV screens. One might as well be a robot, flashing dials on a console on the *Starship Enterprise*. What about the patient, dammit?

Well what *about* the patient when all you have to offer are a fistful of pills, each a scintilla of hell in itself, a wheelchair, a respirator and a cartload of compassion he can do without? What about *him*?

Yes, yes, we learn, we learn.

Four years into neurology and one knows nothing, *nothing* is like what we think it is. Forty pages of fine print won't tell you the first thing about a tremor. The patient knows more about the tremor than you do because he's got it and you don't and possession is nine-tenths of the law. He doesn't want that tremor and he'd like to wish it on you, on his wife, on his kids, hell, on the rest of the world, but he can't, he's stuck with it. Meanwhile, he's got you.

The best you can do is show him the face of the enemy. Where it lurks, how it plans and moves, how it will conquer, crush and ultimately nullify him. After a time, the questions change. The cautious 'Will I die?' becomes the peevish and querulous 'When will I die?' That's when you put all the heroism and forbearance *he's* supposed to have into *your* smile that says Not yet. That's also when you begin to run.

If you stick past those four maybe five years, things change. You see the choice you have to make. You can choose not to see men, women and—God help us—children. You need only see symptoms, elicit signs, deduce a diagnosis and leave the rest to fate. Or you can do the other thing. As I did. Or maybe I never had the choice. Whatever. And now I'm stuck with *people*.

People are tough. People are angry when disease hits them. Their rage shames them. Every doctor knows that patients have their own brand of professionalism. They come to you heavily disguised. They're never themselves, but the roles they've decided to play: wife, husband, brother, son, parent, sister, niece, girlfriend, boyfriend. They hold these derived identities like umbrellas, and my job is to thrust their naked faces into the harsh rain. How else will I know them? How else will they know their rage? Sometimes I succeed on the first visit, sometimes the second. It seldom takes longer than the third.

I have seen Clarice Aranxa six times, alone on four of those occasions, and I still don't know who she is when the guests have left.

I try to picture her, quite literally, in that situation. (There is a daughter, but for the sake of convenience, let's delete her for the moment.)

The guests have left. What will Clarice wear when she takes off her party dress? Something equally creaseless and elaborate. Clarice must also eat, piss and maybe shit, but it is unlikely she enjoys any of these activities. She has a smile like a coiled spring. It leaps out in a jagged flash of rage when I allude to bodily functions. If I didn't know better I'd think she was a cylinder of vinyl and wire beneath that impeccable dress and the satin camisole. The camisole was a surprise: I expected something starched.

Clarice has suffered two pregnancies so it is likely she also suffered the late Mr Aranxa to impregnate her. Maybe he gave her general anaesthesia on those two occasions (there couldn't have been more). Clarice would have kept on her lace-edged manner when she woke up. Imagination fails me. The domestic life of Clarice Aranxa is a total blank.

Yes, there it is—I am totally out of sympathy with Clarice. All this while I gave her my most dispassionate and professional counsel because I thought there was nothing remotely human about her. It needed only this revelation to free the woman from the robot she sold me.

I injured Clarice, I cannot dodge that. I subjected her to a trauma so violent as to dissociate her from reality. I should have made certain she met Justin herself here in Bombay, before risking her removal to Goa. I should not have left these decisions to Marion. Clarice's trauma didn't have to do with Justin dead. It had to do with Justin alive. His death was merely the snapping point.

It would be easier for all of us to call Clarice mad—as Marion had. Marion's harshness is nothing more than a very human dread of chaos. Now, after she hears the truth from Clarice, her feelings are likely to be even more turbulent. She has made one suicide attempt already. Should I not have stayed to counsel her? No. She would think me intrusive. And in the strict legal sense of the matter, I am not her doctor.

Draw your lines and never cross them, says Hippocrates, and your conscience shall stay pellucid. Surely the old guy couldn't have been that defensive in his own practice.

I think I know now what to do. Writing all this has cleared my brain. I'll wait for a couple of days and then phone Bougainvillea House.

No, that won't help. What if I can't gauge from Marion's voice what my patient has been up to? She's Clarice's daughter, after all, and can be smooth as oil when she wants to be.
What then?
Speak to Mrs Borges?
Damn.
Damn.
Damn Damn Damn Damn. I shall have to speak to Sharifa after all.

Sharifa surprised me. She said it was right of me not to see Justin's mother again. Why should you carry tales from Clarice? Mother and daughter are both chudails, she says—the old one should die.

A great gift to a doctor, I said, a wife like you. I speak the truth, she said, who's to police what I say? What do I care for that old fart Hippocrates?

Clarice, Tape 4

A little silence does one good. *You* should know. Born that way, were you? What's the use asking, you're not going to answer me. Tell me, no you're not going to tell me—did you always have that waxy calm, or did you assume that with the veil? Lay Sister. I've heard that term before. You're no nun, and you don't wear a veil, but you do have a waxy calm. Mendonca won't have to do a thing on *you* when you die. You could step into a coffin right away and the congregation would file past the tapers and lilies not knowing this sweet-smelling effigy still carried the stink of life. I want to say things to you. Bad things. Cruel things. Ugly, twisted things. Things I can hurl at you and watch as they break you. Things Clarice wanted to say every day of her life and never could, these things I can say to you, you, deaf as a post, deaf as a dead man, dumb animal, cat got your tongue, stone face—JesuMarieJoseph, what am I saying! Holy mother of God forgive me, forgive me, Sister, put it down to the ravings of the sick.

I am not raving. And you cannot hear me. So let me begin where I left off. A little silence does one good. A lot of silence—three weeks of it—has done me a lot of good. But I have to speak now because my tongue is growing heavier by the hour. My jaw sags. Already I choke on water, on tea. (I told Dr Khan this when he telephoned, and he told me to drink thick fruit juice instead! I never heard such rubbish in my life.) Soon I shall choke on spit. That will be unpleasant. I have asked Marion to keep my flannelettes ready, I have a pile of them in the armoire, but practical Marion has provided tissues. I don't like wiping my face with bits of paper. I'm not so old that I can't tell the difference between top and bottom, never been one of that filthy sort, thank God. I shall insist on my flannelettes. Lovely rose-point I've edged them with, none of your knotty stuff that Pauline makes with tatting. Pauline can wash out the stains. Pauline is good with stains. She's always kept me fresh and neat.

Yesterday I asked Pauline to bring me the box I have made ready for Cajal Mendonca. As I suspected, there was no hair spray. I knew I had overlooked something: shampoo (Clairol) and conditioner, yes, and a colour rinse, soft auburn, my usual. I must leave instructions that he blow dries, but I like a touch of spray to keep the wave in place. Clive liked my wave. It's a lazy wave, like the slow lift of a bird's wing. Clive liked my hair ...

Marion went away when I told her the truth. I was disappointed. But then, Marion has always disappointed me. Melissa pleases without effort. Marion has always tried very hard to anticipate my every wish. And Marion always fails.

What is to be done with Marion?

When Marion went away after hearing the truth, Pauline and I were afraid. Pauline thought there was more between Justin and Marion. You can't blame Pauline, that's just the kind of thought she's likely to have, they're all like that. Turn your back on them for a moment and they're at it like rabbits. Hot-blooded, these Indians are all hot-blooded, and the Pope ought to know that. You can't cool your blood with a good dousing in holy water. So it's babies, babies, babies, and what are you going to do about it.

That's what Pauline thinks. Let her. I know my Marion better. Even after Keith signed that settlement for the flat she didn't let him advance an inch, did she? I only found out later that he'd signed it already. She was so cool you'd never guess.

All the same, I was afraid. I was afraid she might do the foolish thing she had with Keith. She swallowed those tablets knowing it was a mortal sin. She didn't swallow enough. Marion can be trusted to do things by halves. But her intent was to commit that mortal sin. Marion has Clive's muddy streak in her. Nothing I do can wash it away.

In a way, I was glad Marion had gone. My long hibernation had left me eager to move about and to do as much as I could. Marion would have stopped me. Pauline and I were allies.

We often spoke of Justin, Pauline and I. We spoke of that strange evening when the power of the Lord was in my limbs. We spoke of Justin's discovery, his hot-headedness, his wrath against his mother. We spoke of her confusion, her anger, her despair. We spoke of him threatening her with that red belt. We spoke of the past flaring up, of Clive standing between them at that well. At that point we would be overcome. Nothing further would be said. We would sit out the hour in silence. One of us might begin a prayer. By the time we said Amen, we felt a little exalted, a little lifted above the common froth of things.

By now I believed this version of the truth. It was much the best for all of us: Pauline, Marion, I. It was right. It was fitting. Marion and Pauline could get on with their lives, and I could get on with the protracted business of dying. Like the churchyard with the sleepy crosses all askew, it comforted me. It was cozy.

But Marion would come back, and I knew I must hurry. I didn't have much time.

I'd told Dr Khan about her, Justin's mother, but now I found that he had done nothing at all about it. For a while I expected the police to question her. I made Pauline bake a cake and take it to the nuns at St Anne's with a warm note of thanks to sister Domenica. But if Pauline heard any gossip there, she didn't tell me.

I waited. I waited. I heard nothing. At the end of the week I sent for Xavier's taxi. We went to St Anne's. Leaving Pauline to pray, I went to make my confession. It was more than a year since I had confessed.

As always, I spoke the truth. I spoke the truth that Pauline and I told ourselves every day. I spoke the truth I told Marion, the truth of Justin's discovery, the truth about Clive. That was more, much more than I had told Sister Domenica. This priest, this shadowy form crouched behind the trellis, had been there that evening. He had been there too with the sisters who plied me with stale cake and strong tea. He had heard what I had to say that evening, and he heard what I had to say now.

I wept a great deal as I spoke. 'Do not grieve,' the voice behind the trellis said, and I believed it.

'Pray and you will be comforted.'

I prayed his prescription out and was absolved.

Only then did it strike me that I needed no absolution.

The sins I had recited were not my own. The prayers I had whispered were for Clive, for the servant girl in the red dress, for dead Justin. Clive's was the sin of lust, Justin's the sin of wrath. All the other sins were hers: the sins of envy, greed, sloth, falsehood. And now the sin of murder.

I tottered back to Pauline, collapsing on the bench, completely drained. A great peace enveloped me. I looked up at the vaulted ceiling and imagined a host of angels, chubby little cherubs with rosy bottoms and tiny wrinkly weenies curling like little earthworms that were always going to stay that way, even when they became great broad-shouldered men-angels in pastel robes. I could hear their music. Tears rained down my cheeks. I had spoken the truth, and was at peace.

Once more I felt the nearness of divine grace. I was empowered. I was being directed. I had read the signs right. Very soon I would be called upon to do what I had to do.

On the way home, I asked Xavier to drive past the Baga promontory. It was not yet dusk, but the rain-washed light had begun to thicken. Xavier asked if I would like to drive to the top of the cliff. Yes! I cried with a lift of heart. A lightness like a bird's winged me out of my old disobedient body.

Yes! To the top, then!

Pauline looked surprised. Whether she was surprised at my delight or at Xavier's suggestion, I cannot say. This much is certain: I never asked to go up there. I didn't even know there was a road to the top of the cliff.

I did not ask to go up there.

'Too much lovering after dark,' Xavier said.

I did not respond, but a swift current of anger thrilled me. Pauline giggled. Xavier, catching her eye in the mirror, said something in Konkani. I didn't understand. To me he spoke Pauline's brand of English. The lower classes have completely forgotten Portuguese these days. Pauline, having by this time recollected herself—or me—looked away.

Even that unpleasant moment could not spoil my mood. Xavier's old taxi wheezed breathlessly up the slope. Banks of weed and silvery plumes of thistle brushed the window. All the old unhappy, knotty days fell off me like soiled linen. Fresh, scented, lacy, soft, the evening waited. All I had to do was step into it.

Xavier stopped the taxi at a clearing. Beyond, the road simply curved downhill. From below, the cliff looked absolutely flat, and, but for the outline of a few small trees, completely featureless. Now I saw why. All the bushes at the side of the road had been cleared away across the width of the cliff. The road swept parallel to the unguarded edge. The few castor bushes that had escaped the scythe could not completely obscure the sea. 'Before, when too much trees, people were walking straight off from this road to watch sunset,' Xavier said in his native's English, just like Pauline's. 'One step, then one step, talking, talking, too much grass and too much bush, one more step—then *dhoop*! Into sea!'

The view was worth going over the edge for. Beyond the black rim of the cliff the sea billowed like a silver skirt, and as it rose the wind patted it down modestly, smoothing out its ruffles. The sound of the sea comforted me. It was the muted hum of a vast piece of machinery. It gave me the same feeling as domestic appliances do. Back home, in Bandra, the fridge, the AC, the fans, the washing machine gave me the feeling of being cherished. As they went about their efficient lives, these machines made certain of my own security. The sea was even better. It had a longer guarantee.

I missed that hum of cherishing in Bougainvillea House. I heard instead the drip of a leaky tap. The creak of a rusty fan. The fridge was a new one, and hardly breathed. There was no AC. The body of the house disowned me. I was an occupant on leave and licence. It waited, preparing slyly for my machinery to fail.

It was silent, the house, so that I could hear more clearly the falter in my footsteps, the catch in my breath, the dry hot cough that signals death by choking. It did not care for me. It was waiting for my lease to expire, and then it would rid itself of me. Marion would return to Bandra. Pauline could go—I can't imagine where. My clothes would be given away, my shoes would hold up other feet. Bougainvillea House would stretch itself, snap its knuckles and yawn. It was waiting for that moment.

I was safer by the sea.

'I want to walk a little.' I stopped Pauline who was preparing to accompany me: 'Just a little by myself, to feel the peace of the evening.'

'Don't go too far from here, madam,' Xavier fussed. But he helped me out of the taxi and led me to the clearing. There he left me.

I have often relived that moment. Yes, I did will myself alone. Why, I cannot say. They too let me go. Again, I cannot say why. At some time one has to stop clutching at reasons and surrender completely to chance.

Chance led me to the cliff. Chance made Xavier park there. It was chance that I should feel this sudden kinship with the mothering sea and want to lose myself in it. Chance led me through the clearing. Chance, too, that a clump of castor with its palmy leaves should cut me off from the view of Xavier and his taxi. I tell you these silly details only to show you how little I can be held responsible for the events that followed.

That evening set the pattern, I willed very little, but I surrendered entirely to chance.

The lightness had left me. To the left, the sky flamed with colour above the smoky sea. To the right, the crowding castor bushes grew thicker and more secret. The sky lowered its arch till it seemed no higher than the ceiling of St Anne's. From its scatter of painted clouds fat little cherubs called down to me. *Clarice! Clarice!* Where had I heard those baby voices before? *Clarice! Clarice!*

The years before Clive, the lost years, the easy years, opened like gates, and the distance was hazy with beautiful things. When had I lost all that? Why had I wandered out of those gates and blundered into my harsh unforgiving life, when? How had I arrived at this point?

Clarice! Clarice!

They waved their fat arms at me, calling out with plump little voices, higher, fainter, they were lifting me up with their voices, rushing me, reaching through my blouse, slipping between my ribs, grabbing with their baby hands till they found my heart, slipping, holding, slipping, holding, squeezing, squeezing my old heart in their small greedy fists till I felt my feet leave the ground and the sky turn.

Then all at once the gates clanged shut, and she stood before me.

For a moment I was still, bedazzled. The sky roared with flame, clouds smeared and clumped like bloodied cotton-wool. The sea switched off its hum. There was only this scream of colour, and at its centre the thick black figure of this woman.

The moment passed. My eyes cleared. The sea resumed its hum.

We saw each other.

I saw a girl in a red dress. A girl no longer, no longer in a red dress. But I saw a girl in a red dress.

What did *she* see?

She never told me.

I can guess, though.

She saw a lady in a yellow Tricel skirt and a headband, who walked with her shoes in her hand for fear of muddying them. The lady's face was young—ah so young! Her eyes were full of hope.

And she, the girl in the red dress, she was waiting to murder that hope.

This is what she saw that day. Though, I must repeat, she did not tell me so.

We recognized each other, shocked by the live current that leapt between us. But we had both seen life. We recovered our calm. We smiled at each other.

'Good evening.' It was my responsibility to cue her.

'Good evening.'

'Enjoying the sunset?'

'Yes. It's very peaceful here.'

Words came easily to us. Neither was willing to walk away. Our eyes probed, trying to mine the hidden years.

'Do you walk here often?'

'Almost every day.'

'This is my first visit.'

'I hope you will come again.'

'And I hope to meet you again.'

'I shall look forward to it. Goodnight.'

Did she turn away, or did I? I don't remember. I only remember finding myself back at the clump of lantana, Xavier's taxi gleaming in the sun's last rays. There was a flutter of voices as I neared them. Xavier hurried up to help me inside. Pauline only watched, she did not move towards me. She had changed, Pauline. I couldn't help feeling a twinge of pain when I thought how the old Pauline would have fussed over me. Oh we were allies, she gave me every attention, but something in me repelled her now. All too often she turned away at the moment our eyes brushed. All too often of late she avoided my gaze.

I did not allow that irritation to last. In fact, Pauline's coldness was of some help to me. The girl in the red dress was my secret, and I wanted to savour it deliciously in silence. It filled my mouth with caramel, tough and sweet and sticky. I rolled it on my tongue till it grew into a flat brown slab of clarity.

That girl! She spoke English! How was that possible? She

couldn't have, she shouldn't have. She spoke to me as an equal. In English. She addressed me in English as an equal. No matter how I turned that inside out, I could not get over the insult of it.

Her voice was calm, distant. Had it been as calm and distant when she swarmed all over Clive? I saw myself at the coconut grove, I saw my young and frightened face, I felt my life crumble beneath my bleeding feet. I saw those things as Xavier's taxi wheezed its way back to Bougainvillea House.

That night I asked Pauline to take one of my new nightgowns out of its satin case. Soft silky apricot, with deep scallops of lace. 'You tire yourself too much,' Pauline sighed as she undressed me. But it was a token protest. 'Why did you go alone? Suppose you fell? Right into the sea, sank like a stone?'

'Good for all of us if that happens, Pauline.'

Two old women exchanging wounds. We did not talk of my health anymore these days. It seemed understood that since I had unburdened myself to Dr Khan and later to Marion, there was no further danger of my going blind and deaf and dumb again. I wasn't so sure myself. There were moments when I yearned for that safe blackness, but there was too much to be done.

After Pauline left me, I walked to the window. A full moon glared down at me. The whisper of silk against my skin set up an ache so deep I could not tell where or what it was. I was deathly tired. By every law of nature, my knees should have buckled. But they held me up hour after hour as the moonlight mocked me, slapping with white palms my fallen tits, punching in my belly, hammering my hips, mocking me, mocking me.

My knees held me up because I knew I had been mocked for too long. I had brought this disease on myself because I had let myself be beaten down and shamed and had done nothing about it. The moonlight pulled at my tits, pulled them off my chest, I saw them float like white clouds outside my nightie. I crossed my legs quickly before the moonlight did anything worse. I crossed my legs and gathered up my nightie, wadding it between my thighs as hard as I could. I made myself as rigid as a pillar, a marble column, white and pure and solid. I made myself safe. I locked myself tight till the moonlight grew tired of whimpering like Clive and sulked and moved away. Only then did I make my trembling way to bed. There my legs failed me. The effort of climbing into bed nearly killed me. But a single thought penetrated the fog of exhaustion: *I must see her again.*

The next day, Marion returned. She fussed over me as of old. Cross-questioned Pauline about my medication, my meals, my exercise. Asked if she should call Dr Khan for another visit. What's he going to do, I asked, waggle his beard at me and say Clarice you are going to die and charge a fat fee for it?

That wasn't true, Dr Khan never said that to me, I take that back. This is the truth, isn't it, I have to speak the truth to you and I take that back because it isn't true. Till I run into real trouble, I have no use for Dr Khan. But I am grateful to him for explaining my blindness.

Neither Marion nor I mentioned Justin. Pauline murmured, 'Baby is acting as if nothing happened.'

I did not think it necessary to explain to Pauline that Marion was not going to let it hang out like an Indian. A very vulgar expression, I've always thought, it used to be a favourite of my mother's: *Don't go letting it hang out like an Indian, Eustace, nice girls won't let you.* Eustace was my brother, and a lot of nice girls did let him.

'More than that Keith, she was sweet with Justin,' Pauline persisted. 'Laughing and making eyes the whole time.' Nonsense. Marion's never made eyes at Justin or at any other man. She wouldn't know how.

'She won't go running to Justin's mother now,' Pauline said with satisfaction.

My heart stopped.

'When you went blind and all, again and again she told me it looked so bad we did not go to see her.'

I was so exhausted by what I heard that it was only after Pauline settled me in bed that I was able to whisper, 'Send Marion to me.'

I roused myself when she entered. 'Sit here, Baby.' Marion was surprised, but she settled herself next to my pillow eagerly. I took her hand. Such beautiful hands! So tender, so strong! We were silent. Marion's tears fell *plink! plink!* on my hand. It made my skin itch, but I didn't move away.

'Let me have peace, Marion,' I said as though I was praying to the Blessed Virgin. 'I've had thirty years of pain. I want some peace before I die.'

'Don't talk of dying, Mamma.'

'I'm quite content to die, now that all this is almost over.' I said that aloud, but she did not ask what *all this* was. Marion had taken off the engagement ring Keith had given her, a sapphire set with diamonds. Now she wore a plain gold band with her initials on it. She had a new sort of nail paint. Her nails looked like mother of pearl, colourless, with a flash of light. Not like real opal.

Marion will have my opal brooch when I'm gone. My brooch came from Australia, one of Clive's early gifts before he grew stingy. I loved that opal the moment I saw it, a drop of milk with heart afire.

I've always thought of myself like that—a drop of milk with heart afire.

What had Clive given *her*, the girl in the red dress? What more did she get out of Clive besides that spoonful of slime? What would she have got out of Clive if he hadn't died? What would have happened to us?

We would have crouched in the mud, in the rain, in the filth on the roadside, we would have crawled there and starved and waited to die while she ruled the house like a queen, while she ran about barefoot, sat around with her feet up leaving dirty marks on the furniture. And all her relations, half-naked, spitting, rolling about and rutting on the floor. *This* would have been our fate if Clive hadn't died.

I didn't tell Marion this, of course not, but I held her hand as these thoughts raced in my brain, and then I said: 'I must go up that hill to get peace. Tell Xavier. Tell him to take me there every evening. Tell Pauline she needn't come. Sometimes, Marion, I'm so sick of Pauline. Everywhere I turn, there's Pauline. More like a shadow than a servant. Tell Pauline she needn't come. Xavier will take me. He will wait while I walk a little, watch the sunset, feel the sea. Such peace, Marion! Such peace!'

'Hush, Mamma,' Marion soothed me, 'don't worry yourself over it. I'll look after it.'

'That's my Marion,' I said. 'Always my girl, Marion,' I said, though she wasn't and we both knew it.

Melissa is not my girl either, but then she has Tom.

Marion has done everything she can for me. But she fails me every time. Too bright, too eager, too loving. How can you trust a child like that? Right from the moment she learned to talk—Yes Mamma, Please Mamma, Thank you Mamma, I love you Mamma.

Too many kisses, too many hugs, too many terrors in the night. Every term she'd bring me the report card with huge scared eyes and yet she was always top of the class, not right on top—I wouldn't have liked that, it never does for a woman to be too clever, scares the boys off, doesn't it?—but third or fourth, certainly. She'd stand there with that report card, her small face so worried that I would feel simply forced to tell her she must write more neatly, spell better, behave more like a little lady. Of course I would have said these things anyway, even if she hadn't looked so scared. I said these things out of anxiety, fearful lest the good report go to her head. The only thing worse than a clever woman is a woman who knows she's clever. Marion is clever. Where has it got her? With half her brains and at half her age I had Clive, rich, handsome—there were those who thought that!—and well born. Well born. I had Clive, and Marion hasn't even caught herself an Indian, poor thing. Still, I said to her that night, feeling her hands smooth my hair, 'That's my Marion. That's my girl,' and saying that, I fell asleep.

Soon after that, the whispers began. I heard them everywhere. Pauline coming in from the market, whispering with Marion behind the door. The gardener coming in by the front door, quite without permission, right into the living room, the gardener, whispering in full view of the house, whispering to Pauline. Pauline padding up the stairs with her heavy tread, pulling Marion out of the bath, Marion rushing down without her robe, her tits all bouncy for the gardener to see, whisper whisper the three of them, though what the gardener whispered I had no idea, he was so struck by Marion's tits.

When Pauline came to dress me, she gave nothing away. When I strolled in the garden to work up an appetite for lunch, the gardener wouldn't meet my eye. Some Indian name he has, I can't say it, I just call him the gardener, that's what he is, that's what he will be to me.

When I reminded Marion about Xavier's taxi, she shrugged and left the room.

Pauline brought me lunch on a tray. An omelette, a small helping of rice and *doll*! Indian food, imagine! But bread was getting difficult. It clotted to a dry wad on my tongue. I ate the Indian food, humbled by my need and angry at my humiliation. But there is just so much Clarice Aranxa can take. The day I am forced to wear flip-flops like an Indian I'll simply stop walking. I had decided that long ago. I remember saying that to Justin. He laughed and promised me that day would never come. 'Have you thought of sandals—with velcro straps? You won't need chappals.'

'Baby shoes!' I said scornfully. 'You'll be giving me squeaky shoes next.'

Justin.

Justin!

I loved that boy! How I loved that boy! I loved him as I could never love his father, as I could never love the children of my own body. Justin!

Pauline set down my tray and went away without offering to cut up the omelette (another difficulty). Then, again, whisper whisper behind the door.

Marion: We should tell her, I think. You tell her.

Pauline: No, no, Baby. You tell.

Marion: I can't! I'm going back to Bombay now.

Pauline: All right. Okay, Baby. Let her eat first. Then I'll tell her. You go pack your suitcase. But better you don't speak any more about this. Don't tell anyone, Baby.

Pauline came in and helped me with exaggerated anxiety. She asked if I would like some pastry from Fortino's, she could send for it. The thought of a lemon tart filled my mouth, but I saw it for the bribe it was and said no.

She stood there like a boulder. 'What is it, Pauline?' I asked finally.

Her hands fluttered to her face, as if she would fence the words in with her fingers. 'They're talking in the village. They're saying Justin was Clivebab's son.'

I cried out then. It was a howl of grief torn out of my centre, a wild and desolate sound that brought the gardener tearing into the house in alarm.

The truth was about. Memory, that mangy cat, had burst its cage, thrust its claws in the nearest face, drawn blood and scampered free. What would it do to me? Suddenly I realized it could do nothing. I was safe from it. It would find its prey elsewhere.

'They're saying Justin found out. They're saying he got into a quarrel and somebody called him a bastard.'

'That's what he told me.'

'They're saying she was there—'

'That's what Justin asked her to do. Justin asked her to go there.'

'They're saying that she—'

'*She?*'

'She!'

There! It was out! And we hadn't said a thing.

Pauline shuddered. 'What will they do now? Police and all?'

'Definitely.'

'JesuMarieJoseph. Her own son.'

'Don't judge her, Pauline. Remember, we don't know anything for sure.'

'You are too good, Baby, too big your heart is—'

And that fool Pauline burst into tears, all her grievances forgotten.

'The poor woman has had enough grief in her life,' I said gravely. 'I know what it's like. I have suffered. I have lost. I have mourned.'

I was well into my mood of exaltation. It was exciting to discover how easily I could slip into it now, that lightness of heart, that lift in the spirit, that golden hour of scattered clouds and cherubs calling out in plump sweet voices—*Clarice! Clarice!*

I was well into that mood.

Sternly, I quelled it. 'Where's Marion gone?'

'To meet Sister Domenica.'

'What for?'

'To offer our help—'

'We don't want to give any help,' I told Pauline. 'Marion has no business meddling in this. You had no right to let her go without telling me.'

Pauline sighed. She rolled her eyes. 'It will look bad, Baby, if she doesn't go.'

It will look bad. Hasn't that been the deciding factor for everything in my life? It'll look bad if I say no to Clive. It'll look bad if I don't give him children. It'll look bad if I notice the girl in the red dress. It'll look bad if I reproach Clive. It'll look bad if I don't cry my eyes out. It'll look bad if—

It'll look bad if you sit with your knees apart, Marion. It'll look bad if you pick your nose, Melissa. It'll look bad if people find out it's your time of the month, Melissa. It'll look bad if you seem so eager with boys, Marion.

Maybe that's what I'll get them to carve on my gravestone: *She never looked bad.*

Marion was back soon. Sister Domenica said the police had taken the woman for questioning. That doesn't mean a thing. Here in Baga, where everybody is related to everybody, the Inspector is only your nephew in fancy dress.

By night we had more news. Sister Domenica called from St Anne's to say Justin's mother was back home. The formalities were over. Naturally, she was upset, but now we must pray that the matter is closed.

I asked to speak with her, calling loudly across the room, so that Marion could not refuse me.

'How are you, Clarice?' Sister Domenica, relishing every syllable of tragedy. 'Clarice, what can we say? We didn't want you to know, but Marion told us you knew already.'

That was just to protect the fool priest who spilled the beans. Nothing loath, I put in my bit: 'How is the poor lady, Sister? All this trouble on top of her grief. How much suffering she has endured!'

'You have the heart of a saint, Clarice. May Our Lady protect you, dear. We're praying for you, Clarice. Every day we say a prayer for you.'

'Thank you, sister. That means so much to me.'

'Anything you need, Clarice, anything at all, just call us. Tell Pauline to call us. I know Marion will be getting back to Bombay. But we sisters are here for you, Clarice. Anything at all—'

'Oh sister, actually, there *is* some help I need. Could you send Xavier to me? I want to make a regular arrangement with him as soon as I can. There's so little time left for me to get about.'

'I'll send him right away. I don't mind telling you, Clarice, it will be a great help to Xavier. With all this environment rubbish you know what a tourist slump we're facing. These days Xavier doesn't get a fare for weeks. His taxi gets a flat tyre just sitting around. I'll send him in the morning.'

There! I walked back to my chair avoiding Marion's eye. Time enough to show her how she had displeased me.

The next day I made my arrangement with Xavier. I paid him well. I had a small stock of money with me. I was not likely to need it in the future. It would have to do for now. I did not involve Marion in the transaction. Pauline was present, but when she broke into the conversation, I asked her to leave.

Xavier would call for me every evening at five. He would take me up the cliff, help me out of the taxi and wait as long as I wished to walk. That was the deal.

Pauline protested later. Why did I want to go alone? What if I stumbled on uneven ground? Why not go to the beach instead as we used to?

Because I don't want to go to the beach, Pauline. And, if I remember right, we didn't have such a good time there. Because I need some time to myself, Pauline, some time away from you, some time to make peace with myself before I die.

I didn't say this to Pauline. I merely closed my eyes and pretended sleep. Next it was Marion's turn. I had resolved to stop talking to Marion. When she spoke to me, I turned my face away.

'I will have my tea at half past four,' I told Pauline. 'You can dress me then.'

I stretched out in bed, my heart hammering, praying for strength to win this last battle, to achieve this final bid for freedom from Marion.

About an hour later, Marion stole into my room. She stood by my bed a long while, staring down at me. My eyes were shut, my fists clenched, I was afraid she might hear the tumult in my heart.

That evening I chose a yellow dress as pale as the five o'clock sun, a simple sacque with a silver chain for belt. I would need jewels. I asked Pauline to open my safe and took out my favourite necklace. It has tiny beads of garnet strung with seed pearls between small gold flowers. A very delicate cross for pendant. You should see it sometime. It was Clive's mother's. Real Portuguese gold. I put on earrings that went with the necklace, too flashy for an evening stroll, but very necessary for what I had to do. A pinkish blush, very light, with a touch of aubergine in the cheek's hollow. A brush of bronze over the eyes. My lipstick that evening was a deep red, matte and soft as the inside of a rose. A generous spritz of *Anais Anais*. I have saved my last precious drops of *Joy* for Extreme Unction. Shoes—ah, trouble, I thought, but the soft moccasins Marion had insisted on buying were very comfortable. My feet felt safe in them. And so, in the end, even Marion abetted me.

Xavier was disposed to chat. I told him I wanted quiet. He shut up very quickly. It's best to be direct and definite with menials, I always find. No point letting them get familiar. When we got to the top of the cliff, I made him stop a little further away from the castor bushes so that I would not feel his eyes bore into my back as I walked.

He hung back like a scolded pup after he had helped me out. 'If you get tired, I'll come fetch you, madam,' he muttered. I could almost picture the questions coming to a boil in his slow brain: *How will I know when you get tired? How will you call out to me? What if you fall? What if you fall down dead?* But of course he said nothing.

I laughed. I was exhilarated, I was free, I was going to walk away from this frightened man, leaving him in a froth of worry till I returned. I had forgotten how heady that feeling could be. This petty triumph took me back to the victories of my youth: I used to leave Clive in just such a froth when I went out without him, even if it was only for a game of tennis at the gym. All the time that Clive was cheating on me, *he* could never trust *me*. Think of that!

I was exhilarated, but that lightness of heart I anticipated did not visit me that day. The sea kept up its vast domestic hum. The sky was scrubbed and dry. The tops of trees swished lazily like dusters. It was an evening when time had stopped. The day was brushed and tidied, but had nowhere to go. The sunlight glazed everything. I wanted peace, but I felt only waiting.

Then the waiting was over.

I saw her.

She stood just ahead of me, staring at the polished bowl of sea. She did not turn at my approach. I have a very light tread. Nor did my shadow scythe her down.

She stared at the sea as though her eyes strained to pick out something beneath the crisp ruffles of water. I was tempted to help her get a closer look, but I did not do it then, not that day. I coughed and prepared my face for greeting.

She looked up with a distant, almost bored look that wiped the smile off my face.

'Good evening.'

It was she who said it first, hastily recovering manners, forcing warmth into her voice. But I had seen her eyes. I did not let her know that, though. I smiled, and if my smile had frost on it, she did not notice. I joined her contemplation of the sea. So we stood, side by side. Who would speak first?

Neither would, it seemed, that evening.

We stood close, so very close to the grassy edge of the promontory. The ground sloped down from our feet, the sky roared down at us, the sea swooped up every minute. Everything urged us towards that margin of grass and still neither she, nor I, advanced.

Xavier was glad to see me back, and I was gracious. Pauline and Marion sulked. I sat in my bed in a puddle of moonlight and dreamed.

The days passed. I went up to the cliff every day. We met every day. We paced the cliff together. We stopped to enjoy the breeze. We exchanged words that meant nothing. Of what lay between us, we did not speak.

Sometimes I felt she awaited the hour with as much eagerness as I did. She too felt the rush of days overtaking her, the speed of running down the slope, knowing it would be free fall very soon. I found that exciting. It charged me with energy. Next to her I was not Clive's delicate wife or Justin's dying patient. I was myself. We were both bystanders watching ourselves in the coconut grove: she in the red dress, arching over my husband. I in the shadows, crouching in the mud. She spied on me as I spied on her. In our silence we walked the deep green shadows of the ruined temple, we waited at the well. It was not the sea we stared at, never the sea. We stared down at the still and the parted waters of the well.

Sometimes words surfaced, completing a thought that connected us. Neither asked for explanation.

Once I said, 'I saw you together.'

Another time *she* said, 'I never told him.'

We never thought of Justin. He might never have existed. It was Clive who stood there with us. It was Clive, Clive, Clive every day.

There was an evening when we stood side by side, closer to the edge than we had ever gone before.

There was no more than a hand-span of air between us.

I asked. 'Are you afraid?'

'No. Are you?'

'No.'

The air between us tightened. The slightest movement would snap it, and when the air cracked, one of us, only one of us, would fall.

The days hurried.

Marion had returned to her job. I rested all day in bed, storing strength for my secret hour of life. Pauline was respectful, caring. Somehow, by isolating myself, I had gained in importance and dignity. Xavier never intruded. He couldn't have seen her—or I would have heard about that from Pauline.

I knew I was growing weaker. I could walk, but the stairs were getting difficult. Some days I choked on the merest sip of water, though I willed myself to swallow food.

The days hurried, the days hurried.

The last time I saw her the sky was red as her dress. It raged down on her, lighting her like a flame that floated down, down, a spark soon to be extinguished by billowing night.

That evening I could not get out of the taxi on my own. Xavier had to lift me out and carry me up the steps.

It took me some time to brave the arduous journey from living room to bed. Pauline fussed over me. She sponged and powdered me, massaged my feet, brushed my hair.

But when she brought my nightie, I could no longer see what I was supposed to wear. She pulled it over my head. I surfaced, but the world was still black.

'Pauline! Pauline!' I shouted. 'Pauline, I cannot see!'

If Pauline answered, I did not hear her. Darkness, clean, cool darkness, poured into me. The world as I knew it had ceased to be.

Liaqat

The telephone woke him. He stared stupidly into the dark, letting it shrill. The street light cast a watery film on the ceiling. Sharifa stirred and hurriedly he picked up the phone.

'Dr Khan? Dr Khan!'

His heart gave a sudden knock, reminding him of its relentless beat.

'Yes. Yes, Marion.'

'Oh, thank God, thank God, Doctor. Thank God I got you now. It's happened again. I just got a call from Pauline. It's happened again. She can't see, she can't hear, she can't talk. She wasn't talking to me when I left, she was angry with me, oh God, what if she never talks to me again—'

'Hold on, Marion. Take a deep breath and wait. I'm here, we'll see what we can do. You can't help her if you break down now.'

'Heavens. It's past midnight. I'm sorry, Doctor, I had no idea—'

'That's all right. The time doesn't matter. Just collect yourself and tell me slowly. Take your time, tell me what's happened. What did Pauline tell you?'

'She—she's become like last time, she's become—like quiet and lost.'

'All right, Marion. I will talk to Pauline right away and tell her what's to be done tonight. We'll deal with the rest in the morning.'

Pauline shouted in his ear. He found himself shouting back. When he put down the phone at last, he was shaking.

'*Now* what has she done?' Sharifa muttered. 'Why do you let these people get to you like this?'

He padded angrily to the bathroom, overtaken by a senseless rage towards his wife. He came back contrite.

Sharifa was awake. 'No point getting huffy in the middle of the night,' she said. 'That chudail will wait till morning.'

He took the two o'clock flight to Panjim. Marion had reached ahead of him. He was shocked by her appearance. She had lost more weight, her hair had thinned, her eyes were tortured. Pauline was inscrutable. Clarice lay in state, draped in satin and lace, her face curiously childlike without make-up.

He took her hand.

'Clarice.'

No response.

The hand, soft and pampered as a fallen flower, lay limp in his grasp.

Her eyes, blank and distant, roved the room.

Catatonia. Whatever its cause, catatonia.

He left the room, followed by Marion and Pauline. He searched his brain for words while Marion spoke—'. . . upset with me . . . wouldn't talk at all the last few days.'

'Any reason you can think of?'

The two women exchanged looks. Then Pauline nodded and Marion said sullenly, 'I went to St Anne's to enquire after Justin's mother. That hurt her, I think.'

Pauline said, 'Very grand she became, like maharani. Pauline now only for bring this, do that. Then all this taxi business.'

For a woman who was losing her limbs to motor neuron disease, the patient was certainly a notch above active. Should he reconsider the diagnosis? Aloud he asked: 'What taxi business?'

'She's arranged for a taxi to drive her every evening to the top of the cliff to watch the sunset. Sunset! I don't think my mother ever looked at a sunset all her life. I can't think why she wants to begin now! However, there it is, she wants to go, she goes. Makes all the arrangements herself.'

'All the time alone, alone. Leave me alone. I want to be alone.' Pauline touched her temple significantly when Marion was not looking, and in case he hadn't got it, muttered, 'Screw loose. Maddy!'

He went over Clarice's responses. She permitted Pauline to sponge and dress her. That morning she had accepted a bed pan. So far she had refused food and drink. Marion said she had coaxed her with broth first and then ice cream, but she remained unresponsive, her jaws clenched tight.

When he was alone with her again, he pulled down the blinds and darkened the room. He drew up a chair and forced himself to relax.

The room breathed around him in half light, curiously womblike. Muscle by muscle he loosened with grim volition, emptying his mind of thought. This was an exercise he had learned during vigils beside the comatose, a discipline urged by a need to reach a plane of communication. Illogical, perhaps, but it worked sometimes. 'Om' was not good enough; he tried for the circular vowel 'Au-uu-um', the final whiplash at his navel punching in his abdominals. 'Au-um.' He said it silently, though the sound echoed in the vault of his skull and he had a momentary vision of its glistening and emptied interior, the arching aqueducts of blood in a tense hammock of membrane. He had it now. He kept at it, feeling his burdens drop away one by one.

He became aware of her, beneath the fruity scent of her talc, the dry, scrubbed odour of her skin. He heard her stir, the shifting of a muscle, no more. He found her hand and waited.

Her fingers slid, curved, locked into his own.

'Clarice.'

Wait, he told himself, and returned to the cycle of emptying his brain.

Her fingers kept up their touch against his own.

His voice came easily. He had found it helped not to get too chatty. It was useless to pretend familiarity. It was a bit like prayer. She was, in her silence, almighty. He was the supplicant.

'Clarice, you can hear me. I know you can hear me now. I understand you want to be alone. I understand you don't want to talk. I want to help you, Clarice. I want to make certain you can do what you're trying to do. No, I do not want to know what that is. I only want you to be able to do it. You must let me help you. You must help me to help you. I understand you cannot trust yourself to speak, Clarice. I'm going to tell you a few things. If you agree, blink once. If you disagree, blink several times. Is that clear, Clarice?'

Clarice blinked. Once.

'Your heart is so heavy, you cannot trust yourself to speak. is that right, Clarice?'

Blink.

'Shall I ask Marion to stay on here?'

Rapid blinking.

'Shall I ask Pauline to be here with you?'

After a long interval, blink.

'You are thinking things over, aren't you, Clarice?'

Blink.

'After you have thought them through, you will be able to talk again, you will be able to see again. You do understand that, don't you?'

Blink.

'But now you need to be undisturbed, you need to concentrate on your thoughts.'

Blink.

'You need strength to concentrate, Clarice. You won't be able to concentrate if you feel weak. You need food, Clarice.'

Rapid blinking.

'You need food to help you think clearly. To help you sort out what's weighing on your mind. Do you want to return to Bombay?'

Rapid blinking.

'All right, Clarice. I'll make sure you stay here. I will instruct them to leave you alone if you promise to eat. Try Clarice.'

Blink.

'You must be hungry now. It's past lunchtime.'

Blink.

'Shall I tell Pauline to bring you something?'

Blink.

'I shall tell Marion you are not to be disturbed, you need absolute peace and quiet.'

Blink

'I shall see you a week from now, Clarice.'

Blink.

He wrote out instructions while Pauline fed her.

'I expect her to stay in this state for a few days,' he told Marion. 'Please call me in two days. Till then I want her to be completely isolated. Pauline can feed and sponge her. No conversation. Unless, of course, she wants it. If she begins to talk, reply. No questions. I suggest you keep out of her room for a while.'

'Why? How can you keep me from my own mother?'

He sighed. He searched his vocabulary for balm. He said, 'You're too close to her. Your presence makes her feel observed. She wants privacy. You're an intelligent lady, Marion. You must be patient. The more patient you are, the quicker she'll return to normal.'

'What's normal?' Marion asked bitterly. 'A creeping paralysis that will make her bedridden before the month is out? What if she can't swallow, doctor? What if she chokes? What if she dies when I'm out of the room, because she can't call out, she can't breathe? What will I do if that happens?'

Marion knew all the answers. She wasn't asking for information. It took him an hour to extricate himself.

Then there was a further half hour with Pauline.

'Everything locked inside heart,' Pauline said, 'everything locked and key thrown away. Lost. Now she want to look inside. Can't open!'

Which, he thought, was as good an analysis as any shrink could give him.

'You can help her, Pauline, I think she has always depended on you. Just make sure nobody bothers her. No questions. No conversation. No gossip.'

'I will take care.'

Then the taxi drew up at the gate, and he was free.

'Same taxi,' Pauline muttered, with a dark look at the driver. 'So much money she paid and just only three trips. Now Xavier's head become swollen.'

He met Xavier's impassive eye in the mirror with every bump on the potholed road. 'Very sad Madam is not well.' Xavier opened the conversation delicately, scanning his face for the flicker of disapproval.

Liaqat must have passed the test, because Xavier continued in a higher gear. 'Every day take me up the cliff road, she says. Every day. Who knows what she want to see, same sun setting same place every day. But no. Take me up the cliff road every day. Three days I took her, then she became sick. Too much strain.'

'Yes, I suppose so,' Liaquat got the feeling, once again, that this was as sound a second opinion as he was likely to get. 'She is completely exhausted.'

'That Pauline said Madam is going to die. All nonsense, Sahib.

Dying people are not walking up cliff, I tell her. You have given strong medicine this time, eh? Injection? Injection is best. So many tablets, taking, taking all the time, all colours, all shapes, no use. That's why I tell our doctor, give injection please. Fifty rupees, hundred rupees, never mind, for my children I get money somehow. But you give injection.'

Liaqat cringed. He fought the momentary guilt of not confessing he hadn't given Clarice any medicine at all. In his head Sharifa clucked impatiently, 'Go explain, explain, explain to every beggar who knocks at your door . . .' He laughed inwardly and focussed again on Xavier.

'No help from me, no help from anybody she wants. "Wait in the taxi, Xavier." Only English, not like our Goan people—Konkani, English, Portuguese—all mix. Madam I put chair for you near railing, you sit and watch sunset, I tell her. "Wait in the taxi, Xavier." No—"*Please* wait in the taxi, Xavier." When she is saying "please" I say bas, Xavier, now no more telling. Half an hour I wait. Sun go down, she come back. "Thank you, Xavier." Then when I leave her at the house, "Good night, Xavier." Like that. No other talking. Three days only, then too much it became, I think.'

'She might feel up to it again once she's a little better. Now she needs bed rest. Is that the cliff there?' He looked up. The promontory jutted, a dark block of solidity against the luminous sky.

'Yes. Road go up that way. We take down road now.'

The road hugged the beach. The choppy sea glittered with unease. Over the rocks it sparkled like a giant scrap of tinsel, a chocolate wrapper afloat in the wind.

His eyes still mesmerized by that aerial chunk of earth that cut off the sky, Liaqat did not notice the road block ahead. Xavier swore, pulled up and was out of the taxi and running barefoot in the sand before Liaqat could protest.

A confused scatter of men appeared over the rocks. They swarmed, then settled in a stillness as absolute and immoveable as the rocks themselves. *Petrified*. The word rattled in Liaqat's skull as he scrambled out, ran, slipped, fell, shuffled, kicked his way through the sand. Xavier's khaki back with its wide maps of sweat had found a place in that still throng. Now all his quivering urgency was stilled too.

Liaqat saw all this in jerky frames, interrupted by blanks of sea and sky as he fought his way through the sand. Were his feet really so clumsy, or was he trying to postpone the inevitable moment when he too would take his place among the men on the rocks?

How ancient it was, this ring of male backs stilled into unity, frozen in one long moment of shock. How ancient and predictable that posture. No need to break past them to see what lay beyond—

Yet here he was, scrambling for foothold next to Xavier. Xavier turned, his eyes focussed, widened in intelligence. Liaqat found himself trapped in Xavier's brawny arms, and steered to face the sea. 'Doctor's here!'

Liaqat felt their relief as the ring broke to let him through. He had been sent to take this burden from them. They thrust him out there, where the unthinkable awaited—just a few feet ahead, yet a galactic distance away. The sea's cold breath mingled with a familiar reek. They propelled him forward on the rocks, Xavier's hand a restraint on his arm as though they feared more violence. They urged him because he was a doctor, licensed to restore life.

But his pitiful knowledge of life was useless now. All they could use was what he knew of death.

Sodden, bunched, broken, and knotted anyhow in the rags of the sari that had once draped it, a woman's body lay shattered at his feet. Death had claimed her first. Then the assaulting sea had turned predator. There was little left to recognize in the face, bloated, bitten, gnawed, macerated. But a person is more than her face, and somehow Liaqat knew her. They all knew her, all these witnesses. Her life had passed through theirs and now she had plucked it away. She had not trusted them. The quality of their silence hardened. Even as Liaqat stared at her, he sensed that. Their silence was no longer resonant. It had gathered into a sullen clot, it had passed from horror to censure.

He crouched in the sea spray, picking foolishly at the clump of grey hair matted on her face. He remembered her look of bewilderment. Justin's death had baffled her. Did she know now? Had death brought her the knowledge her son had kept from her?

He felt a touch on his shoulder. He allowed Xavier to lead him back over the rocks. His eyes prickled from the sea spray, his nose leaked. It was only when he found himself unable to speak that he realized he was sobbing.

Twenty-four hours later, he was still in those sand-stained clothes. Sometime in between—on entering the house, probably—he had slipped off his shoes, peeled the soggy socks away.

Xavier had got him to the airport on time, steering to the right counter and racing ahead to a vending machine to grab a scalding cup of tea for him. The sear on his tongue ended a long, numb hour. 'You want I will phone your house.' Xavier was worried. 'You will take taxi from airport, no?'

Throughout the panic of that brief flight he drew comfort from the memory of Xavier's creased face. It was something real, something that had no part in this masquerade of silence and sudden death.

It was a relief to be on firm ground again, and out of the swing of the sea. The rickshaw ride home was interminable. The warm odoriferous soup of Bombay air laved his lungs without comforting him.

Sharifa took one look at him and stepped aside. Their eyes tangled, but there were no questions. He collapsed in a crumpled heap on the sofa. 'I'm okay, just leave me alone.' Sharifa had heard the words before and took them seriously. In their twelve years together there were some privacies they honoured.

She left food on the table, a carafe of water, towel, t-shirt, shorts. He ignored them.

She had gone to bed at eleven. He had sensed, rather than seen her, in the doorway before she turned in. She'd left the lights on in the kitchen. He sat the night through in that sub-fuse glow. He did not feel the night end or the day begin. Sharifa hovered in the periphery of his vision, replenishing the water on the table and clearing the untouched food before she left for work.

It was three in the afternoon now. He still lay on the sofa, hungry, sleepless, his bladder straining for release. As always, that protest finally roused him. His knees buckled on the way to the bathroom, but he made it sternly. He switched on the geyser. And with the first needles of hot water, life returned. He emerged ravenous. The house was empty. He fried a couple of eggs, found milk in the fridge, cut himself a slice of melon. When he had eaten, he dressed in some haste, scrawled a note for Sharifa and left the house.

The city punched him in the stomach, driving air out of his lungs. His eyes burned. His nose watered with the first dry ammoniac whiff of the hot afternoon. God, I need that, he thought savagely, yanking back his collar to feel the sun's teeth on his neck.

Liaqat had every intention of going to his clinic. He was about to turn into Hill Road when he thought sourly how predictably his life moved between home and work. Nothing ever deviated the pendulum from its path. Not even death. He crossed the road angrily and hurried into a small lane he hadn't noticed before. Like all small unnoticed lanes, this one was a labyrinth. Tenements jostled, crowding out the sky. Pavements bulged with merchandise. Children on their haunches dotted the roadside, rising abruptly to inspect their small steaming productions and waddling away importantly, pants bunched carefully between their knees, in search of older sibs who would wash them.

Everywhere, the cacophony of haste. Oddly, the chaos soothed him. He kept walking, dodging elbows, handcarts, rickshaws, toddlers. He found himself crossing a street. Suddenly the road widened, and just as suddenly he was part of a crowd milling in a bottleneck. Over the street sounds arched the sonorous notes of the azaan. Four-thirty. Liaqat walked faster. He was not a praying man. Further on, a brassy clangour of bells, God persistent in His many guises. A sting of jasmine in the hot air, a fleeting thrill of desire. Faster, faster. His shirt swelled under a faint current of breeze. He stopped at a fruit cart and bought an orange, tearing it apart, cramming its tart sweetness into his mouth, careless of the dribble of juice on his chin, walking away without his change. Faster. Faster.

Faces blurred. The sky opened. Salt stung his tongue. Tears. Sweat. The bitter air of the sea.

He had walked right back into the nightmare. He was back on the beach. Soon he would take his place among the men on the rock, sea spray in his eyes blurring the broken figure on the sand.

Liaqat stopped, sick, giddy, close to blacking out. There was a restaurant just ahead, dark and shadowy. He dived in.

He was almost blind indoors. He groped his way to the table against the far wall. The blackness before his eyes was eerily lit by red and green thumbprints of sun. He sat down. Light returned blearily. Shapes returned, their margins melting in a mozzarella fringe of luminescence. The edge of the table was reassuring, solid, cool. Eyes closed, he read the cracked table top with his palms.

Marble. He opened his eyes knowing what he could expect. An old Irani restaurant, round marble-topped tables, delicate wooden chairs. Kashmir on the wall, complete with snow cones, waterfalls, pines and flower-laden shikara. Bun-maska, double omelette, chai in thick white crockery.

'Lemon lao.'

Good idea. But he couldn't trust himself to speak, not yet. Then magically the bottle was between his steepled hands, icy, moist, hard. Someone took it from him and he heard it glug into a glass. He drank.

'Sun got you.'

A statement, not a question. Liaqat focussed on the voice. The man was at the next table. His chair was tipped back against the wall, his long legs stretched out into the stripe of sunlight that slunk in, tamed by the trellis outside. His face, in the shadows, was almost invisible.

'Sun got you,' he repeated.

'Yes, I've been walking for some time.'

'Nowhere in particular.'

Liaqat did not reply, concentrated on his lemonade, faintly resentful of the intrusion. He would pay for the lemonade and leave.

'Story got you, then!'

'Story? What story?'

'How would I know? It's your story, not mine. First the story gets you, then the sun.' The man laughed.

'What's *your* story?' Liaqat demanded aggressively.

'Drink. "A" for alcohol. Burned me out. Now I'm dry as a twig.'

'Good for you.'

'Not so good. No more story. Bottle empty. Life empty. Now I listen to other people's stories.'

Not mine, you don't, Liaqat thought fiercely. Aloud he said, 'Okay, tell me what's my story?'

'Not money trouble. Not love trouble. Not health trouble. Right?'

'Not too off the mark.' Might as well play along, though he wondered what kind of bill the man would stick him with.

'Only one kind of trouble left. Woman trouble.'

'Why? Could be family trouble. Kids.'

'Not old enough. How old? Forty? Forty-two?'

'Forty-five.'

'Time hai. Now only one possibility. Woman trouble.'

The old windbag wasn't that wrong.

'Not wife trouble, not love trouble. Woman trouble.'

'Okay, wise guy, tell me.'

'Because it's turned you inside-out, and only woman trouble can do that. Not love. Not conspiracy, plotting, twisting your arm till you do what she wants—not that. That's simple. You have only two options—yes or no. But silent suffering—not knowing what's happening—that's a killer. That one's a stone on your chest, won't let you breathe, won't let you sleep. That's woman trouble.'

Liaqat was used to café philosophers. Twenty years of medicine can't be lived through without meeting the Canteen Freud, the oversexed Ayn Rand, the hairy de Beauvoir, the Drunk Poet, the genius hopped out of his head on speed. They were ageless, a permanent twenty-four, frozen in a time warp when the world was young and there were stars in their eyes. The haze of drugs or drink came later. Sometimes it was simply the haze of bewilderment. The merciless world chewed them whole and spat them out on the pavement.

'Want to tell me?'

What the hell, the man belonged to a threatened species, and all the rescue he needed was the price of a cup of tea—

'For me coffee. Nescafe, not filter. One bun-maska.'

Liaqat ordered. He couldn't face another lemonade, asked for tea instead, resolved not to touch it.

'There's this lady I know,' Liaqat heard himself say, 'dying of a slow disease—'

'Incurable?'

'Incurable. Dying, I said.'

'Ah. Beautiful?'

'Not exactly. I can't tell you if you keep interrupting.'

'Continue.'

'This lady is dying of a slow disease . . .'

The grave notes of maghrib rose as Liaqat stopped talking. The air was a dusty gold with the last scatter of sunlight. The lights hadn't come on within the café. His audience of one, still obscure in deeper shade, sighed. It startled Liaqat. It was a sigh of pleasure.

'You tell the story from inside,' the man said. 'I see your story from outside.'

'What do you see?'

'Too many dead people. Husband dead. Son-in-law dead. Doctor dead. Husband's mistress dead. How many left? Daughter. Plus maidservant. One or the other's next.'

'But that's ridiculous.'

'Ridiculous. I agree. Finally, beautiful lady dead. End of story.'

Liaqat drew out his wallet angrily. What was he doing listening to this drunk?

'No more drunk. Yes, I can read your mind. Now I'm dry. No more drunk, no more detective, only plain Perera.'

'You were a detective?'

'Security. Snooping, bugging. That kind of work. Dirty work.'

'Thanks for your company. I must be going now.'

'Go, go on. You'll be back. Ask for Perera.'

Like hell I will, Liaqat swore silently as he strode out of the café, ears burning.

He was going home now. Its gravitational pull yanked him past the seductive sounds of dusk. Past the slowing rhythm of things, it hurried him angrily. Dusting off the irrelevancies of the past hour, it drew him to his centre, the moment where Sharifa waited to claim him.

It was easy talking in the dark.

Liaqat often wondered if it was this ease that kept him content with life. He thought about it as he padded to the fridge, and returned with two tall glasses of icy water. For Sharifa the act of love was incomplete without this finale. He held the glass while she raised herself on one elbow and drained it in one long draught.

For Liaqat these hours opened like wild flowers in the grass, unexpected in shape and colour, unknown by name.

Now, after he had parked his own glass on the bedside table and let in the moon, he would begin to talk, and all the hard, crooked, rusty things that had clogged him all day would tumble out.

He asked himself often enough why Sharifa had nothing of her own to unlock and set free in these quiet hours. He worried that she held back her fears because he let his own prowl so hungrily, snapping at the air till he had them tamed. He worried, but he didn't ask.

He was intimidated by his wife's fragility at these moments, the smallness of her, the compact grace so different from his rogue presence, large, clumsy, all over the place. His feet, particularly, embarrassed him, and he dug them deep under the bedclothes to get them off his mind.

He worried, he did not ask, and he feared that one of these nights when he felt like this, unburdened of lust, sluiced with icy water, feet hidden, heart open, one of these nights he would ask: Sharifa, what is it you hide, what is it you don't tell me?

And she would say: What? I don't have anything to tell. And with that, slam the door in his face.

This was one door he was resolved not to knock upon. The dread was too great.

Khuda ke waaste purdah na Kaa'be se utha zaalim
Kahin aisa na ho ya'an bhi wohi kaafir sanam nikley.

Tonight he was not going to worry about any of that. He set the glass aside, hid his feet and prepared to talk.

The words wouldn't come.

They lay in silence, staring into the dark. Sharifa said, 'Maybe she won't suffer now.'

'Won't suffer? How can you say that?'

'I meant Justin's mother.'

Liaqat felt a stab of guilt. He had almost forgotten Mrs Borges. In the silence, he felt Sharifa's heart harden.

'You're still worrying about that chudail.'

'Yep. She's withdrawn completely now, lying there like a statue.'

'All natak—as the maid told you.'

'Sharifa, no. Think of the intensity of her suffering.'

'Why? What is she suffering?'

Sharifa sat up, knees drawn up to her chin. 'Liaqat, who suffered? The son-in-law. Justin. Justin's mother. These people suffered. They died, Liaqat.'

'Sure they died. You don't suffer when you die. It's the survivors who suffer.'

'But why do you think of Clarice as the survivor in these tragedies? In her place, would you suffer? Let me put it another way—would your pain be greater than that of your daughter who has lost a lover, greater than that of a mother who has lost her son?'

'I don't believe that you have to be related, formally, by blood or civil contract, to feel for another person. I thought you didn't believe that either.'

'I won't be drawn into that argument. Answer my question. Can you explain her suffering? No, you can't. You're silent. Nobody can explain it. She's simply asking for attention.'

'She has ALS, for Godssake.'

'ALS now, but I bet she's always been this way. Withdrawal is a tantrum of sorts, isn't it? It's her personality.'

'Catatonia isn't personality.'

'I wouldn't know about that. But it's one hell of a way of getting people to notice you.'

'You're tough.'

'And getting tougher. Think of that girl Marion. What a life! No wonder she swallowed those pills when her boyfriend died. I remember you saying Justin was interested in her. He may have been, but what about her? Naah. Who notices Justin when Mummy's around.'

'You don't know anything about Marion, Sharifa, you're only building on what I told you. She has a busy career, makes a lot of money.'

'So? Since when does that give you a life?'

'She's a dutiful daughter.'

'Maybe her mother doesn't want her to be that dutiful. Maybe that's why she's gone statue on her.'

Liaqat sighed. He was a fool, sometimes.

'Move a bit to the left, Sharifa.'

'Why?'

'The moonlight falls there. I like to look at you in the moonlight.'

'Really, Liaqat?'

'Really, Sharifa.'

It was no use. He would have to think this through for himself.

Liaqat's Diary

Got in early to write this. Strange how guilty I feel, how disloyal to Sharifa, sneaking in here to get an hour alone with Clarice. And that Gracie! One day I'm going to strangle her. Don't disturb me till six, I said, and she gives me a look straight out of the gutter. What does she think I do in here? Masturbate?

Takes me a while to get down to writing what I want to say. Takes time for the guilt to wear off. How do men have affairs? Think of all the planning and time management. I know now why Sharifa married me. One look at me and she knew I'd never cheat on her—too much of a darpok!

But it's funny how she feels threatened by Clarice! Can't expect any help from her there. Never known Sharifa to be cruel before, but she's really ferocious when it comes to Clarice.

What should I do about Clarice?

What has driven her into this? Are her bereavements enough to explain her withdrawal from life?

I mean—*aren't they*?

The body count is four, if you include Clive. And of course one must include Clive—he is the root of all her griefs, the bastard. I can never forgive myself for introducing Justin to Clarice. What that moment of recognition must have cost her!

She should be able to speak of what's oppressing her. But whom will she speak to? Marion? When Marion's own injury goes as deep? Clarice told me when I last called Bougainvillea House that she had revealed the story of Clive's infidelity to Marion. What has that done to the girl? I do not know. Marion has simply gone back to her old life. She does not speak about it to her mother.

And this is the core of the problem—they don't talk to each other in that family.

What about Pauline? She's family too. She's Clarice's shadow, they're of an age, they've been together for the larger part of their lives. Don't social distinctions blur with circumstance?

Not to a woman like Clarice.

Clarice, Clarice, Clarice, what's in your fucked-up mind!

Why haven't I called in a psychiatrist?

True, Marion's reaction was immediate and violent when I suggested it. But I could change that.

Well, frankly, I don't want Clarice pumped with zany molecules that will blast the last shreds of sanity from her mind. She has too little time left to waste on virtual bliss. I owe her that respect. Every psychiatrist I know would medicate her.

But there's also a darker reason—a selfish, mildly unsavoury one: curiosity. Yes—I'm curious. I want to know what's driven a thorn in her soul. I want to know.

Maybe there isn't any thorn. I want to know that too.

I must be good enough to unlock Clarice.

From the first, Clarice AranXa has annoyed me—I need only glance at my case notes to see that. Her lack of vulnerability offended my physician's sense of propriety. At first, around the time we discussed her diagnosis, she hurt my ego by refusing to lower her defences. She kept her lace-edged manner on all the time. Now that circumstances have altered, the lace-edged manner is put away, but I'm still supposed to swallow any old story she pitches my way.

It's the iceberg effect.

All I see, all I'm told is the one-eighth on the surface. The seven-eighths that lurks unexplored is what makes up Clarice's life.

The one-eighth I see is doom. A woman in the shadow of slow death by suffocation. And how can I know what that feels like? Perhaps everything—every event, every grief, every disaster—is made peripheral by the enormity of imminent death.

But there's Justin's back-story.

That may well explain everything: Clarice's over-controlled manner, her puppet-like daughter, her refusal to trust me even as she relies entirely on me, her ambivalence.

The psychiatric opinion would be 'flat affect'.

I'm come full circle now: Clarice's manner is strange because of her intense unexpressed grief, her catatonia and flat affect may add up to an incipient psychiatric illness.

So what?

So bloody what?

How does that explain my dread?

Because this is about me, Liaqat, and I'm scared. I'm shitting bricks.

It's time I put a label on that dread. No point evading it anymore. My fear has a name: Unexpected Death.

What did that dry drunk Perera say yesterday?—'Too many dead people.' Eerie, that guy. What kind of guy makes a living out of spying on folk, with video cameras and bugs? Wanted to tell Sharifa about him last night, but couldn't, and won't now.

He looked at the story from outside, he said. Too many dead people.

I'll qualify that. Too many unexpected deaths.

Three sudden, unexpected deaths in a family within six months—no, none of the deaths were strictly in the family.

Interesting, that.

A mathematician would make something of that—call it random clustering or some shit like that. Wish I knew some maths, but I've always bombed on that. Sharifa's a whiz of course, I could ask her, but I don't want to. I never want to bring up the Clarice matter with Sharifa again. Never.

These deaths are clustered, but not necessarily linked. Their only link is Clarice. That too might be deceptive. These dead people whose lives have brushed Clarice's, they may have touched hundreds of other lives as well.

Let's leave Clive out of this for a moment. He was her husband, for Godssake, and drowned himself out of guilt or despair.

Take Keith instead. Death on the tracks—he was just one of the hundreds of railway accidents every year.

Justin. Justin is the most difficult.

Clarice made a mistake with Justin. She built up a life for him. Listening to her it's easy to believe there was nothing to Justin's life but the comings and goings to Bougainvillea House. That's nonsense. She may have been no more than a very small part of his life.

Clarice's story may have nothing to do with Justin's suicide.

Clarice thought Justin had accidentally discovered his illegitimacy on the evening of his death. He wanted to 'confront' his mother.

But in a small place like Baga, the story of Justin's birth must have been common knowledge. It may not be considered significant. Mrs Borges was respected, not shunned. Surely Justin must have arrived at the truth long back!

Even if he had discovered the truth just then, a thirty-five-year-old man of fairly decent sensibility will not talk of it to a 'stranger', nor threaten to 'confront' his mother. The injury would be too deep for such a superficial demonstration of wrath.

If Justin had wanted to 'confront' his mother, there must be more behind his rage than Clarice knows, or is willing to tell. Nothing in her account says that Justin had learned who his real father was.

The man Clarice met that evening was angry and cruel. What had happened to Justin?

Whatever killed Justin, killed his mother too.

Their griefs are linked.

I might even have dismissed Clarice's story about Clive's involvement with Mrs Borges as the fantasy of a neglected woman, if she hadn't shown me that photograph.

Justin is Clive recycled.

Was. I keep forgetting. I can hear his laugh, his big, happy lungful of merriment. How young he was!

And now all these clustered deaths have driven Clarice into a shell of silence where she listens to the trapped echoes of her lives.

What do those echoes say?

I'm certain Clarice's dissociative reaction—withdrawal, complete lack of response, total inertia—is situational. Nothing suggests a psychotic breakdown.

She needs to set down her burden.

She won't talk to family. She won't talk to a priest. Marion refuses a psychiatrist point blank. Who's left?

A stranger.

A stranger whose integrity is above reproach. A medical professional, trained not to meddle.

I know that stranger.

After all these years, it's going to be hard to find her, though.

Sister Abby

Liaqat sat on the edge of a shiny sofa, sipping tea. Sister Abby gently steered a plate of home-made biscuits in his direction. Liaqat took one, nibbled appreciatively. Sister Abby, the ironic twinkle in her eye not one whit abated, waited.

Liaqat ate those biscuits with dedication. He was thinking, as he ate, of the last twenty-four hours he had spent tracking her down. Finally, when she opened the door of her small flat, he almost thought it was the wrong woman. Sister Abby had shrunk.

She wasn't wearing the imposing armour of a ward nurse, crackling uniform and that bizarre sculpture of starched linen, half veil, half helmet. She was dressed in a cotton sari, comfortable, homely. He guessed that even if he hadn't phoned, he would never have surprised her, found her in a housedress. Even if she were dying, Sister Abby wouldn't wear a Mother Hubbard.

He remembered the first time he had seen her in 'off clothes'. He had sailed past without recognizing her till she recalled him with a tart comment. How abashed he'd been! And how young! Sister Abby, though, seemed ageless. The face was the same, sharp, ironic, the eyes belying the stern mouth. But she was tinier than he recalled. Her iron-grey hair was knotted clumsily in a bun, giving her a vulnerable look. Her feet were puffy and he was reminded that she suffered from varicose veins. Her movements, however, were as brisk and contained as he remembered them from twenty years ago.

When he registered in Neurology after his MD, he lost sight of Sister Abby. She belonged to that earlier time of stomach pumps and Tik 20, solitary night vigils, lumbar punctures and liver biopsies, a time when he had been pitched heart first into the maelstrom that is critical care. Sister Abby was there. She threaded the collapsed vein nobody else could, coaxed the frightened and the fussy into accepting tubes and needles, taught Liaqat how to put in a chest drain and made certain no bed ever had sheets that were anything less than snowy. In her ward, patients had eggs for breakfast, while the rest of the hospital dragged a ragged slice of bread around a puddle of daal. In her ward, staff nurses renowned for their fierce contempt toward resident and patient were pliant as plasticine after a look from Sister Abby. Student nurses adored her. She had once nursed a girl with sixty per cent burns, a bride of two weeks, organizing a rota for her friends to sit vigil, clean, dress, feed, while she and two senior nurses took over actual medical management. The girl refused to make a statement to the police. The husband leered and told all who would listen that his bride was insane, they had burdened him with a madcap, and what dowry could be sufficient recompense! But that was before Sister Abby arrived on the scene. Half an hour with the man and she had the havaldar recording his statement. Student nurses were full of stories about Sister Abby, half of which were untrue.

But it was neither her skill nor her compassion that had compelled Liaqat to find Sister Abby. It was the small flesh-coloured piece of plastic she wore behind her ear.

Sister Abby was deaf. She announced the fact every time a new tubercular patient entered the ward. 'Look at me,' she'd tell the houseman as he made his notes, 'stone deaf. Streptomycin toxicity. Some fool has that on his conscience, remember that.' How long back that was! They were still using strepto then—

'So, Doctor Liaqat. Tell me, why you need a deaf nurse?' Sister Abby said.

Liaqat was disconcerted by her question.

She smiled. 'It's one talent I've always wanted to use, Doctor. There are good nurses and bad nurses, and you could have your pick of them. When you asked me on the phone if I would be willing to take on private duty, I knew it was something else you wanted. There are very few deaf nurses. Perhaps I'm the only one you know.'

'You haven't changed, Sister.'

'Nor you, Doctor. I can still read you like a book.'

They laughed, and in the kindliness of shared memory, his resentment left him.

He found it easy to tell her about Clarice. He edited out the story of Clive and Mrs Borges and the origin of Justin. These were Clarice's secrets and he would keep them that way. He told her about all the deaths, though, and about Keith's accident and Marion's suicide attempt to make her see how fragile the situation was. When he stopped, his head still buzzed with words.

'I can see you haven't changed a jot, Doctor,' Sister Abby sighed. 'You've kept back a lot, I can see that. I don't blame you, that's the doctor-patient privilege. But you've taken Clarice's burden on yourself. Her daughters don't seem much use either. Are you sure your plan will work? Will she really talk?'

'It's worth a try, Sister.'

'If she does talk, Doctor, she will certainly be easier in her mind—'

'I'll make certain the fee is good, Sister.'

'Thank you, Doctor. I'll let you know what it will be. A whole week you say? And only two hours every day?'

'Yes. Also, it's important that Clarice feels you go there to listen to her alone. Pauline will make an attempt to fraternize, I think you should avoid that. I'll ask Marion to book a room at a nearby hotel for a week for you.'

'Oh, don't do that. Baga, didn't you say? That's very close to Calangute. I have a cousin there, she'll put me up. And I always make it a habit not to have anything to do with the patient's family, even in the way of tea, coffee or sharing a meal. Socializing makes it easier for them to complain and quarrel about the fee. I can't stand that.'

She walked with him to the door.

'Will next week be all right, then, Sister?'

'Yes! All days are alike to me now, since my husband died. Your offer comes as a relief, Doctor, I won't pretend otherwise.'

Liaqat knew words of sympathy would sound hollow to her.

'As I said, Doctor, I'm sure Clarice will be relieved if your plan works. She will be relieved—but what about you?'

Sister Abby's parting words rankled in his mind. Finding Sister Abby had brought back a part of himself that had atrophied from disuse—a part that Sister Abby remembered in the resident she knew: Daring. The need to push the envelope just a little further, to nudge open a door that was considered hermetically sealed— always at detriment to himself, always risking disapproval, defying rules.

For an instant, Liaqat saw himself with Sister Abby's eyes: pompous, complacent, comfortable in the mapped range of his skills. This far I can go, she must have heard him say, this far and no further.

Bullshit.

He called the clinic on his mobile and told Gracie he would be late. Then he parked at the kerb, and leaving the main road, began to walk towards the sea.

Liaqat's Diary

I've done it.

What have I done?

It is actually a mad, half-assed idea I've put into action.

Sister Abby, by her very presence, might help, even if not in the way I've planned. There's always the risk of her backing out when I tell her exactly what I have in mind. But I rather think she won't. She'll see it through.

But what of the rest? I've laid myself open to action, blackmail or worse. I can see the lot of them, Medical Council, Consumer Court, the police, all swooping down on Liaqat Khan, ex-neurologist, now selling water purifiers from door to door for a living.

Heck, who'd give me a job as a salesman? Too old. I don't have any skills except neurology.

What have I done with my life?

A totally bullshit question. We don't do it to life. Life does it to us, every which way, it fucks us to a frazzle. The All-Seeing Voyeur up there is splitting his blessed sides with merriment.

If this thing backfires, never mind my job, I'll have Sharifa to deal with. That's the Medical Council raised to the power of n. I can just picture the scene.

Time enough when that happens. Can't be running scared now.

I wouldn't have dreamt of doing it but for Sister Abby's parting comment.

I too need some relief.

Dr Liaqat Ali Khan's Casebook

Monday, 8 a.m.

Clarice Aranxa

72 hrs now since the onset of catatonia.
Marion called to say she has accepted food, used the bed pan. No change otherwise in her level of response.
Diagnosis of psychomotor disturbance seems valid.
Lorazepam 1 mg orally.
Sister Pednekar in attendance.

8 pm. Sister Pednekar reports change. C is rolling her eyeballs and responding to her name. Adv lorazepam 2mg bid. Observation.

Tuesday, 8 pm. Sister's report: C woke up around 6 pm. Addressed her as Sister. Asked for Pauline, attempted some conversation, but returned to catatonic state within half an hour.
Impression: response to lorazepam suggestive of dissociative reaction—stupor may change into uncontrolled excitement. Stopped lorazepam.

10 pm. M called, requesting my presence. Is it too late to call Sister Abby?

Midnight: Just put the phone down. Sister Abby agrees. She will have arranged things by tomorrow evening when I am to call.

M didn't mention Justin's mother's death. But then of course, she knows I'm aware of it—Xavier must have told them I was there. M has booked me on the 8 a.m. flight.
   Back to Baga then.
   Sharifa. I will have to tell her the chudails have got me again!

Liaqat

It had rained overnight at Baga. Little puddles steamed in the morning heat. He was used to the landscape now and could pick his way past the small whitewashed shrines and winding paths. A magenta flare of bougainvillea lit up the house, its flamboyance isolating it from the more modest cottages in his path. He wondered what Justin's days had been like here—unhurried and peaceful, or dull and stagnant. The rickshaw driver seemed reluctant to get to his destination. The rickety engine sputtered uncertainly, then stalled as he slowed for no apparent purpose but to squint at the landscape. Everything was *susegade*. Even the sun was only halfway up the sky at noon.

Marion appeared at the gate. She looked as if she hadn't slept in a week. He reminded himself that he had seen her just three days ago. Pauline took his bag. The house seemed bigger and chillier than before. He entered the parlour with a strong sense of déjà vu—what was he soon going to be hearing again, what tale of pain or loss? Marion's anxious voice pecked at him irritatingly. Less than a fortnight ago—no, it was more—he had sat here listening to Clarice's story. But there was more where that came from. Something told Liaqat she would never let that go.

'You must get her back to normal, Doctor,' Marion was babbling. 'Stroke, coma, those things we can understand. Those things happen. But this is too much! I have never heard of such a thing before! Blind and deaf and dumb! Everything at once. It's too much. You must make her normal.'

He heard his voice say, 'You must understand what's happening to your mother, Marion. We will find a way out—if we're lucky. If not, we must come to some sort of working solution.' I'm doing fine, he thought, just keep the phrases rolling. Working solution, yes, she should buy that. 'You have your job to return to. A few practical arrangements will have to be made.'

Marion left the room to tell Sister 'to get Mamma ready'.

Ready for what, he thought. How do you prepare a woman who's not there?

Pauline hovered with iced water. 'Something? Tea, coffee?'

'No, no thanks, Pauline. They fed me on the plane.'

'Ha. That food fight inside your stomach.'

'Started already.'

'I make you nice pomfret for lunch. You Mussalman not eating vindaloo.'

He smiled. Pauline was a relief. She looked conspiratorial now. 'Big trouble inside.' She jabbed a finger into her décolletage.

'Yes?'

'No talking. Marion made rule: no talking. Marion told you? Justin's mother, Arula? Xavier told me you saw. Jesu forgive her, all her life she suffer, poor girl. Marion heard and immediately gave order: don't tell Mamma.'

'Clarice does not know?'

'Nobody told her. Only me and Marion she sees, no? We didn't tell. But something she knows, she knows before she became like statue.'

'How did Justin's mother drown? What do they say?'

'She jumped from the cliff. Suicide. Everybody in the village find out about Mr Clive. Everybody knows Justin find out. Some are even saying she killed Justin.'

'No! That's a terrible thing to say.'

'It went to her heart. She jumped. But who can blame her? Mother and son together now. Everybody happy.'

'What lies has Pauline been feeding you?' Marion had returned. 'Mamma is ready for you, Doctor.'

'Pauline has been telling me about the tragic death of Justin's mother.'

'What? Oh yes, yes. Very sad. What else could she do? Oh—Mamma doesn't know. You won't tell her, will you?' She said that with a grating laugh that worried him more than Clarice's catatonia.

'Clarice?'

No response.

'Can you hear me, Clarice?'

Blink.

'You're very tired, Clarice, very tired.'

Blink.

'But you've kept your promise to me, Clarice. You've eaten. You've let Pauline take care of you.

Blink.

'Sister gave you a new medicine yesterday. How did you feel after that?'

Rapid blinking

'Wake up now, Clarice. You're really not asleep now. You can hear me. You can see me.'

No response.

He stopped. This would go nowhere unless he took decisive action. Damn Marion. He was going to do what he had to.

He had been shocked when the thought first came to him. He thought it would be brutal. But he was after the truth, and how could he reach it unless he gave Clarice the complete truth?

He said: 'Clarice, I have bad news. It is something you should know. It will cause you pain. Are you prepared to hear it?'

Blink.

'I'm sorry to have to tell you, Justin's mother died a few days ago.'

Her lips made a whirring sound, urgent but unintelligible. He raised her gently and held some water to her lips. She drank thirstily, making him wonder if they had been subtly negligent of her needs. He had seen it often enough: forgetfulness, oversight, omission—all respectable forms of violence towards the helpless.

Clarice's hand moved towards his own. When he held it, the fingers dug into his palm.

'What happened?' Clarice was looking at him now. She repeated the words, clearer this time.

'She committed suicide.'

'In the well?'

'No.' That shocked him. 'No, she jumped off the cliff.'

'She had nobody left.'

'May she rest in peace.'

'No peace for the wicked! Remember that, Doctor. No peace for the wicked.'

'I'll remember that, Clarice. You've had a long rest. How about letting me examine you. Let's see how your muscles are doing.'

She sat up, then flopped back in bed, dizzy. He wondered if

she had really eaten all they said she had. He let her set the pace. It took more than an hour for him to complete the assessment. As expected there was marked deterioration. There were definite signs of cranial nerve involvement now. Soon there would be trouble swallowing. She would need a tube—a feeding gastrostomy would be too much trouble to nurse. No, a nasogastric tube would be best. It wouldn't be for long, anyway. Perhaps he ought to tell Marion right away.

His years in neurology had taught Liaqat one necessary skill: humility. It was a skill, not a virtue. It was a necessary skill if half your patients had illnesses that defied diagnosis and the other half were hurtling towards a lifetime of indignity that would end, most often, in a welcomed death. He no longer worked to prolong life, but he did his damndest to cherish it. And humility was needed for that, or you couldn't do the job right. You had to forget all you knew and begin to learn from your patient. Strange that it should be this woman whom he disliked, this stranger who refused him houseroom in her soul—strange that of all his patients she should be the one to rely so utterly on his decisions.

'Am I better, Doctor?'

'No, Clarice.'

'Will I be able to walk now?'

'Yes. Of course. Don't tire yourself, though.'

'I don't want to go blind again, Doctor. That's all I ask of you, please.'

'We'll try, Clarice. That's what I want, too.'

'I'm less trouble to them when I'm blind and deaf and paralysed. Less trouble for Marion. Less trouble for Pauline.'

'That's not true, Clarice.'

'Don't argue. You'll tire me. It's true.'

'Okay.'

She held his hand. Her nails, he saw, were perfect ovals, painted blood red, stigmata of her suffering.

Liaqat returned to the hotel after Pauline's pomfret lunch. He had declined Marion's offer of a room in Bougainvillea House. That house was oppressive. He could not endure the thought of spending the night in it.

Lunch had been a subdued meal. Marion seemed too upset for conversation. Pauline served them absent-mindedly.

'Do you think it'll happen again, Doctor?' Marion eventually asked. 'Will she become unconscious again?'

He noted the new label Marion had chosen over the older ones: attack, blind, paralyzed, mad. Pauline hovered, waiting for his answer.

He deliberated. Once before he had chosen for Marion, and he had chosen wrong. Now Clarice had made her choice and he must get Marion to respect it.

'It must have disturbed you deeply to see her like this.'

'Not just once—twice! The worst is not knowing what's happening to her.'

'Clarice is very upset about it. In fact the only thing she wants is to prevent another bout like that.'

'It's the only thing all of us want, Doctor. It isn't easy for me, you know. I want her to get the best, no matter what it takes, you know that, you've seen that, I've done everything she wants. But it isn't easy. It isn't easy on me, it isn't easy on Pauline.'

Pauline put her arm around Marion's shaking shoulders. Marion sobbed angrily, clumsily, letting her nose drip into her plate. She was more like an angry ten-year-old than a woman of thirty-eight.

'Clarice counts heavily on you, Marion. She's very proud of you. She's very sad that you should go through all this.' His words were meant for the child sobbing. 'Your mother needs some help, Marion, if she's to get over all this.'

'What kind of help?'

'I suggest a trained psychiatric nurse.'

'Psychiatric? She's mad, then.'

Liaqat sighed. He tried again. 'No, she isn't mad. But her overburdened mind needs relief. She needs to be alone. I would have suggested hospitalization—in a nursing home for a week or two, but I don't think that is practical. Clarice does not want to leave Bougainvillea House. And one more thing, Marion—she's going to need help with eating, very soon. We may need to feed her through a tube.'

'Tube? You'll make a hole in her stomach?'

'No. For her a soft thin tube through the nose might be better.'

'You're kidding. In her *nose*? Mamma won't let you.'

'We won't do anything she doesn't want, Marion. If she thinks a tube in her stomach is better, we could do that instead.'

'That means an operation.'

'Yes.'

'She won't agree to that. She's against operations, all operations. She wouldn't let them remove Melissa's appendix even when the doctors said it would burst—remember, Pauline?'

'Two weeks Baby suffer,' Pauline said. 'Fever, vomiting, crying day and night with pain, but Missy said trust in God, make Novena, Pauline, I am not allowing operation. Then Baby became cold-cold, Lucas Doctor saying put in hospital or she will die. So hospital, middle of the night, ambulance, oxygen, and all the time Missy like stone. Lucas, fat man, like pudding shaking inside his shirt, all wet-wet with sweat. You will lose her, he says, let us operate. No operation, Missy says, Jesu will heal. Then Lucas, he goes out of the room, I think maybe because bad words are coming. Baby's fever going up to 104, 105, then Lucas comes back and says, all right, Mrs Aranxa, one more injection is left. This is last I am trying, so much faith you got, so one last injection. After he gives injection, Missy and I are kneeling, praying whole night. In the morning when light comes, Missy, she cries loudly and I think—finish, all finish, Baby gone to Jesus! But Baby fast asleep, so sweet, like angel. No fever, no pain. No operation.'

Liaqat endured this bit of lore without comment. Then he returned doggedly to what he had to tell Marion. 'I think we should leave the choice to Clarice. She will pick whatever she's comfortable with. Though that's still some time away.'

'Is she worse, Doctor?'

'Yes, Marion. All the more reason why we should do what she wants.'

Marion pushed away her plate and rose angrily. 'What does she want? What more can she want? Haven't I done everything she wants? What more does she want me to do?'

Pauline tried to soothe Marion and was pushed away. It was developing into a first-rate row. It only needed Clarice there to be complete. *How do these things always happen to you?* Sharifa's voice said in his head.

'Sit down, Marion.' Quite without intention, there was steel in his voice. 'The first thing she needs is peace of mind. If you want her to have a few happy days before she gets worse, we must give her that peace. I would like you to have a trained nurse here for a week. Let her spend at least two hours with Clarice every day—more if she wants to. Clarice may not want to talk much during this time, she may ask to be left alone. We must respect that.'

'What will she do?'

'Give your mother the ease she needs to come to terms with what's burdening her mind.'

'What kind of burden can she possibly have? She's lacked for nothing all her life! She's had everything so easy! Of course my father died so early in their marriage—and now I can see how much of grief he must have given her. Is it that sorrow, Doctor? Can that last for so many years?'

'I can't say, Marion.'

'And if she doesn't have this nurse she'll play dead again. Is that it?'

'It may happen, yes.'

'Okay, get that nurse, then. Do you know somebody?'

'I've made enquiries about a sister who has worked with me before. I should hear from her this evening at the Palm d'Or.'

Lies! He'd been through a lot of lies that afternoon. He had no idea how he had entangled himself so inextricably with the Aranxas. He thought enviously of how most of his colleagues would have dealt with Clarice. A placebo for mother, tranquillizer for daughter, and back to the GP with his cut of the fee, the ingratiating phone call or the bottle of Scotch that would keep the patients trickling in.

He had opted against that game. I'd rather be an honest pimp and work Foraas Bridge, he told Sharifa. Very well, shrugged Sharifa, you do what you think is right. Meanwhile, we can starve.

Starve they never would, but they had to strive for small comforts. He wouldn't make it to the seven-star corporate hospitals that were springing up like chrome and glass fungi everywhere. The mantra that got a consultant in there was: put 30 lakhs down first, and we're talking. He didn't even have 30 K in the bank. Money, money, money. A CT scan for every headache—Why didn't you order an MRI, Doctor? Don't you know the kickback is one grand? I've married a stupid man, Sharifa said when he told her these stories, a stupid, stubborn man, and I'll kill you if you change.

That was how he'd got here. He'd never be famous, he'd never be rich, but by God he'd be the best—even if nobody knew that but he. Most days it was enough to know he had used his skills and used them well. When the voice of ambition demurred, he silenced it.

He had been right in telling Clarice about Mrs Borges. The thought of somebody else's pain had been enough to jolt her out of her trance of self-absorption. But he wouldn't have done it even a week ago. He would have kept it from her as the others had.

There was an STD booth in the foyer. 4.30. Sister Abby must be home now. He would call her before talking to Sharifa.

She picked up on the first ring.

'Doctor Liaqat?'

'You were waiting for my call?'

'Yes. I was curious. How is Clarice?'

'Unresponsive. Catatonic.'

'Oh.'

'Till I told her about Mrs Borges. Now she's herself again. Terribly weakened, but calm, well-oriented.'

'Aha. What does she say about the nurse?'

'All Clarice wants is that she shouldn't get catatonic again. I think she'll agree to the nurse. The daughter has.'

'What about Clarice's physical state? Do you anticipate problems there?'

'Not immediately, no. I've told them the nurse should be there for a week. This is what I'm going to tell Clarice too. Some kind of time frame is necessary, or she won't feel the urgency to respond.'

'Yes, I agree.'

'So when can you come, Sister? I'd like to meet you first before I take you over to Clarice.'

'The evening bus gets to Calangute by five in the morning. I'm packed and ready, Doctor. All I have to do is leave the house. Where are you, and when should I meet you?'

'I'm at a hotel called the Palm d'Or.'

'Right. I'll meet you in the foyer at eight. Will that be too early?'

'No. Eight is fine. We'll need to talk a bit, first.'

'Yes. Yes, of course. What about the daughter? Will she be around?'

'I think she should get back to Bombay. I'm going to suggest that—diplomatically.'

'That's a good idea. And what are your plans?'

'I think I should be here till tomorrow evening to see how Clarice takes to the nurse.'

'That's wise. Till eight o'clock, then!'

She had hung up before he could say goodbye.

He called Sharifa, and, they enjoyed being miserable together for half an hour.

The evening stretched interminably. He decided to call Marion later about the nurse. Nothing, he felt, nothing could drag him to Bougainvillea House a second time that day. He swallowed a cup of over-boiled tea and strolled out of the Palm d'Or.

A pleasant vacuity overcame him, dispelling the weariness that had tortured him all day. Last light was still an hour away, but already the air held the soft melancholy of dusk. A yellow slant of sun gilded the maize fields ahead of him. A path parted the field, but his feet refused it, seeking instead the grassy unevenness of fallow land. Beyond that a row of coconut palms brushed the sky.

Save for the flap and flutter of crows settling down for the night, there was no sound. The muffled sough of the sea breathed around him. He crossed the picket of coconut trees and found himself within a grove. The palms here were tall and gracile. Their feathery heads meshed at the sky. The gentle melancholy he had savoured but minutes ago hardened into something more severe and unforgiving. Here, time was advanced: it was almost night, though there was still light outside.

He felt uneasy. He wanted to turn back, but a mulish defiance forced him forward. He found himself walking stealthily, his footsteps noiseless on the hardpacked ground. He was drawn deeper within the grove.

In a sudden clearing between palm fronds, a pane of sky.

Even as he watched, the clear gold of its span was webbed by a bat. He had the eerie feeling that the bat hung there, on the other side of a glass pane, staring down at him.

He blundered on, half running, half hesitant, his feet trying to keep time to the thundering in his ears, till a dark shape that loomed ahead forced him to a standstill. His knees buckled, he sank to the ground. He sat there hugging his knees, staring his eyes out at the darkness, trying to see beyond the pale stripe of the police cordon, wondering what power of good or evil had dragged him here, the site of Justin's doom.

How long he stayed there, he did not know.

He was roused—not startled—by a cough. He turned in its direction with some relief. A thick figure stood black and stolid in the gloom. Pauline.

Had she followed him?

'Come away, Doctor, this place, it is not good,' she said heavily. 'I also come here so often. What drag me here? Who can tell?'

He followed her numbly out of the grove.

It was not dark yet. The sky was bleached by a lilac light. A sliver of moon was curled like a nail paring from a giant hand.

'Missy go mad because of Justin doctor,' Pauline said with sudden energy, 'because of my mistake.'

Liaqat, about to speak, was silenced by her next words.

'You are going to give treatment for madness, no? Then you must know—let me speak, please, don't say never mind, never mind.'

He was silent.

'That day, suddenly Missy becoming holy like. Jesus is making miracle for me, she says. Go to Panjim and make Novena, I can feel sickness going from me. Go, go. Very urgent she became. She told you that?'

'Yes.'

'But she never told you what happened after, because she don't know. She think we, Marion and I, we go to Panjim. But we never go. No!'

'No?'

'Little bit we walk and Marion says, today only we have to go or what. I say same thing in my mind also—never mind, Jesus never hurry. Tomorrow we go. Today your Mamma making too bad-bad. Let her get calm. Then tomorrow we go.'

'And so?'

'Marion gave me fifty rupees and says, "Pauline, you go bring the bazaar, take rickshaw. I am walking little bit." So I take rickshaw half distance then I get down and walk—money grow on trees or what! Seven o'clock I come back and Marion is in the kitchen making tea. Where is Justin doctor, I ask, I think you go with him walking. No, Marion tells me, Mamma gone with him. You sit, Pauline, I will make tea for you, cut one slice palm cake for me, no. So chatting chatting we be—'

'But weren't you worried that Clarice was not home?'

'With doctor in pocket, what for we'll worry? Chatting chatting we be then Marion says, Pauline, it is eight o'clock! And then the taxi sound came and one nun comes out, one driver, and last of all Missy, so weak, cannot stand even, but quickly she climb the steps, then I catch her before she fall. Then they tell us how Justin doctor left Missy in church to vanish—serious patient, Sister says. What about Missy, I say, she is also serious patient, no? Shh, Pauline, Missy told, tomorrow Justin will explain. Well, what do we know—Justin is explaining from bottom of that well?'

'But—'

'Please wait, Doctor. If you don't mind. Why Justin died? Missy's wishes we did not respect. Go make Novena she say. We do not go. We make a mistake. Don't tell Mamma, Marion says, please Pauline, don't tell Mamma. So till today, swear upon God, I don't tell Missy. Finish. Now you say, Doctor.'

'Pauline, I know you feel bad about it. But—' Liaqat shrugged. How was he going to counter Pauline's punitive morality? They were on the road that Justin had walked to his death. What could he say to comfort her?

'Mr Clive also, same well,' Pauline said in a low voice.

'Your Missy is still suffering from that tragedy,' Liaqat said.

'She suffering? You think only she is suffering? Nobody else? What about Arula?'

'She suffered even more.'

'Maybe you understand. Maybe you don't think she burn in hell.'

'Of course not, Pauline. Why should she burn in hell?'

'Here all people say she burn double-double. First time for adult only, this time for suicide. Both big-big sins. But not for me, I don't think Arula was sinner.'

'Me neither.'

'When you are young, man make soft-soft eyes at you, what can you do? Mr Clive never look my side. Too scared of Missy. But Missy not scared of him. Put him in a crate and post him straight to father-mother in Bandra. Old people, not knowing what big parcel is bringing. Missy come later with the girls and me, three-four days later. Missy always do things different from other people.'

That Liaqat could well believe.

'Every time something happen, Missy know before, like something come and catch her before only. Mr Clive time also, Justin time also, Mr Keith time also. You know Mr Keith? No, you only know after Marion ate poison. Listen, I will tell you.'

They had reached a culvert. Pauline sank down and dusted the space next to her for Liaqat. She began speaking in a low dreamy voice and he had to strain to catch her words.

Pauline

You have called special sister to make Missy's madness go away? I tell you she is not mad. I know Missy day she came with Mr Clive from church. Mr Clive's mother, she brought me from village. Look after Missy, she tells me. Mr Clive also: Look after Missy. So all my life I look after Missy. No matter what happen, I look after Missy. Now Missy is become blind and deaf and dumb, on-off like electric. Madness come and go like that or what? No. Madness permanent, lifetime guarantee.

If Missy become like statue, there is reason. What reason, she will not tell you or me or that special sister. There is reason, but not for us to know.

We only *do*. Pauline, do this, I do. Pauline, do that, I do. Why? Because of Mr Clive? Maybe. Because I got nowhere else to go? Maybe. Who can tell?

Missy will not tell, but she know why.

When Marion's going to marry Keith, I told Missy, now give my savings, I will pay my brother and take one room for rent. Talk to brother first, she say, what kind of woman your sister-in-law is, that you know and I know. Talk to brother first, she say.

Then all this trouble, no wedding for Marion, Missy is sick and dying, where I am going to leave? My savings still with her. How can I ask? I won't die so soon, Pauline, she tell me, your money is safe with me.

What will happen when she die? Whom I can ask? Miss Marion, please give my savings from your Mamma's safe? What safe, Marion will say, so shameless you are, all money-talk and Mamma not yet cold in her grave. What money? What savings? Mamma never told me anything.

So I stay. Lips are sealed. Missy says do, I do.

Now Marion says tomorrow special sister will make Mamma's heart light, and I am thinking, but this thing is like stone inside me, Justin dying because we do not go to Panjim. So better I tell doctor this also. So I come after you to tell. But one thing more. Whatever Missy will tell special sister is lies. All lace and silk and make-up and scent these Aranxas, everybody think they are so great, so high, their shit don't stink, but I know.

I know! I know their stink, I know their stains! I wash them. I wash out all Missy's stains.

So big clever doctor you are, with daari and all, still you do not understand Missy's mind. I will tell you what happen when Keith died and you will understand.

This Keith, he was East Indian. Handsome, big, like hero. But Missy said no Indian, no black Indian is going to marry white Aranxa girl. No!

Then who is going to marry, I ask.

Now Marion is forty. Thirty-seven they say last so many years, but I can count, no? Forty. First all boys are buzzing around, but that time Marion says shoo-shoo, like they are flies. Now no nice boys come. Only old men, bald, second marriage, widower, that kind. Because Marion got money, got job, and also old virgin girl, what *she* knows—will not want too much jhanjhat in bedroom. So old men bring proposal. Missy quite happy, but Marion say no, no. Then Keith come, so handsome, so rich. Marion's heart really gone this time, I see. Go girl, I tell her, run away with him. But Marion so much Mamma's girl, no?

Missy finally listen. Keith bring mother-father—old people, nice, simple, very rich. Missy make importance: Oh we are so old family, straight Portuguese, not wanting to make marriage with Indian, but what to do if young people insist. What you are going to give my Marion to make it okay? Something to make her safe even with Indian husband?

I can see Keith mother-father don't like this talk, but they very polite, and next day Keith bring papers of new flat he bought in Worli. But Missy throw papers back at him. What is the use, she say, flat is yours, not Marion's. All the same, Marion say—please, Mamma, it is all the same.

Silly girl, Missy say, go to your room.

Then Keith, he promise to make new paper with lawyer in Marion's name and Missy agree to wedding. Then he bring engagement ring, big diamond, and Missy say, let me have the receipt from the jeweller, Keith, one never knows when Marion may need it.

Very unlucky to talk like that.

Next day Missy taken to you, Doctor, and disease found out. Now for one week all the time mother daughter quarrel, quarrel. Every day Missy ask, have flat papers come, have papers come, and Marion say tomorrow, tomorrow. Missy tells me, Pauline, force Marion not to tell Keith I have this disease. If he knows, he will break engagement. Better she tell him then, I say, better engagement break than marriage break.

But Missy, she after Marion all the time not to tell Keith.

Then the day come when Marion and Missy have big fight before Marion leave for work. Marion cry till her eyes like coals. Then she go out banging the door. Whole morning Missy very nervous. Looks at watch, looks at clock, switches TV on and off. Finally, one o'clock she tell me, 'Pauline, quickly go to Marion's office and stop her meeting Keith. Today he is taking her some fancy restaurant for lunch, she will tell him about my disease. Stop her. Tomorrow I know the papers will be here, Keith told me yesterday. After that if she tells him, never mind, even if he leaves her, the flat is in her name. That much she got. Run, Pauline, run! Take rickshaw.' And she give me twenty rupees.

Go fast, I tell rickshaw-man, all the time thinking—how to stop Marion?

But when I reach her office, Marion gone already, left early, her friend say, her Mummy got important medical. Girls make story like this only when meeting boyfriend, I think.

So I come back and tell Missy Marion gone, but by now Missy become cool again. Never mind, Pauline, she say, I am feeling tired, I am going to lie down.

Then three o'clock. Bell ring. Marion outside with some girl, not one word, just push me like this, go fast-fast into bathroom, bang the door. Then her friend tell me Keith became accident. How bad? I ask, but I know from her face—finish. I run to Baby, and friend, she go away before I can ask more. Inside bathroom Marion vomiting and vomiting and suddenly I am thinking maybe Marion not so much Mamma's girl, maybe she opened legs without taking permission!

'Baby not in trouble, no?' I ask when she come out and she give me such bad-bad gaali in return, my ears burn, I never think Marion know like this words.

By then Missy come out. She take charge of Marion. Go in

and lie down, she say. Take your tablets, get calm. You always helped Keith do his duty, she say, now you must do your duty. Missy always say hard things like this when Marion sad.

After some time she come to me and ask—what happened? I don't know, I say, only this much friend said. She look at me, I look at her. What to do about Keith mother-father?

'Pauline, you go,' she tell me. 'Six- six-thirty, take rickshaw, go to Malad. Tell them Marion got shock, became serious, I call doctor and could not come. Find out what happen there. At such a time, the house is full of people, everybody talking. Listen to what they are saying. You also talk. Innocent-like, you bring up flat paper matter, see what they say.'

Fifty rupees she gave me, rickshaw only one way, coming back, I catch local.

Trembling-trembling I enter Keith house. First time I am going, very old-fashioned it is, very big, but old-fashioned. These people are eating with hand, I think, no knife-fork here, no toilet paper. Trembling-trembling I go inside. Mother-father both gone statue. Everybody crying. I also. Next to me one old lady, she say they brought Keith head in towel to mother-father. Then I nearly faint. What for police so cruel to mother-father, I ask, angry, why not call some uncle, cousin to look? No, she tell me, it is law, closest relative must look and identify. They take mother-father in van to dead house. Please sit, they say. Old people sit in one room. Inspector brings in one bundle, like this, like this one on my lap, and put it on table in front of them. Mother-father poor thing still looking at door, thinking now it will come, now I will see my son in trolley or stretcher.

Please look, Inspector say.

And open bundle—like this.

Keith head.

Now I do not believe, but that time, so shocked I was, I believe fully.

Then, suddenly, Keith mother, she look at me and point. 'Enough!' she scream.

All think she is gone mad.

I become so frightened I think I will pass water there only and bring shame upon Missy. Very hard I pray, JesuMarieJoseph protect me till I find bathroom. Lord send me idea to cry and sob and wail very loud, and kind ladies take me inside to another room, force me—drink water, drink water—and I say I giddy, want to wash face, so they take me to bathroom and I become okay. Then quickly-quickly I leave when nobody is looking.

Next day big packet come from lawyer with flat papers in Marion name, also receipt from jeweller for ring. And also one letter saying with this all is finish between Keith family and Aranxa, all is settled, now no more talk.

But by then so many things happen!

Marion swallow poison, you come, Doctor, and then you know all what happen.

After Marion came home from hospital, mother-daughter chup-chaap. No talking. How sad it is, no crying, no taking Keith name. If any stranger come, he can never guess such a thing happened only two days back in this family. Keith become chhumantar, vanish. Only sign of him, flat papers in safe. Ring, also in safe.

You want to understand Missy, how she think, that is the reason I tell you how Keith time went in this house.

My savings also in her safe. Thirty years every month one-two hundred rupees I keep, rest she take back to keep safe for me. If I keep back more she will ask: What for you want money, Pauline? We give you everything! You need to save some money, Pauline, keep it with me.

You only tell me doctor, what I can say?

The day hadn't yet ended for Liaqat. After he parted from Pauline, he wandered by the river, a silver thread of zari in the moonlight. Dusk had been full of omen. Night was surprisingly friendlier. The talk with Pauline had eased him in a way he couldn't yet explain. Clarice's cupidity shocked him, but it was not unexpected. Besides, he reminded himself, Pauline's account was not entirely without prejudice.

There was one more encounter ahead, before he could turn into Palm d'Or for the night. He awaited it with impatience, a forgotten excitement vivifying his every sense.

'Oh here you are, then,' he said with relief when the wait was over. 'All set? Let's go.'

Sister Abby

Sister Abby was following instructions. She entered Clarice's room with a curt nod of dismissal to Pauline.

She had been briefly introduced to the patient the previous day by Dr Khan, mainly to confirm the duties he had earlier outlined to her. This would be her first time alone with Clarice.

Clarice was in bed, sitting up in a fluffy bed jacket of palest mauve. Her face was carefully made up as though for a formal and public audience. Her smile, when it briefly touched her face, was less of a greeting than a grimace. Sister Abby noticed the slack cheeks, the uncontrollable twitch at the corner of the mouth. Clarice looked apprehensive and yet her manner mocked any attempt at ease.

'Sister is simply going to sit here with you, Clarice,' Dr Khan had said. 'She will begin with a quick examination tomorrow, so that she knows the exact state of your health every day.'

Now, alone with Clarice, Sister Abby was following those largely useless instructions. She took the patient's pulse and blood pressure and made a quick assessment of her reflexes. Yesterday she hadn't really noticed the muscles wasting in Clarice's hands. Lying like discards on the sheet, today Clarice's hands looked almost skeletal.

Clarice lay back resentfully, glaring at Sister Abby.

'Are you a nun?'

'Lay sister.'

'Thought so. Where are you from?'

'Sisters of Charity.'

'No, no. Where do you belong? Not Goan, are you?'

'No.'

'Thought so. Where are you from, then?'

'I'm sorry. We're not allowed to speak about ourselves.'

'Against the rules, eh?'

'Yes.'

'Sorry. That's why I never became a nun. Too many rules. I make my own rules.'

'Yes?'

'My daughter now, Marion. She's a nun. Pure in heart and body.'

Sister Abby looked appreciative, but said nothing.

Clarice shot a look at the clock. 'What am I supposed to tell you? What does Dr Khan expect me to say?'

Sister Abby responded with a curious gesture. She removed a piece of flesh-coloured plastic from behind her right ear and held it out to Clarice. 'Sometimes words don't come when we're with someone. And we can't talk aloud to ourselves. If you like, Clarice, I can take off my hearing aid. I'm stone deaf. But I can lip-read, so I shall sit with my back to you and you can say what you want to—I won't hear a thing.' She replaced the hearing aid, and waited.

'Is this some sort of game? I'm not a child!'

'There are times when we have to trick ourselves, Clarice. My job is to help you set down your burden. This is one way of doing it. It usually works.'

'Usually? You've seen patients like me before? Patients who turn blind and deaf and dumb, and then return to normal again?'

'A few, yes.'

'And did they recover?'

'Two of them entirely. Not the other three.'

'Even Steven. Almost.'

'Yes, you could say that.'

'Okay, let's take a shot at it. You put that hearing aid here on the table and sit with your back to me and I say the first thing that comes into my head—is that it?'

'Yes.'

'And we do this every day for a week?'

'Less or more often, as you wish. But I have to be elsewhere next week.'

'So either I speak now or forever hold my peace.'

Sister Abby smiled. She rose and turned her chair to face the window. A rosary clicked in her restless fingers.

Clarice watched the clock, hands cupped over Sister Abby's hearing aid.

There were twenty minutes left for Sister Abby to leave. In the last hour Clarice had tested the nurse's deafness for the first ten minutes, for the next ten she had talked about her illness. Then she had fallen silent.

Sister Abby had not moved.

Clarice said, 'Sister, turn around, turn around and look at me, Sister, I can't breathe, Sister, something's happening to me, I'm dying, Sister! Sister!'

Sister Abby, a black pillar against the flaming sky, did not stir.

Clarice said: 'It's the house. It's this house. Bougainvillea House. I was never heavy-hearted till I came here. Everything happened here, inside here. Inside this house, inside my heart, inside my head. When did it happen? How long ago? How recently? What was the date? Never mind. It's enough that you should know it rained.

'It rained the night they brought me to Bougainvillea House...'

Liaqat

The week passed slowly for Liaqat. He found himself tired by mid morning. He forgot chores, earning himself more than the occasional grouse from Sharifa. He was unable to sleep, waking in the early hours with a dim consciousness of great unnamed danger. He tried to distract himself by switching on the TV the moment he got home. It worked sometimes as a defence against conversation. He took to getting to the clinic an hour before his appointments began, to give himself the solace of solitude.

He toyed briefly with the thought of medication, rejected it and decided to confront his anxiety. He found a cheap little name for it—curiosity. He wanted to know what was happening at Bougainvillea House.

On Wednesday Sister Abby called to say that Clarice was talking.

Liaqat wondered what Clarice could have to say—once she'd begun talking, the pressure to get it all out would be intense. Would it tire her? Would it cause a sudden deterioration? Would she—to put it bluntly—die as a result of his possibly hare-brained scheme?

He wondered if he should call Bougainvillea House, but decided against it. Night after night, jolted out of sleep by the sound of Justin's laugh, he lay awake in the dark, smelling the sea, his eyes turned away from the crumpled heap washed up on the rocks.

If only he hadn't brought Justin into the case—

He stopped the thought almost as soon as it arose. After all, Justin's suicide had nothing to do with Clarice. He had died without discovering how his unhappy birth was linked with Clarice's history. And as for his mother, the loss of her son had brought the sorrows of a lifetime to the surface, making it impossible to continue.

The villain of the piece was long dead. Clive, who had thought suicide would stop the implosion in their lives. He had reckoned without fallout.

How quick and easy it must have seemed to end it all by plunging into the well. Was it?

Liaqat shuddered. What a mess Clive had found himself in! The girl must have told him she was pregnant. That would have been in the early sixties, no precautions, being Catholic and all. But precautions or no precautions, it was just the sort of situation where pregnancy was a sure bet. He saw that every day. Couples grinding themselves to powder to make a baby that never happens. While some pathetic teenager, eager at the first rush of desire, cruelly finds herself with child.

What would Clive do? He couldn't have married the girl. That would have meant a scandal. He wasn't the sort of person who'd risk a scandal—neither was Clarice. What then? He was not cruel enough to dump the girl. Correction—he did dump her, but sneakily, when he jumped into the well. Ugly, but neat. He'd got away.

Try as he would, Liaqat could not equate the dignified woman he knew as Justin's mother with the local girl Clive had seduced.

Had she been any less dignified or any less of a woman then, he asked himself furiously. He realized with dismay that he had been using Clarice's appellation for Mrs Borges—*local girl*.

Oh well, what else could the injured wife say? A real bastard, that Clive.

There was something eerie about Justin choosing the same way of death. It had destroyed his mother.

It had devastated Clarice.

Poor Clarice. She had lived all these years with that knife in her heart, and he, Liaqat Khan, the man she trusted most in the world, had thrust her straight into the hands of her torturer. For what was Justin but Clive resurrected?

Marion

Two days after Sister Abby's call, Liaqat was surprised to see Marion in the foyer when he entered his clinic. He was a little late, delayed by a house call at Mahim.

Driving back through the causeway, the silver bloat of the sea, like a vast dead fish floating belly-up in the sun, had filled him with sadness. He had a momentary glimpse of his old life, now cast away like a soiled garment. Sharifa, their moments of love and laughter, their wondering explorations in post-coital calm, all these seemed alien, from another time. He saw these things beautiful and diminished in the receding scenery of a life left behind. In a little while he would no longer bother to turn back for a look.

The dwindling, inconsequential, uncertain life of Liaqat Khan was no longer small, no longer predictable in its limited excursion. But this knowledge did not take away the sadness he felt.

God knows what I'm up to, he had thought.

Ego trip, Sharifa's voice had snapped in his brain. Feel-good compassion.

Ego trip? His head was on the block, for Godssake.

Feel good? He felt rotten.

Compassion? This was cruelty. Calculated cruelty.

If Sharifa knew what it had cost ...

Five thousand. He'd drawn it from their account. He told her. He told her he'd banged into a brand new Ford and the owner had stuck him with the bill for the headlamp—five thousand, not a paisa less. 'I paid him,' he told Sharifa miserably, 'what else could I do?'

A complicated lie. He was shocked to discover the pleasure of it. Sharifa could do nothing but commiserate. Accidents happen. Thank God it was nothing worse than a headlamp. What's money, after all, forget it, Liaqat, don't kill yourself.

It was even better because they couldn't afford the expense right now. The guilt was spectacular, and he didn't have to pretend that.

That one was easy.

What lay ahead wasn't going to be anywhere near as easy. There were only two ways it could go: It could boomerang on him. Result: Disaster.

Or it could fizzle out, an exercise in futility. No bones broken, 5K down the drain.

There was, of course, a third possibility. A week, a lifetime ago, it had seemed the only possibility. Now he regarded it in the same light as three wishes, new lamps for old and fantasies of that sort. The possibility being that the plan actually *worked* and, khulja sim-sim, the mystery of Clarice lay revealed, setting his maddened mind at rest.

Liaqat didn't doubt for a moment that he was maddened by Clarice Aranxa. She provoked him to the degree reserved for psoriasis and like pruritic ills. She was an itch he couldn't keep from scratching, though she left him bloodied and ulcerated every time.

He was surprised to see Marion.

He called her in at once and told Gracie to hold all calls.

The change in Marion's appearance that he had noted in Baga last week was even more marked today. She had evidently come straight from work, still in her uniform of navy suit and rainbow scarf. As usual, she was heavily made-up, but the morning's careful effort had been thwarted by a slapdash overlay of rouge. Her lipstick was awry, the colour, an unfortunate matte purple, leaking past the carefully pencilled maroon outline. The rouge, intensely pink, had taken on the blotchy appearance of a rash—the butterfly rash of lupus, if he was going to be clinical about it. Only her long legs, taut calves seductive in sheer black nylon, impossibly poised on six-inch stilettos, were in character. Her hair was dull and stringy, her nails bitten to the quick. The lovely eyes were restless in a nystagmus that always excluded him.

He poured her a glass of water, but she pushed it away and shook her head.

'I heard from Sister Abby,' he opened the conversation. 'She's happy with your mother's progress.'

'Happy?' Marion shrugged. Her hands played with a box of paper clips, spilt them, swept them off the table, wandered towards a block of paper, peeled off a page, crushed it, tossed the crumpled ball off the desk. 'Sister Abby is happy with my mother? Why? What has my mother been telling Sister Abby?'

Liaqat fought an insane desire to pick her up by the lapels of her boxy jacket and throw her out, simply hurl her into the foyer and bang the door shut. He said with heavy patience: 'How would I know, Marion? Sister Abby does not know what your mother is saying. As I explained to you, Sister Abby is stone deaf. The deal is that she removes her hearing aid during sessions. Your mother is not likely to start talking till she has convinced herself that she will not be heard. Knowing your mother, I'm quite sure she won't rely on hearsay—she will satisfy herself that Sister Abby really can't hear, before she utters a word of what she has to say.'

'I can't understand that!' Marion broke in belligerently. 'She must be mad to go on talking to nobody. What else do you call a deaf woman in an empty room? I call that nobody.'

'You could call it that.'

'Then my mother's mad.'

'Not in the medical sense of the word, no.'

'You said she'd be paralysed. But nothing of the sort seems to be happening.'

'But it soon will, I'm sorry to say.'

'I think you're making a mistake, Doctor, please don't feel bad, but I think it's my duty to inform you that you're making a mistake. Didn't you say Mamma has the same disease as this American scientist, the guy who's in all the papers now?'

'Stephen Hawking? Yes. He's not American.'

'You're wrong about Mamma, then. When I saw the report in the paper, his photograph and all, and read motor neuron disease, ALS—the names you told us—I said, let me go take a look at this guy, and you know, that's what I did. Yesterday afternoon I took off to Colaba. I had the address of that institute, I went there and they were all out on the lawn and waiting for him. There he came in his special little car, creeping like a king's cavalcade slowly across the lawn, one nurse holding an umbrella over him, two people in front, two behind as if he's a celeb or something—'

'Oh but he is! He's a marvellous writer, too—'

'Frankly, Dr Khan, I am *not* interested. I'm *not* interested whether he writes well or badly, whether he's American or not, I'm *not* interested. I don't want to know anything more about the guy. I saw for myself, thank you very much. What I saw was a man kept alive by gadgets. My Mamma doesn't have anything that needs even one solitary gadget. She can walk, talk, eat, dress. What more does she need to do? Why don't you admit it, Doctor? Why don't you admit you've made a mistake and tell me, go home Marion, it'll be all right, your Mamma's going to be fine, it's only a little weakness. Why don't you?'

Marion's voice had long lost its vengeful edge of anger. Now there was only despair. Despair and denial.

Stifling his own pain, Liaqat answered her earnestly. All the while, though, he could not quiet the stubborn pulse of guilt. For the first time in his utterly blameless career, he had lied during a consultation. That could not but detract from the sincerity of the truth he now told her about the disease and its merciless eventualities. Guilt beat on in his head, a migraine that wouldn't go away.

Marion moistened a tissue with some water from the glass she had pushed away, and gently dabbed her eyes. He stopped talking, fascinated by the delicacy of her movements, examining the tissue with almost as much care as she did for the tell-tale trace of colour. She hadn't been listening to him, anyway. He didn't think she had ever doubted his diagnosis. She had simply needed to get that tantrum off her chest.

Her haunted eyes jumped about the room.

'I'm thinking of resigning,' she burst out. 'I can't keep up with my job, it's all become too much for me.'

He was aghast. How much more specific could he get, to tell this woman her mother would soon be dead and she, Marion, needed something, a job, an affair, a dog, a parrot in a cage, something, for Godssake, to hang on to, if she didn't want to also fold up and die.

He said slowly, 'That's not a very good idea, Marion. Your mother is well looked after by Pauline, and you visit her very often. You too have suffered much of late. You must see to your own life too, Marion. I don't think giving up your job to spend all your time with your mother is such a good idea.'

'More time with Mamma? No, no, Doctor, I wasn't thinking of that.' Then, with the petulance of a tormented child, she exclaimed, 'Mamma doesn't want me there!'

He was a neurologist, dammit, not a sob sister. He did the best he could. 'Why don't you ask your sister?' he asked clumsily, 'she should share your responsibility for Clarice.'

'Melissa? Oh Mamma can't stand her. I mean, she loves her and all that, but having her around—forget it! Whenever she comes to Bombay, Melissa is a party animal, we hardly ever see her. Nothing will induce her to come to Baga! All these months that Mamma's been ill, what do you think Melissa's contribution has been? One phone call! One measly bloody phone call on Christmas Day. That's it. Forget Melissa!'

Her tone was almost jaunty. The mention of Melissa had driven the megrims out of her.

'What about her swallowing problem, Doctor? It's only occasional.'

'We'll cross that bridge when we come to it. Right now, let's see if the sessions with Sister Abby make her feel any better. Marion, at every step our decisions must be based on what Clarice wants. Right now, she desperately wants to be free of bouts of catatonia—the statue-like spells she's had. They caused her intense suffering. I can help her once her mind is unburdened. We can then deal with the ravages of the disease.'

A bitter smile injured Marion's violet lips. It wiped out the indignities of powder and paint and lent her a grave dignity that belied her childish manner. Liaqat was compelled by the beauty of her lined brow and tormented eyes. The woman herself had retreated behind this classic mask of grief.

'Everybody has their burdens, Doctor, even you and I. How come we don't get this special treatment?' Their eyes locked in a complicity of bitterness.

Then she freed her eyes and left.

The encounter did nothing to lessen Liaqat's disquiet.

The call Liaqat had been waiting for came on Sunday afternoon. They could meet on Tuesday, if Liaqat was free.

'Why not now?' Liaquat demanded. 'Why not tomorrow?'

'I'm not free till Tuesday, Doctor,' the voice said gently, too gently to convince. 'Tuesday afternoon at two, then?'

When he agreed, he was further irritated. He was asked to turn up at a car mart in Andheri. 'You'll find me waiting at the gate,' the voice said—and had hung up before he could respond.

Liaqat fumed with resentment. 'Don't go if you don't want to,' Sharifa said reasonably. 'It is that Sister Abby, isn't it? You can say you're held up with an emergency.' But he wouldn't agree. 'Have it your own way then,' Sharifa flounced out of the room, adding, 'heartburn and bellyache, headache and heartache, Y'Allah what a man I've married!'

She came back with a glass of milk for him. 'You think I don't know what's eating you? Maybe this lady will tell you something that will drive that chudail out of your brain. If you can't be trusted to be there at that car mart at two, I'm going with you.'

Anything but that! He did nothing to correct her misunderstanding. All he'd told Sharifa was that Sister Abby (the famous Sister Abby he raved about so often) was going to be nursing the chudail for a week. He had told her nothing about the rest of his plan.

On Monday morning, Liaqat met Sister Abby's bus. She alighted looking relaxed after her brief holiday.

After a quick exchange of courtesies, he took her bag and they walked to the parking lot in a silence that betrayed their anxiety. Finally, Liaqat blurted out, 'Did you—'

'Oh, every day. I told you not to worry about that. But the cross around the neck, though . . . She asked if I was a nun. No, lay sister, I said. No more questions.'

'A crucifix! We messed that up!'

'Let's hope the rest is okay, Doctor. When will you meet the technician—the sound man?'

'Tomorrow, at two o'clock. Would you like to come too, Sister?'

'I was hoping you'd ask. I leave it to you, though. I'll understand if you change your mind.'

'No, I want you to. Perhaps I'm selfish, perhaps it's wrong to burden you with it. But I'd take it as a personal favour if you came.'

'I want to. I can' tell you what it felt like, sitting with my back to her day after day.'

Once that was out of the way, both of them relaxed.

'Clarice is going to need a feeding tube soon. Sputters her way through a glass of water. I've told the woman who looks after her to purée her meals, but that one runs Clarice like a dictator.'

'Who, Pauline? I thought she was a devoted slave!'
'Works both ways, doesn't it?' Sister Abby said mysteriously.

So here he was, a little after two, coughing in a cloud of exhaust, turning in at the gate of the car mart, and there *she* was, Sister Abby, soignée in a silk sari. Her eyes were remote, the eyes of a stranger, amused, but secret. She looked—electric.

No greeting passed between them. He parked and followed her into the building. As he passed the showroom he almost lost her, distracted by the seduction of a bright red sedan.

Sister Abby seemed to have vanished through the blank wall. He wheeled around, but there was no sign of her outside.

When he turned, a voice said from the shadows, 'Dr Liaqat.'

The blank brown wall had opened magically, and Perera materialized from the gloom. Liaqat followed him into the cavern. The mountainside closed behind them. They were in a dim vestibule, made gloomier by the few yellow spot lamps in the ceiling. A row of moulded chairs nailed to the wall enhanced the prison motif. Sister Abby sat in one of them. Everything was a despondent shade of brown.

'Disorienting, isn't it?' she read his mind. 'Why does everything have to be this sickening shade of brown? It's only a sound lab!'

'Sound lab?'

'The best in Asia, Mr Perera says. We'll have to wait a bit. Look, he's disappeared again.'

Liaqat sank into a chair. Things were moving too fast for him. 'You know Perera?'

'Sure. I caught him one of those afternoons, squatting in the maidan behind Bougainvillea House. I thought he was doing his job, you know—there are always one or two of them on the fields in the afternoon, and no wonder—with all that drink, their bowels aren't going to be regular bright and early. I did wonder why he needed the umbrella, though. I had a good mind to yell at him, but just then he straightened up, and I saw he was fully dressed. Not the kind of man who would squat on the grass for his daily job. So who else could he be? After I turned the bend in the road he came up and talked with me. Coming through loud and clear, he said.'

'I wish he hadn't done that.'

'I might have blown the whistle on him if he hadn't. I'd imagined quite a different kind of man.'

'What do you make of him? I'm curious.' Liaqat wanted to ask: Is he a sleazeball? A gob of slime? A blackmailer? Will he hang me, betray me, see me in jail?

'Oh he's harmless,' Sister Abby said breezily.

His jaw clenched, he stared at the wall.

'I don't want to hear the tape.'

'Don't leave now, Liaqat.' Sister Abby sounded cold and remote.

'I don't want to hear the tape.'

'Oh you do, you do. You've been killing yourself all week to find out what Clarice had to say. Now that you can, you suddenly turn holy.'

He shrugged. 'It's only natural to be curious. But I didn't tell my patient her words would go on tape. She trusted me.'

'She still will.'

'I wish I hadn't done it.'

'Yes, I know you do.'

She nodded and looked away. They sat side by side, impassively like Egyptian deities on their thrones of stone.

Presently they were led into a room with padded walls. The carpet was so springy he bobbed rather than walked forward. The walls were concave, the ceiling bulged down. At the far end of the room a console winked in unreadable Morse. There were overstuffed chairs, upholstered in the same dead shade of brown. Sister Abby perched on the edge of a chair, but Liaqat sank like a dead weight drawn deep by the muscular suck of its springs. At any other time he would have extricated himself angrily, but he was too confused to move.

The door opened. A tall man with glasses greeted Liaqat. Sister Abby was introduced.

'Tea, coffee, something cold? Playing time is two hours.'

'I thought it might be longer,' Sister Abby said.

'Your tape was about four hours. After editing, cleaning up, reducing distortion, two hours.'

'Where's Perera?' Liaqat asked.

'Perera's gone. He said he'd call you tonight.'

'Let's begin, then!'

The sound engineer (the best in Asia, no doubt, Liaqat

thought sourly) left the room. Sister Abby moved to the chair furthest from Liaqat. A cold look of dislike passed between them. Liaqat's scalp prickled. What had he done to Clarice?

The lights on the console winked again. A low hum enveloped them. They were sitting within an enormous seashell and now there was the sound of tides: The rustle of her breathing—shrill, amphoric—quietening down to a snuffle.

Then, Clarice began to speak.

'It rained the night they brought me to Bougainvillea House...'

The glare outside made them blink. They had left soon after the second replay. Sister Abby carried a package: a small tape-recorder with headphones that Perera had left for Liaqat, a copy of the edited tape they'd heard, and the original unedited version. She held the package out to Liaqat. He shook his head, still too bemused to speak. She followed him to the car.

He drove in silence for a while, aggressively, till they were past the snarl of traffic. His anger had been dissipated by what he had just heard. He wanted to tell Sister Abby that, but he could not find the words. Oddly enough, he felt as though he had shamed her in some way.

'Where can I drop you?'

'At the next signal. Don't turn, it's a two-minute walk.'

He changed lanes.

'Come with me,' she said.

Liaqat's Diary

It's been five days now, since I heard that tape, and I can't rid myself of her voice. Stray sentences spring out of my memory to sting me out of sleep, out of joy, out of concentration. Clarice! What do I know of her? I cannot understand how her thoughts can be so completely amoral or her morality so completely skewed. She feels nothing—nothing! Nothing for that poor boy Justin, nothing for that unfortunate Keith!

It's all delusional, of course—she couldn't possibly have pushed them.

Or did she?

My first feelings were horror, shock, revulsion.

The facts began to sink in during the replay.

Initially I was distracted by all her bullshit about make-up and clothes—the woman knows she's going to die, what sort of vanity is this?

And then it hit me.

This woman was describing *murder*. She pushed her husband down that well. She pushed poor Justin, she killed him. She did not physically push that unlucky Keith, but it was murder, just the same. And Justin's mother? She doesn't say—but it's implied, isn't it?

I left that sound lab completely brain-bashed. I drove on autopilot. I was no longer angry with Perera. Or with Sister Abby. I didn't want to leave her. I didn't want to face Clarice alone. Sister Abby sensed that.

Big, BIG problem there. She has been kind and gentle with me and I have treated her boorishly. I can't apologize—what's the use? An apology takes nothing away. I behaved like a pig. I went with her to her flat. I wolfed down the food she set before me, not noticing that she did not eat. When she had cleared away, I fell asleep. Just like that, on that shiny sofa, I crashed in this strange woman's house, and the next thing I knew it was dusk and Sharifa was in that room listening to the tape. At first, because the room was in that delicious lilac haze of twilight, I thought I was dreaming. Then Sister Abby came in, and I remembered where I was.

I felt horrible, thick-tongued, heavy-headed. But another look at Sharifa frowning at the floor as the headphones filled her skull with Clarice's nonsense sparked off a white rage in me. I could have throttled Sister Abby!

Though my hands stayed at my side, she saw my intent. For a moment her face changed. Eyes widened, a pulse twitched at her temple, jaw tightened. It lasted no more than a second, but it showed me how dangerous I could be. Almost instantaneously a swift pain crossed her face and her eyes were lit with tears. She turned away.

I had been shouting all this time. Yes, shouting. I had lost every shred of decorum. How dare you, how dare you, I kept saying, how dare you give that to my wife, how dare you betray Clarice again and again.

'Shut up, Liaqat,' Sharifa said quietly. 'You've said enough for one day. Let's go.'

Then I turned on *her*. 'Oh, already? What about all that bheja masala you've got between your ears?'

Just go, Sharifa said. Just go, Sister Abby's rigid back said. Just go, Clarice's shocked voice said. Just go, just get out of our lives.

I walked out. Sharifa did not follow me. I waited almost a quarter of an hour in the car before she came down. By then the fight had gone out of me. I wanted to be silent, to be alone.

Of course, that was not possible. All the way home Sharifa let me have it, her favourite J words dotting every sentence. She had never dreamt I was such a jahil. Sitting in this lady's house, gulping down her lunch, burping and farting and falling asleep on her sofa with my legs sticking out and my belt undone, waking up like a jungli and shouting, yes, shouting, I could be heard three streets away, shouting at the person whose house I was sitting in, whose food I had swallowed, whose sofa I had snored on with my legs sticking out and my belt undone, a great gross jungli, etc.

Except to state here in writing that my belt was not undone, I let all that pass without argument.

To make things worse, Sister Abby phoned a couple of hours later. I held the receiver dumbly, waiting for her to speak.

'I suppose I was wrong, Doctor Liaqat. I presumed your wife would be better off knowing what was worrying you, and I took the liberty of calling her.'

'No . . . I couldn't face up to what I'd done, I just lashed out at everybody. You particularly. Forgive me, please.'

'Of course. So, are you going to let Sharifa hear the tape?'

'Let? Let? Haven't you met my wife?'

'Well, then. Don't shut her out. Consider what she has to say.'

'Oh, she isn't talking to me.'

'Naturally not. Till dinner time. You take it easy, doctor.'

Perera phoned at eight. I didn't give him a chance to speak. 'What was the need to go to that sound lab?' I demanded. 'What was the need to accost Sister? Now the matter is over and done with, it's all over the city, they will be talking about it on buses and trains. Thank you very much.'

Perera sighed. 'Why are you so frightened, Doctor? For me this is everyday business, man. That Sister would have come poking into my business if I hadn't explained. Besides, you had already told her the plan when you gave her the microphone. And why the sound lab? Because it's the best in Asia, man, we always use it for our work. Best reproduction. You got the package? I thought you may not have a recorder, so I left that for you. Give it back when you finish, okay? Now you relax.'

'Relax? Perera, you heard that tape!'

'Yes, Doctor Liaqat. I heard that tape. Take your time, Doctor, take your time to consider the tape. Take it easy. There's one more tape. Not fit for lady's ears, last two days' recording. Shall I bring it to your place, or will you come here?'

'Can you come here?' I asked Perera.

'After dinner okay? Nine o'clock?'

'Okay.'

As I put the phone down, I realized I would have to list all my lies for my wife.

She turned the eyes of a judge on me. 'Was that the headlamp?' she asked.

I could have denied it, I suppose, but that lie was sickening us both. 'It was,' I said. 'I know you've heard something from Sister Abby, but she doesn't know all of it. This is how it happened.'

How foolish it sounded, right from the moment I ran into Perera in that Irani cafe, his chance remark, Sister Abby's shrewd comment and then my mad decision to record what Clarice had to say. My guilt and fear Sharifa had witnessed all along. Disapproval was written all over her now.

'I would have told you, anyway, if Sister hadn't called you,' I said, and I meant every word. 'I lost it when I heard the tape, I blamed Sister Abby, I blamed Perera. That was unforgivable. *I* made them do those things. The responsibility is mine.

'I got the idea the day I met Sister Abby. That evening, I went back to the Irani restaurant to look for Perera. Will you do this job for me, I asked. Perera agreed to record Clarice for five thousand, all said. I thought it was cheap. He met me at Baga the night before Sister arrived, showed me what he'd be doing. Then he messed it up. He'd installed the microphone in a crucifix, and he expected Sister to wear that round her neck. My mistake, actually, I used the word *Sister*, he thought I meant a nun. Still, Sister Abby passed it off.'

'But Liaqat can't. He can't live with the fact that he's done the dirty on Clarice.'

'No.'

'Even though Clarice seems to be our popular neighbourhood axe murderer.'

'Sharifa! She's delusional.'

'Delusional, my foot. That woman did it. Ask Sister Abby.'

'Since when is Sister Abby such an ally of yours?'

'All right, I'll ask Perera when he comes.'

'You'll do nothing of the sort. I don't want you to be here when he comes. I don't want you meeting such riff-raff.'

'So now suddenly he is riff-raff? What is he, anyway? Policeman?'

'No, he was some kind of security chap, surveillance expert he calls himself.'

'Oh, a professional bugger.'

We both burst out laughing, and that was the end of our quarrel.

Perera came promptly at nine. He declined Sharifa's offer of sharbat, and handed me the tape. He might have been as deaf as Sister Abby, for all the reaction he showed to Clarice. 'Take it easy, Doctor,' he said, irritating me no end. 'I'll meet you when you finish.' And after making small talk with my wife, telling her of his days of alcoholic glory and the empty present, Perera took his wraith-like self away.

'So?' I demanded.

It was basically all the questions I had kept from asking Sister Abby.

'Naah,' Sharifa said. 'The man's harmless. Come on, let's give Clarice another hearing.'

'He's brought another tape. Not fit for lady's ears, he says.'

'Good. Let's start with that.'

Clarice, Tape 5

I am here. I am talking to you. I am back in the world of touch and smell, speech and hear—oops! Sorry. Forgot your deafness. Forgot your handicap, as they call it nowadays, handicap, like golf. Clive used to play golf. There were golf links on Carter Road those days. Handicap. Makes it sound like a game. I dare say this doesn't feel like a game. What does it feel like, Sister, being deaf?

Wait! I know! But you couldn't have known what I know. I can't imagine you've ever known that delicious rushing silence that filled me like cool water when I turned deaf. No. Not you. For you, deafness is a block of wood hammered into your skull. Square peg in a round hole. I can tell that from the blocky set of your shoulders, from your short thick neck with its tenniquoit rings of fat. From that ridiculous bun. Your deafness is a block of wood hammered into your skull. It can't be any different for a woman as ugly as you.

Ugly Puglee.

Funny, it's been a long time since I said that.

Ugly Puglee. That's you, Sister. Born ugly, turned puglee with a lifetime of wiping bottoms, sticking tubes through every hole, Ugly Puglee. That's what I call you. That's what the boys used to call my sister Florence. Flossie. Go 'way, they'd yell at her, go 'way, Ugly Puglee. Dark she was, you know, all skinny like an Indian, knobby elbows and knees. Mummy used to say the devil had changed her. She was born pink like all Aranxa babies and then suddenly one day they found her turned black like an Indian. Black.

Ugly Puglee. Dead now, isn't she? No more loaves in the oven for Flossie. Got her first one at fourteen, didn't she? The luck of the devil she had, too—lost it before they could find out. Sunday afternoon. Right after lunch. Coconut pudding for dessert. I heard her crying in the bathroom, but I didn't go, not at once. Then she called me, and she hadn't latched the door—and the coconut pudding flew straight out of my throat, shattering the scarlet windowpane on the floor. Rich red glass from a cathedral window lying there on the bathroom floor. I shattered it. There was red glass everywhere, tiny red spots on the white tiles. And all those clumps of coconut, soaking it up, turning a strawberry pink.

But Flossie didn't care, did she? Not she!

She was crouched over the shiny slimy lump in the middle, sticky red strings leaking out of her stretched over it.

She turned all screechy when it twitched on the tiles. I slammed my hand hard against her face and she shut it.

The lump twitched again. *'Don't touch it, don't touch it—'*

Stupid Flossie. Wouldn't let me flush it, Stupid Flossie. I had to clean up. I had to give that bloodied bundle to the gardener and threaten to tell Daddy if he didn't bury it. He did it like a shot. Maybe it was his. Yes! That is an idea! Funny it's taken me all this time to discover that. Heavens. The gardener! Flossie never told. My God. She'd done it with an Indian, then. Depraved. You hear that? My sister was depraved.

Ugly Puglee. The boys never asked her to please please fix the balloons for the party, right up on the ceiling, we'll hold the stepladder, promise you won't fall, Clarice, please please, nobody can do it so pretty like you! They never asked Flossie. Up the stepladder then I'd go. 'Higher, higher, Clarice!' There I was, right on top, stretching right up with a bit of Scotch tape as they handed me the balloons.

Six boys round that stepladder to catch me if I fell. Six pairs of eyes peering up my skirt. Six little willies standing at attention inside six pairs of shorts. And not one of them ten yet. Disgusting.

But when Flossie went up the ladder, all the boys ran away, though I know for a fact she hadn't any panties on.

That didn't last long, did it? By next Christmas, they'd stopped calling her Ugly Puglee. They followed her around like dogs. Flossie was younger than me, but she knew a great deal more than I did. Because of Walter.

She'd found this dirty, dog-eared book stuffed away at the back of Father's wardrobe. Always a snoop, Flossie! The cover was torn off, except for a bit on the spine that had only one printed word: Walter. So that's what she called the book. Walter. Flossie sneaked into Father's room every afternoon and had her fill of Walter. She was always red when she came out. Every night she boasted about all the secrets she knew till I bribed and bullied and threatened her I would tell Father unless she told me all she knew.

Flossie was clever. She offered to 'lend' me Walter, knowing I wasn't much of a reader. But I was smarter. I said I would go with her to Father's room and she could read Walter out loud to me.

We crept in, and she took out the book from its hiding place. 'Here's a part for you,' she says, 'you can see there's nothing to tell about.'

And then she read out a surprising bit about how all this was instruction for young people. I nearly left, it was so boring, just like Religion.

But she kept on and there they were. There they all were. All the wicked rude ugly terrible words. She said them all. She read them out of the book. She read them as if she were reading a lesson. She said them all. She said them all.

How they're burnt into my memory! They are branded in my brain. When I close my eyes in the cool velvet dark they fume like fire and brimstone. They drip blood. They throb like a heart laid open, twitching, dangerous, till the cool water of darkness puts them out. I know they continue to smoke unseen in the darkness, a breath of smoke from a cigarette stubbed away.

I can't understand that. I cannot understand why those words stay.

I'm not a nun like you. Nun, lay Sister, whatever. Celibate by destiny if not by intent, that's you. But not me. I had Clive, remember? I had Clive, every time he could get me, I had Clive. But all that has nothing to do with these terrible, horrible, ugly words, the really bad words, the wicked words that Flossie read out to me.

Can you understand that, Sister? These words are something else.

I never did that, never. Never. That was what *Flossie* did.

I've seen to it very carefully that Marion never hears or reads or sees such wickedness. I showed the girls a crochet hook when they were ten. 'Don't make me use it,' I told them. It was the same hook Flossie used on me. She was much older then. I was much older then. She was sixteen. I was nineteen. It was an accident. That's what I told Flossie. That's what I'm telling you. Flossie laughed. Was it the one with the moustache? she said. Or his brother? Did you even notice his face?

As if I should have, as if they were people.

They're labourers, I explained patiently. They don't have faces. They don't have names. They must be whipped and sent away.

I saw to that.

I went crying to Daddy. He had them whipped, all the way to the gates. Everybody said they were lucky he didn't hang them.

They didn't touch her, I promise you, Daddy told Clive. They didn't touch her.

I was already engaged to Clive. Would I have let Flossie otherwise?

I was engaged to Clive. So Flossie pinched the crochet hook. It was Mamma's. Flossie pinched it. I trusted Flossie because it was just that once, I told myself, I never need trust her again.

I didn't, you know.

After I married Clive, I wouldn't give Flossie the time of day. My sister is a slut, I told Clive. Please keep her away. She was dead by the time Marion was born, what do you expect. She wrote to me, you know, she had the nerve to do that. I never read the letter. Maybe she put those words in the letter. Maybe she did. She was that sort of person.

I remembered those words all over again when I got that letter. I remembered her face when she read them out from that Walter book, her face all puckered with laughter.

She laughed, she found it funny. She said the words again when she used the crochet hook.

I can hear them now as I watch her turn the hook round and round and round and up and down and crosswise.

That didn't hurt so bad did it? she says. As though she's a nurse or a doctor or something. And she giggles the way she did when she read from the Walter book. She giggles as she says the Walter words. She giggles as if we're both on the same side. As if it's our secret. But we are *not* on the same side. It was an accident.

Do you hear that, Sister? We're *not* on the same side. We never can be. Flossie couldn't see that. She kept saying those words with a wink even after I took the hook away. She said the words on my wedding day. And she laughed.

She never understood those words could never ever have anything to do with me.

I kept the words from both my girls.

There were times when the girls were growing up when I'd lie rigid all night, afraid to close my eyes lest the words flame up and throb in the dark. I'd keep my eyes open and think of Flossie Waltering away in the dark, jiggle jiggle in the bed next to mine, but I never sank so low. I kept myself pure. I kept Marion pure, so help me Jesus.

The words are choked up somewhere inside me. Sometimes I want to shout out the words on top of my voice in a closed room. Hullo! Sister? Sister! Hello?

Sorry. Forgot you can't hear me.

This is a closed room. The door's shut, the window is shut too. And you are deaf as a post.

I shall say those words out now.

Listen carefully with your deaf ears as I pour poison into them.

I want to dirty you, Sister, to pollute you, to smear my shit on you till you stink with the stink that is mine, me Clarice, Clarice Aranxa, me, me, me!

If I had a willie, I'd pee on you.

There, I said willie, that's okay, that's safe, that's not dangerous as the words I'm about to say.

Here they are. Here's Walter. It starts, as you'll see, with a holy word. Providence. Providence. That's no more than Satan quoting scripture. Satan knows his scripture, give the Devil his due.

Providence has made the continuation of the species depend on a process of coupling of the sexes called fucking. It is performed by two organs. That of the male is familiarly and vulgarly called the prick, that of the female, a cunt. Politely, one is called a penis and the other a pudendum. The prick, broadly speaking, is a long, fleshy, gristly tube. The cunt a fleshy, warm, wet hole or tube. The prick is at times and in a peculiar manner thrust up the cunt and discharges a thick fluid into it, and that is the operation called fucking.

There, that's it.

I remembered all of it, even the bits like *broadly speaking*. I wonder why. *In a peculiar manner*—that too. It's important.

Not so bad, was it?

Mucked about in the dirt, did we?

But then you're used to mucking about in the dirt, aren't you? Whore. Harlot. Bitch. Motherfucking bitch. Whore. Whore.
Enough.
I'm finished.
My words are finished.
Go away.
Go now.
Go away.
Go.

I'll start with an apology. I'm sorry I sent you away so rudely yesterday, though perhaps you don't know that, you only turned when I flung a cushion at you. That was a good throw for me. I can't usually manage to pitch things that far. Not anymore. My shoulder seems to have got stronger these last few days. But my legs feel week. I tell Pauline not to give me such hard things to swallow.

Everything is difficult.

Dr Khan has warned me that speaking will soon be difficult. Soon. Very soon.

Before that I must tell you all that's dammed within me, I must flatten you with my rushing cataract of words. Not because Dr Khan has said so, but because when you leave the room, Sister, I feel a peace, a comfort I have never felt before.

I am angry when I see you.

The sight of you fills me with hate.

But you cleanse me. You heal me. You are ... like that stupid book Marion's always reading. You are chicken soup for my soul.

Dr Khan told me the news. It was fated. It has happened. The girl in the red dress is dead. I waited very long for that to happen, but justice is now done. The girl in the red dress is dead. Clive is dead, the fruit of their sin is dead.

It is time to put that story behind me.

The dead are a closed book.

Time enough to open it again when I'm dead. Maybe they'll be waiting for me, the three of them, maybe it will all begin again.

Till then, though, I put them behind me.

I must look to the living.

I must look to Marion, to my child, the fruit of my womb. I worry about Marion. I've worried about her day and night, as long as I can remember. I don't worry about Melissa, I never have. Melissa has Tom. Marion will have neither Dick nor Harry. I even tried to look out for a boy for Marion, the way the Indians do. But who will marry a girl with such bad luck? All that education, all that beauty, all that money, of what use are they all if she can't catch a boy?

Marion will never catch a boy.

Too clumsy, too careless, too eager.

Marion must be made to see her responsibility.

Marion must do her duty.

My illness has been good for Pauline. It's got her to behave. She was getting a little out of hand ever since we came to Bougainvillea House. But she can't get very far with me. I've always seen to that. Sometimes she forgets herself. I forgive her, we've been together so many years! But I put her in her place. A servant is a servant and must know her place.

Grumble, grumble, grumble. That's Pauline. But she's reliable. All these years and she's never let me down. I can always count on her. Pauline is faithful. Pauline will stay. She isn't going anywhere. She won't leave me till Mendonca puts those pumps on my feet. Maybe he'll send for her to help. She's the expert, she's been easing my feet into shoes these forty years.

Pauline will stay not because she wants to, but because there's nothing else she can do. I've taken care of that. All these years, I've insured against her going away. That's foresight. All her money is with me. I have her savings in my safe.

I must look to the living.

I must look to Kansas, to my child, the future of my child. I worry about Vinton. I've worried about it day and night, as long as I can remember. I don't worry about McBratney ever. Mebbe not Tom. McBratney will bear fruit for Dick much larger, I ever up to Dick can not show for Mattie. She's not the Indians to. But who will marry a girl with a bad idea? All that education, all that beauty, all that money. Tis what else are they all at the start can't a boy.

Mattie will never catch a boy.

Too clumsy, too broody, too earnest.

Mebbe that he made to see her responsibility.

Vinton must not be a slave.

McBratney has been good for Pauline, dey not her to behave. She was getting a little out of hand ever since we came to Edmondville, I mean, but she can't act out on early me, I've always seen to that, but she is. She forgets herself. I forgive her, we've been together so many years, but I think she forgets sometimes I'm a servant and must know her place.

Grouchy, grumble, grumble. That's Pauline. So she's a biddie. All these years and she's never let me down, I can always count on her. Pauline is useful. Pauline will age, she won't gone anywhere. She won't leave me till Vinton is gone, those pounds of hers, McBratney, and for her family. She's the expert, she's been caring on her own shoes that long, sure.

Pauline will care not because she wants to, but because there's nothing else she can do, we won't get rid of them. All these years, I've counted against her going now. That's foresight. All her money is with me. I have her crushed in my palm.

Liaqat's Diary

I've taken my time to consider Clarice—and I'm still in the dark.

Sharifa says, I told you she was a chudail. Now forget about her. Let her die.

I'm not stopping her, am I?

But the truth is that Clarice will never die. She will live as long as I do, a constant thorn throbbing in the flesh of the soul—unless I learn the truth.

After we heard the last tape, Sharifa came around to my view that Clarice was delusional. All the sex stuff convinced her. Frankly, the hate in Clarice's voice scared me.

The very next day I sent a copy of the tape with detailed case notes to B.K. Joshi. Of course BK is mad, but he's the only psychiatrist I know who thinks beyond fluoexetine. Doesn't medicate, doesn't shock, doesn't confine. More than that you cannot ask for your patient. The rest one must endure. (BK once told me the spleen is a pelvic organ, but then, he's basically Freudian.)

Naturally, I had to find Perera.

Back to the café, and there he was, face lost in the gloom, legs sticking out in the sun. Maybe I'm the one that's delusional and Perera's a figment of my brain. I gave back his tape recorder.

'So, Doctor, problem solved?' he asked after the token bunmaska and Nescafe had arrived.

'Problem started,' I corrected. 'How do I explain all this? I knew she was disturbed, but I had no idea it was so severe—'

'You think she's—how do you say—mental?'

Mental. He would call it that, wouldn't he?

'Of course.'

'There's no of course about it, Doctor. She might be mental. Or not.'

'Perera, she's my patient, I know her, I know what she's capable of.'

'You knew all this, then? You knew she had all this on her mind?'

'That's not what I meant. How could I possibly know her fantasies? But I do know her real life, her real everyday life.'

'And these deaths happened in her real everyday life.'

'Yes, but—'

'What does Sister think? Does she also think this lady is mad?'

'I haven't asked her. What do *you* think, Perera?'

'I never give opinion on subject. Perera is here to help.'

'Big help, that! I'm not supposed to discuss my patient with you, either.'

'Supposed, not supposed. Who makes the rules?'

'Medical Council for one. Common decency for another.'

'Listen, Doctor. Forget Medical Council. They're not going to hear of this one. And common decency led you to help this lady in the first place. Why should you bother about what's troubling her? Dope her with an injection and everybody's peaceful. Why didn't you do that? Because you're not that kind of person, and therefore not that kind of doctor. Gentleman like you gets a concession. Other clients I charge ten thousand.'

He called for a chai.

'You know ACP Kher, I think? Tennis partner?'

'Suresh? Sure. Haven't played tennis in a long while, though. Friend of yours?'

'I do his surveillance. Play tennis, Doc. Good for paunch.'

'I don't have a paunch,' I said indignantly.

'Some more Goan ladies, and you'll get one. Take my advice, Doctor, play tennis.'

How's that for our mystery man?

That rattled me to begin with, and when I got home, I was greeted by the sound of laughter and women's voices. O God, I thought, Sharifa's catclub. But it was only Sister Abby.

I kind of froze the laughter off their lips as I entered. They had a look as they caught sight of me—part embarrassment, part dislike—that told me I was under discussion. Then of course they were all over me, Sharifa getting me a glass of water as though I had lost the use of my limbs, Sister Abby asking comfortable questions about sleep, appetite, etc. (I stopped her in time; bowel movement would be next on the list).

It just told me, didn't it. Sharifa never discusses me with her friends, I know that for a fact. I mean, I hope so. But here she was, laughing over me with Sister Abby. It's all the fallout from that miserable Clarice. Is nothing sacred anymore?

Sister Abby didn't waste too much time. 'So what are we going to do about Clarice, Doctor?' she asked. I forgave her that *we*. Heck, I welcomed it.

She looked a bit sceptical when I told her I'd sent the tapes to BK. 'I was staff nurse in Psychiatry for five years before I got promoted to Sister,' she said. 'Can't say I've seen any case like this. There were schizos growing wild in that ward, every second bed. We had Gandhi and Hitler and Dev Anand all at the same time once. And then we had women, three of them, who had murdered their babies. But you could sense their madness a mile off. Clarice is so sane!'

'Let's wait for BK's verdict. If Clarice is not what Perera calls mental, are you suggesting she actually did all those things? Murdered Clive and Keith and Justin—and perhaps Justin's mother as well?'

'I suppose so.'

We digested her reply in silence.

Finally, I asked: 'What about her ALS, Sister? Can you imagine her walking a mile or so and then pushing a strong young man into a well? I can assure you, long before she left for Goa, the power in her arms and shoulders was pretty bad. She couldn't even push open a door.'

Sister Abby nodded. 'I don't doubt that for a moment. Now she can barely walk a few steps before buckling. And her story is she walked on that cliff every day, standing at the edge with Mrs Borges. Lots of unbelievable things in her account, certainly. But Doctor, the reasoning is so logical.'

I don't know what she meant. There's nothing logical about Clarice.

'Why don't you let someone listen to these tapes, Doctor? Someone who's an expert, I mean. I know some people.'

'Expert in what? Murder?'

Sharifa shot me a warning look, but I was too far gone now to stop. 'You know a panel of experts on murder, Sister?'

'Yes, Doctor.' Sister Abby was unfazed. 'The police. I know some people, pretty high up. They call me now and then, you know, for dowry cases.'

'I didn't know the police brought in their own nurses!'
'No. Not to nurse the victim. To talk to the relatives.'
'They call you to talk to the relatives?'
'Don't talk like a parrot, Liaqat. That's what Sister just said.'
'You counsel the relatives?'
'Counsel, hell. I get the truth out of them.'

It sounds like a boast written down, and it sounded like a boast when she said it. I was aghast. An A to the police for talent spotting.

'I bet you get them every time, Sister,' I said sincerely.

She smiled with satisfaction. 'Every bloody time.'

It then turned out that Mr Abby had been in the police. 'I've known men like Perera all my life,' Sister Abby said. 'Something breaks inside them after they've seen human ugliness day in and day out for years. No resource inside to hold them together. Get a life, my husband used to say. He built ships.'

In bottles, she meant.

All my life I've wanted to make a ship in a bottle, but I've never figured out how.

You see how everything hits you in one bloody day?

First the tennis partner, then Sister Abby as avenging angel, then the ship in the bottle.

But the day wasn't over yet. As we were going to bed, I remarked idly, 'Wonder what that Walter book was.'

'*My Secret Life*,' Sharifa said promptly, 'the sex diary of a Victorian gentleman, known only as Walter. First published in eighteen something. Banned, of course. Very tedious porn.'

'How do you know?'

'I looked it up. It's there on the Net.'

The Net! Scandalous, the kind of stuff you find there. Must check it out.

Meanwhile, there have been two phone calls from Marion. The first was to tell me that Clarice's swallowing difficulties are on the rise. Thick soups and custards are all she can manage. She keeps asking for Sister Abby. The second call was to ask me when I planned to visit Clarice again. Sister Abby had told them I should be called if her swallowing worsened—and it had, hadn't it? 'How long can a person live on custard?' Marion demanded tetchily.

I almost asked: How long is she going to live, anyway?

Clarice will need assisted feeding. A nasogastric tube will be best. I shall have to go to Bougainvillea House, after all, I cannot shrink from my responsibilities. But I cannot bring myself to face Clarice again. Not after the tapes. The nasogastric tube is such a trivial thing, that Sister in Panjim should manage it.

But Clarice wants Sister Abby.

It's been over a week now since I heard that tape and I haven't yet come to any conclusions about Clarice. She couldn't have killed her husband, not the man she loved so deeply. And Justin—yes, his very existence was an insult, but was that enough to make her kill him? Can a person store hatred for so long?

I see it somewhat differently.

Clarice feels guilty about her illness, for being a drag on her family. Her guilt makes her take on the onus of these tragedies. She feels guilty about her anger towards her husband, guilty about not forgiving his infidelity—so she makes herself responsible for his death. She's guilty about Marion's anxiety of how to reconcile marriage with filial duty. Perhaps Marion had expressed the wish not to marry so that she could care for Clarice. And so Keith, crossing the railway lines, is killed in a roundabout way by Clarice's terminal illness. Justin's discovery of his illegitimacy makes Clarice feel guilty about Clive. So his suicide makes her feel responsible again. And Mrs Borges—that's easy to understand too.

I expounded my theory to Sharifa. She said I was a good *neurologist*, stressing the last word.

Pauline

Pauline walked heavily into St Anne's. She didn't like coming here.

The grandeur of the interior, the gilt mouldings, the imposing altar, the ornate tabernacle awed her, as did the tall candles with their slender wavering flames, the long-stemmed lilies, the chill rebuke of holy water at the font. Pauline had never sought comfort inside a church. This was not a place where she came to pray. Pauline prayed often, loudly, publicly, and very often just to pass the time. JesuMarieJoseph in her imagination looked like larger, more dignified versions of herself. She thought of them as elderly relatives whom one could rely on for sound advice. She would not have known what to say to the Blessed Virgin inside the Church. Here, the Blessed Virgin, Marie, would be sitting next to her in the pew, too nervous to do more than whisper, painfully conscious that she was not grand enough to mother the magnificent Christ at the altar. Pauline and the BVM would have exchanged glances, shrugged and hurried out to the nearest grotto where they could have their cozy hour together without fear of being patronized.

Jesu was another matter altogether. Pauline always shut her eyes when she saw a picture of the Sacred Heart. He looked like a tourist: yellow hair, pink cheeks, itty-bitty beard, blue eyes. He was all right for the Aranxas of this world. But Pauline's Jesu was a worried-looking man in a sweaty singlet, the one you instinctively called when there was trouble nobody else could fix, like when the gas ran out over the weekend or the plumber couldn't unblock the toilet.

As for Joseph, he was a good soul, but you could tell straight off he hadn't had much experience. The BVM shielded him from life.

Of course, for really big trouble, Pauline knew you had to pray to the three of them together if you wanted it to work.

Pauline was not here to pray.

Nevertheless she was prepared for a long vigil. She made herself as comfortable as she could in the pew. One by one the other worshippers slipped out. Now was the hour when the tall candles would be snuffed, the flowers refreshed, the blinds pulled down, and the church would drowse till evening service. It was siesta time.

Pauline was not drowsy. In fact, she felt as though she had never been as awake in all her life as she was these days. She was alert—but as she watched the door of the vestry, her mind was far far away. It wandered, as it often did these days, to the first time she had come to Baga.

Thirty, thirty-five years. Maybe more. My! Had she lived all these years! She was a girl then, just a slip of a thing, pretty too, though he hadn't had eyes for her. He had eyes only for his doll. And when he found out the doll was just a doll—without heart or guts or blood—just a porcelain doll, what could he do but look elsewhere? You look after Missy, Pauline, he said, make her happy. So Pauline had begun that lifelong endeavour for Clive's sake.

At first it had been for Clive's sake. Then because she was used to it. And finally because there was nowhere else to go. And now, when deliverance was finally in sight, she didn't want things any different. She was worn out.

She had had a lifetime of doing things for Clarice, for Marion, for Melissa. Now she was here to do something for herself, something she owed a woman whose uneasy life—if fate had worked differently—could have been Pauline's own.

Pauline gazed uneasily around. She didn't particularly want any witnesses—

There was just one other worshipper, and he seemed sunk in his devotions.

She turned back just in time to see a thin cassocked figure emerge from the confessional. Despite the gloom, she had no trouble recognizing him. Not so very long ago, she had seen him at this very hour, slipping back into the dark belly of the church as Clarice tottered back after her confession. There was no mistaking him—it was the same man.

'Hoi Padri!' Pauline's voice, harsh, belligerent, shocked the still air. A bird squawked, flapping out hurriedly into the sunshine. Even the plaster saints looked startled out of their painted calm.

The priest, who had picked up the long-handled extinguisher to snuff out the candles, now gripped it like a weapon. Pauline had made her way down the aisle and was now within a few paces of him.

'Hoi Padri, caught at your filthy tricks, huh? What are you up to, listening within that little cage? You get an itch maybe, huh? Between your legs something wakes up, huh? What do you do when women tell you their sad stories? What do you do when you tell them to make Hail Mary? Rub and rub and still nothing, so go running and tell all your eunuch friends what you heard inside. That's what you do, huh? Tell the whole village who sleeps with whom. Khus-phus, khus-phus all the time, in this one's house, in that one's house, khus-phus, khus-phus, no other work you got. For this your mother made you Padri? Eunuch! Motherfucker!'

Pauline's vocabulary ran out, and she aimed a kick at the cowering priest. He staggered and fell. Pauline took a deep breath as she towered over him, brandishing her bag of shopping. 'Think of what you did to her! You killed her! As good as if you pushed her off that cliff! You killed her! All the village kids ran after her shouting "Whore Whore!" Every morning somebody makes shit on her verandah, every evening children throw stones at her when she walks to the cliff. Who made them do that? Their parents or you? You! Take this from me! Take this from her! Take this from her son!' Pauline spat richly, thrice, splat on the priest's trembling and upturned face. Then, with a contemptuous shove of her foot against his jaw, she picked up her bag and stalked out.

I've put in my papers.
That's all for the best.
Everything's for the best.
I've told nobody.
That's for the best too.
We all have to do our duty.
She taught me that.
And we have to help the weak do their duty. I did.
They were all weak, and the old woman the weakest of them all.
So frail with her hair all fluffed up to a silver halo by the wind.
She looked like a saint.
That messed me up.
I lost my nerve.
I lost my wits.
So I had to make two trips.
I shouldn't have made two trips.
It was wise to put in my papers.
I shouldn't have made two trips.
She'll know about it.
She'll find out, she always knows when I've been clumsy.
It's better if I tell her myself.
If there is time.
If there is time.

Sister Abby

Sister Abby was checking out fares to Madagascar. The girl at the counter looked blankly at her as she nattered about vanilla forests and Aepyornis eggs. '... and of course it's mainly because of Ricky Martin,' she finished breathlessly, hoping she had the name right.

'What about Ricky Martin?' the girl asked suddenly.

Sister Abby sighed. The sphinx had spoken. The plastic tab on the girl's uniform said *Vivica*. Sister Abby noticed with pity that her eye shadow had caked into warty mauve clumps. 'Somebody sent me tickets, dear. The concert's on the 5th, and the ticket's so terribly expensive, I simply must go.'

'You've tickets for Ricky Martin Live?' Vivica's squeal left a flutter of curiosity in its wake. Customers at other counters were ignored. The airline staff, to a woman, had its eyes glued on Sister Abby. 'I do hope I qualify for the Seniors' Concession,' Sister Abby said worriedly. 'I'm just one month short of sixty-five.'

Vivica caught her neighbour's eye. 'Why don't you come into the office, madam. We'll see what we can do for you.'

Of such small change are miracles wrought, thought Sister Abby, fervently blessing the jactitating Mr Martin as she made her way round the glass cubicle.

'Actually, I was hoping to meet Marion,' Sister Abby began chattily as Vivica scanned her papers.

'Marion? Marion Aranxa? You know her?'

'I've been nursing her mother, you know.'

'Oh! Actually, that's why she isn't here. She's in Goa—went just for the weekend, actually, but couldn't make the eight o'clock flight. She'll be here at four. Forget it, I told her, just stay on till your mother wants you to. I'll cover.'

'That's sweet of you.'

'It isn't allowed, you know. They're very strict here. But her mother—it's serious, isn't it?'

'Very serious, I'm afraid. It's a noble act to risk something for a friend, dear ... Vivica, is it? What a lovely name!'

'Do you think so? My dad invented it. It's after that actress. You know, *Gone With the Wind*.'

'Ooooh. We were crazy about it when I was your age. I saw it five times.'

'Yeah? You won't believe this, but I've seen it ten times. It's that Clark Gable.'

'Such a charming rogue. It's always the wicked ones we fall for.'

'Yeah. Real devil, that one.'

'Umm. You look a bit like her.'

'Naah! You're kidding.'

'The eyes. The eyebrows. The eyes, mostly.'

'Her eyes are her best feature.'

'Of course your nose is like hers too, and you have the same heart-shaped face. But there the resemblance ends! You've got a kinder heart than Scarlett, covering for Marion like that.'

'I got caught once, you know. Last month it was, here it is on the roster, right here, the 12th, look, MA, 8-14 hours & 20.00 hrs. Two shifts she had that day. At 11 a.m. she phones me at home, her mother's taken bad and she has to rush, and can I cover. So of course I say yes, because the next shift's mine. I rush down here, she's already left by the 1 p.m. flight. I really didn't now what to do about the night shift, but she calls from Goa and says she'll be on the 6 p.m. flight, pukka. So here I am, from 11.30 am, waiting to be relieved, but no Marion on the 6 o'clock flight. No Marion on the 8 o'clock flight either. My Mummy's phoning, worried. Boyfriend's phoning, furious—you want to spend your whole life in office or what. No end to it! And that supervisor! Finally at 10 p.m. Marion comes. Indian Airlines she had to take, poor thing, didn't even go home to freshen up. Straight to the desk to relieve me. She's a very good person, Marion. Very nice to us younger girls though she's so senior and all, you know the story, I expect—'

'Keith?'

'Yeah! Handsome, really dreamy guy he was! We were all so thrilled for Marion, after waiting for so long, a really good catch. Rich. Crorepatis, his family are. Two-bedroom flat he bought in Marion's name when they got engaged. In Worli Sea Face, can you imagine?'

'Costs quite a bit.'

'Lovely diamond ring. They were to go to Switzerland for the honeymoon—and look what happened. I just can't understand that. The guy used to zoom around in a Toyota, what does he need to cross the railway tracks for? My, I'll never forget the day. Only a week after she got to know about her Ma and all.'

'Yes, that's what Marion told me, poor thing.'

'Yeah. In fact Marion had just told us that morning, she had to go early for lunch, to collect some special test results. Like a CAT scan, she said, only more, you know, special.'

'MRI?'

'That's it. I forgot you're a nurse. Ran all the way, poor thing, ricked it up and down, only to discover the results were so bad they asked for a repeat. Five thousand bucks gone down the drain, imagine. No wonder she came back so flustered. Hadn't eaten anything either. Why don't you grab a sandwich, I said—nice sandwiches they make in the canteen, chicken, Russian salad, really fresh. No, she says, I'm really tired, I'll just go freshen up. She comes back looking her old self. She's very good with make-up. You must have noticed. Must have looked glam when she was young. Wonder why she got left behind. Anyway, there she was, back at the desk when the phone rings and I pick it up. That's right. I took that call.'

'No!'

'Yeah! I was the one that took that call. Even the thought of it now makes me ice all over. I wasn't scared a bit, the police call often enough, flight timings, passenger lists, that sort of thing. But this time, I sensed right off it's different. The guy had a cultured voice, spoke in English and all, asks if Marion Aranxa is in. Just a moment, I say, but he interrupts and says are you her friend he says, just stay with her, I have bad news. By then I'm shaking all over, the mother is gone, I think, though why the police, I have no idea. It's different when they give it to you face to face, it's horrible on the phone. What's your name he says, I nearly told him, but got my sense back, luckily, just in time. Never give your name to the police, if you can help it. I give Marion the phone. The next thing I know she screams and drops the receiver. Then she picks it up and says, all trembling like, "Yes, I can give the address. Sabrina, 24, Charvi Road, Malad West." See, I remember every word, my memory is that clear. And she puts the phone down.

'"What's happened, Marion?" I rush to her with a glass of iced water. "What did the police want?" She speaks like a zombie, like a computer tape. "Keith's had an accident. Keith is dead."'

'Shock. She must've been shocked.'

'Totally. Like stone she became. Come on, I'm taking you home, I say. No, no, she starts pushing me away, I'll go on my own, don't worry. But I remembered how ill her Ma was, and this on top of everything else. So I just told the supervisor, and called a rick. She never wants to trouble people, Marion. Very independent nature. Short of throwing me out of the rick, you can't stop me, I say and jump in with her. At her place, I told the rick to wait, had to get back, hadn't I?

'Servant opens the door, Marion just pushes past her. Servant asks me with her eyes, kya hua? So I tell her, and she dashes after Marion leaving me there. I wait for sometime, then I call out I'm going, bye. Meter was running and all so I didn't stay.'

'Naturally. One doesn't like to intrude.'

'Exactly.'

'And then Marion's on leave for a week. We didn't visit because we didn't know where we ought to go, with her Ma being ill and all. They didn't invite anybody to the funeral. Keith was the only son. Huge property they have. Not that Marion cared for that.'

'Oh no. She isn't the worldly sort.'

'Exactly. Spiritual. That's the word. Now especially, since her Ma's so serious. It's tough on Marion.'

'Yes. Poor girl . . . Oh—what a pretty scarf you're wearing! I noticed because it's different from what the others have on. Black and gold. Very elegant. Goes with the navy uniform.'

'What a coincidence, me wearing it today and you telling me all about Marion. That scarf's a gift from Marion. It's genuine Dior.'

'Oooh!'

'Yeah. Look at the label. I didn't want to accept it because I knew Keith had bought it for her. But she insisted. And who can say no to Dior?'

'Who indeed!' agreed Sister Abby.

Dr B.K. Joshi, MD. Dip. Psych.

Dear Dr Liaqat Khan,

Thank you for your reference. As you know, it is difficult to assess a patient without actually meeting her. But as you have given a detailed history and findings, I am willing to hazard an opinion on the taped statement of the patient.

The catatonia you observed, I agree with you, was mainly a dissociative hysterical reaction. We could go with that, except that the tape betrays certain features suggestive, if not completely pathognomonic, of latent schizophrenia. A morbid narcissism seems to be the overwhelming personality trait. In the earlier part of the account, there is a definite flat affect. (I am presuming, of course, that the events are entirely delusional, or at least her role in bringing them about certainly is.) But to somebody who does not know the patient's physical condition, the flat affect in the earlier part of her statement may be mistaken for the cold-blooded callousness of a professed killer. Although she reports no 'voices', some of the conversation she conveys may be hallucinatory.

Her 'exalted' state, the 'state of grace', marks the onset of frank paranoia. The first bout, ending with the death of Dr Borges, brought on a catatonic episode. Its long duration (three weeks in the first instance) suggests an underlying psychosis. Its method of resolution, though, is more like that of a dissociative hysterical reaction.

Subsequent events are narrated in language that shows a rapid loss of inhibitory controls, a greater pressure to talk aloud, a higher degree of paranoia, all suggesting a full-blown psychosis.

In view of her neurological status, neuroleptics may not be advisable. Although the catharsis has been remarkable, I cannot say with any degree of certainty that it will have any bearing on the prognosis. I would suggest medicating her if there is an acute psychotic crisis like another catatonic episode.

You note that the patient's only request is that she be spared further attacks of catatonia. This makes me wonder if we should be less rigid about medicating her. Perhaps medication will be more compassionate. On the other hand, these sessions with a trained nurse appear to have afforded some relief. It would be wise to continue them.

But all my comments are merely educated guesses based on the tape and on your history. Were I to assess the patient independently, I might conclude differently.

Do let me know the follow-up on this interesting case. Thank you once again for sharing your case notes.

Regards,
B.K. Joshi

PS: That nurse seems quite a find! Let me know if she restricts herself to a known practice, or if her services are available. I am at present exploring cognitive behaviour therapy as the sole method of managing unresponsive schizophrenias. Your colleague sounds an ideal candidate for training in CBT.

Liaqat

The moment he read B.K. Joshi's letter through, Liaquat called Sister Abby. 'I'm on my way to Bandra now,' she said, 'I can come by your clinic if that's all right.'

She was there in twenty minutes. While he dispatched his last patient he gave her the letter to read, making her comfortable in an ante-room. His patient, with nothing worse than neuritis, was well into her usual litany of complaints. He heard her out with scarcely disguised impatience and bought his freedom with a prescription.

Then he called Sister in.

She sat down with an air of finality that told him she was about to make a statement. She tapped the letter. 'You agree with this?'

'Yes. I too think there are many features of a psychosis.'

'I don't think she's delusional.'

He laughed. 'You don't think she committed all those murders, do you?'

'They happened.'

'Her delusion may be built *after* the fact. For instance—'

'For instance, Justin's death. Justin drowned in that well. Clarice was with him that evening. That well had special meaning for Clarice.'

He was standing now, leaning across the table, his hand punctuating his words with hard knocks against the glass top. 'I'll match that. Justin drowned in that well. He was in a disturbed state of mind, having just learnt the truth about his parentage. That well had special significance for him too. And for his mother. Whom, incidentally, he had summoned to that very well.'

'Your facts are from Clarice's statement to you. You're discounting the tape. And even Clarice did not tell you that he had summoned his mother to the well. She merely said Justin had asked his mother to meet him at St Anne's.'

'I think she suppressed all her delusions, they made her catatonic. Then she let them all out on that tape.'

'She spoke the truth to begin with, and then, when she was certain nobody was listening, she came out with all these delusions? Perhaps. That could be possible.'

'It's more than possible. It's probable. In fact, it happened exactly that way.'

'Oh yes. The whole thing was delusional. Clive didn't drown in the well, Keith didn't get hit by a train, Justin didn't drown in that same old well and his mother got blown over the cliff on a perfectly calm day.'

An angry silence separated them.

Sister Abby rose to go. 'I'll keep a Xerox of this, if I may? There's a machine downstairs, I noticed. What news of Clarice?'

'She keeps asking for Sister Abby.'

'So soon?'

'Your fatal charm. She's going to need help with feeding very soon.'

'Nasogastric tube?'

'Maybe I could call a sister from Panjim if you don't want to make the trip?'

'Only if you don't want me to, Doctor.'

At the door she relented. Her eyes lost their steely glint. 'Give me a couple of days, Dr Liaqat. I have a few things to clear up here before I make a trip to Clarice. Meanwhile, try answering this: Why is it so important to you that Clarice should be delusional?'

Liaqat's Diary

Why is it so important to you that Clarice should be delusional, she said.

Is it?

Let me break that down.

If Clarice is not delusional, she is speaking the truth.

Since she believes her words are unheard (and unrecorded)—and necessary therapy to avoid another catatonic episode—she will not lie.

If she's speaking the truth, then, she is a murderer.

Enough! Just the thought makes me laugh! That frail 5'2", 40kg and dwindling woman—a murderer?!

If it were poisoning or any other sort of remote controlled killing, sure, she could have done it. But her 'murders' are physically strenuous acts.

She *pushed* her victims. Yes, she may have caught them off guard. But even considering she caught them off guard, could she have managed that push?

Let's leave Clive out of this—that was a Clarice I never knew. Let's leave out Keith, too. He wasn't pushed, exactly.

Which leaves just Justin and his mother. Could she have pushed *them*?

Just before she left for Goa, Clarice didn't have enough power in her shoulder muscles to pull the door shut behind her. I remember distinctly her vexed exclamation when she entered my room and couldn't get the door to shut.

No way could she have pushed a strong young man.

She couldn't have pushed Mrs Borges either, though the element of surprise cannot be discounted.

Final reckoning:

Clive's death: Undetermined.

Keith's death: Ditto.

Justin: Suicide/Accident.
Mrs Borges: Ditto.

And of course that's just the physical possibility. *I* could have pushed the lot of them with my little finger—but what for? Motive bhi koi cheez hoti hai ki nahin? All these people—except Mrs Borges who was a decided thorn in Clarice's dwindling flesh—all these were people she wanted in her life. They were family.

As for Mrs Borges—

Wait a moment. There's something I have to check on, something on that tape I remember. I've got to check that tape. Now. I don't give a damn if Naeem's irritating wife and incontinent brood are swarming the house—I'll announce I have the runs, pick up that tape and listen to it on the throne.

I was right! She's delusional. What she says is this: she went to the cliff for days and days, spending each of those evenings with Mrs Borges, till suddenly the world shut down on that last evening. She's trying to tell us that she pushed Mrs Borges and then turned catatonic.

But the time frame doesn't fit.

Xavier, Pauline, Marion, all swear that she made no more than three visits to the cliff. The flow of time in Clarice's imagination can be nothing but illusory.

I told Sister Abby on the phone, and she bit my head off! 'Of course I know the time frame's unreliable,' she snapped. 'So are many other things on that tape. She says Marion told her on the evening Justin died: "We'll go in the morning, Mamma. We'll take the car." What car? They don't have one. Plenty of discrepancies like that one. Marion's ring—Clarice says it was a sapphire surrounded by diamonds. Everyone else says it was just the one diamond. Things of that sort. That doesn't make her delusional.'

'Then you think it all happened as she said?'
'Did I say that?'
'You think she's lying?'
'Could be.'

What kind of low mind would think that?

I haven't been able to work out Sister Abby's mind. It seems made of some incredibly tensile metal that won't snap. Imagine not feeling compassion for a woman who is dying of a creeping paralysis—even without all the other tragedies that she has been forced to endure through life. Even I, a cold-blooded observer, am badly shaken. But Sister Abby hasn't turned a hair.

How can Clarice not retreat into a dream world where she can punish herself for suffering? Guilt and pain are strong moulding forces, and often interchangeable. To a controlled personality, the lack of personal happiness may seem a personal failure. Clarice blames herself for failing to control events.

I've discounted much of Pauline's chatter, I don't recollect it all now. I wish I did. Perhaps I can make sense of Clarice's words by recalling Pauline's. Pauline is Clarice's echo. They are the same age, one is the pampered darling, the other her slave—Pauline's resentment is only natural.

But a balance has been struck. Clarice is dying. Pauline must do her living for her. Pauline must be her hands, her legs, her eyes and ears. And if the events in the tape are true, wouldn't Pauline have been Clarice's voice too?

Liaqat

Playing tennis at the Gym meant waking up at five, a luxury Liaqat could do without. The initial high of post-exercise endorphins never lasted beyond breakfast, and mid morning found him grumpy and maddened by the least intrusion. It didn't take long for Sharifa to rule that tennis was bad for his health.

But she was beginning to wonder.

A week of considering B.K. Joshi's letter had taken Liaqat no closer to understanding Clarice. 'There's nothing left to understand,' Sharifa said patiently, 'there's nobody left to die.'

'Clarice is just one of those secrets we must learn to live with,' Sister Abby told him. 'At least till she pulls one more rabbit out of her hat.'

There wouldn't be time for more rabbits, Liaqat reflected. He'd give her a few months more, a year at most. But who could tell?

Perera had phoned once to ask if all was well, whatever that meant. Liaqat had the uncomfortable feeling that he had called to check the body count.

With three of the four people in the know turning their thumbs down on Clarice, Liaqat felt an urgent need for an ally. He called B.K. Joshi. BK was clearly nervous about having committed a written opinion on a patient he hadn't seen. Could there be a remote possibility that Clarice was not delusional, Liaqat asked. This threw BK into a panic. 'I hope you won't quote me,' he said. 'If there is any legal complication, please don't quote me.'

'Nobody knows the contents of the tapes besides you and me,' Liaqat lied glibly.

'Medicate, medicate,' urged BK. 'The less you have to do with her the better. Just get her peaceful. Don't wake up too many ghosts.'

Too many ghosts.

They clamoured for attention every time he tried to shut his eyes. He fell asleep towards dawn, if the wasteland of dread he toppled into could be called sleep. Most days he had to be woken at seven and sat staring at his cooling coffee for the next half hour, the paper unread on his lap.

These, and other factors, made Sharifa revise her opinion. Tennis, she said, might just be what was good for his health.

Liaqat set the alarm for five but he was awake at half past four. He left the house ten minutes later, racquet in hand, with absolutely no intention of playing. The slatey sky had the chill brittleness of glass, a pane misted over with cloud, beyond which a brighter room beckoned in thin spatters of light. The air cleansed him like water.

It was a long time since he'd been out this early.

Half a lifetime ago, the small hours had been filled with electric zeal. His years as a resident had been his happiest, and most solitary. He grew to enjoy the ward at night and often strolled in after midnight. The house physician would be long gone, the staff nurse asleep over the drugs register, obligatory cardigan over her shoulders. A student nurse padded noiselessly, checking vitals. The wardboy snored on a trolley. Liaqat would step through all this into the ward. Bathed in the blue glow of nightlight, the cots had a complicated geography—peaks, hillocks, tablelands rising-subsiding as if he stood witness to a seismic orogeny. Hours ago there was a noisy clamour of life, more life. Rogue hearts on autopilot, thudding downhill to doom. Squeaking lungs scavenging stray molecules of oxygen. They were all gagged now. Rocked or shattered, helpless in the hypnosis of dark. All the endeavour of day was diminished beside this greater force, all his science trivialized. For Liaqat, these were moments of understanding, though if asked what he understood, he would have found it impossible to say.

He missed those hours now. He realized his need to talk the night through with Sharifa was an attempt to reclaim that earlier epiphany. It never happened. He did not allow it to happen. He no longer drove himself so close to the edge of things.

He could now. Clarice had driven him to this, close, closer still to the glittering edge of things. The abyss roared up at him, urging him to that hypnotic moment when he would stare into it, past the prismatic distractions of pain. He would come to it, no matter what it caused in him.

He lad lingered longer than he meant to. It was half past five when he reached the court. The floodlit concrete was horrific in the wet dawn, like a cinematic frame of Auschwitz or Belsen, *Schindler's List* for sure, black and carnal, death silvered over with ash.

His quarry was on the court, playing as usual, a wimpy game. Liaqat liked Suresh Kher because he misled people, not deliberately, but because he was like that—a man of uncertainties. There was a shimmer to him as if it wasn't really him there but a hologram, his more solid self locked away for security.

He caught Liaqat's eye and nodded, allowed himself to be trounced off the court, and hurried up after exchanging a word with his partner.

'Too sleepy to play, yaar. How are you? Where have you been?' He led Liaqat away into the shadowy enclave. 'Hate these early morning sessions. Man my age should wake up to a walk and a cup of tea, not this slam bang thank you sir. Every morning this guy fucks me.'

'You let him,' Liaqat smiled.

'Yeah, sure, I let him. Makes his day. So you want to play now?'

'No.'

'I thought not. Don't sit, the chairs are all damp with dew. Want to walk?'

They strolled out on the deserted promenade, Liaqat taming his brisk stride to match Kher's. The sea lashed its plumy tail lazily. 'You're here about Perera? Reliable man, nothing to worry about,' Kher said.

'Not about Perera, exactly. I'm not worried about him. He's told you about this patient of mine?'

'Mrs Sanchez.'

'Mrs Aranxa.'

'Sure, same thing. Cancer patient.'

'Neurological disease, ALS, motor neuron disease. The muscles gradually get paralysed.'

'Polio.'

'No, not polio. Never mind that. Recently, she showed changes of behaviour. Became withdrawn, catatonic—'

'Brain cancer? Cat scan is done for brain cancer.'

'—completely shut off from her surroundings. There have been two such episodes. Thinking that a catharsis might help, I—'

'Listen, Liaqat. Use simple language. I am listening, yaar, with complete attention, but I can't make out one word of what you say. Look, let me recap: This Mrs Sanchez, suffering from polio and brain cancer had a Cat scan. Fine, so far. What's next?'

Liaqat grinned. This would last another minute or so, then the guy would start ticking. It had taken him a long time discovering that.

'No, let *me* recap. This Mrs Aranxa who has a rare nervous disease becomes like a statue from time to time. Blind, deaf, dumb, paralysed. This is not part of her disease. It is seen in people who are reacting to trauma. So I ask myself—what is her trauma?'

'You ask what is her trauma? Husband dead, son-in-law dead, doctor dead, doctor's mother dead, and you ask what is her trauma? How much more trauma do you think a human being can stand?'

'So you know all about it.'

'Sure I know all about it.'

'I thought you said Perera was reliable.'

'Hundred per cent. He told me everything, didn't he?'

Liaqat gave up and laughed. Suresh grinned uneasily and said, 'Don't take it badly, Liaqat. Tell me, what does the psychiatrist say?'

'So Perera left that out? The verdict is psychosis. Mental, as Perera calls it.'

'Schizo?'

'May not be. Maybe just the reaction to trauma. B.K. Joshi feels she's built up these delusions following the trauma of the actual event.'

'And the actual events were what? Accident? Suicide?'

'Whatever. That's not our problem.'

'I can't believe what I'm hearing! That's not your problem? Woman says she's killed so many people, and that's not your problem? You might be next on the list.'

Liaqat laughed. 'This is like a telephone diagnosis. Always faulty. Because you haven't seen the patient, your diagnosis is based on the *patient's* judgement, not yours. You're overlooking the one fact I know—Clarice is too weak to move easily round the house. Even when Justin died, she lacked the strength to have pushed him, to have taken that walk from the church to the well. I'm taking for granted Perera gave you the tapes—she describes all that. But she simply didn't have the muscle power for any of it.'

'And yet, under special circumstances, people have been known to commit acts requiring extraordinary strength.'

'Multiple murders from a wheelchair? You wouldn't suggest it if you saw this lady.'

'So you agree with the shrink. Then why are you here?'

'Perera advised me to play tennis.'

'Liaqat, in matters like this, let me tell you what we do. We check the files on these deaths, to make sure we haven't missed anything. The slightest suggestion of foul play is followed up. Meanwhile, we check out the people in the story, motive, opportunity, alibi ... you know the way it goes. After all that, if we find nothing, we keep an open mind till—'

'Exactly. Till what? That's what I came here to find out. The shrink feels Clarice's fantasies shouldn't be given free rein. Medicate her, he says. Clarice wants to be free of her catatonia. I want to respect that wish. She hasn't long to live. During this short time left to her, she must be sane, in touch with reality. If her spells of catatonia are an escape from her truth, then she must confront the truth. But in her own way. I don't want to dope her.'

'What if more people die?'

'You're not serious!'

'No, just a hypothesis. What if there is one more death? Will she become catatonic again?'

'How can I say? From the pattern, it does look as if she might.'

'Then we must ensure there are no more deaths.'

'What the hell is that supposed to mean?' Liaqat demanded angrily. 'Don't play God, Suresh.'

'Wish I could. No, I don't know what I meant. Except that if I were you, I'd keep listening to Clarice. I wouldn't dope her either, though not for the same reasons as you. Let me know if you come up against anything that worries you. Take my mobile number, call at once, don't hesitate even if your worry seems trivial.'

'You don't usually do this. You're taking this seriously.'

'Very, very seriously. Is that nurse likely to see her again?'

'Yes, she'll have to soon. Clarice is going to need a feeding tube, she isn't able to swallow too well.'

'Horrible! Poor thing. Send Perera.'

'What? Instead of Sister?'

'Now who's being dumb? *With* Sister.'

'No.'

'Just like that? No?'

'Can't afford it.'

'We'll see about that. Could be police business, you know. I'll deal with Perera.'

Liaqat walked home dissatisfied. The day had begun badly. It looked as though the world was eager to take up arms against Clarice, no matter where he turned.

It was seven thirty. Sharifa was in a whirl, getting the day to rights before she left for work. He got breakfast, packed her lunch and helped finish chores. She left at eight, and he had a clear hour to himself before he left on his rounds. He made himself a cup of coffee and sat down to think.

There's very little time left. I knew that the moment she saw me. I shall have to wait till I know it's time.
There's very little time left, but I've done almost everything. There was very little to do.
Is that because I have always been orderly and well organized? Or is it simply because there is very little to take care of?
Questions. I shouldn't ask any more questions.
I hope it doesn't take too long.
I hope I know soon.
I haven't bought any groceries for the month.
I paid the milkman off too.
I hope I know before the toothpaste gets over, it will be such a waste to open a new one.
The phone bill's paid. If the electricity bill comes in soon, that'll be tied up too.
What is soon?
It could be tomorrow. Or tonight.
The phone could ring now.
I wonder if I'll get a day to get ready.
Better not ask.
It'll just cause an upset.
I am expected to be ready.
I have had enough warning, I should be ready.
I am ready.
I won't leave the house in case the phone rings.
If I say I'm sorry I was out, I missed your call, it will just cause an upset.
I'm always sorry.
I've been sorry as far back as I can remember.
I don't want to be sorry till the phone rings, when it rings, or after that.
I don't want to be sorry anymore.

Liaqat's Diary

I've been on edge all day, unable to concentrate. I was late for my rounds, perfunctory with patients. When Sharifa called I was short with her. When I get home this evening, I'm going to walk straight into a quarrel.

This torment will last till I know the truth.

I've spent the afternoon listening to the tapes again. Clarice speaks the truth every time.

There are no absolutes. There's nothing like absolute truth. Truth is what one perceives. Ask Clarice. Isn't that what she's been saying all along on that tape? This truth is for Dr Khan. This truth is for Sister Domenica. This is the truth for Pauline, and this the truth for Marion. All wrapped and labelled like Christmas presents, different brands of *truth*.

Perhaps I'm being too literal. Accounts vary—with the audience. Consider this example. I'm uncomfortable. If Gracie notices and asks what's bothering me, I say I have a headache. But if Gracie left the room and Perera were to ask me that question I'd say I need to find a bathroom. If Sharifa were to ask me that question I'd say I've been flatulent all morning and in agony lest I fart in public and why the fuck are you feeding me chana dal anyway?

Poor analogy. That tape is not a recital of body functions or social embarrassments. It is the story of her life.

All the more reason to believe it's the truth. What else can a dying woman speak but the truth?

If the tape's a lie, look at what those lies accomplish. Those lies make Clarice guilty of every possible crime. Doesn't that suggest a pathological self-loathing? Isn't that one of the prime features of any psychosis?

Which is it to be, then? Is Clarice's story the truth, or a lie?

Liaqat

Liaqat was surprised to hear from Suresh Kher a little after midnight. He had just returned from Baga, he said. Some official work had taken him to Panjim, and finding he still had a couple of hours on his hands before the evening flight back, he had made the detour.

The Goa police was quite satisfied with the verdict of suicide. Runs in the family, Inspector Rozario said. The nuns of St Anne's had given him an incredible story of Pauline assaulting a priest. Then he had met Pauline herself, rambling on about the Aranxas. There was a lot he had seen and heard, so much of it utter rubbish. He'd visited Mrs Borges's sad little house, boarded and locked now. Somebody had drawn a crucifix on the door. Somebody else, probably, had chalked 'WHORE'. Then the long hours at Panjim checking lists, timetables, without quite knowing what he should be looking for.

An idea, he said, had been growing in his mind all the way back from Baga, some scrap of information floated just beyond his memory's grasp. A name? A place? It buzzed in his skull like a trapped gnat. Could he come over early tomorrow?

Suresh Kher turned up at seven. He set Sharifa's anxiety at rest with some inane banter. He read the paper while Liaqat got breakfast and waved Sharifa off to the station.

Liaqat brought his tape recorder to the breakfast table, and made fresh coffee as Clarice began to speak.

At noon they were still hard at it. They had gone over Clarice's statement line by line. Mad as a bat, thought Liaqat. And yet—

'This Clarice must have a lot of power,' Kher said slowly. 'Justin seems to have fallen for her. Pauline will do absolutely anything she says, and the daughter seems a total doormat.'

'Suresh, Clarice is a pathetic creature, half paralysed, soon to stop breathing, about to die.'

'She certainly has a high-funda way of talking. Like an actress or something. This truth is for Justin, this truth is for Marion, this truth is for Pauline . . .'

'You're making a mistake. All those versions of truth, all of them, Suresh, are meant for me.'

'Why? Besides, she doesn't know you're listening.'

'No, but I'm the one she's talking to, just the same. Like Dear Diary. It's called transference. And as to why she has so many versions—why does someone say the same thing over and over again?'

'To be heard?'

'Not unless they're remarkably stupid. If they're not heard the first time, it's unlikely they'll be heard the third or fourth time.'

'Why then?'

'To convince themselves. Auto-hypnosis.'

'And what is Clarice trying to convince herself of? She's saying—I did it, I did it, I did it . . . She's taking on guilt? Or confessing? One or the other. If she's the killer, she's confessing. If she's taking on the burden of guilt—why should she? Anyway, who'd believe her?' Suresh tapped the tape recorder thoughtfully and answered his own question: 'Nobody. Nobody will believe she killed Mrs Borges, as we all know she was a prisoner of catatonia when the death occurred. Nobody can believe, either, that she pushed a strong young man into the well after walking half a mile on paralysed legs. And that's the whole point of her confession. Nobody will believe it. Clarice can confess because nobody can possibly believe she committed these murders. Confession makes her safe. Confession absolves her.'

'What's there to absolve, if she's committed no crime?' Liaqat broke in irritably. 'I don't see why you use the term 'murder'. There's nothing to tell us Justin and his mother did not commit suicide.'

'You must realize, Liaqat, Clarice is a very moral woman.'

'At least we agree on that,' Liaqat's scowl relaxed. He looked around uneasily.

He took a deep draught of coffee. 'What if . . . No, forget it.'

'Go on.'

'What if she were afraid she'd done all the things she reports on that tape. What if, in a state of fugue or hypnosis, she did all those things?'

'Tell me, will a person like Clarice, weak and almost paralysed, show increased muscular strength, better coordination, more endurance in a state of fugue or hypnosis?'

'I don't know. I don't think so.'

'Maybe she's got multiple personalities!' Kher broke in excitedly. 'Clarice 1, Clarice 2, that sort of thing?'

'NO! That's not how a Multiple Personality Disorder presents,' Liaqat said. 'Clarice retains a very strong sense of her identity throughout those tapes. Her opinions are the same, her point of view unchanged.'

'Clarice is very persuasive,' Suresh said slowly. 'So—whom will Clarice persuade? She persuaded you, for one.'

Liaqat said: 'Not true. I didn't buy into her story of murder. I am unpersuaded of her crimes. I reject them as delusions. I do not participate in her mind.'

Suresh Kher nodded. 'You're thinking very clearly, Liaqat. You were not persuaded. But perhaps somebody else was.'

Liaqat was furious. '*Whom* could she possibly have persuaded, for Godssake! Who would commit *murder* at her command?'

Suresh Kher shrugged. 'There's only one way we can find out. We can ask her.'

Liaqat felt himself turning cold. Every moment took him further away from his principles as a physician.

'I don't propose to interrogate her, Liaqat,' Suresh smiled. 'She's likely to tell us. She wants us to know. This is Clarice's story, and we must wait till she's ready to tell it. Let's hope by then it's not too late.'

Marion called soon after Suresh Kher left. She wanted to know when Sister Abby could go to Baga. Pauline had called this morning to say Clarice was refusing food. Should she book Sister Abby on the seven o'clock flight? Yes, Liaqat said, without thinking. If he couldn't locate Sister Abby, he'd go himself.

He did get Sister Abby, though. She was a little huffy at having to leave that very evening, but agreed. 'And what about Perera, Doctor?' she asked. 'Is this to be with or without?'

'I'll get back to you, Sister. I'll pick you up at five o'clock and we'll talk on the way to the airport.'

He skipped lunch and went in search of Perera.

'He's taking the bus,' Liaqat told Sister Abby as they drove to the airport. 'She may be too dehydrated. It might be best to hydrate her intravenously first. I've packed IV fluids and the drugs you're likely to need. You could pass the tube once she's more comfortable.'

'And if she wants to talk, to have one more session, what should I do?'

'You have your crucifix. Perera will have set up shop by 6 a.m. tomorrow, though personally I think it's a waste of time and money.'

'You still think she's psychotic, Doctor?'

'Why would I change my opinion, Sister? Let me see what you think this time. See if your earlier sessions have improved her; once she's fed and hydrated, you can judge that. If she's better, more together, our job's done.'

'My job's done, Doctor,' Sister Abby corrected him gently. 'I'm afraid all this has only made your burden heavier.'

Liaqat had expected Marion to meet them at the airport, but she'd left the ticket for Sister Abby at the airline counter, where, to Liaqat's surprise, Sister Abby was greeted like an old friend. 'I'll get back to you next week to confirm,' Sister Abby sang out gaily as she waved to a girl inside the glass cubicle.

'They seem to know you here,' he remarked.

'Oh because of my trip to Madagascar!'

'And when is that?'

Sister Abby laughed. 'What would I do in Madagascar! No, I spent an hour chatting up those girls. I miss my students, you know.'

Like most men his age, Liaqat had a deep distrust of computers. When he wanted information, he made a trip to the library. Sharifa was just the opposite, and they had agreed to disagree till very recently: Liaqat had been impressed by how quick and sure the Net was in getting Sharifa the details on Walter.

It was five-thirty. He called the clinic and told Gracie he was taking the day off. He got himself a glass of water, and putting Sharifa's sceptic smile out of his mind, he switched on the computer. As the screen lit up, his fingers moved automatically, his thoughts far away from the blue flicker. Damn. VSNL again. He was twenty minutes getting that connection. He typed in a Google search, hoping he had the spelling right. He remembered a glimmer from all the unnecessary thrilling reading he had done as a resident. Bloody French, what do you know.

There!

Induced Psychotic Disorder, infectious insanity, psychic infection, contagious insanity, collective insanity, double insanity, epacti psychosis, dyadic psychosis, influenced psychosis, mystic paranoia, induced psychosis, associational psychosis. Lasègue-Falret syndrome—

There it was.

A shared madness. *Folie a deux.*

Yesterday the words would have read as gibberish. Today they clanged and clamoured within the echoing dome of his skull. *A pathological relationship in which the dominant party strives to maintain a link with reality while the other fulfils dependency needs.*

Whom did Clarice depend on? Who was the closest to her in thought and action? Who did what Clarice could no longer do? Who was her legs and hands, her ears and eyes? Who was her shadow?

Dismissing the thought, he read further. Case histories, first person accounts, reviews, analyses. *Two minds but with a single thought* took on menace as he read about *folie a deux* cited as an explanation for partners in crime.

There were dozens. The British serial killers, Ian Brady and Myra Hindley, Frank and Rose West. Karla Homolka, petite, soignée, colluding with her husband Paul Bernardo to rape, torture and murder young women, among them her own sister. And most revolting of all, the 1954 story of teenagers Pauline Parker and Juliet Hulme who battered to death Pauline's mother because she disapproved of their friendship. In recent years, judging by the spate of 'studies' cited, the case had become a cause celebre for the gay and lesbian movement. The ugly connect made during the trial between homosexuality and crime led to a backlash of suspicion and hate in New Zealand in the late fifties. The innocent were scarred, winkled out of their quietly decent lives, held up to public disdain. The story distressed Liaqat. The perpetrators, after five years in jail, had gone on to lead new lives—one of them becoming a bestselling writer of crime stories. They became heroes of a sort.

Brutish, insensate, subhuman. How could people like these be compared with Clarice? It was all a load of rubbish. Myra Hindley's repeated claims that she had been 'persuaded' by her boyfriend into participating in crimes sounded more like a mitigation than a psychological truth.

He read further: *Symbiotic psychoses (induced delusions) are marked by 'solitude by twos'—together in alienation to the environment. This may lead up to symbiotic suicides. The pre-suicidal symbiotism of two cases is described ...*

Damn! The rest of the paper was in German.

What if Clarice, innocent in her delusions, had led her doppelganger into acting out her fantasies? Ridiculous!

Clarice would be better for medication. Liaqat had reached that conclusion when Sharifa returned. He switched off the computer hurriedly. Time enough to go back to all that later. Right now, he wanted a more domestic brand of *folie a deux*.

Sister Abby

'Clarice, try and swallow, please.'

Clarice's eyes, terrified, dilated, singed Sister Abby's cheek with their heat as she bent over her. The soft tube slid smoothly down Clarice's parched and slackly stirring throat. Its free end swung ignominiously out of one nostril. Sister Abby taped it down securely. 'There. That wasn't too bad, was it, Clarice?'

Clarice's hands eased their grip on Sister Abby's dress. The eyelids relaxed. The parched lips made a flutter of soundless movement.

Sister Abby took a glass of iced water from Pauline and let it flow slowly down the tube. She touched Clarice's lips with an ice cube. Clarice tried to suck at it, but her lips slipped away. She found Sister Abby's free hand and tried to clasp it, but the fingers would not curl. Her eyes bristled with messages.

'Morning she was okay,' Pauline said stolidly. 'Speaking and all. One egg I make, soft-boiled, no use. But yack yack yack on the phone to Marion.'

'Oh, that's nice you got to talk to Marion, Clarice. You're weak because you've been thirsty a long while, and your body has lost all its water. We'll have to get your strength up by giving you food and water through the tube, and you should soon feel better.'

'C-ccc—'

Sister Abby bent closer. 'Cool.'

'Ah, stomach is feeling cool now we put water,' Pauline said eagerly, 'that right no, Missy?'

Clarice's hand sought Pauline now. Pauline dropped the towel and sank on her knees, sobbing.

Sister Abby had been shocked by Clarice's appearance when she arrived at Bougainvillea House. She had been met at the airport by Xavier's taxi, and on the way, Xavier had expressed his conviction that Clarice was about to die. Sister Abby had booked a room at the Palm d'Or, guessing she might have to stay on for a couple of days—for her own sake, if not Clarice's. She had meant to talk to Clarice, persuade her to agree to a feeding tube, and do the procedure itself next morning.

But what she found changed all that. Clarice was a husk of her former self, emaciated beyond recognition. This was not the attrition of disease, but the attrition of neglect. Very soon Pauline spoke her apologia. 'Missy drink water? No. Missy eat something? No. Full-full tray she sends back. Try, Missy, I tell her, please try. No. Stubborn she become. Stubborn.'

'Soup? Blancmange? Custard?'

Pauline looked stupidly at Sister Abby. 'Sweet things bad for health, no? Toast I make for her, hot-hot.'

Sister Abby lost it. She glared at Pauline. Clarice's eyes intercepted that glare. Clarice shook her head. At that moment, Sister Abby understood the loyalties of Liaqat Khan.

She pulled up a chair and began to talk to Clarice in a low voice. Quickly, she completed her examination: the blood pressure was low, but the heartbeat was strong. There was a strong ketotic taint in the breath. The eyeballs were sunken from dehydration. Despite all this, the kidneys were hard at work: Pauline held up a small dark puddle in the bed pan with pride.

Sister Abby had seen too many starvation deaths not to know what was happening with Clarice. As she went about her work, she pondered the cruelties of forced intimacy. She understood exactly what had happened. As Clarice's swallowing became weaker, Pauline's menus became harder to swallow. There would be no other sort of neglect. Clarice's body was clean, well cared for, her clothes as dainty as she herself would have wished. And Pauline, that gifted cook, feasting alpha males on prawn balchao and stuffed pomfret, used to tempting children with puddings, jellies, custards, Pauline the chef, now made toast.

Well, she was crying now, tears of contrition, probably, head nestling in the slack embrace of Clarice's tired arm.

Sister Abby left the room. For the next hour she made notes and busied herself teaching Pauline how to feed Clarice. Now was the time to praise—with more than a hint of menace—the skills of a woman she would simply have to trust. The truth was, without Pauline, Clarice would die. Sister Abby believed cruelty was a universal trait. Perhaps Pauline had no more than the usual share of it.

At the end of the hour, Pauline had melted completely. She told Sister Abby about her savings in Clarice's safe. 'If I tell Marion afterwards, she will not believe, but how I can tell her now?'

'I'll tell her, Pauline,' Sister Abby said. 'I must talk to her anyway about her mother's condition.'

'She'll die soon, Sister?'

'I don't think so, Pauline. Once we start feeding her, she's bound to get stronger. But she's not going to last very long.'

'She phoned Marion. Very weak, but very clear. Before that she's telling me not to tell Marion about you coming and all. She's telling Marion she got sore throat, so voice is becoming bad. Then she says, Do your duty, Marion, stay there, do your duty. Then she tell me how much leave Marion is taking, too much, so only call her if something happen. Otherwise they will cut her pay. What Marion will do if they fire her? Too old for another job. Marion must keep her job, Missy tell me, must must. Because of me too much expense is becoming.'

'Shall I call Marion now, Clarice?' Sister Abby asked.

'No.' A whisper, but the lips made it this time. 'Not yet.'

'Tomorrow, then.'

'No. One more day. Wait.'

'Sleep well, Clarice. I'll see you in the morning.'

'No!' Clarice grew agitated. She pulled herself up on the pillows. 'Don't go. Please.'

So Sister Abby stayed. Clarice slept fitfully as water trickled into her. At midnight Clarice woke again. Sister Abby was amazed once more by the resilience of the human body: worn out, battered, wasted, paralysed, but the will to live made all that inconsequential. Clarice's blood pressure had risen to 100/60. Good.

Sister Abby called Liaqat at a little after midnight, and they discussed Clarice's treatment. 'Should do, Sister, without a drip, I think. It's mostly hunger. Lots of sugar in the fruit juice, and milk as soon as we can. We'll reassess in the morning. Kidneys are fine, you say?'

'Yes, Doctor, but I do think you should speak with the daughter. Clarice has absolutely forbidden me to phone Marion. What should we do?'

'If you think she's improving, we'll wait till morning. I'll call her myself, Sister.'

Clarice drowsed and muttered restlessly in her sleep. By dawn her blood pressure was satisfactory. She woke and mouthed a few words noiselessly, before drifting off again.

'Get some rest, Sister,' Liaqat said when she called him at eight, 'you're doing a great job. Just don't overtire yourself. She's going to sleep most of the day, so if the Palm d'Or will allow you some silence, get a nap. I'll call Marion later.'

As Sister Abby walked towards the hotel, she caught sight of Perera. He raised a solemn hand in greeting and looked away.

When she returned late in the afternoon, Clarice was still asleep. Her colour was better, her blood pressure and pulse normal, her breathing more peaceful. Sister Abby spent the next hour or two with Pauline, teaching her how to plan and process meals for tube feeding. 'Let's see if she can swallow some custard when she wakes. If she can, it's a good idea to give as much of mushy food as we can by mouth and give her fluids, water, juices, milk, by tube,' she explained.

Pauline remarked it strange that Missy could not swallow water and rice, but all fancy things seemed to slip in easily. Just her way, she told Sister Abby. All natak. They spoke in low voices in the kitchen while Clarice slept. Pauline told her about Justin and Arula. Sister Abby remembered to look shocked.

Clarice asked for the phone at eight o'clock. Pauline returned to the kitchen muttering that Missy could hardly talk, nobody would believe it was a sore throat, not even Marion, who believed everything her Mamma said. Clarice didn't speak for long. When Pauline went in again, she was fast asleep. Like a baby, Pauline said, so soft, so innocent, 'like first time Mr Clive bring her, so young.'

A little after midnight Clarice woke and asked for food. Pauline spooned soft-boiled egg which she swallowed successfully.

Pauline went back to the kitchen. A while later, Sister Abby rose to go. Clarice held up a hand imperiously, stopping Sister Abby from leaving the room.

'Listen.'

Her voice had a nasal twang because of the tube, but she seemed to have no trouble enunciating her words.

'I spoke to Marion today,' she said with great deliberation. 'Marion. My daughter. You have met her, Sister.'

'Yes, Clarice.'

'Marion has done her duty to me.'

'She's a loving daughter, Clarice.'

'No time for all that politeness now. Listen to me, Sister. Listen.'

'I'm listening, Clarice.'

'Marion has done her duty to me. It is not her fault if she failed me. You understand? She always tried. She always failed.'

'But she has done her duty to you.'

'Yes. She—has—done—her—duty—to—me. Do you understand, Sister?'

In the long silence that followed, Clarice's voice rose an octave.

'Do you understand? Sister?'

'Yes.' Sister Abby's voice was that of a stranger. 'Yes, Clarice, I understand you.'

'She has done her duty to me. Now she must do her duty to herself. I spoke to Marion yesterday. Do your duty, I told her. Stay there and do your duty. Don't come here. Have some consideration for my condition. I spoke to her today again. I told her not to come here. Stay there and do your duty today. Today. I said: Do your duty today. You heard that, Sister?'

'I heard that, Clarice.'

'Good. Now leave me alone. Go!'

Sister Abby left the room. She hesitated as she passed the kitchen, but Pauline was fast asleep at the table, her head pillowed on her arm. A room had been prepared for Sister Abby, but she didn't go there immediately. She squinted worriedly at her watch, then decisively reached for the telephone.

Liaqat

Strange animals cavorted across burning sands. Liaqat could name a wombat and a wallaby. The rest were nameless. Lizard-like, but winged, they rushed up and down like extras on the sets of *Jurassic Park.* Two girls ran shrieking after them, turning now and then to shake their blood-spattered skirts at Liaqat. He was in a park, grassy, unkempt with bramble and weed, stumbling as his foot struck something soft and warm and wet. The girls shrieked, over and over again in strident bell-like notes.

The telephone shrilled.

'Dr Liaqat? I'm so sorry to bother you this late. Really, I have no business calling you, but I'm so uneasy, Doctor.'

'What is it, Sister Abby?'

'Clarice woke up a little while ago and said the strangest thing, over and over again. I have no idea what she meant. She said she had spoken with Marion and told her to do her duty. To do her duty today. She repeated it with such distinctness, Doctor, it's quite scared me. Did you speak with Marion today?'

'I called, but she wasn't at home. I don't know what Clarice means, perhaps she's—'

'No, she isn't wandering, Doctor. She's as clear as a well person. You're right, though, it's probably nothing. Shouldn't have called—'

'No, Sister, I'm glad you did. Let me see if I can get Marion in the morning. Don't worry too much.'

When he put the phone down, Liaqat was surprised to feel his heart hammering. He was getting really jumpy about Clarice. But so, apparently, was Sister Abby. He wondered briefly if Sister Abby were frightened of being alone with Clarice.

Alone with Clarice and—

Good God, he should have seen it before!

Mouth dry, he shot out of bed and rummaged through his

desk till he found his diary. There it was. He dialled rapidly. Pick up, pick up, he willed, pick up, damn you—

At the fifth ring, Suresh Kher said sleepily, 'Hello ...'

'Sister Abby,' Liaqat babbled, 'she's—she's alone there with the two of them. What have I done, Suresh, it should have struck me earlier!'

'Hey, take it easy man, tell me slowly.'

Liaqat forced his voice to slow down. With awful distinctness he conveyed to Suresh Kher that Sister Abby might be in some danger.

'Perera's there, he's on the scene, Liaqat. She'll be safe. I'll call Perera right away. But what got you scared?'

'Sister sounded scared,' Liaquat said slowly. 'Yes, that's it, that's why I lost it. She sounded so bloody terrified.'

'What did she say?'

Liaqat recounted the conversation.

'And have you called Marion?' Kher asked sharply. 'Now? Have you called her now?'

'No. I called you.'

'Okay. Call her right away, call me back.' He hung up.

Liaqat found Marion's number and dialled. The phone shrilled on and on tirelessly, without answer.

He called Kher. 'No answer.'

'I'll be downstairs in five minutes. Be ready.'

Liaqat bumbled to the bathroom. Be ready for what? What did Kher mean to do? How could he be so certain Perera would guard Sister Abby? And from what?

He moved slowly in a fog of questions, then hurried, and just as the jeep braked at the building he emerged at a run, shirt still flapping unbuttoned. He jumped in and the jeep shot forward. There were two constables in the back.

'What's happening?'

'Let's call on Marion.'

'And what happens if Marion opens the door and demands why we're disturbing the peace?'

'I don't get sued if you can think up a good excuse.'

Liaqat was surprised by his own resentment. Suddenly, all he wanted was to be back in bed.

They parked at the end of the street.

The four of them walked in silence. Liaqat almost missed the place in the unfamiliar dark. Ground-floor flat, on the left as you enter, he reminded himself.

Kher rang the doorbell.

They waited.

No response.

Again.

Silence.

At a nod from Kher, one of the constables stepped forward and bent over the keyhole. The door swung open with a faint click. They stepped into the living room. The constables stayed back at the door.

The house had been brightly lit the last time he was here—the first time, too, Liaqat corrected himself. Now the house was wrapped in sleep, and his every step was a violation.

This was her bedroom.

Somewhere in his skull Sharifa's voice whispered: *You idiot, Liaqat. You only needed this. The woman is asleep and any moment now she's going to open her eyes and find you and yell rape. You only needed this.*

Shut up, Liaqat said sternly, shut the fuck up.

Kher's hand clamped over his mouth.

Liaqat groped the wall for a switchboard. Again, Kher restrained him. Kher stood absolutely still.

The white expanse of the bed was dappled with deep night shadows. A thin watery gleam of street light came in through the window. The lace curtains stirred uneasily. Liaqat took all this in before he could look at the centre of the bed. Suresh Kher blocked his view.

Then the lights blazed, and he saw.

The first thing he saw was his right foot. He had blinked reflexively, and in opening his eyes, looked down. The first thing he saw was his right foot in an unfamilar shoe. It was not the soft brown corduroy slip-on, shabby with wear. This one was something jazzy, a splash of colour growing across the toes. A red splash. He was standing in a pool of blood.

It was spreading slowly, fed by a thread of crimson that swung endlessly down the side of the bed.

Suresh Kher's hand on his elbow urged him forward.

Marion was sprawled across the bed. A sheet was drawn up over her chest. Only the top of her nightdress showed, its unstained white cotton pathetically childish. She wasn't breathing. Her eyes were open, fixed on the ceiling with a look of ardent yearning. The sheet that partially covered her was black with clotted blood. Her splayed arms were no longer bleeding from the slashes on the wrists, but the blood pooled at her side was still warm enough to flow. It dripped to the floor in a thin trickle.

Suicide.

It could be nothing else. The wounds were self-inflicted. The initial cowardice, the slight slashes on the wrists, then, as determination grew, a deeper, more vehement statement from the knife, trailing off on the right as the exhausted hand extricated itself from intent and fell back to consider its next move.

Mechanically, because it was expected of him, Liaqat went about his business. He slipped the wide neck of her nightdress down her shoulder, easing it off till one heavy breast emerged tiredly and flopped aside. He felt beneath it for her heartbeat, knowing it would be his own pulse he'd feel. He held the compact from the dressing table against her still lips, flashed a torch at pupils that stared back frozen in defiance. He did all this only because it was what Kher expected him to do. She was dead. She had been dead an hour, at most.

The blood loss was too great to have come from the meagre cuts on her wrists. Both men exclaimed as they peeled off the sheet. Her nightdress was a sodden mass of blood. Kher raised it. Her thighs glistened with slippery clots. The black web of her panties was stretched across two crimson craters. The left wound was larger, more jagged. In its wide red gape a clot glistened like a throat of black glass. The puddle of blood had gelled, but in vain. There was nothing that it could seal off anymore. No longer renewed by the pumping heart, the torn blood vessel had emptied itself. Large clots had welled out and slipped stringily down her thighs where they were beginning to crust. But there was still a patient seep from beneath.

Suresh Kher raised one thigh and picked up the kitchen knife, its serrated edge gummy with congealing blood. The tip spun out a long sticky thread of black from the clot that covered it. The femoral veins on both sides had been sliced open. The arteries had escaped. She had bled slowly, relentlessly. There were more slashes on her abdomen, but these were superficial cuts, radiating off her navel as if undecided what direction to take.

Liaqat pictured her gaining in courage as she tried cut after cut, till finally she summoned nerve enough to drive the knife deep into her groin. The spiteful thought smote him that even then, even at that terminus, she had been careful to keep her panties on. Then, as the blood gushed out, her quick determined push into the other side, the knife plunged in with both hands. Finally, when she was certain it would be enough, she had fallen back, waiting—

'Liaqat!' Suresh was jogging his elbow for attention. 'Liaqat, go home. The constable will drop you. Nothing more to be done here.'

He was rooted there, trying to make sense of it all.

'Liaqat!'

'Come on, Doctor.' One of the constables practically pushed him into the jeep.

'Why can't I stay?' he protested. 'She was my patient.'

'She has another doctor now. Poor thing. Boyfriend trouble.'

'Was it?'

'Always is. Kill themselves over useless fellows, all these lovely girls.'

It was still dark, getting on for four o'clock. The jeep drew up outside his building.

'You get some sleep, Doctor sahib.'

'You too.'

'I have to go back.'

Liaqat walked slowly inside. Then stopped. I can't go into the house like this, he panicked, I've got her blood on my feet. He was a long time out there on the road, wiping his feet on the dewy grass, scraping his soles on the gravel until sleeping strays came bounding up to him, woken by the sweet scent of her blood.

Sister Abby

After she had made that call, Sister Abby lay down. Her heart hammered painfully. Don't let me go now, she pleaded with the dark, not yet, not with so much unfinished. It was a bit of hyperbole she used to bully herself into calm. It worked. The burst of palpitations quietened. She went into the bathroom and splashed water on her face.

Pauline knocked. Clarice wanted her.

Pauline looked frightened. 'Too much bad-bad, Sister. You want to give injection, maybe?'

'No, Pauline. Let me talk with her.'

Clarice was sitting up in bed. 'Am I going to die tonight?' she demanded abruptly as Sister Abby entered.

'How can I say, Clarice? It doesn't seem very likely, though. Your body seems to recover fast. I don't think you'll die tonight. But who can tell?'

'Sister Abby, I must talk now. Now. Just now. Before it's too late. Tell Pauline to go away. Pauline, don't answer the phone. No. Put the phone off the hook. All calls must wait till I have finished.'

Pauline gaped at Clarice as though she was completely insane. Sister Abby led her back to the kitchen. She disconnected the phone. 'Listen to Missy, Pauline. Let's do as she says. Who's going to phone us in the middle of the night, anyway? Go lie down a bit, it's almost three o'clock.'

Pauline went away. Sister Abby returned to Clarice's room and latched the door.

The action seemed to afford Clarice some relief. Her face relaxed.

Sister Abby reached behind her right ear, but Clarice raised a languid hand. 'Not this time, Sister. This time, the truth ...'

Aftermath

Sister Abby was hurrying to make the 6:30 flight home. Xavier's taxi was at the gate. She was checking out of the Palm d'Or when the bellboy said there was a call for her.

'Dr Liaqat?'

'Sister Abby, thank God. We couldn't reach you. Marion—Marion's dead.'

'Yes.'

'She cut herself, she—'

'Are you at home, Doctor? Just stay in, I'm coming to see you straight from the airport.'

She reached the airport. There was no sign of Perera. Time enough to worry about that once she got to Bombay. The flight was being announced now.

She looked over her shoulder, seeing once more a thin grey face at the window, a wan hand raised in farewell. But there was nothing behind her, only the blank glass door misted over with rain.

The body of Marion Aranxa was autopsied that afternoon. Liaqat attended the autopsy. The cause of death was haemorrhagic shock following self-inflicted wounds to both femoral veins. The right and left radial arteries had been merely grazed. The cuts on the abdomen were non-penetrating.

Marion Aranxa had died in perfect health. In his report the pathologist had underlined the words *virgo intacta*. 'That's for the family,' he told Liaqat with a leer. 'They always ask.'

Quick as thought, Liaqat hit him, an uppercut that felled him on the pink-stained marble floor.

He strode out, leaving ACP Kher to mop up the mess.

Suresh Kher came inside heavily when Liaqat opened the door. He seemed to have aged overnight. Perera rose to meet him. The two men shook hands, a curiously formal gesture. Condolence or congratulation, wondered Liaqat. He himself was completely bereft of any feeling but exhaustion. The air smelt of coffee. Liaqat's stomach churned. He sat down, waited for Kher to speak.

'Pauline will let Clarice know,' Kher told him. 'I spoke to her a while ago. The other daughter arrives tonight to take charge.'

'This will kill Clarice.'

'No, Doctor,' Sister Abby spoke for the first time since her arrival half an hour ago. She had called from the airport to say she would come in a little later. The truth was, she was desperate to go back to her own safe flat and rest. The memory of the past few hours still brought on bursts of palpitations.

After a brief nap and a good lunch she felt equal to facing Liaqat. Sharifa had led her straight to the kitchen for a quiet word. When they returned to the living room, Kher was already there.

Sister Abby said gravely, 'Clarice was expecting this. She knew Marion would kill herself.'

'Marion threatened suicide?'

'No, Doctor Khan. Clarice told me yesterday that Marion would kill herself. She told me she had ordered Marion to kill herself. She told me this after I called you. I was desperate, I didn't know what to do, I simply stayed on, trusting Mr Perera would get in touch with you.'

'This is too much!' Liaqat exploded. 'All of you are against Clarice, making her out to be some sort of demon—'

'You believed that too for a short while last night,' Suresh Kher said dryly. 'Here, read this. It's a Xerox of the suicide note, left, predictably, on the dressing table.'

Dearest Mamma,

I am going to do my duty now. I did my duty towards Keith and Justin and his mother. I helped them because they were too weak to help themselves. But you have raised me to be strong and, Mamma, I will not disappoint you.

Thank you for giving me a beautiful life and forgive me for failing you so often. I shall not fail you now.

Your loving daughter,
Marion

Liaqat looked up bleakly. 'Marion? Marion killed Justin? And Keith? And Mrs Borges?'

The faces around him regarded him with pity. For some time nobody spoke. Finally, Suresh Kher broke the silence.

'Marion kept a diary of sorts,' he said, 'mostly tortured jottings. Nothing you can call a confession, but there's enough proof even without that. Police procedure paid off. All the tedious work of matching time and place and alibis worked. At least with Mrs Borges's death, Marion was careless. She travelled under her own name on the day of Mrs Borges's death. The Baga police would have picked up the trail if only they'd cared to look. Apparently, she'd made the trip to Goa two days earlier as well. Perhaps for the same purpose, but her nerve failed her. She was seen with Keith shortly before the accident. She was wearing that scarf Clarice spoke about—Sister Abby discovered she had gifted the scarf to a young colleague of hers after Keith's death. And I think there's no doubt about Justin's end either. She pushed him.'

Liaqat walked slowly to the sofa and sank down. His shoes had been cleaned, but he could still see a shred of scarlet at the edge. He shuddered. 'But all this is still surmise, isn't it?'

Suresh Kher smiled. 'You'll never have faith in anything I say, will you, Liaqat. Don't listen to me. Like all great criminals, Clarice wants applause. Sister Abby and Perera have heard her already. Now *you* listen to her.'

He switched on the little tape recorder, and Clarice's voice, surprisingly strident, rang across the room—'This time, the truth...'

Clarice, Tape 6

This time, the truth, Sister.

I have spoken it often enough to you. You are deaf, but you have heard it. You have heard it, I know, and you have not believed it, but the truth I am about to speak, this truth you must believe.

When you return home, there will be news of Marion.

Marion is gone.

I felt her go. As I had felt her leave my body, ridding me of hours of pain, I felt her go, ridding me of a lifetime of pain.

Marion has left me, and I am empty. I must rest to recover my strength.

For what?

I don't know. But I will, soon enough. Something always remains. Pauline will tell me. Pauline will show me what's left to be done.

Sometimes I feel Pauline has led my life for me. But that's not true. Pauline has lived her life the way I wanted her to live it, not for my sake, but for Clive's.

Pauline. Now don't laugh, Sister. I'm beginning to see it might be dangerous to laugh. Pauline—she had something in her heart for Clive. For my dead husband, Sister, in case you didn't hear earlier—Clive was my husband. Pauline sinned against me—in thought, not in deed, but she sinned against me.

That afternoon at three o'clock in the coconut grove—

I forget you don't know anything about this, Sister, this truth.

Let me say this now, once, without fear. I am free now. Let me say it: That afternoon at three o'clock I pushed my husband Clive into the well. I don't remember very much about it except that it happened quickly and easily. I caused him no suffering, JesuMarieJoseph, I caused him no suffering. I was not vengeful. It had been raining and the ground was slushy. After I pushed Clive

I bundled my shoes in my skirt and crouched in the mud like an Indian. I don't know why I did that. All these years and I've never understood that.

I got home, the clock struck four, I remember that. Pauline took care of me. She bathed me and tucked me into bed with a hot toddy. I was in a swoon, almost in a swoon. I didn't see Marion come in. She was small, so very very small, my Marion, my little sweetheart, barely two!

She came in and stood staring at me with those big brown eyes. I've looked at those eyes for thirty-seven years, Sister. I've seen them happy, I've seen them sad, I've seen them angry, I've seen them plead, but all they have ever said to me are the words my baby uttered that day. She said those words as she stood there staring at me. She said: 'Mamma push.'

She climbed up on the bed and butted me playfully. 'Mamma push!'

I could have passed it off as a game, I suppose. But not at that moment. She turned me cold. I screamed for Pauline to save me.

Pauline came running just as Marion gave me another playful push. This time, caught off guard, I toppled on the bed and Marion clapped her hands and crowed, 'Mamma push! Mamma push!'

Do you know, Sister, all these years and I can still hear her!

Sweet mercy of God, grant me freedom from that voice. For thirty-seven years, Sister, I've heard those words in her baby voice. No matter what Marion had to tell me, that's all I ever heard: Mamma, push. Surely, Sister, the Lord is merciful towards those who suffer? Surely I will be granted a few days of freedom in the life left to me?

Pauline came in—and when I caught sight of her face, I knew. I don't think it ever crossed Pauline's mind to threaten me. She could be nothing but accomplice. You see, she too was injured by Clive.

Pauline saw me do it. That afternoon, Melissa was asleep, and once the rain stopped, Pauline had come out looking for me, carrying Marion on her hip. She told me now what she had seen. She told me what Marion had told me minutes ago. They had seen me push Clive into the well.

Marion soon forgot her new game. Certainly, of what she had witnessed, she has no memory.

Sister, I'm telling you this so that it's easier for you to understand—when the girls were growing up, I told them their father died of typhoid fever. Pauline colluded with me in this. You must remember this, always.

We didn't talk much about Clive. I quarrelled successfully with his family. We kept his photograph on the piano. The girls never asked about him.

But Marion—

Marion, my baby, was lost to me the moment she entered the room that day. The Marion who stayed was not one I knew. She tried, so hard, so hard. She never pleased. She would do anything to please me.

When she was six, there was that bother about the Bai's baby. We had a Bai, Indian, you know, with a squalling brat I couldn't stand. She'd bring it to work with her every blessed day. I'd had enough, I can tell you, so it was just as well.

One day, Bai takes Melissa to the park, Pauline is out shopping, Marion is playing quietly in her room, and Bai's baby left asleep on the kitchen bench.

Suddenly—you know how these things are, you simply feel something's wrong—I hear something and go into the kitchen to check on the baby.

The baby is on the floor, and Marion is bending over him.

I know at once what has happened.

Marion's big brown eyes are searching mine for approval.

I go down on my knees and pick up the baby. It's so still, I know it won't ever move again. I tell Marion, 'Poor baby, stupid baby, rolled off the bench! We won't tell Bai or she'll shout at poor Baby. It's our secret, Marion!'

Marion claps her hands and jumps, delighted. I put the baby back on the bench and hurry out, dragging Marion. Luckily, we meet Pauline coming home and I tell her we're off to the park.

That's how I handled it the first time, Sister. That Bai tried to gyp me for funeral expenses. Not one paisa, I told her, first of all your baby goes and dies in my house and on top of it you expect me to pay for it? Forget it, I said.

Marion was thrilled with her secret for a long time.

There were many little secrets, Sister, many, many.

Melissa found a boy. But Marion, always sticking to me, always crowding me with luxuries, trying to bribe me, Marion never ever left me alone.

Then there was Keith.

And soon after the engagement, this motor—motor whatever disease.

Think clearly, I told Marion, don't tell Keith about my illness till the flat papers are signed. Get the flat in your name, then tell him. You never know with men, Sister. All they want is one thing, and that my Marion never gave Keith or any other man. I told Marion, what if he breaks the engagement? Then you still have the flat and nothing is lost.

That morning I spoke with her again. There's no shame in safeguarding your rights, I said. See a lawyer if necessary, do what's necessary. For how can you be certain what life with Keith will be like?

Think clearly, I told her, act wisely. Do what's necessary. She was going to meet him for lunch that day. They'd planned to look for furnishings.

I can't explain what happened to me that morning after Marion left. Perhaps it was the dread Dr Khan's diagnosis had put in me—to choke slowly to death is something to dread, isn't it?

I was overcome by fear. I tried to ring Keith and tell him not to keep his luncheon date with Marion—but even as I dialled I knew how foolish that would sound. So I didn't call Keith.

I tried. Sister, I tried. But life and death are ordained by heaven, as you doubtless know. I tried, but knew even as I did that in trying I defied what heaven had ordained.

I asked Pauline to go to Marion's office and intercept her. Pauline missed Marion—that too was ordained.

I was past caring. I simply waited.

At one-thirty the phone rang. Marion's voice, quiet, hushed like a prayer: 'I've done it, Mamma. I've done what was necessary.'

She lacked character, Marion did. When she got home I told her, 'You helped Keith do his duty, now go do yours.' I am a religious woman, Sister, I feared for her salvation. But she botched it. You must have heard of that from Dr Khan. I don't like to speak of that. Marion was good at heart. It was not her fault that she was poor in spirit.

When did Marion know about Justin? I've often wondered. She met him before I did. Did she notice he resembled Clive? She couldn't remember Clive, surely. I don't know. When I told her, later, about the girl in the red dress, about the red belt that had been found sticking to Clive's body when they pulled him out, I watched her to see if there was any glimmer of memory in her eyes. There was nothing.

But I think she understood the grief I felt every time I looked at Justin.

Make no mistake, Sister, whatever her faults, whatever her shortcomings, Marion always understood me.

I knew that evening Justin took me to church, Marion would hear the Lord's command to me. I had to trust Marion. Trust is the foundation of love. Marion often felt I did not love her. Perhaps I did not.

But I trusted her, didn't I?

I trusted her to find Justin at the church with me, I trusted her to walk with him into the coconut grove. After that, whatever took place between them was ordained.

I was unprepared for the grief Justin's death caused me. It wrecked me. It blinded me. It made me a deaf mute. It turned me into a pillar of salt. I looked back, riven with grief, I looked back, riven with anger that I had to pay for Clive's sins and those of that servant girl. There was no justice in that. Vengeance is mine, saith the Lord. That's right, but what about justice? Tell me, Sister? Should we not hope for justice?

No, don't tell me. I must finish. Let me finish while there's still some breath left in me.

I told the story. I tried to buy myself the justice that was owing me. I told the servant girl's story to the priest knowing he would blab and it would be all about Baga. I did it to punish her. I did it to save her. They punished her, but not enough. And so I did not save her.

Marion knew that. I told her the girl had cheeked me, talking in English and all—Mrs Borges she called herself, very stylish, though everybody knew what went on underneath that red dress.

I told Marion. And because the waiting was unbearable, I went away again, for a little while.

Then I did my duty for my child and made up truths that were easier to believe in.

I told you all those, Sister, your detached celluloid earpiece was in my hand as I spoke, but somehow I think you heard me.

And now Marion has done her duty, as you will soon discover.

She was always a clumsy child, but I hope she has been considerate and not left too much of a mess. I had to insist on it, Sister, or Marion would have left it till I was too far gone to care.

Marion has done her duty. I hope I will not be bothered with formalities. I have told her to leave a note. You will find it on the dressing table.

It is strange how much stronger I feel now that Marion has left.

Will you tell Pauline I shall enjoy an egg for breakfast? Lightly boiled, with just a dab of butter.

And you must go now, Sister Abby, whoever you are, go back to wherever you came from. I do not think we shall meet again.

I think I shall die with this tube in me, but Pauline will see to it that it's removed before Mendonca's men arrive.

But I think that's still some months away.

We are old friends, now, this house and I, and Pauline is there to care for us.

You are leaving now? I shall wave to you from the window. Take an umbrella. It often rains at dawn.

It rained, ah how it rained the night they brought me to Bougainvillea House . . .

Marion

I've written the note that she dictated, but I don't think I'll leave that. That's not what I want to say.
The last words in my heart can only be for her.
I wish I could die with her arms around me, my head in her lap and the world barricaded away. All my wasted years, all my tears and pain would be worth it if I could only do that for one moment.
But she would not wish that. She will wish me to do as I am about to do. This time I am certain I will please her.
I'm very tired.
I'm very hungry too, and that's so strange, isn't it?
I haven't eaten all day.
I took those laxative pills as she told me last night, and today I'm clean and pure.
I haven't eaten all day and after midday I haven't drunk any water.
I think that's precaution enough. She would be disgusted if she found out I'd made a mess. I shall go to the bathroom once more at nine o'clock.
I could have taken pills, I suppose. They would have been easier. But I can't afford another mistake. And pills are too easy. What's the point in simply falling asleep and waking up on the other side? She was angry with me last time. 'You must suffer,' she told me, 'there can be no salvation without pain.'
I will feel pain. I will not flinch from pain. I will think of the pain Our Lord suffered on the Cross and bear my own.
It is almost nine o'clock. Her voice on the phone was hoarse, as if she had a sore throat. I want to tell Pauline to be sure to give her soft easy things to swallow. I want to tell Pauline to look after her.

But she won't like it if I call now. She will want me to do my duty and will not speak till it is done.
It is nine o'clock. I must go now. I will go to the bathroom and then write my last note to her, the one she wants.
I will kneel and say my prayers as if she is by my side.
Then I shall go into the kitchen and find that knife.